"SHELBY, I'VE TRIED NOT TO TELL YOU—"

Donovan's words were broken with passion. He sat on the edge of the bed, and his hands went to Shelby's ankle and encircled it. With excruciating slowness he drew them slidingly along her calf, up her thigh. Then he bent closer. His lips touched her cheek, her ear, her eyes. He kissed her everywhere, awash in the same sensations that engulfed her.

"I love you," he said, so low he seemed unaware he was even speaking.

"And I love you," she said. "I'll never leave you, Donovan. Never."

He tensed suddenly at these words. His hands had been stroking her hair. Now they stopped, and he let out a sigh of frustration and self-anger.

"What is it Donovan?' she pleaded. 'What s wrong?'

But his only answer was silence.

LISA LENORE
is also the author of
SUPERROMANCE # 18
DANCE OF DESIRE

No ballet dancer was more electrifying than Nikolai Sharmanov. And when producer Tiffany Farrow was assigned to film him in Moscow, she should have been overjoyed.

Instead, she was shattered. Years earlier she'd had to give up her own dance career under tragic circumstances. Now she wanted nothing to do with the ballet world—especially with an arrogant superstar like Nikolai. She resolved to do her job and leave immediately....

But Nikolai had other ideas. He captured Tiffany in a dance of love—a passion so strong that even the threat of death could not destroy it.

LISA LENORE LOVE'S HOUR OF DANGER

A SUPERROMANCE FROM
WORLDWIDE

TORONTO · NEW YORK · LOS ANGELES · LONDON

Published November 1982

First printing September 1982

ISBN 0-373-70039-3

Printed in Canada

CHAPTER ONE

Washington, D.C.

FROM THE REACTION she was getting, Shelby figured it was probably unheard of for a U.S. State Department officer to be doing what she was doing. And for good reason, she decided finally.

She raised her head from behind the open duplicating machine she was fiddling with, her expression sheepish. Her hands were streaked with blue duplicating powder, and some of it had smeared across her cheek and onto the neck ruffles of her blouse. Her rich chestnut hair was pulled back in a loose chignon, a few strands falling forward onto her face.

Mrs. Markle, holding Shelby's tailored suit jacket, was trying hard not to giggle. The two secretaries in the administrative office were also trying not to giggle. No one spoke.

"This was a *big* mistake," Shelby admitted ruefully.

Everyone broke out in laughter. Shelby smiled, wiping a few wisps of hair from her face, smearing the blue streak across her cheek even further.

"Shelby," laughed Mrs. Markle, "whatever possessed you to think you could fix a duplicating machine? Is a college education, plus eight months of training here at the Foreign Service Institute, supposed to qualify you to do *that*?''

"I guess not," Shelby admitted, shaking her head in wonderment at her own motives. "I just thought a few sheets were stuck together and I could pull them out to unclog the works. Boy, was I wrong.'' She gratefully accepted the paper towels offered by one of the secretaries and tried to get her hands clean.

"You're just impatient to get your copy of your new overseas orders," Mrs. Markle said knowingly.

"Well, it *is* my first assignment, and I have been waiting for it ever since I graduated from the institute and all through the first year of my probation period.''

"You'll just have to wait an hour longer," said Mrs. Markle good-naturedly, "while I call the repairman. Besides, you know it's very rare for a new State Department officer to come down to administrative to collect her own orders. Usually Mr. Davidson sends his secretary over to pick up all the orders at once.''

"Oh, I know," said Shelby with a make-believe moan as she kept trying unsuccessfully to wipe the powder off her hands. "My father always told me that patience is a virtue. I just never listened."

One of the secretaries said brightly, "At least you won't have to be bored while you're waiting for the duplicator man, Shelby. I'll let you fix the transmission on my car. The way you look now, you could pass for a real grease monkey."

Everyone laughed, including Shelby.

At that moment the door to the office burst open and in came a tall, physically imposing man in an expensively tailored dark blue suit. He had black hair and a strong firm jaw. As he glanced around the office with a glowering expression, an image came into Shelby's mind of a military commander from the days of the Roman Empire assessing his field position for a coming battle. He had a powerfully masculine face that was almost too rugged to be really handsome. He seemed in his mid-thirties.

"I was told there's a girl in here who speaks German," he said. His voice was quite deep.

"I speak German," Mrs. Markle acknowledged.

The tall man looked at her and frowned. His eyes scanned the women again.

"And Shelby does, too," finished Mrs. Markle nodding toward her.

As the man focused his gaze upon her, Shelby felt as if she had been pinned to a board by a butterfly collector. What depth there was in those sea-blue eyes!

"Sprechen Deutsch?" asked the man.

"That's *sprechen Sie Deutsch*," Shelby corrected.

"Good, you'll do. Come with me. You're my date for this evening."

Shelby straightened up. "I most certainly am not."

"I'm sorry, honey, but I really don't have time to

argue." He checked his watch—a gold Rolex.
"We're due at a reception at the West German embassy in two hours. I want you to go outside to my
driver. He's in the black limo parked at the west entrance. Have him take you home so you can change.
Then he'll drive you to the embassy. I'll meet you
there." He looked Shelby over with a critical eye, not
very pleased at what he saw. "The affair is semifor-
mal. I don't expect you know how to dress for an occasion like that, but...well, try to be neat. I suppose
that's the best we can hope for."

Shelby glared at him icily. "You can hope for
whatever you like, but one thing you're not going to
get is me attending any sort of social event with
you."

"If you don't have the proper clothing," he continued, as if she had not even spoken, "have my
driver stop and pick you up something. I know this is
on a moment's notice, but I'm afraid it can't be
helped."

His entire attitude infuriated Shelby. "Didn't anyone ever tell you," she said, "that the gentlemanly
way of conversing with people is to introduce yourself first, and not to act like some loutish boor who
doesn't know the meaning of the word 'manners'?"
Mrs. Markle, watching, appeared shocked, but Shelby continued heedlessly. "I don't suppose you'd
know anything about manners, though, would
you?"

The tall man flashed her a sudden grin of amusement so overpowering and self-assured that for a mo-

ment it made Shelby lose her fire and become disoriented.

"No, I don't suppose I would," he agreed. There was a glimmer of admiration in his eyes for the way Shelby was talking back to him. He seemed the sort of man who was accustomed to being obeyed without question and did not often find people who challenged him.

The last thing Shelby wanted from this infuriating man, however, was admiration—or anything else for that matter. She started to tell him she had no intention of going out with him when he interrupted her.

"Look, I really enjoy our pleasant little chat here," he began wryly, "but this isn't the time for it. You go do as I told you, and I'll see you at the reception in a few hours. Meantime, tell me your department head's name so I can explain to him why you have to leave early."

Shelby raised her chin defiantly and said nothing.

The tall man looked at Mrs. Markle.

"Shelby just finished her first year internship, Mr. Hawkes," she explained in a respectful tone. "She's assigned to Bill Davidson's department while waiting for her first posting overseas. Her orders just came in for assignment to our embassy in Brazil."

The man nodded and walked out. He was gone now, but his aura still lingered—like the aftereffects of a destructive hurricane. Shelby looked at Mrs. Markle with perplexity, feeling betrayed.

"Sorry, Shelby," the older woman said, "but that's Donovan Hawkes."

The name meant nothing to her. "Whoever he is, he's in for a rude awakening if he actually expects me to show up at that reception as his date. This is the U.S. State Department, not some backwater white-slave ring. The man acts as if I were his personal property."

One of the secretaries applauded Shelby's indignant stand, but the other said with lowered eyes, "I wouldn't mind if he wanted me for his date tonight— or any night."

Shelby went to the rest room to wash up, and when she returned, Bill Davidson was in the room waiting for her, looking somber. He asked her to follow him back to his office, then left. Shelby looked at Mrs. Markle in puzzlement, but all the older woman could say was, "Good luck, dear."

Bill was the executive in charge of training and orientation for officers about to be posted overseas. He was a stout middle-aged man with black-frame glasses. Though he was the superior of most of the officers he trained, he was an unpretentious man who preferred to be called by his first name. He lost no time in getting down to business when Shelby reached his well-appointed executive office. He motioned for her to be seated opposite his desk, near a large potted palm.

"You'd better go change, Shelby. You're off duty as of now. You've been commandeered for the evening."

"You're not serious?"

"I'm afraid I am. That man you just dealt with is

Donovan Hawkes. He holds the rank of deputy minister—meaning, if he says he needs you for the evening, you're his.''

Shelby was appalled. "Bill, he can't order me around like that, no matter how senior he is, and I have no intention of—''

Bill Davidson waved his hand, trying to calm her down. He spoke in a sympathetic but disheartened voice. "You're one hundred percent right, and I agree with you completely, but frankly, Shelby, there's not much either of us can do. This Hawkes has a reputation as a man who...uh....'' He didn't know how to phrase it diplomatically. He clearly disapproved of the man but didn't want to let it show. "He gets what he wants,'' he concluded firmly.

"Well, not this time. I'm twenty-three years old, and I didn't spend my entire childhood as a foreign-service brat without learning a few things from my father. I know my rights, and one very basic one is that I can refuse a 'personal' request—which this clearly is.''

Bill Davidson swiveled his chair to the side so he could gaze out the window. Shelby had the feeling he didn't want to meet her eyes right now as he said, "Yes, you're within your rights to refuse him, but I wouldn't advise it. The fact is...look, you've just received orders to be posted to Brazil. You know how important that first overseas assignment is to your career. You wouldn't want anything to happen to... ruin it.''

She was shocked. "Are you telling me this man is

vindictive? That he'd actually use his rank to inter-fere with my assignment?''

Bill turned back to her abruptly, and she could see he was clearly upset. He hated the position he was be-ing put in. ''You're a big girl now,'' he said a bit scoldingly. ''Let's not be naive. You know a man of that rank can do anything he darn well pleases. Well, it so happens that Donovan Hawkes has a reputation for being a ruthless s.o.b. who stops at nothing to get what he wants.'' His voice was bitter. ''I don't like him; hardly anyone in Washington likes him. He's an abrasive maverick who refuses to play by the rules. This thing you're experiencing now is just one exam-ple of that.''

''I don't see how a man like him can stay in the department.''

''He's good at what he does. But don't think his bulldozer tactics haven't hurt his career; they have. With his brains and talent and drive he'd be an am-bassador by now if he'd been willing to give in a lit-tle, to compromise.'' He shook his head. ''But not Hawkes. He won't give an inch.''

''What does he do that he's so good at?'' Shelby asked. She knew his rank, but that didn't tell her what ''cone'' he was in. The State Department was divided into four career areas called cones: political, economic, consular and administrative. Each cone performed its own function in attending to the tasks of implementing America's worldwide foreign pol-icy.

''He's a troubleshooter in the political cone,'' said

Bill. "The department sends him out to problem areas wherever crises arise that can't be handled by the resident officers."

Yes, thought Shelby ruefully, he would be very good at that. Most diplomats were dignified, conservative and... well, "professorish." They were not action oriented, and troubleshooting was just not in their natures. This Donovan Hawkes, though, seemed more like a rough-and-tumble sort than a diplomat—no matter how conservatively cut his three-piece suits were.

Shelby's anger was beginning to lessen slightly as her curiosity grew. "Bill, I don't understand why he wants me as his date tonight. He doesn't even know me."

"Here's the story," he began, standing up and moving around to the front of his desk and leaning back against it. "He's got a girl after him. But this isn't just any girl. It's Gretchen Bruckner, the daughter of the West German foreign minister. She met Hawkes during one of his missions to Germany. He's not interested in her, but Gretchen is a very headstrong girl and has never learned to take no for an answer."

"So let her learn now."

"The problem is that she carries a lot of weight with her father. You know a petty thing like a perceived insult to one's daughter can get blown way out of proportion if the man happens to be a doting father. And Herr Bruckner is."

"I still don't understand. So what if it gets blown

out of proportion? It won't be the end of the world.''

"Normally, no. But Hawkes is about to be posted to our embassy in Bonn on an urgent mission—something about someone named Lion. Anyway, he'll have to work with Bruckner, and if there's antagonism between them, it would hinder him in accomplishing his mission. And that would be bad for the department.''

At last Shelby began to understand, but still it didn't make all that much sense. "So I'm supposed to show up as his date,'' she ventured, "so Herr Bruckner can see there's a good reason why Hawkes isn't available to court his daughter, that he's already 'committed'?''

"Exactly.'' Bill looked uneasy as he said this, though, making Shelby wonder if maybe there was really more to it. "In fact, Bruckner insisted Hawkes bring his date to tonight's reception, which is being given in honor of Bruckner's visit here.''

"Why me? Why can't he ask some other girl?'' She reflected with displeasure on his ruggedly handsome face and broad-shouldered build. "That sort of man always seems to have enough girls more than happy to go with him anywhere at all.''

"He backed himself into a corner by mentioning that his, uh, 'date' speaks German. You've spoken it fluently since the time you lived there, when your father was stationed in Bonn.''

Shelby sighed with displeasure, but she didn't protest further. She noticed that Bill was relieved to see she was at least considering this proposal now, rather than dismissing it out of hand. He didn't want to see her career ruined before it got started any more than she did. Still, she was having such a hard time assenting to this. It wasn't just her pride that was at stake. It was that this was such an unscrupulous abuse of power. Normally she would never agree to go out with such an overbearing unethical man. But. . . .

"Well," she said, shrugging in unhappy resignation, "I guess it's time I started living in the real world. I knew when I joined the department that it wasn't going to be all sweetness and light."

"Then you'll do it?"

"I won't like it, but I'll do it."

"Good." He seemed relieved. He hesitated, then reached into his desk drawer and withdrew a small blue velvet case. He looked guilty, as if having been forced by Hawkes to withhold an important piece of information until the last minute. "Incidentally, you're not going as. . .uh. . .just his date. If that's all you were, Hawkes would still be expected to court Gretchen, since he wouldn't be committed." He handed the case to Shelby, who was amazed to find a glittering ruby ring inside.

"Hawkes said to give this to you. It's an engagement ring. You're his fiancée now—for tonight only."

CHAPTER TWO

SHELBY WAS STILL SEETHING several hours later as she arrived at the West German embassy, where her wrap was taken by a butler. Officially this ballroom was part of the "ambassador's residence," which was where social affairs were hosted. The nerve of that man, Shelby thought, fuming. Not only was he ordering her to be his unwilling date at a major diplomatic function—and on only a moment's notice—but he expected her to pretend to love him, as well.

Her indignation began to recede slightly as she reached the threshold of the sunken embassy ballroom and looked in. She gazed at it from atop the wide burgundy-carpeted stairway landing. The ballroom was a stunning sight to behold, and she could not help but be captivated by it.

The ceiling was very high and adorned with inlaid mosaics. The walls held huge, vividly colorful murals depicting historical scenes. A great crystal chandelier sent splinters of bright light in all directions. Down on the floor of the ballroom were perhaps a hundred elegantly dressed couples, laughing, talking, mingling. Against the background of spirited baroque music being played by a tuxedo-clad string quartet, the sound of their voices rose up to Shelby. Liveried servants bearing trays of hors d'oeuvres circulated through the crowd.

As she began descending the stairs, Shelby reflected on how the gay atmosphere of the ball did not tell the entire story. True, there was genuine glamour here, but she knew also that the serious business of nations was being discussed at this ball. This was the case with all balls hosted by members of the international diplomatic corps at embassies throughout the world. Such social occasions served an important purpose. They allowed diplomats to get together to make contacts and informally feel one another out about business that would later be formalized at the conference table.

Shelby was halfway down the carpeted stairway when she noticed men turning their heads up to gaze at her, some discreetly, some more boldly. Though she had long ago resigned herself to being a focal point of the affairs she attended, it still bothered her the way men stared at her so insistently. In fact, ever since she had blossomed into young womanhood, she had felt intimidated and a bit frightened by the attention. In Europe, as a young debutante attending balls at embassies where her father served, she had at first tried to minimize her looks, dressing in a bland manner and adopting a meek reserved posture. But Shelby had had a wise elderly governess during that time, who told her that such behavior would not do.

"Be grateful for your beauty," her governess had

said. "Do not demean it. Do not let men frighten you into demeaning it." The kindly woman had raised Shelby's chin then and uttered words that had a strong effect on her at that moment and ever afterward. "Think of your mother, dear. If she had lived, would she have wanted her only daughter to be so apologetic about the looks she gave you?" Shelby had seen pictures of her mother. She had been a great beauty in her time—much more so than Shelby.

Ever since that advice from her governess, Shelby had carried herself proudly and unapologetically, as she was doing now. She noticed the awed look on the upturned faces of several of the men on the ballroom floor. She knew her looks were considered quite stunning by some. She gave herself credit for her vivid green eyes, which were slightly almond-shaped and which she considered her best feature. Others, though, told her it was the deceptively fragile-seeming arrangement of her rather delicate features that gave her her beauty—that and her dark chestnut hair, which Shelby wore in a shoulder-length style with bangs. Several people had told her she looked the way Audrey Hepburn had looked early in her career.

She reached the floor of the ballroom and began making her way through the crowd in search of Donovan Hawkes. A jumble of conversations in a variety of languages filled the air. Shelby was arriving late and therefore had missed the formal receiving line. She had also missed meeting Hawkes at the

ballroom entrance, where Bill Davidson had said he
would be waiting for her. She had deliberately taken
her time showering and dressing, knowing she would
be late, and now, as she glanced around, she was glad
she had made the effort to dress properly.

She saw she had been right in assuming the reception would be more formal than Hawkes had led her
to believe. Most of the women wore fashionable
gowns, and their wrists and throats were atwinkle
with jewelry. A fragrant hint of their expensive per-
fumes hung in the air. The men were attired in evening clothes—dark jackets and ties. A few wore
tuxedos.

Shelby knew that in the diplomatic corps semifor-
mal meant more than that, and formal meant ultra-
formal. If she had been some other girl, though, who
had not grown up in the foreign service, she would
have taken Hawkes's instructions at face value.
Shelby thought of how embarrassed that other girl
would feel. Donovan Hawkes had shown no consideration.

Shelby herself was wearing a shimmering emerald
gown of a shade that matched her eyes. The dress
highlighted her slender but shapely figure without being too revealing. Its rich color contrasted with her
fair skin. At her throat was a modest gold pendant on
a gold chain, and on her finger the unwanted lovely
ruby ring.

Shelby saw Donovan Hawkes before he saw her.

He was engaged in conversation with a thin mus-
tached man whose looks and attire appeared to

Shelby to be French. Hawkes himself looked quite handsome in a double-breasted charcoal gray suit and a blue tie the color of his eyes. She was annoyed at the way he appeared so comfortably at home in his expensively tailored clothing. It shouldn't be this way. His broad-shouldered masculine physique seemed not at all the sort that should go so well in civilized dinner clothing.

The Frenchman noticed Shelby first and began staring in the sort of worshipful fascination for beauty that only the French seem to have. This irritated Hawkes, who was trying to carry on a serious conversation. He turned to see what was causing the man's distraction.

For one of the few times in her life, Shelby was glad, rather than disturbed, at the effect her looks had on men. Donovan Hawkes was staring at her, transfixed; and best of all, Shelby mused with satisfaction, there was a look of nonrecognition in his gaze. He didn't realize whom he was looking at. He had no idea that this poised vision he was watching was the same rumpled blue-powder-smeared girl he had invited to this reception.

As Shelby came toward him through the crowd, she saw him frown in anguish, struggling to recall where he had seen her previously and whether she was someone he would be expected to know. In the diplomatic corps, where social etiquette was strict, to forget a previous introduction could be a grave transgression. Diplomats often spent hours at their files, memorizing names and faces, to avoid giving such offense.

Shelby came directly up to him and stood staring up into his face. She enjoyed his distraught look. She prolonged the moment of his discomfort for as long as possible. Finally she relented, smiling and saying, "Hello, darling." She stood up on her tiptoes to kiss him lightly on the cheek.

At first he frowned even harder, but in an instant he realized who she was. He was clearly surprised. Then he grinned at her wryly, in a way that was quite generous. It acknowledged the victory she had just scored over him and held admiration for the stylish way she had carried it off.

The Frenchman at Donovan's side cleared his throat loudly, calling attention to himself as he waited to be introduced. He was staring at Shelby, smiling politely.

Donovan put his hand on Shelby's waist. "André," he said, "may I present Miss Shelby Everest—my fiancée."

"No!" said André, taken aback. "I don't believe it. Your fiancée? You never told me."

"Didn't I? Thoughtless of me. I must have forgotten."

"You? Engaged? Donovan Hawkes, the playboy of the seven continents? I don't believe it. Of course—" he glanced at Shelby "—I do believe it now that I see what has made you change your ways." He bowed over Shelby's hand, raising it to his lips. "*Enchanté*, my dear. My name is André Forchette. I am a good friend to this dirty dog you are about to marry. In fact, you are far too good for

him. Here, let me steal you away." He reached for
her hand and wrapped it around his arm, then started
across the floor with her.

Donovan pulled him back, took Shelby's hand and
put it on his own arm. "Sorry, friend, I'm afraid
she's already spoken for."

"I still have such a hard time believing this. For
how long has this engagement been going on?"

"Oh, long enough. I'll tell you all about it some
other time. Meanwhile, I think I'd better hunt down
the foreign minister. He is, after all, the reason I'm
here." His eyes became serious as he scanned the
room.

André bowed to Shelby once more. "I am charmed
to have met you, *mademoiselle*. I hope to see you
again soon. Anytime you wish to leave this no-good
scoundrel, I will be happy to rescue you, to take you
away from all this! We will go far away and live happily ever after."

Shelby smiled. "That sounds very romantic."

"Yes," said Donovan, turning to André, "but what
will your wife and children say when you run off with
my fiancée?"

"What wife? What children?" He looked innocent
and puzzled, but under Donovan's grinning gaze he
shrugged and admitted, "Oh, *that* wife and children."

Donovan slapped him on the back, and then he
and Shelby moved off down the floor in search of the
German foreign minister. Donovan's grip on her arm
was firm and no-nonsense as he escorted her. "You're

late," he said, his tone not very cordial. Now that they were out of earshot of his friend, his true colors were showing.

"You're lucky I came at all," Shelby retorted coldly.

"Did Davidson tell you how important this is and how you're expected to act tonight?"

"Yes, he told me how your lying deceitful ways have got you into trouble and how I'm expected to bail you out of it." She looked at him distastefully. "Or rather, how I'm being 'blackmailed' into bailing you out of it."

"Good, at least we've got that straight. Now I suggest you start acting your part. You're my fiancée, not my sparring partner. I personally don't care how you feel about me, but if Herr Bruckner sees you acting hostilely, he'll know the engagement is just a sham."

"What would you like me to do—smile prettily and call you 'darling'?"

He stopped walking and turned her to face him. "If that's what it takes," he said, "then that's what you'll do. This is important to me. I didn't ask you here because I'm crazy about your personality. You're here because I've got a job to do, and I can't let anything interfere with it—not Herr Bruckner's family problems and not your sense of righteous indignation."

A few people nearby were turning to look at them. The music from the string quartet was not quite loud enough to drown out their argument. Shelby said nothing, just continued to stare at Donovan. He took her arm again and started her forward. Several people he knew greeted him in a variety of accents as he continued making his way across the floor. He nodded to them and spoke a few words without stopping.

"You might have told me the proper way to dress," Shelby said. She was still feeling argumentative and wanted to make it clear she would not knuckle under to this arrogant man, even though she was being forced to carry out his charade.

He glanced at her. "You look fine to me—surprisingly fine, in fact. I figured I'd be lucky if you just managed to clean those blue smudges off your cheeks."

"If I look fine to you, it's because I grew up in embassies overseas and know how to dress for an affair like this *despite* your misinformation."

He shrugged. "Sorry if I led you wrong. It wasn't deliberate. I don't know the first thing about how women are supposed to dress." He nodded to a bearded Pakistani in a white turban who called out his name in greeting. He paused briefly to shake the proffered hand of a Russian diplomat who wore his country's ribbons and medals in rows on the front of his jacket.

"You grew up in embassies overseas?" he asked as they continued searching for Herr Bruckner. "Who is your father?"

"Charles Porterfield Everest." Shelby said this with dignity, hoping to put this abrasive man in his place by the impact of the highly renowned name.

Donovan's reaction, though, was just the opposite of what Shelby had wanted. He laughed in amusement. "Charles Everest is your father? I should have guessed. The same last name. I worked for your father once—in Turkey. I was his political-affairs deputy."

"That's surprising. I can't imagine father putting up with having anyone as insufferably rude as you on his staff."

Donovan grinned. "He didn't. He fired me and had me recalled home."

That really was surprising. Even though Shelby knew her father would disapprove of a man like Donovan Hawkes, it was a major blot on an officer's record for him to be sent home from an overseas post. Her father would not have taken such a step lightly. She had no knowledge of the incident because she had been away at school, in California, during her father's tour of duty in Turkey. Still, this colored her image of Donovan. He must be far worse than she had imagined to provoke her father into taking such drastic action.

"What did you do that made him ask for your recall?" she inquired curiously.

They were approaching Herr Bruckner now, and there really wasn't time to talk. "I'll leave that to your imagination," he replied. "You've already got such a high opinion of me, I'm sure you'll come up with a worthy possibility."

"Whatever it is," Shelby said, feeling her father's

integrity must be defended, "I'm sure you deserved it."

"I'm sure I did—that is, if you happen to view the world through the sort of narrow-minded, pompous, inflexible attitudes your father has."

Now Shelby was really outraged. How dare he insult her father! She turned to him in anger, but before she could utter a word, they were directly in front of the German foreign minister, and Donovan was being greeted by him. Shelby managed to restrain herself only through a major effort of will. Inside, though, she was furious.

"Ah, Donovan!" said the foreign minister. "Good, you are here." He was a stocky man with a jowly face, who looked dignified in his diplomatic attire. He spoke with a staccato accent. "Your ambassador has told you of the matter I called you here to discuss?"

"He has, Excellency. He also told me that you insisted I bring my fiancée tonight, that you were very anxious to meet her." He put his hand on Shelby's elbow. "Excellency, Miss Shelby Everest. Shelby— Herr Heinrich Bruckner."

Shelby curtsied slightly at the introduction.

Herr Bruckner regarded her with a critical eye. *"Wie gehts?"* he asked her.

"Sehr gut, danke sehr. Und Ihnen?" she replied.

"I am very well, too, thank you." He turned to Donovan. "So you truly are engaged after all, and she does speak *Deutsch*, just as you said."

"Of course, Excellency. Did you doubt me?"

Herr Bruckner looked at him piercingly for a moment. "*Nein*. Of course not." His expression, though, showed that he had. "It is only that... well, your reputation, Donovan. It is such that one would not expect you to give up the bachelor life to marry."

He turned to Shelby, smiling politely. "I congratulate you on your engagement, *Fräulein*. I must admit that for a period I thought it would be my daughter, Gretchen, who would be the future Frau Hawkes. She desires it greatly. But I see there is indeed a good reason for Donovan not to court her, and I wish you every happiness in your marriage."

"Thank you, Excellency," Shelby uttered in a quiet voice, trying to suppress her anger. She hated this situation. She hated liars, and in particular she hated being forced to tell a lie herself. The only reason all this deception was necessary, she reflected, was because Donovan Hawkes seemed to be such a renowned playboy. Shelby had never admired that trait in a man.

Her hatred of the situation must have shown on her face, despite her efforts to hide her feelings, for the minister looked at her in puzzlement, wondering why she should be so upset when accepting his wish of happiness in marriage to the man she supposedly loved.

Donovan noticed the minister becoming aware of Shelby's harsh feelings and quickly changed the subject. "Excellency, my ambassador told me how urgent this matter is regarding the Lion. My orders have already been cut. I leave for our Bonn embassy in the morning to begin my investigation.''

"Good," he said, turning to Donovan, keenly interested in this matter he had called him here to discuss. His voice was grim. "Donovan, we must stop this man. He has struck again—only last week. He arranged the crossing of a man named Furth and his wife. He stole a tractor from a construction site near the border, had the refugees get into the steel basket attached to the crane, and then he bulldozed his way right through the barricades, right over the antipersonnel minefield, into West Berlin."

"I heard, Excellency. I was in Frankfurt at the time. I read about it in *Der Spiegel.*"

"He gets more daring with each crossing! Now that taking refugees across the wall is almost impossible, he goes through the northern border instead! Or across the Spree River.

At first Shelby had no idea whom they were talking about, but then she recalled a name she had heard in the West Berlin office of the State Department when she had been interning there during her training. The name had been spoken in respectful hushed tones. "Are you referring to the man they call the Lion of Berlin?"

Both men looked at her. "Yes," Herr Bruckner acknowledged. His expression made it plain he was willing to allow her into the discussion in deference to her status as Donovan's fiancée. "You are familiar with the Lion, *Fräulein*?"

"He's the people smuggler, isn't he? The one who

keeps bringing refugees across the Berlin Wall in spite of the strongest efforts of the East Germans to stop him?''

"That is the one." He looked upset.

"I don't understand, though," she said in puzzlement. "Now your government, too, wants to stop him? I thought West Berlin welcomed all refugees who escaped across the wall?"

"We do! But this—it is different." He was very agitated and defensive about the matter.

Donovan said, "Herr Bruckner's government welcomes refugees who flee into the West on their own. This Lion, though, actually sneaks into the East, organizes crossings for the escapers and takes them out. The Communist East Germans are up in arms. They call that a major violation of their sovereignty."

Herr Bruckner began mopping his brow with a handkerchief, quite upset. "To tell the truth, *Fräulein*, this affair disturbs me greatly. We do not wish to arrest this man. In Berlin he is considered a great hero. So far we have tolerated him, despite protests from the East, but on this last crossing he went too far. He wounded a *Vopo*—an East German policeman. The *Vopo* climbed into the tractor cab to try to kill him and a moment later was seen flying out of the cab, wounded by his own weapon. The East went wild at this. They now threaten to blockade our city, to cut off all access roads—to strangle us!"

He turned to Donovan agitatedly. "I am glad you

have been put in charge of the investigation. I have heard you are a ruthless man, Donovan, a man who stops at nothing to get the job done. Ruthlessness is what is needed here to outfox this cunning Lion. You must stop him! For years no one has been able to."

"I'll stop him," Donovan said.

Shelby was appalled at how easily he had uttered the words, as if he had no doubts at all about the justness of such an action. Though she knew how precarious West Berlin's situation was and how it depended for its survival on access roads leading through Communist East Germany, which surrounded it on all sides, still she couldn't help feeling sympathetic toward the Lion.

When Herr Bruckner excused himself to go welcome the French ambassador and his wife, who had just arrived, Shelby said to Donovan, "You sounded terribly merciless just then, do you know that?"

"Did I? I hadn't thought about it one way or another."

"How are you even involved in this? You're not German."

"Neither is the Lion, apparently. Intelligence reports say he might be an American citizen. That's why Herr Bruckner's government asked our State Department to investigate—to find the man and stop him."

Shelby peered at him critically, trying to understand his motives. "Don't you have any qualms about trying to track down the Lion, about having him arrested? This is a man who risks his life to help refugees escape to freedom.''

Now it was Donovan's turn to look at her in a strangely appraising way. Shelby sensed he wanted to tell her something that would make her understand, make her view his role in a kinder light. But his expression changed, and instead of saying such a thing, he declared in a harsher voice, ''I have a job to do. I plan to do it. My career is based on getting results, and that's all I care about.''

She was shocked at such callousness. Until now she had suspected he might have some redeeming traits that, for some reason, he felt he had to keep hidden. She had had a sense of the man based on little things, such as the direct way he spoke, the boldness of his eyes as they met hers. Her intuition had seldom been wrong, but obviously it was wrong in this case.

''You really are a cold-hearted mercenary,'' she said disappointedly. ''I don't think I want to have anything more to do with you, Mr. Hawkes. I went along with this masquerade of yours, but now that you've introduced me as your fiancée, it's over. I'll find my own way out, thank you.'' She started to leave.

He reached for her arm and stopped her. ''Not just yet.'' He nodded toward the side. ''Look over there.''

Shelby looked and saw a very attractive, buxom, blond-haired girl hurrying toward them through the crowd with a radiant smile that did not quite hide her predatory intentions. She had creamy white skin and wore a silvery gown and diamond earrings. Following after her was Herr Bruckner, who had excused himself from the French ambassador.

No one had to tell Shelby that this was the girl who was the cause of this unpleasant masquerade—Gretchen Bruckner.

CHAPTER THREE

"DARLING, IT'S SO GOOD to see you," Gretchen said, laughing gaily. She put her arms around Donovan and hugged him in greeting. "Daddy said you'd come, but I wasn't so sure. Why, you've been avoiding me ever since we arrived in Washington!" She narrowed her eyes in a playfully accusing way. Her hand remained on the back of Donovan's neck, and she was very close against him.

"Gretchen," scolded Herr Bruckner, upset, "is this the proper way to greet an engaged man?"

Gretchen turned to Shelby with cool disdainful eyes—a direct challenge—and then looked back at her father. "Oh, daddy," she said playfully, unrepentantly, "I'm just being friendly. We are the greatest of friends, aren't we, darling?" she asked Donovan.

Donovan grinned at her wryly, saying nothing. His expression made it clear he knew what she was doing and the only reason she could get away with it was that Herr Bruckner was her father.

"Besides, daddy," she continued, "engagements come and go. Marriage—now there's an institution I respect. When a man is married, I draw the line and say he is no longer available. But until then. . . ?'' She shrugged. She looked at Donovan, apparently knowing him much better than her father, for she asked in a mocking, highly doubtful tone, "You *are* getting married, isn't that right, darling?"

"That's right," Donovan replied impassively. He began making introductions then between Shelby and Gretchen. Shelby was aware of Herr Bruckner looking on, embarrassed and upset at his daughter's behavior, and she felt sympathy for the man. He clearly cared for his daughter's happiness, though just as clearly had no control over her.

"So you're the one who gets him?" Gretchen remarked to Shelby, scanning her cattily. "Hold on to him tight, dear. He's a fine catch, but he may be hard to keep." Her hand moved to the back of his neck once more, and her falsely smiling eyes were trained on Shelby in deliberate confrontation.

Moments earlier Shelby had not thought it possible that this horrible situation could get any worse. Now, with Gretchen's arrival, she saw that it had become worse than she could ever have imagined. Because now she was being tested and Herr Bruckner and Donovan were both watching her to see what she would do. She knew what was expected of her. The rules for this sort of thing dated back to the beginning of time, when men and women had first courted.

Shelby was expected to put her hand in Donovan's possessively, or to hug his arm while returning Gretchen's stare, or to give some clear sign of affection—

a kiss, a loving look—to show that she cared for him and was willing to "fight for her man" in the face of this clear challenge.

But Donovan was not her man, and Shelby would never want such an unprincipled person to *be* her man, no matter how dynamic and physically appealing he might be. What's more, Shelby was suddenly sick and tired of the whole pretense—of having to sacrifice her pride, of being blackmailed and forced into pretending affection for a man she despised. All the indignities and resentments of the past hours welled up in her and came to a head as her pride reasserted itself, and in response, Shelby folded her arms across her chest and looked away, refusing to carry on this charade for even another minute.

Gretchen's expression was joyously triumphant; Herr Bruckner's was bewildered—and rapidly turning skeptical. Shelby's earlier coolness toward Donovan had made Bruckner suspicious about whether she truly did love him, as she was supposed to. This display now made him even more suspicious. He pulled his daughter away from her possessive pose near Donovan and began scolding her in German for her behavior.

Donovan took this opportunity to come up to Shelby, very close, and look her in the eyes warningly. She held his stare defiantly, her expression saying, "I'm through with this charade, and there's nothing you can do about it."

His own deep blue eyes answered her with a message that shocked her. "Yes, there is," his eyes said.

And then, without warning, his head came forward, and his firm lips descended upon hers. Shelby's arms went out to her sides in surprised reaction. She tried to back away, but Donovan's arms went around her and embraced her tightly. She felt his hard masculine body pressing against the front of her, from her breasts down to her hips.

She wanted to resist, but was so shocked by the unexpected sensuousness of the kiss that for a moment she could not move. She felt suddenly weak, as if all her strength had deserted her.

From the hushed silence she sensed that Herr Bruckner and his daughter were watching them, but then that thought, along with the music and the sounds of the party, all seemed to fade from her mind as she drifted awash in the sensation of Donovan's kiss. She was lost to it, drowning in it. Nothing seemed real except his lips moving upon hers, his powerful arms holding her against him, her excited breasts crushed helplessly against his hard chest.

The masculine scent of him was in her nostrils, and when she opened her eyes and saw the ruggedly handsome face she had been watching all evening so near now, she nearly swooned. She felt herself melting against him. Her hands went up to try to push him away, but somehow the fingers of one hand found their way into his hair and became entangled there.

After a few seconds Shelby's wits began to return, and she understood weakly why she was so susceptible to him now, so vulnerable. It was more than just the fact that all her life she had been denied any signs of warmth or affection. It was because Donovan himself was so close to all she had ever dreamed of in a man. He was bold and self-assured, strong and bright. As her wits returned to her more fully, however, she remembered that he was *not* what she wanted. He was unprincipled and heartless, too— and self-serving.

She was about to pull away from him, but before she could, Donovan did something that seemed very cruel. He abruptly stepped back a pace, away from her. This had the effect of leaving Shelby's expression exposed for all to see before she could compose herself. Her eyelids were half closed, and her face showed the vulnerability his kiss had made her feel. Her moist lips were slightly parted. Only his firm hand on her arm kept her from tottering, she was so unsteady on her feet.

She knew he had done this sudden stepping-back maneuver deliberately, so that the others could see in her face the passion and affection she had refused to show by her previous actions. And it had worked. He had salvaged his squalid little charade.

"There!" said Herr Bruckner to his daughter, gazing at Shelby's expression. "You see? They are in love. There can be no doubt, no matter how it seemed to you earlier." His tone was one of vindication. "*Now* will you stop with this nonsense of how you consider him fair game until he is married?"

Shelby was blushing with humiliation. She felt so vulnerable; her emotions had been so nakedly exposed. She turned to Donovan with the intention of slapping him stingingly, no matter what the consequences to her career, but something stopped her. On his face as he gazed at her was a look of powerful sensitivity and caring, a lingering aftereffect of the kiss. And there was puzzlement there, too, as if he were astonished to be feeling these emotions, as if the kiss had affected him more deeply than he had imagined it would.

Now Shelby felt confused and helpless, in addition to being humiliated. Oh, God, she thought. She didn't know what to do. She was still blushing pinkly, and everyone was watching her. She turned and fled from the ballroom.

The night was cool and crisp and black. Shelby had not stopped to retrieve her wrap from the butler, and goose bumps were rising on her skin. She hurried down the long circular driveway, past the line of waiting black and silver limousines. She was halfway to the street when Donovan caught up to her.

"Where are you going?" he asked, falling into step beside her.

"Home." Her voice was subdued and icy.

"My car and driver are back that way."

"I've no intention of sitting in the same car with you. I'll find a taxi. I'd rather not be taken advantage of any further tonight, thank you."

He walked beside her in silence, apparently knowing better than to try to stop her at that moment. Shelby heard the clicking of her high heels on the driveway and her own mortified angry breathing.

After a moment Donovan said, "Look, I'm not in the habit of forcing myself on women. You brought that on yourself in there. You were acting aloof and hostile toward me."

"Which is exactly the way I feel toward you."

"Your feelings don't matter. What matters is the impression you gave Bruckner. Which was that maybe our engagement wasn't all it was cracked up to be. So what I did in there was something that had to be done to get him back to believing what I needed him to believe."

"Oh, and I'm sure you didn't enjoy it," she accused him sarcastically, walking faster in an effort to get away from him. "I'm sure it was only an 'operational necessity,' and you hated every second of it."

"I didn't say that." He paused. "How did you feel about it?"

She glanced at him, daggers in her eyes. "You don't want to know that, Mr. Hawkes."

She tried to pick up her pace even more, but this time he grasped her shoulders and swiveled her around to face him, stopping her. They stared at each other. His expression was intense and earnest.

"I know you don't give a damn about this," he began, "but just for the record, I'm not all that disappointed about you. You're a surprising girl. When I asked you here tonight, I expected someone who was female and could speak German, and that's it. What I got is a woman who's bright, spirited, poised and who seems to have a sense of her own mind. Of course, you're also too pigheaded and your temper hits the flashpoint too fast.''

"Thank you very much."

"What I'm trying to say is, there's a chance I could find myself growing attracted to a woman like you—which doesn't happen to me very often—and I don't want that chance ruined by your being upset at me over what happened in there. I want you to understand it wasn't done to humiliate you or to take unfair advantage of you.''

"Oh, I understand perfectly. It was done for a much more noble reason instead—so you could deceive Herr Bruckner into believing a total lie, so he wouldn't interfere with your wretched job of tracking down a courageous man whom you could then arrest and use to boost your career. Is that about right? Correct me if I've left out anything.''

Now he was getting angry. "All right, you're so opinionated about this, you tell me. What would you do if the State Department gave *you* this assignment? Suppose you managed to track down the Lion. Would you turn him in?''

That made Shelby pause. It was a hard question, but she knew how to answer. She had been brought up to respect the State Department's main rule and had seen the wisdom of it demonstrated over and over again during her childhood as she had watched her father in action.

"I believe that our government makes foreign policy and that we, as officers, carry it out. If the secretary of state believes this Lion is causing West

Berlin to be on the verge of a strangling blockade and he should be stopped—then yes, I'd turn him in." She added hotly, "But that's a far cry from your reason! You'd do it just to advance your career, to carve another notch in your reputation as a man who gets the job done, no matter who suffers."

She was so carried away by her anger she couldn't stop herself. All the things that upset her about this man came together at once, flooding her emotions— his arrogance, his callous attitude and bulldozer tactics. The thing that burned her most was the memory of how he had held her in his arms and how she had helplessly responded to his sheer animal presence, unable to maintain her dignity by uttering even the smallest protest. She hated herself for the way she had responded to him and hated him for bringing that about, and now afterward, out here in the cool dark night, he had actually had the gall to ask her how she felt about him.

"Do you still want to know how I feel about you?" she asked, her emotions boiling over.

"I told you I do."

"This is how I feel." She pulled her hand back and slapped him stingingly across the face.

They glared at each other, their eyes on fire. Shelby's nostrils were flaring; neither spoke. Then she turned and stalked off.

He wouldn't let her go off into the night alone, though. He grasped her arm and took her back to his limousine with him, putting her inside and shutting the door while he remained in the driveway. "Get her out of here," he said to his driver, his voice so low it was almost a growl.

As the car started forward to take her home, Shelby turned in the seat for a final look at him. He was standing there in the center of the circular drive, his teeth bared like those of a savage animal. Then the car turned onto the street, and Donovan Hawkes was lost from view.

CHAPTER FOUR

THE MAN WAS vindictive—Bill Davidson had warned her of that. Shelby spent the next morning in a state of constant anxiety, expecting Bill to show up at any moment to tell her that her Brazilian assignment had been canceled, that she would have to spend several more months waiting for a new assignment. He might even tell her Hawkes had filed a formal letter of reprimand for inclusion in her permanent file.

The morning was spent at the Foreign Service Institute's "area orientation" seminar, learning about the Brazilian government and its political structures. In the afternoon she attended a seminar on the Brazilian economy. Shelby's anxiety was just beginning to recede when the door to the small auditorium opened and Bill's secretary came in, looking directly at Shelby.

Shelby excused herself from the seminar, telling the instructor she would be back in a few minutes, but Bill's secretary said, "No, Shelby, I don't think that's right. Mr. Davidson mentioned you wouldn't be attending any more briefings on Brazil at all."

When Shelby entered Bill's office, her temper was flaring. She declined his offer to take a seat, and

before he could even utter another word, she said,
"My assignment's been canceled, hasn't it?"

Bill leaned back in his executive swivel chair and
folded his hands across his stomach. "Yes, it has."
He didn't seem particularly upset about the injustice
of this.

Shelby, however, was upset. "I'll get even with
that Hawkes," she declared, her eyes narrowing. "I
don't know how, but I do know that someone has to
show a man like that he can't walk all over people."
Though she sounded angry, the main emotions she
was feeling were extreme sadness and a sense of loss.
This first assignment had meant a lot to her.

"Calm down," Bill soothed her, not understanding her anger. "Hawkes had nothing to do with this.
He doesn't even know about it. He left for Bonn this
morning, long before Bruckner's request came in."

"Bruckner's request?"

"That's why your Brazilian assignment has been
canceled. Heinrich Bruckner personally requested
you be assigned to his country. We're honoring his
request and sending you out to our legation in West
Berlin."

Now Shelby did sit down, on the office sofa, bewildered. "I don't understand. Why would Herr Bruckner put in a personal request for me?"

"Beats the heck out of me," Bill replied, smiling.
"You must have made quite an impression on the old
boy at that ball last night."

Thinking back on the events of the ball, Shelby
was still puzzled. She couldn't imagine what she had

done to impress Herr Bruckner enough for him to take such an action. Another question pressed more heavily on her mind, though.

"Bill, you say Donovan Hawkes didn't try to get my assignment canceled? Do you know if he did anything else against me—such as file a reprimand?"

"He did nothing. And I'd be the one to know, since you're assigned to my section until we shoot you out to your new post." He gazed at Shelby's concerned expression and said, "Don't worry about that one, Shel. He won't bother you again." He was clearly disapproving of Hawkes. Evidently he had heard about the kissing incident at the ball last night. The Washington diplomatic corps was like a small-town gossip mill in many ways.

"Also," he added, "you don't have to worry about running into him over there in the Federal Republic." This was the official name for West Germany. "Our embassy in Bonn is almost three hundred miles from the West Berlin legation, where you'll be stationed, and as you know, West Berlin isn't even physically connected to West Germany." He shook his head. "You can forget about ever seeing Hawkes again."

Good, thought Shelby with relief. That was the main thing she wanted to do about Donovan Hawkes—forget him, pretend she had never met him and hope she never would again.

"This is going to be a great assignment for you," Bill continued in a cheerier voice. "Berlin is lovely in the fall, and this is the sort of assignment that can

really make or break the early stages of your career."
He came out from behind his desk and went to the
cabinet near the door. He withdrew two goblets and a
bottle of brandy, which Shelby knew he kept to celebrate occasions like this.

As he splashed some brandy into the goblets, Shelby reflected with rising spirits on how this truly was a
wonderful opportunity. The posts in Western Europe
were the most sought after of any in the foreign service. Usually a new officer had to pay dues at less
desirable posts before ever being assigned one of
these plums.

"Incidentally," Bill said as he handed her a goblet,
"if you can, I'd avoid running into Nancy Nash during the next few weeks of your orientation. She's the
one who was scheduled for this assignment until
Bruckner's request came in."

He moved to clink glasses with her in a toast, but
Shelby put down her glass quickly at this bit of news.
"You mean I'm bumping her out of her assignment?
Bill, I won't do that. That's not fair at all."

Bill looked at her. His expression changed from that
of a friendly superior to that of a stern State Department taskmaster. "Shelby, if you somehow had the
impression you were given a choice, I suggest you
change that impression right now. This is the U.S.
State Department's foreign service. We go where
we're told; we serve where we're needed. And on the
rare occasion on which we're personally requested by
a senior minister of a friendly government, we do *not*
tell him, 'thank you, but I can't come.'"

Shelby lowered her eyes, properly chastened. She knew he was right, but still she was not pleased at the situation, and she certainly would not drink a toast in celebration of it.

"Don't worry about Nancy Nash," he said. "She's been in this game long enough to know the rules. Besides, she speaks fluent German, too, so she'll be in line for the next slot that opens up in either of the two Germanies." He put down his goblet without drinking from it. "Incidentally, your language abilities are going to be essential in this assignment. In addition to being a political officer, you'll be interpreting for a senior official of the legation."

Bill began talking about the crash orientation program he would arrange for her during the next three weeks, but Shelby was barely listening. Her mind was on the mystery of why Herr Bruckner had requested she be posted to his country. She was also wondering, with a sense of foreboding, whether she really would be spared having to see Donovan Hawkes again. The hundreds of miles that would separate them seemed like paltry protection. If she had her way, she would not even be in the same country as a man like him— or even on the same continent, for that matter.

DURING THE NEXT THREE WEEKS Shelby underwent a crash orientation course, attending briefings on everything from German history and culture to economics and politics. Since she was to serve as a political officer, many hours were spent briefing her about the key Berlin personalities she might be dealing with.

It was a bit jarring to suddenly be training for the fast-paced important post of Berlin after having spent so much time getting used to the idea of the more low-profile posting to South America, but Shelby found the change exciting and loved every minute of preparing for the new position. She couldn't wait for the day of her departure.

Finally it came. She was driven to the airport in the same car as another State Department officer, a woman named Diana Mercer, who was booked on the same nighttime flight as Shelby. Diana was a few years older than Shelby and about two inches taller—tall for a woman. Shelby's first impression of her was that she seemed a bit hardened by life. She had blond hair, with a washed-out look and features and a manner that were not very feminine. Once they got to talking, though, Shelby saw that she was a good person and had a warm caring personality, despite her appearance of being a bit "tough."

Though Shelby was making her maiden voyage to Berlin, Diana was returning from a brief visit to the United States. She was an officer assigned to the economics cone of the Berlin legation. She had come to Washington so she could personally plead her case for a reassignment request that had been turned down twice already.

Shelby was in a happy excited mood. The only thing that soured her mood—temporarily—was that her father had failed to show up to say goodbye to her until the very last minute. She had been trying to arrange a time for them to get together these past few weeks for a dinner to celebrate her new assignment, but her father had told her he was too busy. He was a foreign affairs consultant at present for a major corporation, working just as hard now that he had taken early retirement as when he had been a full-time diplomat. Though he hadn't been able to schedule time for her in the weeks prior to her departure, he'd promised to arrive at the airport in time for them to have a late dinner together in the skyroom restaurant before her flight. But he didn't show up until it was too late—only minutes before her departure time.

Shelby was disappointed but tried not to show it. It never did any good. Besides, she should have expected something like this after all the previous experiences she had had. If her father had really wanted to have dinner with her, she knew, he could have made time at some point during the past few weeks.

Charles Porterfield Everest came to the outside boarding gate at Washington's National Airport just as Shelby was preparing to board her plane. He looked vigorous and dignified, with hair that was turning silver rather than gray. He wore a brown wool suit with a bow tie. He had been one of the few men in the State Department who could get away with wearing a bow tie.

When Shelby saw him marching briskly toward her from out of the terminal building, out here into the open air, she smiled. She had thought he wouldn't show up at all. She hurried over to meet him eagerly, happy he had come. As she neared him, her eyes automatically searched his expression to see if it would be all right to hug him as she wanted to do. She also wanted to have him hug her back. But no, she saw; that wary retreating look was there in his eyes, as it always was. So she just pecked him on the cheek and settled for his patting her hand as he held it and said, ''I'm sorry I'm late, Shel, really. I tried to make it in time for dinner, but, well, something came up that couldn't be helped.''

''Oh, that's all right, father,'' she replied, trying to sound bright and cheerful. She hid her disappointment at not being hugged in greeting and at his having missed their last chance to be together before the trip. She had no right to get disappointed, she scolded herself. *After all these years, you'd think I'd get used to it...and stop wanting something I can't have.* But she had never got used to it.

''Diana and I had a nice dinner together,'' she said. ''She's the girl I'll be flying out with. She's assigned to the legation, too.'' She would have introduced Diana, but she had already boarded the waiting plane. The jet's engines were warming up now, providing a noisy background sound to the conversation Shelby was trying to have with her father.

''Well, you have a good trip,'' Charles Everest told her, speaking above the noise. ''And enjoy Berlin. It's a fascinating city.'' He gazed at her and added, ''I'm proud of you, Shel, getting a post like this for your very first assignment.''

Shelby felt a pang of joy at hearing him say he was

proud of her, but she immediately chastised herself for being so starved for any signs of caring from him that she would let herself find pleasure in even a small crumb like that. He had complimented her on something for which she could not really even take credit, since she had no idea why she had been requested for this assignment.

"Miss," said the gate steward, "you'd better board. Your flight is about to leave." The jet's engines became louder, and a blast of air made Shelby hold on to her hat.

"Goodbye, father," she said, her eyes bright. "I love you."

"Goodbye, Shel," he said. He kept his distance. Reaching out, he shook her hand, then patted it, smiling at her a bit self-consciously.

Shelby hurried along the tarmac to her waiting jet.

The flight from Washington, D.C. to New York was just a brief hop, but the main leg of their journey—the transatlantic flight from New York's JFK Airport to Frankfurt, Germany—took about seven and one half hours. During that time she and Diana got to talking, but not very freely. Shelby could see Diana was in a somber mood. Something was troubling her. She didn't want to discuss it, though, except to mention that her personal request for a transfer to the East Berlin embassy when her tour of duty in West Berlin ended had been turned down.

Diana's mood seemed to improve when they reached Frankfurt, where they had a layover before leaving on their connecting flight to West Berlin. This gave them a chance to stretch and to walk through the sleek ultramodern corridors of Frankfurt-am-Main's airport. Shelby's excitement seemed to rub off on Diana, for the girl's spirits picked up noticeably.

"Did you know this is the biggest airport in Germany," Shelby asked, trying to get her enthused, "with runways that are *two miles* long?"

"I didn't know they were that long," Diana said.

"That's one for you. But I'll bet you didn't know that this was the airport the passenger zeppelins were launched from during the early days of air travel."

Shelby hadn't known. She smiled. The two of them had a breakfast of *brockwurst* and eggs in one of the airport lounges. Though it was late afternoon here in Germany, due to the six-hour time difference, it was morning back in New York. Shelby's stomach was still on New York time and made no bones about letting her know it. After breakfast they strolled around a bit, then returned to their TWA jet for the short flight to West Berlin.

"We are now leaving West German airspace," announced the pilot's voice over the intercom a few minutes later. "We are entering the territory of the German Democratic Republic—the official name for East Germany."

Shelby, in the window seat, gazed down through the openings in the clouds and saw the broad Elbe River beneath them. It was very blue and lovely, with wide bridges flung across it. Soon they were flying over green forested hills.

Shelby reflected on how interesting it was—and

how strange—that the city of West Berlin was not connected to West Germany, even though it was a West German city. They were now flying across East Germany, flying *away* from West Germany; yet they would soon hit West Berlin. It was situated deep *within* the nation of East Germany—an isolated island of Western freedom, surrounded on all sides by the hostile nation of Communist East Germany.

Shelby knew this strange situation had come about after World War II, when Germany itself had been divided into two parts by the victorious Allies. The Russians took control of the east, and the Western powers took control of the west. Berlin, the capital, had also been divided into two parts, and since Berlin was in East Germany, it found itself completely cut off from West Germany—more than a hundred miles from the nearest West German border.

The pilot's voice again came over the intercom. "We're now traveling in one of the three air corridors," he said, "used by the Allies during the Berlin airlift of 1948."

Shelby remembered the airlift from her briefings. It had been a major heroic feat. The East Germans, controlled by Russia, decided to starve West Berlin. They blocked off all roads, railroad lines and waterways leading into the city The blockade would have succeeded, too, if it had not been for the determination of the United States and Britain to supply Berlin from the air.

Planes flew in to Templehof Airfield around the clock, bringing in food, medicine, clothing and everything else the besieged population needed. The heroic rescue mission began at the rate of ten planes a day, progressed to one hundred and finally—amazingly—required one thousand planes a day, every day. The Russians realized their blockade had failed and grudgingly lifted it after a year.

"There," said Diana, leaning forward to point out of the window. "That's the airlift memorial down there; it's dedicated to the fliers who died trying to supply the city."

It was an eerie sight. Shelby saw a three-pronged concrete wedge reaching high into the sky. It really did earn its nickname, she thought, remembering that it was called the Hunger Rake.

"Well," said Diana, "we're here. We're officially in West Berlin now."

CHAPTER FIVE

THEY WERE FLYING in from the southwest, and as the jet banked toward the north, the sights started coming fast and furiously. They were beneath the cloud cover now, so that Shelby had an unobstructed view of the magnificent city, the largest in Germany.

The sight was awesome and incredibly romantic. The first thing she noticed was the diversity of the land. Her impression of Germany had been based on her stay in Bonn, which had a somewhat consistent terrain. Here, though, below them, was a landscape of great variation. Shelby saw two major rivers, the Spree and the Havel. These ran through Berlin and joined a river system that included a series of lakes awesomely lovely as she gazed down at them.

"Look at all those lakes!" she exclaimed.

"Berlin is a major drainage basin for the Saxony Mountains," Diana explained, "and it's saturated with lakes, rivers and streams. There are more than one hundred and eighty just within the boundaries of the city."

Now Shelby could see, off in the distance, two major forests, their treetops lush and green. "The Tegel and the Spandau," she said aloud, enjoying the chance to finally get some use out of her information she had learned in her briefings.

From their commanding height Shelby spotted something else that intrigued her. Interspersed throughout the city itself were many large areas given over to woodlands and parks. Diana caught her gazing in awe at this harmonious mixture of metropolitan city and wooded countryside. "That's why Berlin is called the 'city in the country,'" Diana stated. "More than one-fifth of the entire city area is unspoiled woodlands and parks. When we get lower, you'll be able to see farms, too—a hundred of them right within the city limits."

As the jet descended, still banking northward, the details of the city became clearer.

"That's the Gedächtnis church, isn't it?" Shelby asked.

"That's right," said Diana.

Shelby would have recognized it anywhere. Its architecture was not just a blending of the old and new, it *was* the old and new. Its Gothic tower rose up high, an unreconstructed bombed-out ruin. It was the only remnant left standing of the original Kaiser Wilhelm church. Around it a new church had been built—an ultramodern construction of glass and steel many stories high.

"They left the original tower standing," Diana explained, "as a reminder to future generations of what the ravages of war can be like. It's supposed to be Germany's most famous ruin."

Off to the side Shelby noticed a tall hill rising at

least two hundred fifty feet high. The amazing thing about this hill and others like it throughout Berlin is that they had not existed only half a century earlier.

"That's the Insulaner," Diana said. "Can you imagine? These hills that are now such a significant part of the Berlin skyline didn't exist before the war. After the war the entire city was rubble, and no one knew what to do with it all. New buildings had to be built, but they couldn't just cart the rubble of the old buildings away—where would they cart it to? It was an entire city's worth. Finally the city fathers decided to make artificial hills out of all the tons of shattered bricks and stones. They piled them together, covered them with soil and planted grass, shrubbery and trees."

"They look so real," Shelby marveled, "as though they'd been here from the beginning of time."

"There's the Siegessäule," said Diana as they flew over a towering monument in the midst of a vast traffic circle. Rising from the center of the circle was an enormous column of dark red granite, sandstone and bronze. The column was composed of tiers of other Roman-style columns, and at the very top was the golden winged figure of the goddess Victory.

"It's beautiful," said Shelby.

"It was built more than a hundred years ago to celebrate the victory over the French in the Franco-Prussian war." Her voice became a shade negative. "That's one of the things you'll see a lot of in Berlin—monuments to military victories. It's no secret that for centuries Germany was a militaristic nation. That seems to have changed now, thank God, but since Berlin was the nation's capital, a lot of the old monuments to military victories are here. The strange thing is, many of them are so lovely, considering what they commemorate.''

That was one of the things Shelby found so fascinating about Germany. Its history was such an unusual blend of brilliant achievements in the arts and sciences mixed with a self-destructive streak of militarism that had got it in trouble time after time. This was a land that had produced greats in every field, but had also produced the greatest madman of the century—Hitler.

"There's the Garden of Eden," Diana said, pointing to a park filled with flowers and trees.

"The *what*?" asked Shelby, laughing. This was something she had not heard about in her briefings.

"Actually, it's officially known as the English Garden, but since it was dedicated by Anthony Eden, everyone calls it the Garden of Eden.''

Now that they were closer to the ground, making their approach to Tegel Airport, the sights seemed to whizz by so fast Shelby could barely take them all in. She was fascinated and excited by all that she saw and couldn't wait for the chance to view these places close up.

They flew over the modernistic Kongresshalle, with its bizarre curving roof that looked like a pie plate folded in half; Berliners called it "the pregnant oyster." Its majestic broad staircase descended alongside a wide reflecting pool. As the jet passed over, Shelby saw its wing reflected for a second. Soon they were passing near the old Reichstag— German parliament—now completely restored. It was a florid Italian Renaissance building, massive in size and architecturally elaborate. They flew by the Tiergarten, Berlin's magnificent six-hundred-acre park, the equivalent of New York's Central Park Then they were passing the Funkturm radio tower, which resembled Paris's Eiffel Tower in its steel-brace construction. Near the top was an observation platform, and beneath that was a fancy restaurant built right into the tower.

It was when Shelby gazed at the dividing line be-tween East and West Berlin—the wall—that the romance and glamour suddenly faded. The wall was like an ugly scar that slashed across the heart of Berlin. It was thirty-four miles long, an average of fourteen feet high and made of concrete blocks and barbed wire. On the eastern side a cleared area ran along its length, filled with various obstructions, rows of barbed wire, guard-dog runs and machine-gun towers.

It seemed impossible that anyone could succeed in crossing it; yet refugees kept trying. In fact, that was why the wall had been built in the first place, Shelby knew. East Germans had been fleeing into the West in droves to get away from the bleak life and the Communist tyranny. During August of 1961, just before the wall went up, refugees were leaving at the rate of one thousand every day. Now, thanks to the wall, the flow of refugees was a mere trickle.

Though the wall prevented refugees from escaping into West Berlin across the middle of the city, there were other obstacles to stop them from leaving at the other frontiers. The East Germans had encircled the entire half-city of West Berlin with tall fences topped with barbed wire. In some places they were electrified, and land mines fronted the fences. At some points vicious dogs patrolled the fences, in addition to patrols by *Vopos*.

The jet was now passing far to the west of Checkpoint Charlie, the main exit in the wall. It was a collection of shacks and guardhouses, with East German soldiers—on the eastern side—guarding the narrow opening.

"What a terrible thing," Shelby said sadly, gazing at the wall, "to make a prison of an entire city. I wonder how many people are trapped there in East Berlin, wanting to get out."

Diana had been fine only minutes ago, but now, as Shelby said these words and then turned to face her, she was stunned to see the other woman burst into tears.

"Diana! What's wrong?"

"I'm sorry," she said, embarrassed by her tears. She tried to wipe them away with her hands.

"Don't be sorry," Shelby replied sympathetically, "just tell me what's the matter. Is it anything I said?" She was fiddling in her purse to find her packet of tissues. She located it and handed it to

Diana, who gratefully took a few sheets and wiped her eyes. Her mascara was smearing.

"It's my...boyfriend," Diana said. The way she uttered the word made Shelby think she was not quite used to saying it—as if she were not used to having a boyfriend. "He's over there," Diana went on, nodding toward the other side of the wall. "He's an East Berliner. I met him when I went into the East to do research for the legation. Hans works in the research department of one of the newspapers. We've seen each other a lot since then, and...."

She had to stop speaking for a moment because her voice was becoming too emotional. She continued wiping her eyes with the wet tissue. Shelby touched her hand, encouragingly, wishing there were more she could do.

"They won't let him out of the East, of course," Diana said. "I can visit him while I'm here, but my tour of duty is up in just a couple of months, and when I leave, I'll never be able to see him again."

"So that's why you wanted to transfer to our embassy in East Germany."

"Yes. I haven't had many boyfriends...I've never had anyone like Hans." She looked up at Shelby. "We're lovers, Shelby. He asked me to marry him, and I want to, but...." She became distraught suddenly and cried out, "How can we? He can't come over here, and I won't be able to go over there, either, soon."

"The State Department couldn't do anything about your transfer request?"

"Oh, they said they'd try, but they made it pretty clear the chances were about zero. You know how the job slots work. A major embassy like the one in East Berlin is a post everyone wants to serve at, and the job slots are filled months in advance, even years in advance in some cones." She shook her head. "I knew even before I went to Washington there wasn't much chance of getting them to change their minds."

"But you went anyway."

"I just had to. What else could I do—tell Hans there was no hope for us and go on my merry way?"

She was very upset. Shelby squeezed her hand, trying to be supportive. Her heart went out to the woman. Diana was trying to get control of herself, clearly embarrassed at breaking down like this in front of someone she'd known only a few hours. Shelby wished there were something she could do to help.

"Well, at least all isn't lost," Diana said, trying to dispel her emotionalism by making a joke. "Hans is almost thirty. If I'm willing to wait until he's sixty-five, there won't be any problem. We'll be able to live happily ever after then." She tried to smile, but the joke wasn't even close to funny. Shelby knew she was referring to the East Germans' practice of letting their citizens cross freely into the West after they reached retirement age; they did this to free themselves from having to pay the pensions the citizens had earned by working all their lives.

Diana had stopped crying and was beginning to pull herself together, though she was still a bit shaky.

She squeezed Shelby's hand and smiled slightly, showing gratitude for Shelby's support.

"Do you have anyone in your life right now?" Diana asked, trying to get her mind off her own thoughts of Hans and how hopeless the situation looked.

Shelby didn't like discussing personal things like this, and normally she would have come up with some polite excuse not to, but she could see how greatly Diana was in need of talking about something other than her own problems, so she answered reluctantly. "I don't have any man in my life now," she said, "and I don't expect to. To tell the truth, I've given up the idea of ever finding a man to suit me—one whom I can love who'll love me back."

"But why?"

"Oh...it's just a conclusion I came to a long time ago." She felt very ill at ease mentioning this. She had kept it to herself for years. "Besides, most men get scared off by my sense of independence. I seem to rub a lot of them the wrong way. That's just part of the reason, though." She shrugged. "I'm not saying I like the fact there won't be any loving relationship in my future. It's just that since it seems to be true, I might as well admit it. I've given up my childhood fantasies of ever finding a man for me."

"But I don't understand," Diana said. "Why do you think you won't find a man who could love you who you'd love in return?"

Now Shelby was really uncomfortable. "Maybe I'm just unlovable," she answered laughingly, trying to make a joke of it. But the word she had used had not been chosen by accident, and she knew in her heart that her statement was the farthest thing from a joke.

She was saved from having to talk about this any more by the seat-belt light flashing on above their heads and the pilot's voice coming over the intercom, telling them they were making their final descent to Tegel Airfield.

Things happened very quickly once they reached the ground. A German national had been sent from the legation to welcome Shelby and shepherd her luggage through customs. A car and driver had also been sent, and Shelby and Diana were whisked to the legation.

The legation itself was housed in an attrative building in the Dahlem district. Diana escorted Shelby through the corridors to the assignment office, and then once she knew where Shelby would be working, she accompanied her to that section.

"It's a good idea to meet your new boss right away," Diana said. "It'll only take a minute, and then we can go check out your residence."

Diana introduced Shelby to Mary Grant, the man's secretary, when they reached the outer office. Mary welcomed Shelby warmly. Then, checking her phone console, she noticed that one of the yellow buttons was lit. "He's on the phone," she said. She looked uncertain. "But he did say to let him know as soon as you arrived." She picked up the handset and pressed the intercom button. "Sorry to interrupt you, sir, but your new political officer just came in. Yes, sir."

She stood up and went to the quilted leather door of the inner office. "You can go right in," she said to Shelby, opening the door and holding it for her. Shelby entered, and the door was shut behind her.

The spacious office was paneled in rich mahogany. At one end was a sofa and coffee table, then a work table and several conference chairs. Across the plush rust-colored carpet, at the other end of the room, was a handsome executive-style desk. One entire wall of the office was dominated by large windows that looked out onto a lush garden courtyard. Shelby's new superior was standing at the windows gazing out, his back to her. He was quite tall. At the moment he was speaking on the telephone, holding the phone in one hand, the receiver in the other.

"I don't care how hard they are to get, Gottfried," he said into the phone, "I need those drugs. I want those drugs."

His voice stunned Shelby. It was deep and manly—and unexpectedly familiar. Oh, no, she thought in alarm. She looked at the man more closely now—at the thatch of thick black hair, the wide shoulders and strong broad back tapering to a trim belted waist. His suit jacket hung at the back of his chair, and the sleeves of the white dress shirt he wore were rolled up to his elbows. When he turned to motion her to take a seat, she saw that hard handsome face and those incredible blue eyes.

Donovan Hawkes, she realized with a sinking feeling.

CHAPTER SIX

DONOVAN HAWKES FROWNED, astonished to see her. "What are you doing here?" he demanded.

It took a moment for her to find her voice. "I . . . I might ask you that same question."

"*You're* my new assistant?"

"Oh, I hope not!" The words escaped her lips before she fully realized she was now speaking to a high-ranking diplomat in his official role as her superior. He was no longer just a forced "date" with whom she happened to be spending an unpleasant evening.

As they stared at each other, they both remembered the last time they had been together. Shelby began burning anew as she recalled how he had publicly humiliated her, taking unfair license in tasting her lips, pressing his hard masculine body against her in an embrace. And he seemed to be recalling the way he had followed her out into the cool Washington night and how she had slapped him stingingly across the face.

Donovan suddenly remembered the phone that was in his hand. "Gottfried," he said into the receiver, "I have to go. See you in the morning at the

Friedrichstrasse section of the wall." He hung up.

He came over to Shelby and stood looking down at her, his hands on his hips. His dark tie was loosened at his neck, his shirt collar open. His rugged face was as insolent as ever as he gazed at her with displeasure. The sheer physical presence of him was so overpowering, Shelby had an urge to step back, to put distance between them. She resisted the urge, though, and raised her chin defiantly instead. She wouldn't give him the satisfaction of seeing her retreat.

"Nancy Nash was supposed to be my new political officer," he said. "It was all arranged."

"Her orders were canceled, and mine were changed. I'm her replacement."

"This is ridiculous. I'm not going to have you working under me."

"Amen to that, Mr. Hawkes. And if you don't mind my breaking protocol by speaking to you frankly...."

"I don't give a damn about protocol."

"Good. Then let me say that you're the last person in the world I want to work for."

He went over to his desk and reached for the phone. "Who ordered these changes?" he said to Shelby. "Tell me, and I'll have his head on a platter."

"Foreign Minister Heinrich Bruckner," she answered. She felt satisfaction at the way he slammed down the receiver and looked off to the side burningly. That took the wind out of his sails. Herr Bruckner's rank was equivalent to that of the U.S. secretary of state.

"That damned romantic," Donovan said, shaking his head. He looked at Shelby. "I saw him a few days ago, and he was hinting about how he had some 'pleasant surprise' in store for me. He was so mischievous about the whole thing he wouldn't tell me what it was all about." He sighed. "So you're what it's all about."

"By no desire of mine, I assure you. May I ask what you're doing here?" She knew she was overstepping her bounds by this question and by the way she was speaking to him without calling him "sir" or showing the proper respect for a senior diplomat, but he didn't seem to stand on formality. He was far different in this regard from most State Department officials, who were loathe to give up even the smallest sign of respect due them. "I thought you were assigned to our embassy in Bonn," she said.

"Too far from the action. I knew the day I arrived I'd have to relocate my base of operations out here to West Berlin." As he gazed at her, his anger seemed to lessen, and he recalled that she had just arrived from a long jet flight. A note of civility crept into his manner as he motioned to the sofa and said, "You can sit down, if you'd like."

"Thank you, I'll stand." She *was* tired, but if there was to be further confrontation, she'd face it on her feet. "So Herr Bruckner asked for my transfer here because he's a romantic?" she continued. At least that answered one question she had wondered about. "Since he thought we were engaged, he figured he'd do us both a 'favor' by requesting our assignment at the same post?"

"Apparently." He made an impatient frustrated gesture. "This has got completely out of hand." He began pacing across the room. "I only came up with this engagement idea to keep Gretchen out of my hair. She was getting to be a nuisance, following me around too closely." He looked at Shelby. "But I never expected *this*. I never expected you to actually show up here. This complicates things."

"It certainly does, and I hope you don't expect me to continue this charade of being your fiancée, because frankly, Mr. Hawkes, I won't do that. I don't intend to see you socially, on some sort of false pretend basis, no matter what your romantic problems are, no matter how many ministers' daughters—or other women, for that matter—you're trying to avoid."

"No," he said, looking at her thoughtfully, "I agree. It's out of the question."

"Then you'll take steps to end this charade?"

"Yes."

"Good," Shelby said quietly, wondering why she felt the tiniest bit of a letdown instead of the relief she had expected. "And as for my working as your assistant—"

"I'll take care of that, too. You don't have to worry about working under someone you consider as objectionable as me."

He had misunderstood her. Shelby was only going

to suggest that they declare a truce so their personal antagonism wouldn't interfere with their professional relationship. After all, as a newly graduated officer, who was she to propose that she be reassigned somewhere else within the legation to suit her own personal needs?

It was too late to say anything now, though. He was already leaning over his desk, jotting down a note. Shelby could make out the bold printed headline at the top of the note pad: TELEX. Well, this was probably best after all, she thought, remembering how she had despised him after that incident in Washington.

"You're probably tired from your long trip," he said in a voice that was much less hostile than it had been. Apparently he viewed himself and her as antagonists who shared the same bad situation through the fault of neither one. They were comrades, he seemed to feel, in the sense that both wanted out of the situation.

"Why don't you go ahead and get some rest? Diana Mercer brought you over, didn't she? She's probably outside now, waiting to show you to your new quarters."

"Thank you," Shelby said wearily, trying to put friendliness in her tone in response to his. "I am rather tired."

He walked her to the door and held it for her. As she was passing through, he said something that was intended to put her at ease but that, for some reason, made her feel wary. "Don't worry, Miss Everest, I'll take care of everything."

Shelby's new quarters were off post in a quaint old building and were comfortably furnished. Married officers in Berlin were provided with individual houses. Single officers were assigned to large one-bedroom apartments similar to Shelby's. All residences for diplomatic personnel were completely furnished, but as Shelby inspected her new apartment, she saw that the furniture was of the usual bland type found in government housing around the world. Fortunately she had brought many of her favorite items, which would lend a personal touch. She looked forward to living here, to decorating the rooms to suit her taste.

"I still don't see how he can do that," Diana said as she followed Shelby on an inspection of her new home. "He actually told you he'd arrange it so you're working for someone else instead of him?"

"Why is that so hard to believe? He *is* a deputy minister."

"But even so, the job slots are all filled. This isn't a major embassy; it's only a legation, here to deal with the specific problems of West Berlin. There are only thirty-one people on staff. There aren't any political officers who'd be allowed to switch with you if it means transferring down to a lower grade." She looked thoughtful. "Besides, Shelby, I don't think we even have any junior-grade officers in the political cone who speak fluent German, so there's no one who *could* switch with you."

Shelby was too tired and happy to be disturbed at Diana's doubts. She kept wandering from room to room, admiring the hardwood floor in her new bedroom, the casement windows in her living room. *My very first residence,* she thought, *on my very first assignment.*

She didn't really want to speak at all. She was very tired and just wanted to admire her new quarters a little longer, then shower and go to sleep. But Diana seemed to want to pursue the topic, so Shelby accommodated her, saying, "Maybe Herr Bruckner's asking to have me here will give Hawkes's request added weight when he tries to change me to another slot in the legation."

"Herr Bruckner asked to have you assigned here?" Diana was surprised. Shelby had told her about the phony engagement in Washington, but not that the reason for her reassignment was Herr Bruckner's personal request.

"Yes," Shelby replied. "Donovan Hawkes says it's because Bruckner's such a romantic."

"Oh, Shelby!" said Diana, laughing, sitting down on the bed. "Herr Bruckner a romantic? He's about as romantic as a rock."

Shelby looked at her, puzzled. "Well, why else would he request my assignment here?"

"To protect his daughter, of course. Haven't you heard of Mr. Hawkes's reputation? Most of the time during the past few years, when he's come to Germany, he hasn't spent the nights in his own bed. A few times he was needed, and contact was tried—but he was out the entire night." Diana raised her eyebrows significantly. "Don't think Herr Bruckner doesn't know about his reputation. The last thing he wants is for Gretchen to succeed in seducing Hawkes, now that there's no chance he'll ever marry her since he's supposedly engaged to you. He doesn't want his daughter used and abandoned by a man who doesn't seem to have any scruples.''

Suddenly it all became clear to Shelby. She remembered how upset Herr Bruckner had become in Washington when Gretchen said she wouldn't respect an engagement, wouldn't look at anything short of marriage as a reason to stop pursuing Donovan. And Herr Bruckner was such a prim proper man.

"So he wanted me over here," she ventured, "to sort of...protect my own interests?"

"That sounds like it to me. If you weren't here, Gretchen would be all over Mr. Hawkes, but now that you are, Herr Bruckner probably figures you'll be able to keep her away from 'your man.'"

Shelby was too tired even to think how she felt about this. The long jet trip, coming on top of all the excitement of the previous days, was catching up with her. She sank down onto her bed and stretched luxuriously, yawning. "Well, all I know is that Donovan Hawkes said he'd arrange it so that I no longer have to pretend to be his fiancée, so that I don't have to work under him. He said he'd fix everything."

Her last thought before sailing into a void of pleasant blackness was that she'd let herself rest here for just a few seconds more before getting up to shower, just a few tiny seconds....

It wasn't until the next morning, when she went to process in, that she learned how Donovan intended to "fix" everything—and learned it was a way that would solve his own problem...at the expense of drastically hurting her career.

CHAPTER SEVEN

THE FIRST STEP a newly arrived officer takes at a post is to "process in." This involves presenting her assignment orders to the administrative officer, then filling out the various forms that cover every aspect of her life abroad—financial forms, medical forms, receipts for furnishings. In turn she receives the documents she'll need to function in the host nation: driving permit, diplomatic ID, privilege pass to the U.S. commissary, et cetera. Afterward would come the briefings by the department heads and her welcoming introduction at the next staff meeting.

When Shelby went to the administrative officer in the morning, poised and professional in her tailored suit, she was told that processing in would not be necessary.

Shelby was stunned. "I don't understand."

The administrative officer, James Stanton, looked regretful but said firmly, "I'm afraid your orders have been canceled, Miss Everest. The deputy minister told me last night that you won't be assigned here after all."

For a moment all she could do was stare. "Did he

say why?'' she asked, shaken by the news, not quite believing it.

"Not to me, but then that's not my responsibility. All I have to know is who's going to be on the legation staff and who isn't.'' He smiled slightly, trying to be sympathetic. "I'm afraid you're not.'' He added in a brighter tone, "Why don't you take the day off and go sight-seeing? We're arranging your flight back to Washington, but that won't be until this evening.''

"Sightsee?'' she wanted to scream at him. "I'm a foreign-service officer, not a tourist!'' But she held back her words. Taking her anger out on James Stanton would not do any good. However, she knew one man who certainly was going to get a healthy dose of it. She left the administrative section and stalked down the hall to Donovan's office.

Before she reached it, she came upon Diana, who approached her wearing an expression that was very sad. "Oh, Shelby, I'm so sorry. I only heard about it a half hour ago.''

"You're doing better than I am,'' Shelby acknowledged ruefully. "I only heard about it two minutes ago.''

"Anthony in Communications told me. Mr. Hawkes prepared a telex to Washington asking that you be recalled and that someone named Nancy Nash be sent in your place.''

"How can he even do that? I was told that when a host government requests an officer by name, the request has to be honored.''

"Usually it does. Mr. Hawkes will be taking a lot of heat for this, but evidently he feels it's important enough to him to make it worthwhile."

Shelby was fuming with outrage. She had known all along that Donovan had negative traits, but she had never expected anything as underhanded as this. She remembered the reassuring way he had said, "I'll take care of everything."

"He did attach a note," Diana said, trying to minimize the damage. "It says he's requesting your recall for administrative reasons, not because of any deficiency on your part."

"That won't matter! They always say that when they send someone home so it won't hurt their career, but it always does anyway. You can't be sent home from an assignment without people thinking the real reason was that you couldn't handle it."

Diana said nothing. She knew this was true.

"Has the telex been sent yet?" Shelby asked.

"No, the priority on it is routine. Anthony doesn't send his routine traffic until after lunch. The morning is reserved for high priority."

Diana was looking at her with sad eyes, she herself suffering as a result of this news. She was losing someone she had hoped to make a good friend. Shelby squeezed her arm in sympathy, thinking how strange it was that she was commiserating with Diana, instead of the other way around. Then she started away.

"Where are you going?" Diana asked.

"To have a word or two with a certain deputy minister."

"Shelby! You can't confront a deputy minister, and besides, he's not in his office."

"Do you know where he is?"

"No, but I do know you'll only make Mary feel bad if you ask her, because I'm sure she won't be allowed to tell you."

"That's all right," Shelby replied, realizing she already knew where he was. The Friedrichstrasse section of the wall—that's where he had said he'd meet that man he was talking to on the phone the previous day. "Wish me luck," she said, starting away.

Diana looked amazed, and her last words to Shelby were, "But you can't confront a deputy minister!"

If the Berlin Wall had looked ugly from the air, it looked even worse close up. It was like a hideous concrete scar, thought Shelby, as she took a taxi along Schlesischestrasse, which for a distance ran parallel to the wall. The appearance of the wall was in such striking contrast to that of the rest of the city. West Berlin was colorful, gay, glittering, with lively shopping and business activity during the day and a nightlife in the evening that was the envy of Germany. In fact, West Berlin was known as the Las Vegas of Europe. Near the wall, though, the glitter and glamour ended. As Shelby now saw, the busy major boulevards—which had once extended all across the city—came to a truncated end at the wall. This was the case with Friedrichstrasse, she noticed, when she reached it. It simply stopped abruptly.

Nearby she saw Donovan. He was standing at the base of one of the concrete observation platforms that overlooked the wall at various intervals along this street. The platforms were there to allow tourists and residents to gaze over the wall and view the captive population of the East. Donovan was engaged in conversation with a thin man who had a gray goatee and mustache. Both men wore light jackets and had somber expressions as they talked. The day was overcast with dark clouds, and rain was threatened.

Shelby had to pay her cabdriver in dollars. Since she had not processed in, her currency had not yet been converted to West German marks. The driver was happy to accept her money, though, as she knew he would be. The American military presence in West Berlin was so strong that dollars were almost an unofficial second currency.

She started marching directly toward Donovan and the older gray-goateed man. Donovan noticed her when she was near and frowned as he watched her approach. "You've got a knack for turning up in the most unexpected places," he said with annoyance. "First in the legation, when you were supposed to be on your way to Brazil, and now here, when you're supposed to be packing your bags for a trip back home."

"I want to know why you're sending me home," she demanded. She knew she was greatly overstepping her bounds. A junior-grade officer just did not challenge a senior diplomat; she was expected to go through the approved chain of command. But Shelby had always been willful and proud. These were traits she had inherited from her mother, or so she had been told. If this man thought he could treat her so high-handedly and have her take it lying down—well, he'd learn otherwise.

"I can't have you working as my assistant," he said unrepentantly. "I thought we agreed on that yesterday. I told you I'd arrange things so that wouldn't happen."

"When you said you'd 'take care of it,' I thought you meant you'd arrange it so I was working for someone else here at the legation."

"There isn't anyone else you can work for here. The slots are all filled." He spent a moment detailing the very same facts Diana had mentioned the previous night. Then he said, "I'm sorry, but that's the way it is. Nothing personal."

"Nothing personal?" she exploded. "Of course it's personal! You're trying to get even with me for slapping you that night in Washington. I was told you're vindictive, but for some reason I couldn't make myself believe that about you. Boy, was I ever wrong!"

He had been willing to let her vent her heated emotions, aware how disappointed she felt about losing out on this assignment, but his tolerance went only up to a point. Shelby realized now, under his stern gaze, that that point had been reached. And he was right, she knew. She had gone way too far.

She glanced at the thin gray-bearded man, who was looking on in amazement and nervousness. Who was he? A high German official? A senior diplomat of another nation? Shelby had not only barged in and interrupted Donovan's conversation with the man, but she had made bitter personal remarks, as well, remarks that could be very embarrassing to Donovan.

But Donovan didn't seem particularly embarrassed, Shelby noticed. Mostly he looked irritated at her presence here. He did not want to have to deal with her now. He seemed to feel, though, that he did owe her this opportunity to confront him, that it ran contrary to some personal sense of honor of his to deny her the chance. Shelby was surprised. She had not thought he *had* any sense of honor to be offended. But now he turned to the gray-bearded man and said, "Gottfried, we'll have to continue this later. Do you have the...items?"

The man looked at Shelby very nervously.

"It's all right," Donovan assured him.

The man reached into the pocket of his jacket and quickly, furtively, withdrew a brown-paper-wrapped package, which he handed to Donovan. He was clearly uneasy about the fact that Shelby was watching the transfer. If Donovan was nervous about it, he covered it up well. He slipped the package into his pocket without expression. The goateed man turned and hurried away.

"Now," Donovan said to Shelby, turning to her, "let's get something straight. I'm sending you home because I have a job to do here and I need a capable cooperative assistant to help me do it. You're not that person. It has nothing to do with anything personal that happened between you and me in Washington.''

Shelby didn't believe him. She thought he was just making an excuse. ''I'm capable,'' she protested. ''And as far as being cooperative....''

Without a word he took her elbow and guided her up the steps to the top of the concrete observation platform. With a sweep of his arm he motioned to the expanse of East Berlin now visible before them. ''Look at that. Let it sink in.''

Now Shelby could fully appreciate the horror of this despised wall, which made prisoners of an entire nation. On this side, the Western side, the wall came flush against the sidewalk with no obstructions. On the other side, though, as she gazed over the barbed-wire top, Shelby saw the famous ''death strip,'' which turned her stomach.

It extended for one hundred yards out from the wall, running parallel to it, and was composed of several barbed-wire fences, with land mines running along one strip and vicious guard dogs patrolling the strip beyond it. There were metal obstructions placed to foil speeding cars that might try to crash through the wire to reach the wall. Guard towers were positioned all along the wall.

On the other side of the death strip, where the streets of East Berlin began, Shelby saw East Berliners going purposefully about their business. A few looked over at her with seeming longing and hopelessness. Their expressions reminded Shelby of children pressing their faces against the windows of an orphanage, able to see the freedom of the outside world but not able to have it.

"It's the people in there whom the Lion is trying to help," Donovan said. "He arranges crossings for the defiant political ones who are about to be arrested— and for anyone else who's willing to risk his or her life to escape. He earned his nickname because he's king of the Berlin Wall, as the lion is king of the jungle. He's made more successful crossings than any man alive."

He swiveled her to face him, his expression grim. "My job is to stop him. If you're my assistant, your job will be to help me stop him. Now is that something you want to do?"

"No, I don't want to do it. I'd despise doing it." She added slowly, "But I would do it." She felt sobered and serious. "As I told you once before, Mr. Hawkes, I believe State Department policy should be made in Washington, not by every officer who takes it upon himself to decide what's best for the country, not even when I want very dearly to take it upon myself to decide what's best—as I do in this case."

"So you'd help track down the Lion."

"Yes."

"And you'd turn him in if you discovered his identity so the police could arrest him?"

Shelby felt torn by conflicting emotions. She believed strongly, though, in the time-honored principle she had mentioned, so there really was only one answer she could give. "Yes, I'd turn him in."

Donovan looked away from her, glowering in frustration.

This was such a puzzling man, Shelby thought. He hated the wall—that was clear. Yet he was willing to stop the Lion, who was the enemy of the wall.

"No," he said finally, turning to face her. "I still won't have you as my assistant."

"Then it *is* for personal reasons after all," she accused, "isn't it?"

"Think whatever you like. You're going home on this evening's plane." He started descending the steps.

"If I am, then a formal protest will be going along with me, which I'll file the minute I get back."

For some reason that hit him where it hurt. He turned abruptly, midway down the stairs, and glared up at her. For a moment he didn't speak. Then he said, "I can't have you doing that. I can't have you drawing attention to my situation right now, the way a formal inquiry would do."

"And I can't have you ruining my career for vindictive reasons of your own." She told him something then that was very personal and that she didn't really want to share with him, but she did want to let him know why she was refusing to back down. "I joined the State Department because I wanted a career in which I could do something important with my life, in which I could make a difference. I can't let you ruin that for me before it even gets off the ground."

She didn't tell him the rest of it, though—which

was the most personal part of all: that she had long ago given up hope of ever finding a strong, bold, kind man with whom she could fall in love, a man who would love her deeply in return. Her most cherished dream in life had always been to find the right man for her, to marry and raise a loving family. She knew she would make a good mother, and she wanted this so much. Shelby's children would be raised in an atmosphere of caring and affection in which they would never want for love. Unlike Shelby, her children would never have that terrible gnawing suspicion in their hearts that they were really not cared for. Shelby's husband and children would have all the love in her heart, all the love she was so eager to give. . . .

She had to shake her head to bring herself back to reality. There would be no children; there would be no strong loving husband, and because of this, now that that "silly fantasy" of her childhood had been shattered, her career took on added significance as the most important part of her life.

"Look," Donovan said, "there's more at stake here than you realize." He seemed almost desperate to persuade her against filing the formal protest. "There are things far too important for me to take the risk of your ruining them by my having you along as my assistant."

"Such as?"

He wouldn't tell her. He clenched his teeth and glared at her. Shelby could see he had never expected her to present such an obstacle. He must have thought that she would be easy to walk all over, that she would take the situation lying down. She felt a glimmer of satisfaction at proving him wrong. This evaporated, though, at the look of animosity now radiating from him. He bounded up the few steps separating them and stood directly in front of her, glaring down at her.

"All right, Miss Everest," he said, his voice cold steel. "We'll play the game your way. I'll withdraw my telex; you can stay. But I'll tell you this: I'm going to do everything I can to make your life unbearable here. I'll put so many demands on you—legitimate demands—that you'll be begging me to send you home. I'll do everything I can to make you resign from this assignment and leave voluntarily."

She was stunned by the unexpected force of his anger, but she found herself raising her chin defiantly in the face of it. "I'm a big girl," she said. "I can take whatever you can dish out."

"That remains to be seen." He turned away from her. "Go process in today," he called over his shoulder, "and report to me tomorrow morning." He descended the stairs, then stalked off toward his waiting black limousine. He did not invite Shelby to join him for the ride back.

Watching him go, Shelby wondered just what she had got herself into. Her words to him had been confident and defiant, but she didn't feel so confident right now. Here she was, she reflected, on her first assignment, in a new post, in a foreign land, and she had made an enemy of the powerful high-ranking man for whom she would be working.

And worst of all, she didn't even know why. Why was he so determined to get rid of her? The mystery burned like a glowing ember in her soul.

CHAPTER EIGHT

DURING THE NEXT FEW WEEKS, true to his word, Donovan did everything he could to make Shelby's life miserable. If Shelby were not so prideful and strong-willed—Diana called it stubborn—she would have quit and given up after the first few days. But something within her told her it was important to stick it out, to not give him the satisfaction of seeing her broken.

Donovan went about his mission of hunting down the Lion by going to the locations at which the Lion had made crossings. He went to investigate clues and to try to detect some telltale patterns in the Lion's method of operation. He also traveled throughout Germany to interview people who had information about the Lion: witnesses to the crossings, government officials, sometimes even the refugees themselves who had been taken across. Donovan also worked closely with the West Berlin police.

Shelby's role as his assistant was to accompany him on his trips, to act as interpreter when required and to assist him in any way he thought necessary. This gave him even greater power over her than a man in his position normally would have had.

Under ordinary circumstances, Shelby's role as political officer would have involved a variety of interesting exciting tasks. For instance, she would have been assigned to "areas of mutual interest" between the United States and West Germany and would have met with her West German counterpart to solve problems in these areas. She would also have been involved in deciding on the agenda for treaty conferences and in laying the groundwork for ambassadorial negotiations. Now, though, due to the importance the State Department put on catching the Lion, she was assigned to this one task exclusively.

Still, her duties were varied. She went with Donovan on interviews and made a detailed report at the end of each one. Later these were typed up by one of the legation secretaries. She also made phone calls and side trips to track down information Donovan said he needed. For instance, one of the Lion's most daring types of crossing involved taking people out of Berlin through East Germany and then into West Germany by swimming under the icy Baltic Sea. This required securing wet suits and scuba gear and having great endurance and stamina as a swimmer. Shelby's role was to try to discover where the Lion had got his scuba equipment. Donovan had her contact every sporting goods store in West Berlin.

Donovan assigned her enough of these tasks and others, to fill up not only her days but her evenings, as well. She knew he deliberately gave her more work than was necessary. She also knew, from the grapevine, that James Stanton had suggested he accept a second assistant to take the load off Shelby. Donovan had refused. For some reason he didn't like having even one assistant, and the idea of having two was out of the question.

What pained Shelby most was not the work load but the cold way in which Donovan behaved toward her. He treated her as an enemy, not a colleague. He never offered her a word of praise or any small bit of human warmth.

This was especially hard on her, since it had been this way all during her childhood. Her mother had been a woman of delicate features, like Shelby, but also—unlike Shelby—of delicate health, too. She had died when Shelby was only nine, from a series of hepatic infections brought on by the rigors of the constant traveling involved in Shelby's father's career. Much of the traveling had been to inhospitable outposts not suited to a woman with such a fragile constitution.

Her mother had been a wonderful woman, who had given Shelby much love. When she died, all affection suddenly ceased. Shelby's father was not at all a warm person. Though she thought he probably loved her, he was not the sort of man who knew how to show it. He felt very hesitant about ever expressing feelings and looked at displays of affection as somehow uncivilized. He never offered a caring gesture or an endearing word, and he never seemed to have any time for her.

As a child, Shelby grew up with a powerful sense of loneliness and longing. She had wanted so badly to be held in her father's arms, to be kissed good-night the way other children were, to be hugged a little—maybe even just on her birthday. But these things never came, and finally the young Shelby had taken to heart a belief that had never left her: that she would never have any of these things because she was an unlovable human being. It was her fault. There was some horrible thing about her, she was sure, that simply made her unlovable.

The way Donovan treated her intensified this feeling. The previous night had been an example. Since their investigations took them to the far reaches of both Germanies, it didn't make sense to return to the legation at the end of each day. Often they would have two days of interviews in the same outlying area. Because of this, Mary would arrange hotel accommodations for them in the regions they visited.

Since they were two fellow Americans away from their home base, the natural thing at the end of the day would have been for them to dine together rather than separately. But Donovan made a point of never inviting her to have dinner with him. And the previous night had been even worse. By coincidence they had eaten at the same restaurant. Neither had realized it until they were seated at separate tables. Then they saw each other. Their gazes locked, but instead of inviting her over to share his table, Donovan turned away and pretended she was not there.

Shelby had felt all the old feelings of loneliness and emptiness rushing up to flood her. Was it so much to ask that he should unbend just a little, indulge in a tiny bit of companionship with her after the day's work? He could always go back to treating her coldly in the morning.

But no, whatever mysterious reason he had for wanting to get rid of her, it was important enough to make him maintain his harsh attitude, even if he didn't want to. And strangely, Shelby sensed he really *didn't* want to. Once partway through the previous night's meal Shelby caught him gazing at her across the restaurant without his realizing she was noticing. There was an unexpected look of torment in his eyes—and almost of gentleness. She sensed that he hated treating her this way—that it actually pained him to behave so coldly toward her.

Then why was he doing it? What could be of such importance as to make him act in this terrible way that was so painful to them both?

DIANA COULD COME UP with no answer, either, when Shelby told her the situation over a late lunch the day Shelby got back. They were seated at a window table in the Funkturm restaurant, which was a more expensive place than Shelby would have gone to on her own. Diana had taken her and insisted on paying for her, partly to cheer her up and partly as a welcoming gesture, for it was their first lunch together since Shelby's arrival in Berlin.

The restaurant was located in the four-hundred-ninety-foot radio tower of the Messegelände Fair Grounds. The view from their spectacular height on this bright sunny day was astounding. A panoramic vista of the entire city lay beneath them. To the west was the huge Olympic Stadium where the 1936 Olympics had been held. Off to the side was the world famous open-air Waldbühne Theater. Near them, at the edge of the Messegelände, was the altarlike Theodor Heuss monument, at the top of which burned an eternal flame. Shelby could also see Wannsee Lake, with a dozen white billowing canvases of sailboats skimming to and fro. All about them stretched the busy teeming metropolis of Berlin.

Shelby had wanted only something light to eat, but there seemed to be nothing light on the menu. When Diana told her that the *Gefullte Schwienerippchen* were small pork chops, she ordered those. They turned out to be huge, sliced open and stuffed with raisins, apples and croutons, then laced with rum. They were delicious, but Shelby could barely finish half her plate. Diana had ordered a dish of such conflicting tastes that it amazed Shelby. Called *Labskaus*, it was a stew prepared with salty herring, potatoes, pickled beef and topped with a fried egg and slices of sour pickles. Diana seemed to enjoy it, though all Shelby could do was watch her eat in astonishment.

"I've never heard of Mr. Hawkes being so hostile to anyone else," Diana said in perplexity when Shelby told her of her situation. "In fact, he's one of the few senior diplomats who seem to be really concerned about people. Everyone I know thinks he's basically a very decent caring man—everyone except the top State Department brass, that is. They've never liked him because he's not a team player and he won't kowtow to anyone.'' She narrowed an eye quizzically. "Are you sure this isn't all the result of something personal between you and him?''

"I'm not sure at all,'' Shelby replied, thinking back to the incident in Washington. "But he says it's not.''

Diana reflected on the harsh way Shelby said Donovan had been treating her. "I don't see why you even put up with it,'' she commented. "It sounds to me as though you'd be better off going home and awaiting reassignment, even if it does hurt your career.''

Shelby had been toying with the idea but had dismissed it. In a strange way it was partly Donovan's very coldness to her that kept her going, that made her willing to face each new day of hardship. His hostility fueled her determination to resist. She wouldn't have resisted so hard for just anyone, but somehow she felt it important to show this particular man that she was a worthy adversary, that she had the strength and character not to cave in to him.

"Maybe it has to do with his career problems,'' Diana suggested. "Maybe he's so worried about doing well on this assignment—since his career is so shaky—that he's unintentionally taking it out on you.''

There was nothing unintentional about his behavior, Shelby knew, but what she said was, "I wasn't aware his career was shaky. What makes you say that?''

"In the early part of it, when he first became a State Department officer, he was a department whiz. Did you know that during the Vietnam War he was posted to our embassy in Saigon?"

Shelby shook her head.

"That's how he started as a troubleshooter. God knows what he did there, but he managed to stay on while other diplomats were being replaced as though through a revolving door. They couldn't handle the stress of working in a nation at war. Hawkes could. He was one of the last Americans to leave from the roof of the embassy just before the fall of Saigon."

Shelby remembered seeing a striking Pulitzer prize-winning photograph of a helicopter taking off under heavy fire, carrying away the last contingent of Americans. She could have had no idea that Donovan had been on that helicopter.

"His career went wonderfully after that," Diana continued, "until something very bad happened to him during his assignment to Turkey. I don't know what it was because I don't have access to those particular records, but I hear it put a permanent ceiling on his advancement."

Shelby knew what had occurred. Her father had demanded his recall. Could that be why Donovan was treating her so badly—to strike back at her for what her father had done to him? Shelby began wondering anew why her father had fired him. The only way to find out was to call. She checked her watch. It was only one o'clock, meaning it was seven A.M. in Washington.

Diana was refilling her wineglass with white Riesling, and Shelby realized that her hand was shaking. Glancing at her face, she saw how distraught Diana appeared. Suddenly Shelby felt very guilty. Here she was so obsessed with her own problems she hadn't even noticed that her friend was in need of consolation herself. Shelby reached across the table and covered Diana's hand.

"How is Hans?" she asked softly.

"Oh, Shelby," Diana cried her face anguished, "I'm so worried." Now that the subject had been broached, her emotions seemed to pour out. She leaned closer across the table so her words would not be overheard.

"He's threatening to cross," she went on. "He says that if my transfer request isn't granted, he'll do it. He doesn't want to live without me, he says, and he's willing to risk his life crossing the wall to be with me." She looked deeply distressed. "Well, I don't want to be without him, either, but. . . you know how few people make it across the wall these days. It's only the professionals, such as the Lion, who bring people out alive. Most of the ordinary folk who try crossing end up dead, or captured and sent to prison."

Shelby squeezed Diana's hand sympathetically. There was nothing she could say, though, because Diana was right. If Hans tried to cross, he would probably be killed in the attempt. The East Berlin Communists did not play games. Crossing was a life or death matter.

"I haven't told him yet that the reassignment orders were turned down," Diana said. "I'm afraid to. If he knows, he might try crossing right away."

"You'll have to tell him sometime."

"Oh, I know," she moaned. "But I'll hold off as long as I can. Maybe something will come up."

Shelby was trying to think of something to say when just at that moment a commotion occurred that turned all eyes toward the front of the restaurant. Two stiff-faced West Berlin policemen had entered and were marching through the dining room directly toward one of the tables. Shelby looked at the table they were heading toward.

A tall youngish man sat there, leaning back in his seat, watching the approach of the police with a wry, amused grin. He had a handsome angular face, with gaunt cheeks and a contemptuous mouth. His blond hair swept rakishly low across his forehead. He was not broad-shouldered like Donovan, but instead had a long lanky body from which emanated an aura of suppressed menace. He was dressed casually in an expensive tan jacket over a blue shirt and appeared no older than about thirty-five. Beside him at the table sat a beautiful red-haired girl who, unlike him, was clothed fashionably. A lit cigarette hung from the corner of the man's mouth.

The uniformed policemen stopped at his table. One of them said in a no-nonsense voice, "Baron, you will come with us, please."

The tall blond man looked at the policeman and grinned in a way that was quite world-weary, then he

stood up, very cool under pressure. He summoned
the dining-room captain, who hurried over, clearly
eager to please him. The man folded several bills and
slipped them into the captain's pocket. *"Rufen Sie
einen Taxi fur meine Freundin,"* he told him. Call a
taxi for my date.

The dining-room captain nodded.

The blond man bent forward and raised his date's
hand to his lips, kissing it. Then he winked at her.
The girl was looking at him rather dumbly, Shelby
thought, not knowing quite how to handle the
strange situation. She certainly did not have the poise
he did.

The man, flanked by the policemen, walked out of
the dining room to the elevator. He limped slightly as
he walked. When he passed Shelby's table, she saw
his eyes. They were brown, cool and aloof, with a
look that made him seem somehow quite dangerous.

Everyone in the restaurant had been watching the
scene in hushed silence. Now that it was over, a buzz
of conversations erupted.

"What was that all about?" Shelby asked Diana.

"That's Wolfgang von Heller. He's one of the
most successful, most notorious black marketers in
East Berlin."

"He's from the East? What's he doing here?"

"Probably buying up goods to smuggle in and sell
on the black market over there. He has a strange relationship with the East German government that
makes it worth their while to let him cross into the
West whenever he wants to."

"He's a very cool customer," Shelby said with grudging admiration for the way he had handled himself.

Diana shuddered. "You don't know the half of it. From what I hear about him from Hans, he scares me."

"Why did the police arrest him?"

"It wasn't really an arrest. They'll take him down to their headquarters, question him and frisk him to see if he has a large amount of currency on him for illegal transport into the East. Then they'll let him go. They do it to harass him. He's a currency speculator as well as a smuggler. The West Berlin government doesn't like him because he brings strong West German currency into the East, where it's badly needed to bolster the economy. The police can't really do anything to stop him, though—he's too smart ever to be caught with anything illegal on him—but they do harass him as much as they can."

Diana's comment about smuggling goods into the East triggered a thought in Shelby. She remembered the incident at the wall several weeks earlier when she had interrupted Donovan while he was receiving a package from that nervous gray-goateed man.

"Is there a big market for smuggled drugs in the East?" Shelby asked with studied casualness, looking down at her wineglass.

"There certainly is. Drugs are tightly controlled over there. Even legitimate drugs such as antibiotics have to be accounted for, so you can *imagine* how profitable the market is for the hard-core drugs that addicts use. Fortunes have been made smuggling those in. Why do you ask?''

"Oh, just curious."

Diana checked her watch. "I have to go, honey. I'm on the organizing committee for the industrialists' cocktail party we're hosting, and we're having a meeting today. Don't you have to leave soon, too? I thought it was this evening you and Mr. Hawkes were interviewing Eric Furth, that man the Lion took across in the basket of a crane?''

"Yes," said Shelby. "And I do have to work on my preparations." She thanked Diana for the lunch and tried a small smile of encouragement to reassure her about Hans. That didn't work very well, though.

After Diana left, Shelby went to the enclosed phone booth in the restaurant's lobby. She didn't really want to talk to her father now, but she did want to find out just why he had demanded Donovan's recall. She was sure it was due to some unprincipled action on Donovan's part.

Not wanting to bother with a fistful of change, she told the overseas operator to bill the call to her residence. It was now just before eight A.M. in Washington. It took two minutes for the call to be placed, and then she heard her father's familiar voice answering the phone. It sounded tinny, due to the overseas line, and there was a slight echo.

"Hello, Shelby. Good to hear from you. So how is your new assignment?" Before she could respond, he added quickly, "I only have a minute—I've got a speaking engagement this morning—but do tell me how the assignment is going.''

Shelby felt a twinge of sadness at his words and scolded herself for feeling this. She knew she should have long ago got used to the fact that he did not have much time for her. So why did she still let this have the power to hurt her—after all these years—each time she had evidence of it anew?

"Things are going fine, father. I won't keep you long, I promise." She paused. "I met someone here who worked under you in Turkey. Donovan Hawkes is his name."

There was a moment of silence. "Stay away from that one, Shel. He's nothing but trouble." His disapproving tone was just what she expected, but what he said next surprised her. "That man has more integrity than almost anyone I've worked with."

"Integrity?" she repeated in amazement. "That's the last word I'd expect to hear associated with him."

"Well, it's an odd sort of integrity—the sort that gets you in trouble without doing anybody any good. I've never approved of people who have their own sense of right and wrong and to hell with what the rest of the world thinks. That's Donovan Hawkes." Her father sounded reflective. "He called me rigid on more than one occasion, but the fact is, he's more inflexible, more uncompromising. He feels he can do whatever he thinks is right no matter who else thinks otherwise—even if it's contrary to State Department policy."

"I understand you demanded his recall?"

"I had to do that. He interfered with the Turkish police in an internal political matter."

"What happened?"

"You know the police over there are quasi-military. They were arresting a dissident on the street after a political rally. The man resisted, and three policemen started beating him with nightsticks. Hawkes saw it and told them to stop. When they ignored him, he waded in swinging."

Shelby was amazed. Could this be the same man they were talking about—the mercenary who cared about nothing but the advancement of his own career, the man who had been willing to ruin Shelby's career by sending her home for selfish reasons of his own?

"He saved the man from injury," her father continued, "but after that, there was nothing I could do but ask for his recall. You know how strict the department is on the noninterference rule. When an officer is a guest in a host country, he does *not* interfere in that country's internal affairs." He sighed. "If it hadn't been that, though, it would have been something else. Hawkes was constantly following his own head, completely ignoring the rules of diplomacy. As far as he's concerned, the world should be run the way he wants it to be run, and he'll do everything he can to try to make it do just that."

Now that sounded more like the Donovan Hawkes Shelby knew.

"Shel, I've got to go. I'm sorry."

"Oh, that's all right, father," she said quickly, "I

understand." She hid her disappointment at his failure to ask how she was. "It was nice talking to you."

After she hung up, she headed back to the legation, confused and vexed. She had hoped to find answers by calling her father, but all she had come up with were new questions. Every time she turned around, the contradictions about Donovan multiplied. How could he seem so self-serving and callous, yet be the sort of man who would risk his career—not to mention his health—by fighting off Turkish policemen to protect a stranger? Should she trust her father's impression of Donovan's integrity, or should she trust her own—which was that he seemed to have none at all?

Shelby had no way of knowing that the answer to that question would be revealed to her by the end of the night, in a drastic way that would change her relationship with Donovan forever.

CHAPTER NINE

THEY WERE SPEEDING along the road that bordered
the Spree River on an elevated embankment. The
night was cool, and Shelby felt that autumn would
soon be beginning. Donovan himself was driving this
time, having dispensed with his official driver and
even his official limousine. They were in a comfortable Mercedes that did not bear the diplomatic
license plates to which Donovan was entitled.

"That's where we're going," he said, nodding
toward a beam of bright light that sliced through the
black sky off in the distance. "Furth's friends took
up a collection to rent that searchlight for the whole
week to celebrate the grand opening of his riverside
restaurant. People do that here. Whenever there's a
successful crossing, West Berliners chip in to do what
they can to help out the refugee, to show him he's
welcome."

"I like the gesture," Shelby said. "I understand it
was one of the refugee societies that arranged the
loan that let him open his restaurant."

"That's right. He and his wife owned a café in the
East, but when they fled, they lost everything."

Shelby gazed out at the peaceful wide Spree River

they were driving alongside. For a short distance it formed the border between the divided halves of the city of Berlin. A wharf came into view ahead, and Shelby saw a fishing boat and a commercial trawler docked there.

"What I don't see," she said, "is why you think he's going to be any more informative than the other refugees. Almost all the ones we interviewed refused to talk about the Lion. They don't want to cooperate in an investigation that'll endanger the man who risked his life to help them cross."

"This time it'll be different," Donovan said without further explanation.

Shelby didn't understand how he could be so optimistic. She remembered the last crosser they had interviewed. Shelby was supposed to interpret on that interview, also, but her language skills had turned out to be unnecessary. The man had looked at Donovan with a peculiar sly expression when asked about the Lion and shut his lips tightly. Shelby figured the expression to mean, "If you think you're going to get any information out of *me*—not till hell freezes over."

The seafood restaurant came into view then. It was a small wooden building set back only a few feet from the river's edge, with a patio that overhung the embankment. A boardwalk connected it to the nearby wharf. Donovan pulled into the tiny parking lot. He had to maneuver carefully to avoid the trailer on which the searchlight was mounted, its bright white beam slowly, automatically, raking the sky.

"See over there," Donovan said as they left the car. He indicated a part of the river that formed the boundary line. "That used to be a famous crossing point a few years back. Refugees would practice for months to get into good physical shape. Then they'd swim out to those marker buoys at the center of the river, which are the dividing line between East and West, and they'd cross."

"They can't do that anymore?"

Donovan shook his head. "Enough people succeeded at it to make the East Germans nervous. Now they've got swift riverboats that patrol this section of the river. Last year alone three swimmers were shot trying to cross that way."

Inside, the restaurant was cozy and warm, infused with the pleasant aroma of cooking seafood. Burlap coverings adorned the small tables, and the walls were decorated with fishing nets and nautical odds and ends. Earlier in the day, many West Berliners had come to help launch the new venture of the recent refugee. An air of festivity still lingered.

It was after nine now, and the dinner crowd had thinned out enough so that Furth could take the time to sit down with Donovan and Shelby on the outdoor patio that overlooked the river. He was a middle-aged jovial man, wearing a white apron. His wife, however, was less than jovial. She was introduced briefly. Then she disappeared back into the kitchen, refusing to participate in the interview. She didn't wish to endanger the Lion.

Shelby was puzzled about why Furth himself had

agreed to talk. She remembered when she had first heard of his crossing—in Washington, at the ball. Herr Bruckner had told Donovan and her about the bold way the Lion had stolen a tractor from a construction site, then taken the Furths across the mined barbed-wire border in the tractor's steel basket. That was the time the armed *Vopo* had climbed into the cab of the tractor and almost killed the Lion. So why was Furth willing to cooperate in an investigation to get the Lion arrested?

Once they were seated, Shelby learned the reason—and it was a shocker.

"Tell me once again, please," Furth said to Shelby in German. "What is the name of the American magazine this article is for?"

She frowned. "I beg your pardon?" she said in German.

"Which magazine? Herr Hawkes told me through Dr. Rinehardt that this interview is for publication—so the American people can learn of the good brave deeds of the Lion, so support can be gathered for him in America, too. But I forget the name of the magazine."

Shelby turned to Donovan accusingly, not wanting to believe it but not able to disbelieve it, either. "You didn't tell him you're from a magazine?"

"No, I never said that. He just doesn't have a good memory." He looked at her pointedly. "I told him I'm from the *New York Times*."

She stared at him, appalled. "So that's why we came in the Mercedes instead of the limo with the diplomatic license plates. You're lying to this man! You know he'd never talk to you if he knew you were a State Department investigator, so you told him you're trying to help the Lion, instead of trying to track him down and imprison him!''

Furth was looking on amiably, not understanding a word of their conversation. He was becoming disturbed, though, at Shelby's accusative tone.

"That's right," Donovan said. "Now let's get on with the interview. Ask him what the Lion looks like. That description we were sent from the wounded *Vopo* differs from the others we have. Go ahead, ask him."

Shelby glared at him, seething. She was on the verge of getting up and stalking off, refusing to take part in this cruel deception. Then it came to her suddenly, from the way Donovan was watching her so intently, that this was exactly what he wanted her to do. He had set up this situation to make her do it, not letting her know about the deception until the last moment, when it would hit her in such a shocking way. He had failed to get her to quit by treating her hostilely, so this was his new strategy. If she refused to cooperate now, he'd have a legitimate reason for demanding her recall.

"You're despicable," she said to him.

"Probably. What are you going to do about it?"

Shelby was so indignant and defiant that at first she made up her mind to stick it out, to do as he asked just to deny him the chance to get rid of her that he so dearly wanted.

But then, glancing at Eric Furth, she saw how trusting he looked, how anxious to do the right thing. She knew at that point she could not participate in such a sham, no matter how much she wanted to deny Donovan the chance to see her quit. She stood up and walked away from them, retreating to the railing of the planked patio, where she stood watching the river in the bright moonlight. She felt angry and helpless.

"So you're refusing to cooperate," Donovan said, driving in the last nail, stating the fact to make it formal.

"You're such a vile low person," she replied quietly. "I curse the day I ever met you."

He had got what he wanted. He didn't bother to dwell on it but returned to business as usual. He went to the doorway of the kitchen and asked, "Is there anyone here who speaks English?" He returned to the table with a thirtyish woman, who was Furth's daughter. "Would you mind translating for us?" he asked her. "My assistant isn't feeling well."

"*Ja.* Most happy to. I, too, am grateful to Lion for helping father and mother across border so we can be together again. I, too, think American public should hear of Lion."

Shelby felt disgusted. She continued staring out toward the water as the interview began. In the moonlight she saw the East German patrol boat that was slicing across the river, a sleek frightening presence with an automatic rifle mounted on its bow. The craft ran parallel to the marker buoys, extremely near to them, yet staying on the East German side. A blue phosphorescence was churned up in its wake.

With only half an ear she listened to the interview. She heard Furth tell of how he and his daughter had been separated when the wall went up without warning one midnight in August of 1961.

"She was in the western side of the city, spending the night with schoolmates. My wife and I were in the East. The city had thirty-eight crossing points at that time between the Soviet sector and the Allied sectors. People could come and go as they pleased. Then at midnight the barriers all went up—barbed wire at first, guarded by armed *Vopos*.

"The next morning the city woke up, and it was panic. If you were an East Berliner, you weren't allowed to cross to the western side—not even if you worked on the western side, not even if you owned a business there, not even if your wife was there, for God's sake. Parents were separated from children, businesses from owners, workers from places of employment. It was chaos. And most of it is still just as cruel, though now, at least, they allow West Berliners to visit the East—if they pay West German marks at the border. The East is ravenous for West German marks."

Now Furth's daughter made her own bitter comment, instead of just interpreting her father's remarks. "It is terrible how they work it, even now. West Berliners can go in, but East Berliners cannot get out—that is, except for the hardened Communists, whom they know will return, and, of course,

the wicked wealthy souls who can do anything...
men like von Heller.''

Shelby's ears perked up at the familiar name. She
thought of the tall blond man with the contemptuous
mouth whom she had seen only hours earlier. Furth's
daughter had spat out his name hatefully. Now
Donovan added his own clear dislike for the man as
he said, ''That sort of hoodlum exists in every socie-
ty.''

As the interview continued, Shelby turned her attention to a fisherman's speedboat that was just now
pulling up to the dock near the restaurant, its outboard engine idling noisily. Shelby made a decision.
She would tell Furth the truth about Donovan. She
had started to turn back toward the table when she
spotted something unusual that distracted her. It was
far across the river on the East German shore. She
squinted to see it better. She couldn't quite make it
out. Suddenly she realized what she was watching,
and it jolted her.

Two forms were racing across the narrow strip of
beach into the water. At first she thought they were
frightened animals. As they began stroking feverishly, however, it became clear they were people making
a desperate bid for freedom. They had waited until
the *Vopo* patrol boat passed to plunge in, but could
they possibly swim the great distance to the midway
marker buoys before the boat doubled back and
found them?

Others on the riverbank now also noticed the
swimmers illuminated by the moonlight. A commo-

tion went up. Six feet beneath Shelby, the people near the patio's overhang began pointing and gathering. There was tense nervous conversation about how hopeless the situation was. The swimmers could never make it, voices said. The patrol zones were deliberately kept small enough so swimmers would not have enough time to swim to the buoys before the patrol boat returned.

"What's going on out there?" asked Donovan, alerted by the tumult. He came to the railing to look.

"Over there," Shelby said quietly, pointing. "They...they're trying to swim across."

"The fools!" he declared with surprising anger. "It's suicide to do it that way."

Shelby thought this was incredibly insensitive of him. At the moment the *Vopo* patrol boat turned in a wide arc at the end of its zone. It began cruising back upriver toward the two swimmers. The commotion from the West Berliners beneath the patio outcropping increased as they watched in horror. The swimmers must have seen the boat turn toward them, for now they began stroking wildly, realizing how desperate their situation was.

"The stupid fools!" Donovan cried.

Shelby swiveled toward him in outrage, a curse on her lips, but he was not there. His suit jacket was falling to the floor beside her just when her eyes caught a flash of motion as he vaulted over the patio railing. He hit the beach six feet below, crumpling his body as he fell in order to take the weight off his ankles. Then he was up and running with all his might along

the riverbank to the wharf. He roughly shoved aside
people who were in his way.

What was he doing? Where was he going?

Shelby saw the answer as he climbed down the
wharf into a speedboat that had just arrived. The
boat's owner, unaware of the situation, began gestur-
ing angrily at Donovan, his curses drowned out by
the loud idling of the boat's motor. Donovan didn't
take time to explain the situation. He shoved the
fisherman into the water. Then he took the helm of
the boat and roared off toward the center of the
river.

The West Berliners on the beach began cheering
him and shouting encouragement fo the swimmers,
who were far too distant to hear. Eric Furth, standing next to Shelby, was shouting, too, very emotionally, due to his own recent crossing. But no one knew
what Donovan intended to do. What *could* he do?
He could go to the midway line of the Spree; yet once
he arrived he could do nothing but wait and watch as
the *Vopo* patrol boat reached the swimmers—and
gunned them down.

As Shelby watched, she saw what he was intending. Her breath caught in her throat, and she heard
herself whispering, "Oh, no, don't." But he was doing it. He had aimed his outboard on a collision
course with the patrol boat, which was speeding
along the buoys toward the swimmers.

The *Vopos* saw him coming but could not fire at
him, for he was on the West Berlin side of the river.
They waved him away frantically, shouting curses.

He kept coming, though. At the last instant he veered to the side, but not before the patrol boat was forced to veer in the other direction to avoid being rammed.

The patrol boat pulled back on course in a few seconds, having lost only a moment. By this time, however, Donovan had circled around, still on the western side, and was once again aiming toward it. He plowed on so quickly, his aim so true that once again the patrol boat had to swerve off course to avoid being rammed.

This time, though, Donovan had gone too far forward and could not avoid crossing the midway point as he veered to circle back. The *Vopo* behind the mounted automatic rifle began firing, the gun bursts exploding with sound in the clear night air. Bullets raked the bow of Donovan's boat as he desperately arced back toward the West.

Shelby gasped when she saw him sink down into the boat. Had he been hit? Was he alive? The moment the boat roared back across the midway point, however, and the firing stopped, he sprang up again, apparently unscathed. A cheer arose from the crowd.

The air was electric with tension now. The *Vopo* patrol boat had been forced by Donovan to alter its course twice, to concentrate on not being rammed rather than on shooting the swimmers. Now it was back on target; the swimmers were very near the midway, and Donovan was circling sharply back for another pass. The *Vopos* were ready for him this time, waiting. If he crossed the the midway point now, they were close enough and ready enough to aim directly at him. He wouldn't stand a chance.

Shelby glanced around frantically, desperate to find something to do that might help. There was nothing she could do. Nothing! But then she saw it. She ran through the restaurant into the parking lot and climbed onto the trailer supporting the searchlight. She began tugging at the front of the searchlight, furiously trying to pull it down from its sky-sweeping position. She could not budge it. It kept slowly scanning the sky on its preprogrammed pivot, humming electrically.

"What are you doing?" Furth shouted, coming out after her.

"Lower it! Lower it!" she screamed at him. She pointed to the patrol boat.

Furth understood and hurried into action. He didn't waste time trying to pull the face of the giant light down, as Shelby had been attempting. He went to the levers that guided the mechanism and shoved them into a new adjustment. The brilliant white beam of light slashed down across the sky to impale the patrol boat at the exact moment that Donovan was about to intercept it. The swimmers were very near the border now, too, and the patrol boat was aiming to run them down.

The searchlight beam hit the gunner full in the face, and Shelby could see him jerking his hands up to shield his eyes from the bright light. At that instant Donovan came roaring up to the patrol boat, forcing the helmsman to veer sharply once more.

Again Donovan crossed the midway point. For a tense few seconds he was on the East Berlin side of the buoys, turning in his arc. The *Vopo* gunner, though, was temporarily blinded and could not properly aim his rifle. His shots went wild. By the time he was shoved aside and another *Vopo* stood in his place, Donovan was safely back in West German waters.

A wild cheer rose up from the crowd. Eric Furth hugged Shelby with comradely exuberance. Donovan was safe—and the swimmers were safe, too. Donovan's efforts had bought them just enough time, and now they reached the marker buoys and clung to them feverishly, gasping for breath.

Donovan eased off the throttle of his stolen speedboat and pulled alongside. The swimmers tried to climb in. One made it—a young man in dark trunks. The other, now visible as a girl in a one-piece black swimsuit, was too weak from her exertions. Donovan and the boy helped pull her aboard. Then Donovan retook the helm and gunned the boat's engine, heading back toward the dock. The *Vopo* gunboat circled helplessly on the East German side of the buoys like a caged angry animal.

The crowd along the riverbank was in an uproar. Even the owner of the speedboat Donovan had stolen, which was now riddled with bullet holes at the bow, was cheering. A successful crossing was always an emotional event, and no wonder, thought Shelby, since the crossers were almost always the parents, children, or other relatives of those in the West.

When Donovan neared the wharf, he slowed the craft and began idling noisily offshore, not coming closer. He scanned the large crowd, looking disturbed. Shelby suddenly realized what he was concerned about. Several people in the crowd were tourists and had cameras. Snapshots would be taken and would end up in the next day's newspapers.

Donovan, however, could not afford to have his picture taken. State Department policy strictly forbade American diplomats from participating in crossings. To do so would be considered meddling in the internal affairs of a foreign nation. In this case Donovan had not only participated, he had violated East German waters in doing so. If the East Germans learned he was a State Department officer, they would raise diplomatic hell. The State Department would have no choice but to expel Donovan for his well-intentioned but strictly illegal action.

Shelby had an idea. She waved her arms to attract his attention. Then she pointed to an area about half a mile down the beach, where the embankment was less steep and the riverside road came near the waterline. He understood and nodded.

Shelby hurried back into the restaurant, retrieved Donovan's coat from the patio and rushed to the Mercedes. She took the keys from the coat pocket and started the car. Then she drove to the place she had indicated and pulled onto the shoulder of the road at the top of the low embankment. Donovan gunned the boat's engine and raced parallel to the shore, then rammed the boat forward, directly onto the beach. By now the boat had taken so much water from the bullet holes in its bow that it was on the verge of sinking.

Donovan leaped out and raced up the embankment toward the car. The crowd had already mobilized and was rushing down the beach toward him. The two swimmers half crawled out of the boat onto the shore. The girl was sobbing emotionally, shouting, *"Wir sind frei! Wir sind frei!"* We're free; we're free! The boy was on his knees, kissing the earthen riverbank of West Germany, slapping his hands upon it, kissing it some more. Shelby had never seen such emotion.

Donovan rushed into the car, slamming the door, and the others clambered in the back. "Get us out of here!" he ordered, looking toward the rapidly approaching crowd.

Shelby gunned the engine, and the car shot forward onto the road. As they roared away, Shelby glanced at him to see if he had been wounded. His shirt was soaked from the spray of the river, his face bathed in sweat, his black hair a wet tangle. He was breathing in gasps, but he seemed to be unhurt.

"That was wonderful," she said.

"No, just stupid. It's a good thing the boat didn't sink. I don't swim well." He repeated, "It was a stupid thing to do."

Now the emotional intensity of the past supercharged moments—moments of not knowing if he would live or die—exploded in Shelby. "I don't understand you! You do something as noble as this, and then you try to ruin it by saying something like that. And—and you're trying to catch the Lion for helping crossers, but you just did exactly the same thing."

He turned to look at her, and the emotion in his blue eyes made Shelby stop speaking. She felt her pulse begin to race. There was a depth of great caring and affection there. It seemed as if the intensity of the past moments had affected him strongly, too, making it hard for him to maintain the charade of cold harsh un-feelingness. "I saw you by the searchlight," he said. "It was your idea to lower it into the gunner's eyes?"

Shelby nodded.

"Quick thinking. Resourceful thinking." His deep voice became softer. "Every time I'm with you, I see more about you that makes it harder for me to keep pretending that...I don't...." He leaned his head back against the seat and shut his eyes, looking strangely tormented.

"You don't what, Donovan?" she asked gently, eagerly.

He shook his head and kept his silence. After a moment, he unexpectedly grasped Shelby's hand and pressed it against his lowered face, holding it tightly. She felt the hardness of his cheekbone. His lips caressed her palm. There was such need and longing and tenderness in the gesture. But then, fighting to regain control of himself, he released her hand and once more leaned his head back against the top of the seat. He shut his jaw firmly, as if to prevent himself from speaking.

"What is it?" she asked. "What's wrong?"

But for the rest of the drive he refused to speak, lost to a secret torment that Shelby could neither understand nor help him with.

CHAPTER TEN

THEIR RELATIONSHIP CHANGED in the days after that. Shelby could see that Donovan cared for her deeply. She could sense it in his every gesture and expression, though he tried hard to disguise it.

She had seen brief glimpses of it earlier. She had known for a while now that he grudgingly admired her stubborn pride and the way she resisted his efforts to make her cry uncle and go home. The first hint of his attraction had come long ago, in Washington, when he had told her she was the sort of girl he could come to care for. But since then he had tried to deny that, to hide his caring.

Now things were different. After the incident at the river, he seemed no longer able to hide his fondness. The way she had stuck to her principles in refusing to lie to Furth, the way she had responded resourcefully under pressure—these things seemed to meld with all the other aspects of her that touched him deeply. Everything seemed to come together to strike a chord deep within him. It was too much for him, and he could not conceal his emotions, no matter how hard he tried.

Shelby could read the signs. She could see the way

he would gaze at her with intense longing affection—
and then quickly look away when he saw she was
noticing.

TWO DAYS AFTER THE INCIDENT at the river, he was
guiding her along a hillside walkway on the way to interview a government minister at his headquarters.
His hand was touching lightly at Shelby's back, guiding her, as etiquette demanded. As they progressed
along the walkway, though, his hand gradually
moved to the side of her slender waist, firmly and
possessively. Shelby glanced at him sidelong. She saw
that he had not even noticed the change. It was as if
his hand had moved with a will of its own, acting out
the true feelings he himself tried to hide.

How could he not notice, she wondered in amazement. She herself could no more fail to notice it than
she could fail to notice a herd of stampeding elephants. When he did finally see it, he withdrew his
hand as if he had been burned.

Why was he fighting so hard against admitting to
himself the feelings he had for her? The question tormented her. She was not fighting her feelings for
him. She knew how vulnerable she was to him now
and how much she had come to care for him. There
were aspects of him she still was uncertain about,
mysteries that she wished were resolved, but his integrity and character were no longer in doubt. No
matter what he said or pretended to believe—about
being a mercenary and other things—Shelby knew
the truth now. She knew he had been uttering these

things not because he believed them but to provoke her, to make her leave. Deep down he was a man who had a personal code of honor and stuck to it at all costs.

Shelby knew the situation couldn't go on like this much longer. An explosion was coming. He seemed determined not to show his feelings, but the more they were together, the harder it became for him, and to make matters worse, it was not just Shelby's spirit and personality he was attracted to....

The day they visited the minister, Donovan asked him for his notes on the Lion's crossings. The man indicated a binder on an upper shelf of his bookcase. Shelby volunteered to get it. As she reached up for the binder, her cotton blouse pulled taut against her breasts. Turning, she saw Donovan gazing at her. He looked tormented; his brow was knitted. When she handed him the binder, he could not even trust his voice to thank her for it.

The next day, on the eve of the industrialists' cocktail party, which Shelby would be required to attend, the sexual tension between them became even more intense. Donovan and Shelby were staying in East Germany at the Schloss Tauber, a grand old hotel built atop a cliff overlooking the Elbe River. Stone steps led down the face of the cliff to a narrow bathing beach near a treacherous powerful current. Shelby stood at the parapet of the hotel terrace, at the top of the cliff, watching the sunset. It was incredibly lovely. The sun had turned orange and was just sinking beneath the horizon.

She said something to Donovan, but curiously he did not answer. Only tense silence greeted her words. It was then Shelby realized that, since he was standing behind her, he was able to see her slender body quite clearly silhouetted against the setting sun as the bright rays turned her thin dress diaphanous.

When she turned, their gazes caught. This time he was incapable of making any effort to hide his passion, his desire. His feelings were obvious from the look in his tortured eyes. Shelby knew that his deep caring for her had heightened his susceptibility to her beauty and sexuality, and now there was no hiding it.

She did something very bold then. Fighting down her natural shyness, she remained in the light of the setting sun, which was making her dress transparent. She stood straight, her head high. She tossed her hair back and stared at him proudly, letting him see in her eyes that she cared for him and that nothing would be impossible between them, if only he would be honest about showing his own feelings. . . .

He returned her stare for a tense electric moment as Shelby felt a flood of sensation surging all through her. *Maybe,* she thought hopefully, *maybe this time he'll be honest with himself and with me.* She could see she was clearly getting to him—more so than ever before. But then, sadly, the mysterious forces raging inside him seemed to win their battle; he turned sharply and stalked off.

A few hours later Shelby stood in her hotel room, brushing her long chestnut hair at the vanity mirror, preparing for bed. She wore her white satin nightgown—a long lacy affair that buttoned in front. Donovan was in the suite next to hers. Suddenly she heard a crashing sound through their common wall, as if something had been thrown against it in explosive frustration. Her hairbrush was arrested in midstroke as she sat frozen, listening. There was the sound of Donovan's hotel-room door slamming and, an instant later, an impatient banging on her own.

She put on her powder-blue robe but could not find the sash to belt it. Where was it? The knocking came again, and she went to the door and opened it, holding her robe closed with her hands.

He stood there in dark trousers and a tucked-in shirt that looked as though he had thrown it on as an afterthought. Only the bottom of it was buttoned, leaving the top open to reveal his muscular dark-haired chest. His expression was demanding and touched with self-anger.

"We've got to talk," he said, his voice low.

She stood aside and let him into the room. Then she shut the door and turned to face him. They stood looking at each other. His jaw clenched tightly. "We can't go on like this any longer," he said at last.

"No," she replied softly in agreement. She felt a faint thrill of hopefulness. Was he finally going to admit his feelings for her so they could stop this horrible pretense? She gazed into his eyes, encouraging him with her own.

"I'm sending you home," he said.

"What?" Suddenly she was numb.

"When you refused to translate at that Furth interview last week, that was dereliction of duty. That gives me a legitimate reason for demanding your recall.''

All she could do was stare at him, dazed, feeling the strength ebbing from her body. She looked at his expression, which was cold and businesslike, with no hint of any deeper feelings for her at all. Had she been so wrong about him all this time?

''I can put you on report,'' he said, ''but instead I'll let you voluntarily resign your position here. That way it won't be so damaging to you. I'll even include a personal letter that says you were an exemplary political officer. Now are you willing to do that—to voluntarily resign?''

''No,'' she answered weakly, shaking her head.

''You have to do it,'' he shot back at her angrily. ''Don't you understand that if I demand your recall for cause, it'll destroy your career?''

''Yes.''

He ran his fingers through his hair, flustered, disconcerted, before he came to her and put his hands on her arms. He glared at her with an anger that startled Shelby. She had never expected to see such a look from him. Had she been so mistaken in thinking he really cared for her?

''I can't have you around me anymore,'' he said coldly. ''In case you have any doubts, let me make this clear. I don't want to see you. I don't want to talk to you. I don't want to deal with you. Is that clear enough?''

And it was. Shelby felt deflated all of a sudden, as

if her world had collapsed. She shrank from him and sat down gingerly on the edge of the bed. She didn't want to believe her ears and eyes. Yet she did believe them.

A nervous giddy laugh escaped her lips, and she said softly, as if to herself, "What a little fool I've been." Her eyes began to moisten. She laughed that slight anguished laugh once more as she wiped the beginning tears from her eyes.

"You don't care for me," she mumbled, almost unaware she was speaking aloud. "Not even a little bit. It was my imagination, wasn't it, the whole time?" She felt like laughing at herself, and she did, as the tears streamed hotly down her cheeks. "What a silly thing for me to do. Just like a naive little girl. I wanted it so badly, I imagined it was really there... that you really cared for me."

She glanced up at him, a painful anguished half smile frozen on her face—a last defense against breaking down completely. "How stupid of me to think there could be some love for me in this world, just a tiny little bit, just for me; that there could be a man like you in this world who could... care for me." She shook her head and half laughed, half moaned at her own foolishness.

She stood up. "Well, I won't bother you anymore. I'll send my resignation to Mr. Stanton."

She started across the room to open the door for him so he could leave, but then something strange happened. As she passed him, his hand came forward and gripped her arm, stopping her. She looked at him. He said nothing. His eyes were directed straight ahead, not to her. His face was as expressionless as a stone—but like a stone on the verge of cracking. His jaw trembled. Shelby sensed she was witnessing a violent raging battle, and all of it was taking place within himself. His grip on her arm was so tight it was painful, but Donovan seemed not even to notice.

He turned his eyes to her, and they were filled with love and agony. "My God, Shelby," he said, the words torn from his heart against his will, "how much you are to me." He embraced her then so tightly, it was as if he were holding on to her for dear life. Slowly, cautiously, she let her own arms go around him in answer. She felt his hard body trembling.

"Why did you have to be like this?" he questioned. "You're so nearly everything I've ever wanted in a woman. But I can't have you in my life—not now!" Yet he held her even tighter, his body continuing to tremble.

Shelby felt confused and overwhelmed by the immensity of his need and by the mysterious battle he was waging within himself. She knew what had caused his true feelings to now burst through that false exterior of cold uncaring. He couldn't take seeing her cry. He had wanted her to believe he didn't love her, but when he got his wish, when she believed it and broke down in tears over it, it had been too much for him.

Her palms were on his back, her cheek against his chest. "It's. . .it's all right, Donovan," she said softly, trying to soothe him. How could she soothe him, though, when she didn't even know the true nature of his agony?

He raised her chin with his finger and made her look at him. The strength was still there in his face, despite his battle, and there was such depth of emotion there, too, that it almost made Shelby melt, for all her life she had been longing, praying, to see a look like this from a man like Donovan. She had eventually given up hope, believing it would never happen.

His head bent forward, and she saw his lips approaching hers. Then she felt the first touch of them upon her own. At first his kiss was gentle and tender, but soon he became lost to his ardor. His kiss became more intense as he forced her lips apart beneath his. He had kept his emotions, his passion, in check for so long that now there was no holding back. His kiss was violent and yet incredibly tender. Shelby had never experienced such a kiss or such wild soaring responses within her, responses heightened by her deep feelings for this strong, handsome, complex man.

He crushed her against him in a passionate embrace. Shelby became lost to the sensuousness of it, having dreamed of him holding her like this for so long—his strong arms about her, his lips upon hers so possessively. But she had not dreamed she would feel so strangely, as though she were nakedly pressing against him. Glancing down, she saw why she was feeling this way. Her unbelted robe had come open, and her excited breasts were pressing against his hard chest, separated from it only by the thin satin of her nightgown.

Instinctively she tried to pull away from him, a blush coming over her entire body. He wouldn't let her pull away, though. Instead he tore open his shirt all the way, and then his hand went to the buttons of her nightgown.

"No..." she said, looking into his eyes helplessly, the word sounding more like a question than a statement. She put her hand on his wrist to stop him.

"My love," he murmured, his voice throaty with passion. He undid the top button and then the other buttons, ignoring the hand that was failing so dismally in its attempt to yank his wrist away. Then he drew open her nightgown, and the front of Shelby's body was naked before him, from her breasts down to her slippers. She saw his eyes caressing her creamy white form with hunger and appreciation. She tried to close her nightgown, but he wouldn't let her.

"No, Donovan, please," she whispered almost frantically. She cared for him, yes, she loved him... but still, this was happening too quickly. She had never been in this situation previously. No man had ever seen her laid so bare. Her emotions were in turmoil. She had secretly, guiltily, dreamed of being with him this way. Dreams, though, were far different from reality! She felt burningly shy and exposed, embarrassed that her nipples had become so excited under his loving gaze. Things weren't supposed to happen this quickly. It...it wasn't right! It wasn't proper! Wasn't that what she had always believed?

He was holding her wrists down at her sides. He looked in her eyes and said in a manly voice, the words torn from his heart, "Oh, Shelby. Oh, how I love you." Slowly he pulled her near him, inch by inch. Her eyes went wide, and her breathing became rapid and shallow. Her naked breasts moved closer to his chest, and she found she was watching the space between their bodies, unable to tear her eyes away. Then her pink nipples touched his naked chest, and she gasped. The sensation was incredible. He pulled her closer, and her full breasts pressed tightly against him, her rounded belly touching the top of his trousers.

He made her look up at him to see the love in his eyes. She knew she was blushing hotly. She couldn't help it. Her whole body was blushing. Her whole body was tingling, too, with a sensuous excitement electric in its intensity. He bent forward and put his arm beneath the back of her knees, then lifted her up in his arms. She had to put one hand on the back of his neck so she would not fall; with the other hand she quickly closed the front of her nightgown and robe. It took her an instant to realize he was carrying her over to the bed.

Her heart was racing. She wanted to tell him no, to order him to put her down, but her senses were betraying her. The masculine scent of him was in her nostrils, and her fingers had found their way into the hair at the base of his neck. His open shirt had come off one shoulder, and Shelby pressed her lips against it, tasting the salty tang of his skin, feeling the hardness of his muscles.

He laid her down on the rust-colored bedspread and removed her robe. Shelby had to hold her gown closed with both hands, for again it had come open. He stood beside the bed and shucked off his shirt. She had never seen him bare-chested before. His chest was wide, and his physique quite powerful. How had he got such a well-developed physique, she wondered absently. A diplomat like him, with the body of an athlete—it was unheard of.

He sat on the edge of the bed, and his hand went to Shelby's ankle and encircled it. She jerked slightly. His other hand joined the first and then slowly, excruciatingly slowly, moved slidingly along her calf, up her thigh.

No, she thought, her mind blazing, *he won't touch me there. He won't. He won't.* But his hand kept sliding caressingly up her thigh, and when he touched her, she moaned aloud, unable to bear the sensation. She pushed his hand away. She held it away from her, her hand tightly on his wrist, while she lay there breathing rapidly, her eyes wide.

He lay beside her, his trousers still on. Then he covered her with his body. She put her hands to his shoulders to push him away, but instead of pushing, her hands just stayed there, touching then moving over his muscular shoulders to the broad planes of his back. His lips were on her throat . . . brushing over her cheek, her ear, her eyes. He was kissing her everywhere, awash in the same sensations that engulfed her.

"I love you," he said, the words so low it seemed

he was unaware he was even speaking them. "I've loved you for so long. I tried not to let you know, not to let you see it, but I can't help myself any longer. Shelby, I love you more than I've ever loved anyone. I never knew what love was until I met you."

"And I love you," she answered simply, finding that she was crying, silent tears of joy streaming down her cheeks. "I'll never leave you, Donovan. Never."

He tensed suddenly at these words.

She frowned. What was wrong? What had she said? His hands had been stroking her hair and trailing caressingly over her narrow shoulders. Now they stopped. He took in a deep breath and let it out slowly in a sigh that seemed composed of frustration and self-anger.

"What is it?" she asked. "What's wrong?"

He remained unmoving, silent. After a moment he rose from the bed and stood looking at her. His expression was hardening; she could see it doing so. The feelings were deliberately being shut out of his eyes. It hurt to see the love go. *Oh, no,* she thought. *Oh, no, please don't go. . . .*

Seeing him gazing at her now, the love no longer lighting his face, Shelby felt terribly exposed. Her nightgown was in disarray, the hem riding high up on her legs. Her white breasts were fully visible. She quickly pulled the nightgown closed and turned away from him as she rearranged herself. She felt burningly embarrassed and confused. She hurried across the room to her robe and put it on. She couldn't bear to look him in the face until it was fully on and held tightly shut. Then she turned to him with fire in her eyes, deeply hurt but still indignantly accusing. She waited for an explanation.

None was offered. He briskly crossed the room, grabbed up his shirt and put it on. His face was apologetic but stern, as if the situation were out of his hands.

"Are you going to tell me what game you're playing?" she cried finally. "Is this some sort of sport to you, or what?" She felt used and abused, manipulated in the cruelest way, with no idea why.

Donovan seemed furious at himself, but his words to her offered no comfort or explanation. "I shouldn't have let it get this far," he muttered. "I never intended it to. I came here tonight to make you leave me, to *prevent* something like this ever happening. But...." He stopped speaking. He seemed regretful and filled with self-hatred. Without a further word he turned and left the room.

CHAPTER ELEVEN

IN THE MORNING Donovan was gone from the hotel. The desk clerk at the Schloss Tauber handed Shelby a note from him saying he had left the car and driver for her; he had made other arrangements for himself. When she saw him again at the industrialists' cocktail party that evening, he went to great lengths to show he wished to have nothing to do with her. It was as if he desired to prove to her that the previous night's incident had been some sort of fluke and that he wanted to blast it from both their memories.

Though the party was sponsored by the American legation, it was being held at the penthouse garden of a wealthy German financier. The party was an effort to bring together not only industrialists, but also anyone who wielded major economic power in either of the two Berlins.

Shelby hadn't wanted to go. The last thing she was in the mood for was a formal party. But James Stanton had insisted.

"This is your official coming out in Berlin, Shelby," he had said. "You've been on the road with Donovan so often you haven't had a chance to meet the financial or political stars of this city. They'll all be there tonight, and I want you there, too." So she dressed for the formal occasion in her long salmon-colored gown and accompanying jacket, added a designer scarf and fashionable shoes and went with Diana.

The rooftop garden in which the party was held was truly lovely and quite exotic. It displayed small trees and bushes, as well as imported flowers of bright colors and intriguing fragrances. Cobblestone paths wound through the garden, converging like spokes of a wheel at a central plaza. To combat the chill night air, conical gas heaters had been spread throughout. Colorful Chinese lanterns weaved and bobbed overhead, lending a festive air. Musicians strolled along the garden paths, serenading the guests.

When she had first arrived, James Stanton had taken her on his arm and introduced her to several of the financial and political luminaries of the city, all formally attired for the occasion. Despite her glum mood, Shelby made a point of being pleasant and gracious—even to Gretchen Bruckner when she was reintroduced to her. Afterward Mr. Stanton complimented her on the impression she had made and let her go off to mingle on her own.

Her socializing was forced and wooden, though, for her heart was not in it. Most of the time was spent making small talk with Diana, trying to avoid people. Her mind was still on what had happened the previous night, and she still felt confused and uncertain. After another hour she was ready to leave. It was then that she first saw Donovan, who was arriving late. He saw her immediately, and instead of turning away from her, as she had expected, he came directly over to her. He nooded hello to Diana, then took Shelby's arm and guided her along the path with him so they could talk. Shelby violently shrugged his hand off her arm but continued walking with him.

"I'm sorry about last night," he said in a voice that did not sound sorry at all. "I know you don't want to talk to me now, but there's something I have to tell you. Last night was purely physical. I don't want you blowing it out of proportion by thinking anything else is involved."

"Such as?" she asked coolly.

"Any. . . deeper feelings."

"Oh, there definitely are deeper feelings, Mr. Hawkes. Like hatred and contempt, which I feel for you. Those are rather deep feelings."

It seemed so strange to see him now, under these formal conditions, after the passion and intimacy they had shared the previous night. She knew her dress hid nothing from his eyes, nothing that he had not seen already—and caressed and kissed. The sudden memory made her burn with embarrassment and pique.

"I'm sorry if you feel that way," he said. "I don't feel anything negative toward you. I feel. . . nothing."

The strange thing was, Shelby didn't believe him. She didn't believe that the words of love he had uttered were false. Though she knew she might be a fool for thinking this, her every intuition told her that the words of love had been true and straight from the heart and that it was his abrupt change of mood afterward and his show of coldness now that were false.

Donovan seemed to realize she was thinking this, for what he did next seemed aimed at proving he didn't have any deeper feelings for her at all. He directed his eyes at Gretchen Bruckner.

She stood amid a gathering of admirers, very sexy in a shimmering black off-the-shoulder gown that accented her buxom figure. Her voluminous blond hair was swept up and piled atop her head, crowned with a tiara. She had been aware of Donovan from the instant he'd entered, but had not dared to hope he would pay her any attention. Ever since Shelby had arrived at the legation in August, Gretchen had assumed that a romance with Donovan was impossible—especially since he did everything he could to discourage her interest. Now, though, Donovan caught her eyes and smiled at her, nodding briefly.

This was all Gretchen needed. Her face lit up in surprise and pleasure. She excused herself from the men surrounding her—so abruptly that it could not have been in anything but a rude way—and she came toward Donovan, her smile eager and predatory. She glanced briefly at Shelby with narrowed eyes, then put her hand on Donovan's shoulder and kissed him on the cheek.

"Darling," she said, "so you are friendly to me again now, yes?"

"How could I be anything but friendly to a lovely woman like you?"

Gretchen glanced at Shelby's hand, to see that the engagement ring she had noticed in Washington was now gone from her finger. She smiled at Donovan. "So things have changed for you."

"Things have changed," he conceded.

"Oh, my poor, poor Donovan," she murmured. "Heartbroken and alone."

"Yes," he said, "poor me. I guess I'll just have to console myself as best I can."

Shelby wanted to fling her cocktail in his face.

"Tell Aunt Gretchen all about it," cooed the blonde in mock sympathy as she led him away toward the hub of the party. Neither of them bothered to glance back a single time at Shelby, who was left standing alone.

Now Shelby was really mad. She wouldn't put up with this. Did he think she was some weak-willed softy who could be walked all over? Or some sexual plaything whose emotions could be made to soar and then crash, like a roller coaster, for his own amusement? Well, he'd find out differently—and fast.

Instead of leaving as she had intended, she began circulating through the crowd of partygoers very purposefully, casting her eyes about for a particular kind of man. There was one way she knew she could strike back at him, and she was going to do it. Her belief that Donovan secretly did love her meant she could make him jealous. To do so, though, she would have to find a man who was as desirable as Donovan.

Otherwise Donovan would see through her gesture and laugh it off.

Scanning the guests she passed, listening to the jumble of conversations, Shelby became disappointed. Who was there here who even came close to Donovan? Who was as dynamic or handsome or self-assured? She saw distinguished international diplomats bedecked with sashes and ribbons, military officers in full-dress uniforms, business tycoons and captains of industry. But though these were men of quality, none was worthy of comparison to Donovan in Shelby's mind—and Donovan would know it.

She was scowling in frustration when her eyes fell upon a vine-covered latticework bower. There, leaning against a post, was the man for whom she was looking. Her first sight of him thrilled her with a touch of fear, since she realized how dangerous the game would become if she really went up to him. He was a tall solitary figure, smoking a cigarette, gazing at the crowd with scornful eyes. He was also lean, with an angular face and chiseled features. His thatch of blond hair swept low over his forehead. Despite the civilizing influence of his dinner jacket and crimson ascot, he seemed every bit as menacing as he had the first time Shelby had seen him—in the restaurant with Diana.

This was Wolfgang von Heller.

It seemed strange to Shelby to see someone who looked so chilling, yet at the same time was one of the most handsome men she had ever encountered. She knew she shouldn't go up to him. She knew he struck fear into the hearts of even some of the powerful guests who were here tonight. Perhaps that was why they seemed to go out of their way to avoid him.

No, thought Shelby, she definitely should not approach this man or have anything to do with him. But then she remembered how strongly Donovan disapproved of him, remembered his harsh words when von Heller's name had come up during the Furth interview. That decided her. Before she even knew what she was doing, she found herself moving across the garden toward him.

Due to the layout of the cobblestone path, she had to approach him from the side. His eyes were directed toward the front, so Shelby was sure he was unaware of her. But then, just as she came near, he swiveled toward her, pinning her with an unwavering gaze. He had been aware of her approach all along. This was clearly the sort of man who did not let down his guard even for a moment.

"Yes?" said Wolfgang von Heller.

For an instant all her social skills deserted her under his penetrating gaze. Then she found her voice. "Good evening," she replied.

He nodded curtly and said nothing, continuing to stare.

"Are you enjoying the party?" she asked.

"I detest parties."

"Well, why are you here, then?"

"There is a certain satisfaction, *Fräulein*, in coming to a place where you know you are not welcome, where you know you have been invited only because of your position, in the hope that you will be gracious enough to decline."

"But you're not gracious," Shelby shot back quickly.

"I try not to be, no."

He said nothing further, just continued looking at her. Shelby became unnerved. What could she say to this man? Small talk, under the circumstances, would mark her as a fool. Finally, without thinking about it, she blurted something that came into her head suddenly. "Are you really as bad as they say?"

A dangerous look came into his brown eyes. Shelby felt a surge of excitement at the daringness of what she had asked. For a moment she thought he would refuse to respond to her, but then a wry grin of amusement broke over his lips. Apparently she had said the right thing.

When he spoke, his voice was precise and accented in High German. "You are very direct, aren't you? I have always had a fondness for direct women. Coquettes and empty-headed flirts never have appealed to me." He took a drag on his cigarette and exhaled the gray smoke in a thin stream. "Tell me, then, just how bad do they say I am?"

"They say you're a black marketer and a smuggler, a cold-hearted dangerous man."

"Oh, yes? And how do you feel about all this?"

"I . . . well, I don't know you."

"You do not have intuition?"

She looked at him with renewed interest. "I don't think you're so cold-hearted," she ventured, telling the truth.

He nodded, as if accepting a compliment. Then he said, "You're wrong." He flicked his cigarette away. "I believe I also have a reputation as a despicable soul who eats pretty girls like you for breakfast. You would be well advised, *Fräulein*, to heed that reputation."

"Are you trying to scare me away?" she asked. "Are you afraid of me, maybe?"

Now he laughed in amusement. It was strange to see such an open laugh from such a chilling-looking man, but Shelby felt good about having caused it. It was also strange, she thought, for someone so young—not over thirty-five—to seem so jaded and world-weary.

As Shelby gazed out on the terrace, she saw that her plan had worked. Donovan was staring at her and Wolfgang with a sternly disapproving look. Beside him stood Gretchen, her hand on his arm, talking at him, but Donovan's distraught attention was fully focused on Shelby. This made Shelby smile inwardly with satisfaction.

Wolfgang von Heller noticed Donovan's look of disapproval, also, and seemed pleased. "My friend Herr Hawkes—he is not approving of your conversing with me. You are his protégée? If he is to be upset at your talking to me, then I must encourage this. We will have a long conversation you and I, yes?"

"You like seeing him upset?"

He shrugged. "It is one of life's small pleasures."

"You called him your friend, but you're not really friends, are you?"

"We have worked with cooperation on one or two

occasions. There is no love between us, however.''

Shelby was surprised that they could have worked together on any occasion, in view of what von Heller did for a living.

"No," said Wolfgang, "Herr Hawkes and I are not friends. But since you are his friend, then tell me, do you not realize it is not permitted for a friend of Deputy Minister Hawkes to associate with a man of my reputation? Perhaps you should run along and play it safe.''

She raised her chin defiantly. "Perhaps I don't give a damn what Herr Hawkes thinks about whom I associate with—or about playing it safe.''

Wolfgang's expression was approving, but the look in his eyes told Shelby he knew she was speaking more boldly than she really felt.

"I'd like to go to the railing," Shelby said. "Would you care to escort me?"

The railings were at the corners of the rooftop, where the protective barriers had been lowered from shoulder level to waist level to permit a view of the city beneath them. Wolfgang glanced again at Donovan's angry expression, then offered Shelby his arm. He seemed pleased at the chance to upset him. Shelby sensed he was doing this more out of mischievousness, though, than malice.

As they walked through the garden on the way to the railing, Shelby saw that Donovan was not the only one staring at them. Other guests were looking, too, with faces that were almost scandalized. Diana's expression was one of amazement, worry and warning. She kept shaking her head urgently, trying to give Shelby a message without being too obvious about it. Wolfgang looked neither right nor left as he made his way to the railing. To him these people did not even exist.

It was far more secluded at the corner of the rooftop. They were separated from the main body of guests by thick shrubbery and fragrant flowers. Shelby gazed down. Many stories beneath them was Kurfürstendamm, Berlin's busiest boulevard. Sounds of honking and automobile traffic drifted up. Shelby saw the ribbons of white and red lights down on the streets below as the frenzied traffic rushed to and fro. West Berlin was lit up and alive at this time of night. It was very much a city of night, unlike East Berlin, which had hardly any social activity past nine o'clock. The moon above the city was three-quarters full and very bright against the black sky.

Wolfgang put his hands on her arms and drew her toward him. Shelby's eyes went wide. She had not intended this and did not want it. He gazed at her with a wry grin.

"So, *Fräulein*, you have succeeded in upsetting Herr Hawkes, and you have lured me out here alone with you. What is your intention now?"

His message was clear: you've gone too far in your daring little game, and now it's in my hands, not yours. As she gazed at his coldly handsome face, the animalistic aura emanating from him was so powerful and sensual it frightened her. When his head began moving forward, she stepped back quickly, fear in her eyes.

Wolfgang grinned in amusement and leaned casually against the railing. He had been toying with her—that was all.

After a moment Donovan appeared and stalked aggressively up to them. He ignored Shelby and spoke directly to Wolfgang. "Can't you keep your contaminating influence to yourself?"

Wolfgang sneered. He continued leaning against the railing, relaxed and self-assured.

"I want you to stay away from her," Donovan said. "She's not the sort of girl who's fair game for your particular type of company."

"I'll decide whose company I wish to keep," Shelby interposed. "No one has the right to tell me whom I can or can't see, least of all you."

Donovan tried to ignore her, to deal with Wolfgang, but Shelby kept glaring at him insistently. Finally he looked at her. "You don't know what this man is all about. You don't have the slightest idea what you're letting yourself in for."

Now Shelby's temper was really boiling. Who was he to butt into her life when he had tried to make it so clear that he himself wanted nothing to do with her? Her rage got the best of her, and in overreaction she declared, "If Baron von Heller wants to invite me to the *Oktoberfest* with him Saturday, he has every right to. He doesn't need your permission."

Donovan looked at Wolfgang angrily. "Did you invite her to—"

"Yes!" declared Shelby. "And I accepted. Gladly." She glanced at Wolfgang and saw him leaning againt the railing casually, saying nothing, understanding all. He was perfectly content to watch this entertaining show unfolding before him. Shelby sensed that he was so jaded and had made himself so hard that watching the folly of others was one of his few enjoyments in life.

"Do you know what this man stands for?" Donovan demanded.

"Who are *you* to accuse anyone of standing for anything undesirable?" she shot back. "You with your two-faced behavior and playboy instincts."

Donovan did not defend himself. Instead he looked belligerently at Wolfgang, who turned to gaze down at the city below, apparently becoming bored. Donovan said to Shelby, "All right. You're over twenty-one—though you certainly don't act it. Do what you like."

"I intend to, and I'll choose my own friends, thank you." She went to Wolfgang and put her arm through his as she glared at Donovan.

Wolfgang took this, too, in stride. He seemed content to play her straight man for the moment.

"Who are you trying to kid?" Donovan asked scornfully. "You don't care for him."

"Oh, no?" Shelby said. And in defiance she put her hand on the back of Wolfgang's neck and kissed him on the lips. It was an abrupt short kiss, just for show. His lips remained closed, and he did not participate. Afterward Shelby stared angrily at Donovan, her head high, as if challenging him to dispute *that*.

What she had not counted on, however, was Wolfgang's feeling he had played the straight man long enough. Suddenly he swiveled her around to face him, bending her half backward over his arm. He gazed down into her eyes domineeringly, knowing he had the upper hand, knowing Shelby was powerless to stop him. She realized it, too. She had committed herself. She could not back out now without letting Donovan know her kiss had been only for show.

Wolfgang's deep brown eyes were taunting. His handsome angular face, so much like the sculpted works of Roman gods, drew very near—so near she could feel the warmth of his breath and smell the faint scent of his tobacco. Then his lips descended on hers in a savage searing kiss that sent her mind reeling. A sudden wave of emotion surged all through her, shocking her.

When Wolfgang released her, Shelby saw that Donovan's hands had closed into fists and he was about to swing at Wolfgang. Shelby held up her hand, moving quickly between them. "No!" she cried. Nothing could get Donovan booted out of the State Department quicker than swinging at an invited guest at a party hosted by the American legation.

Donovan turned his eyes to Shelby, thinking she was protecting Wolfgang now for the same reason she had kissed him a moment earlier and had invited his kiss in return. In his eyes Shelby could see what she had suspected all along—that he did love her.

There was something else in his eyes now, too—a look of hurt. When he spoke, his voice was subdued.

"All right," he said to her. "If that's the way you want it." He turned and left.

Well, she thought, watching him go, she had done what she had set out to do. She had made him angry and jealous—and had forced him to show in his eyes that his words of love had been true, despite his attempts to pretend otherwise. She had done all this, but at what price?

Forcing her gaze away from Donovan's angrily retreating figure, she slowly turned back to the lean domineering man beside her—the international smuggler with whom she had invited herself to go *Oktoberfesting*. Had he taken her invitation seriously, she wondered nervously.

Wolfgang's expression was knowing and intimidating. He bowed formally. *"Auf wiedersehen,"* he said, bidding her good-night. "Until Saturday, then. At about ten?" He walked off, lithe and graceful as a panther, despite his slight limp. Shelby stared after him.

A moment later Diana came rushing up to her. She had stationed herself nearby, where she had overheard everything. "Oh, my gosh," she cried in horror, "what have you *done*? Shelby. Oh, Shelby. Don't you understand? That is Wolfgang von Heller!"

CHAPTER TWELVE

ALL THROUGH FRIDAY Shelby kept calling Wolfgang's number to try to excuse herself from going to the *Oktoberfest* with him. It was impossible to reach him. She suspected he was deliberately denying her the chance to cancel their date. Finally, on Friday afternoon, Diana offered to have Hans brief Shelby about the baron, on the theory that the more she knew about him, the better she'd be able to handle any situation that might come up. Shelby accepted gratefully.

They left the legation early and crossed into the East while it was still daylight. It took only a few moments to process through Checkpoint Charlie, first through the Quonset-hut-style shacks on the western side, then, after crossing the broad white-painted line that marked the border, through those on the eastern side. Entering and leaving East Berlin was not difficult for Westerners. A payment of West German marks was demanded, except from diplomatic personnel; one's papers were inspected, and then one was passed on through. It was for East Berliners that the journey was so impossible.

Hans Dietrich was waiting for them outside the

customs shack on the East Berlin side. He was a
sandy-haired man a few years older than Diana, with
thick glasses and a rather intense hangdog face. He
was not very good-looking, but he was very much in
love with her. This was obvious from the way he embraced her as if he had not seen her in years, though
actually Diana visited him every weekend. Diana's
back was to Shelby, so Shelby could see Hans's face
as he embraced her. His brow was knit in love and
anguish. Shelby sensed desperation in his look, too,
and suspected he was very near to making the decision to risk a crossing.

After a moment Diana introduced Shelby. Hans
shook her hand, then put his arm around Diana's
waist possessively as they began walking. Glancing at
Shelby, Diana seemed a bit embarrassed at the overt
signs of affection from Hans, but she was pleased,
too, for she glowed. Hans was not embarrassed at
all, though he was a bit shy. He appeared proud of
the fact that someone like Diana could love him as
much as he loved her.

"We will walk to the café, yes?" said Hans. "It is
not far, and the day is nice."

Actually, thought Shelby, the day was typical of
late September—a bit nippy and overcast. All three
of them wore coats. But she didn't mind walking.
She enjoyed seeing the way Hans couldn't keep his
hands off Diana. He would have his arm either
around her waist as they walked or around her shoulders, or he would be holding her hand and swinging it
like a schoolboy. He was not very socially adept and

was not good at hiding his feelings. Shelby liked him right away.

The very first thing Hans said to Diana was, "Your transfer request to your East Berlin embassy—it has been approved?"

Diana looked uncomfortable. "Not yet, honey."

"Why do they keep us in suspense like this?" he asked, upset. "How are we to plan, to live our lives, with such uncertainty?"

"We'll know soon, I'm sure," she said, hugging his arm. She glanced at Shelby. Her eyes said, "How can I tell him the truth?" Shelby could give no positive sign in return.

"I will not wait forever," Hans declared ominously. "If they approve your assignment here, fine. If they do not, we will still be together—one way or another."

As they walked down Friedrichstrasse, Shelby saw a magnificent sight on their left, one that never failed to impress her each time she viewed it. It was the Brandenburg Gate—a massive multicolumned architectural landmark. As the Arc de Triomphe was for France, the Brandenburg Gate was Germany's symbolic passageway of conquest, through which Prussian troops had paraded since the early 1800s. Originally it had been built to commemorate the victories of Frederick the Great.

Shelby glanced up at the famous quadriga as they walked past. This was an enormous gilded statue of a Roman chariot drawn by four mighty stallions carrying the goddess Victory. It was situated at the top of the very high gate. Shelby knew that the original quadriga had been destroyed by World War II bombardment and that for many years afterward the only decoration atop the Brandenburg was the red flag of the Soviet occupying army. Years later the original molds were rediscovered, and a new quadriga was cast—the one they were gazing at now.

"So you wish to learn about Baron von Heller," Hans said to Shelby. "How much do you know of him presently?"

"Only that he's one of the most powerful black marketers in Berlin."

"And if he is still the way he was in his early days," said Hans, "one of the most vicious."

"He seems young to be so successful and powerful."

"He started young; he made his first million before he was twenty-five. He grew up after the war, when East Germany was even more under the iron fist of the Russians than it is now. He became a smuggler when he was only fifteen, bringing in goods for the black market. Before the wall was built, East Berliners could simply walk into West Berlin to buy whatever they needed. When the wall went up, all Western consumer goods were suddenly impossible to get hold of. There was great opportunity in those days for reckless daring men to make a fortune."

"But great danger, too," said Diana. "Not only from the *Vopos*, but from other smugglers, as well."

Hans nodded in agreement. He said to Shelby, "Von Heller carved out a territory for himself in a field that was fiercely competitive among smugglers, most of whom were much older and more established than he. He was only a teenager then, remember. His black-market operation grew, to be sure, because of his intense dedication and hard work, but mostly it was due to his fearlessness. He was willing to make deals and take risks others weren't. Soon he became quite successful, with several others working under him.''

"That was when the big boys stepped in," Diana said, "the hardened smuggling veterans from the war. They tried to muscle him out."

"Yes," Hans added, "and that was when von Heller earned his reputation as a vicious fighter who was not to be crossed. He refused to knuckle under to the other hoodlums. He met violence with even worse violence, matching them blow for blow, refusing to be subdued. For almost a year it was constant war between him and the others."

"Is that where he got that limp?" Shelby asked.

"Yes," said Hans. "Someone tried to run him over with a truck. Von Heller ended up with an injured leg; the driver, according to the grapevine, ended up at the bottom of the Spree River several days later."

Shelby winced. This was the man she was going out with in the morning? She turned her attention to the lovely linden trees lining both sides of the street. They were strolling down Unter den Linden now, a very broad three-hundred-foot-wide avenue that had been the pride of prewar Germany. It was down this street that Napoleon had marched to commemorate his victory over the Prussians; it was here that Kaiser Wilhelm had driven his first automobile. Though it had once been one of the world's most elegant boulevards, the war had destroyed the two hundred forty-six stately linden trees that gave it its distinction. New trees had been planted, however, and now the grand avenue was as lovely as ever.

Shelby turned back to Hans and asked, "How did he get political power? Diana said he's a powerful man politically, as well as financially."

"Some government bureaucrats here are hypocritical and corrupt. They speak of making sacrifices, but they themselves want luxuries." He shrugged. "Von Heller provides them with what they want, what they cannot get through the system. Because of this he has many people who owe him favors."

"But don't confuse the bureaucrats with the hard-line members of the Communist party," Diana said. "The hard-liners hate him with a passion. They hate anyone who works against the system, especially someone who manages to make a fortune doing it. They're constantly trying to set traps to catch von Heller. Once they tried to trap him into bribing an official so they could put him in prison. He was too smart for them, though."

"I don't understand," stated Shelby. "If they hate him so much, why do they give him so many privileges, such as letting him cross the border at will?"

"Again," said Hans, "it is the difference between the bureaucrats and the hard-line members of the party. The bureaucrats know that men like him are a necessary evil. East Berlin is cursed with shortages of consumer goods. Without the black market the system couldn't function; the people would revolt against the privations. They did so once already, in 1953. So men like von Heller are tolerated by the bureaucrats for a very practical reason—the goods they smuggle in are necessary."

"But the party hard-liners don't tolerate him," added Diana. "Those people don't care a whit about being practical. Von Heller's fiercely anti-Communist and runs roughshod over their system, so they hate him and try to trap him into doing something that can get him arrested."

Shelby was impressed by all the people who seemed to want Wolfgang von Heller in jail. Earlier Diana had told her how West Germany constantly tried to catch him smuggling money across the border, and now she learned that East Germany was just as anxious to put him behind bars and had even tried to trap him into bribing an official so they could do so. Yet the man still remained free.

"I wonder why he wants to date me," Shelby said, puzzled. "At first he didn't even want to talk to me at that party. I had to force myself on him."

"I don't know," said Diana, "but I'd be worried if I were you. He uses people for his own selfish ends—or at least that's the way rumor has it."

"Rumor is," added Hans, "that he is as cold as ice and absolutely insensitive, so I do not believe his interest in you is romantic. Besides, he was close to a woman once—a lead dancer with the Leipzig Ballet. Supposedly she was the love of his life, but she left him after only a few months, saying he was too cold a man ever to truly give of himself. He's been bitter about women ever since, and apparently he never dates a girl more than once or twice. No, I do not believe it is romance that is involved.''

They arrived at the café at which they were to have tea. As they were being seated, Diana said to Shelby with concern, ''Honey, why don't you just not be there when he shows up? I don't like the feel of this at all.''

Shelby didn't like the feel of it, either, but she was curious—not just about his reason for wanting to date her, but about the man himself. ''I invited him,'' she said to Diana, ''not the other way around, so if he shows up tomorrow morning, I'll be there waiting for him.''

A bit later, after tea, Shelby thanked Hans for the information and left early. She could see that the moments were precious for him and Diana, and she wanted to let them enjoy their time, alone. She returned home and awaited the morning.

CHAPTER THIRTEEN

SHE HEARD Wolfgang von Heller before she saw him. There was the roar of a powerful engine pulling up outside her apartment, then the screech of brakes. She made out hurried footsteps on the stairs and a knock at her door.

When she answered, she saw him standing there, tall and commanding, in a brown corduroy coat over a rich burgundy shirt. His blond hair was rakishly windblown. A neckerchief was knotted loosely at his throat. His handsome youthful face seemed a bit leaner than it had two nights previous, and quite impatient.

"Guten tag," Shelby said, bidding him good morning.

"Tag. You are ready, I hope. Already we are late."

The day was warm and pleasant. Shelby took a coat, in case she should need it later. She was wearing gray flannel slacks and a cowl-neck royal blue sweater that did not tightly emphasize her figure, but didn't hide it, either. Wolfgang led her out to his car, whose motor he had left running. It was a beautiful old two-seater Porsche—which made Shelby smile in delight. She had always loved restored classic cars. This appeared to be an early 1950s vintage. Its exterior was painted metallic racing green; the interior was glove-soft tanned leather and polished old wood, and surprisingly, it was a convertible.

"I've never seen a Porsche convertible this old," Shelby said admiringly. "I didn't know Porsche even made convertibles back then."

"They did not," he replied, opening her door for her. "When I purchased the car, I took it to the plant to have it modified. The Porsche plant is in Stuttgart. They insisted on doing this as a favor to me."

"I have to get a scarf," Shelby said. "I didn't know you had a convertible. I'll be back in a moment."

He grabbed her wrist as she started to turn away. "We do not have a moment. Please, we are late."

Shelby didn't like being ordered about. She considered ignoring his request and going for her scarf anyway. He had said please, though. She decided to accommodate him just this once.

He closed her door once she was seated, then hurried around to the driver's side and leaped in, not bothering with the door. His slight limp did not seem to impair his movements. Then, with a shifting of gears and in a hail of gravel, they roared away.

The wind whipped through Shelby's long chestnut hair as they raced down the road, heedless of other traffic or the speed laws, and then onto East Germany's main freeway, the Helmstedt-Berlin Autobahn. Wolfgang's gloved hand shifted into the highest gear, then returned to the leather-covered steering wheel. From the motor's sound, smooth under such stress, Shelby guessed that the original motor had not just been restored but completely replaced with a modern high-powered racing motor.

She didn't really mind not having brought a scarf. The feel of the wind in her hair and on her face was wonderful, and the way the trees and roadside objects flashed by was exhilarating Shelby had always loved speed. Though she was by nature a practical girl, she knew there was a reckless side to her, too, buried somewhere deep, for fast cars had always excited her.

Wolfgang glanced at her, then turned his attention back to the road. He seemed preoccupied.

"Where are we going in such a hurry?" Shelby asked. She practically had to shout to be heard above the roar of the motor and the whistling of the wind.

"Oktoberfesting," he shouted back. "Is that not where you wished to go? However, first we must make a brief stop."

"For what?"

He glanced at her again, the wind whipping through his blond hair. His eyes squinted against the rushing air. "A business matter," he said uninformatively.

Shelby disliked the way he refused to tell her more. He returned his attention to the road as they raced along for his late appointment. She decided to ignore him completely, in response to his attitude. She folded her arms across her chest and concentrated on the lovely early-autumn scenery. She glanced at him once, reflecting on how he was a study in browns—from his deep brown eyes to his attractive clothes to the tone of his blond hair.

Soon they were screeching off the *autobahn* and racing down a rural country road. They reached a private dirt crossroad that had a white wooden gate blocking it. Two men stood by the gate, one leaning against it, both looking like ruffians. They inspected Wolfgang—and Shelby, too—as Wolfgang idled the car impatiently before the gate. Then they opened the gate, and Wolfgang roared past. He sped down the private road until he reached a red barn, where three other men were waiting for him. These were burly coarse men, looking just as unsavory as the ones at the gate.

"Who's the girl?" demanded the stubble-bearded one in German as Wolfgang got out of the car.

"That's none of your concern," Wolfgang replied in his native tongue. He grabbed a briefcase from the back of the seat.

"Oh, no?" stated the stubble-bearded man belligerently.

Wolfgang walked the few steps separating them and stood directly in front of him, staring at him. Shelby had never seen such raw menacing power and quiet authority as were in Wolfgang's eyes right then. The stubble-bearded man—heavier and brawnier than Wolfgang—held his stare for only a moment. Then he began looking nervous and backed away, holding up his palms in retreat.

Wolfgang came back to the car and said to Shelby, "Wait here. I will only be a moment." Before she could reply, he had disappeared into the red barn, followed by two of the three men. The third—the stubble-bearded one—remained outside, looking at Shelby hostilely, as if she were the cause of his humiliation.

Shelby felt extremely nervous, more so with each passing moment. Where was she? Who were these men? Obviously they were not friends of Wolfgang's. If something went wrong inside the barn—if something happened to him—how safe would she be?

In only a moment, though, Wolfgang reappeared from within the darkness of the building, striding briskly back to the car. He flung his briefcase in behind the seat and climbed inside. Within seconds they were turning in a sharp arc on the dirt road, spraying gravel, then racing back toward the highway.

After they passed the two men at the gate and were safely back on the *autobahn*, Shelby said, "What was *that* all about?"

"A business matter. . . nothing of importance."

Shelby was becoming perturbed. "I dislike being made a party to business matters about which I have no knowledge, Baron von Heller."

"Wolfgang, please."

"Especially when I feel that no consideration is being shown at all for my safety."

He glanced at her. "You were in no danger—not at any time."

"If this is the way the rest of our day is going to go, I think you'd better take me home."

He surprised Shelby by looking disappointed. For a moment he remained silent. The only sound was the roar of the motor and the whistling of the wind. Then he said in a conciliatory tone, "I am sorry if you felt I abused you, *Fräulein*. I assure you it was not deliberate, and it will not happen again. I was in a hurry. But that is behind us now."

It wasn't much of an apology, but Shelby decided to give him the benefit of the doubt and accept it. "Just what business are you involved in?" she asked, her tone more pleasant.

He glanced at her to see how much she knew. "I am in the import business," he answered.

Shelby remembered Diana telling her he seldom admitted his true profession, even though it was common knowledge in Berlin.

"What is *your* business?" he asked. When she told him that her job at the moment was helping Donovan track down the Lion, Wolfgang grinned in amusement. Shelby thought his grinning at this was rather strange.

"Do you know anything about the Lion?" she asked.

"I know everything about anything that goes on in Berlin, East or West. I make it my business to know."

Shelby realized he might have knowledge of something important that could be useful to her. He did have an intelligence network, after all, to keep him informed of all that happened. "Do you know who the Lion is?" she asked gingerly.

"Yes."

"Will you tell me?"

He glanced at her. "Do you want me to tell you?"

That put her on the spot. The fact was, Shelby didn't really want to turn in the Lion. Ever since the crossing she had witnessed on the Spree River, her feelings about arresting anyone who helped refugees had changed. The image was still clear in her mind of the boy crawling out of Donovan's speedboat and emotionally kissing the bank of West Berlin, the girl sobbing unrestrainedly, shouting, "We're free; we're free!" Also, the more Shelby learned about the Lion, the more she respected him. If she discovered his identity now, she would not turn him in, despite her feelings about the wisdom of the State Department's noninterference rule.

Of course, she couldn't tell Donovan this, for he would seize on it as an excuse to take her off the assignment. She had to be careful. She had already given him one excuse by her refusal to interview Eric Furth. The only reason he had not been able to use that, she was sure, was that their sexual interlude had come shortly afterward. Donovan probably feared Shelby would use that as a basis for filing a protest, saying he was trying to get rid of her for personal rather than professional reasons. She would never do that—but Donovan didn't know it.

"Don't worry," Wolfgang said, showing more perception than she had credited him with. "I will not put you on the spot by telling you who the Lion is. You have heard the saying that there is no honor among outlaws?" He shook his head. "This is false. There is honor between the Lion and me."

He could see how uncomfortable she had become about this subject, due to her uncertainty about where her duty really lay, so he turned her attention away from it by commenting without any prelude, "You are a very beautiful woman. Herr Hawkes must be insane to scorn you."

"Scorn me?" she said defensively. "What makes you think he scorns me?"

"Is it not obvious by the way he encouraged Fräulein Bruckner at the party in so ostentatious a manner? I know he has no fondness for that particular flirtatious lady, and then you, in response, suddenly decide to take an interest in me...." He looked at her, his brown eyes very penetrating.

Shelby had to lower her eyes. She could not deny she had taken an interest in him only to make Donovan jealous. She asked softly, "If you believe I invited myself to go to the *Oktoberfest* with you only for a self-serving reason, why did you agree to take me?"

"Perhaps you appeal to me."

That didn't sound very likely to Shelby, who was quite skeptical of his motives. "You're not very informative. Are you always so closemouthed about things?"

"Yes, always."

"You feel I've used you," she said, "and yet

you've gone along with it. I don't understand why.''

''Perhaps I intend to use you also. Then we will be even, *nicht wahr*? Is it not so?''

He was smiling, but Shelby had no idea whether he was joking. Suddenly she wondered, for the second time today, if she was safe in his presence. She noticed ominously that they were heading east toward the border. ''Where are we going?'' she asked quickly.

''There are many *Oktoberfests* in *Deutschland* this day. I'm sure you know that numerous cities and villages have their own celebrations. I thought I would take you to Idor-Amstein, a village for which I have a particular fondness.''

Shelby did not feel reassured. She remembered how fearful Diana was of this man and how Hans had said he had become embittered toward women after his love affair had ended. Was it possible he felt insulted about her going out with him only to make Donovan jealous? *Was* she in danger? As she watched the scenery whizzing by, her imagination began to run away with her.

Wolfgang looked at her and laughed.

This startled Shelby. She looked back at him.

''Forgive me,'' he said, ''for laughing at you. It is just...your expression, the way you looked so frightened of me. And now here you are bolstering your courage, so that you appear like some scared child trying to be brave. Tell me, am I as fearsome as all that?''

''No,'' she answered too quickly, defensively. ''I wouldn't say you're frightening at all.''

"Then why do you look frightened?"

"I don't, darn it! I just. . . ."

He smiled at her discomfort. It was a pleasant smile, which Shelby would not have expected of him. So the man was not totally cold steel after all.

"Tell me," he said, "what is it you have heard of me that is so distressing? You have heard maybe that I steal candy from the mouths of babies? Or that I push old women into the street?"

Shelby laughed at the absurd images this called to mind. She saw him smile at her laughter and felt grateful that he was deliberately trying to put her at ease. She appreciated warmth and humor now, after all the cold unpleasant days she had suffered at Donovan's hands. And the days *had* been unpleasant, filled with strain and unhappiness. Wolfgang's attitude at the moment was like a ray of sunlight.

"No," Shelby said, "no stories of your stealing candy from babies."

"I assure you I am fully capable of it. It is only that the profit potential seems not so great. Of course, I could be mistaken." He gazed at her with exaggerated mock seriousness. "Tell me, please, have you any candy I could steal?"

Shelby laughed.

"Do you know of any old women, perhaps, whom I could lure to the sidewalk and then ruthlessly push into the street?"

She continued laughing, pleased at his sensitivity in trying to make light of her fear. He was smiling at her, happy that he had made her laugh. He reached out and touched her arm warmly, for only a second, then returned his hand to the steering wheel.

They had turned onto a rural road and were now driving through lovely rolling hills, lush with greenery. There were thickly wooded areas, and here and there stood a wooden building where a family or farmer resided. Some of the hillsides had been cleared of timber and sown with various crops in precise lines that wound up even the steepest of the hillsides. In the United States farmers planted on the east flatlands of the Midwest because there was such an abundance of flatlands. In Europe farmers planted everywhere they could, regardless of the terrain.

The sunlight and the wind felt wonderful on her face. Shelby began to feel happy and relaxed for the first time in a long time. She glanced at Wolfgang, who was lighting a cigarette with a slender lighter that appeared to have been carved from a block of deep purple amethyst.

"You know, you really do have a reputation," she said. "Though of course it's not as bad as you're making out."

"Yes?" he said.

She hesitated, unsure whether to continue. He nodded at her, and his expression encouraged her to go on. "Well," she said, "it's as I told you at the party. They say you're a smuggler and black marketer." Her eyebrows raised quizzically, as if asking, "Are you?"

But again Wolfgang avoided committing himself. All he would say was, "Interesting." They drove on a bit farther.

"I will tell you something of the East German economy," he said finally, "under the Communist system. Many things are needed; few are provided. East Germany is beset by shortages. Several types of goods cannot be legally imported during a given time due to the emphasis on more 'important' goods. Thus there are shortages of shoes, baby diapers, canned fruits, other things. The shortages exist on a rotating basis; usually it is exactly what one wants that is unavailable when he wants it."

He looked at her. "The government is incapable of providing many very essential items, so they must be smuggled in. If one were to become a smuggler under these circumstances, he would really be nothing more than a 'businessman' by the standards of your country—a businessman who performs a valuable service to his fellow citizens."

"So you're a smuggler to help your fellow citizens, then?" She asked the question overly casually, thinking she might catch him off guard and trick him into admitting he was a smuggler.

Wolfgang's sardonic grin, though, showed he had seen through her clumsy attempt. She was certain he would evade the question now, but instead he said, "No, I am a smuggler because of the profits."

She wondered why he had admitted this to her. She respected his honesty, but there was no way she could respect what he was. Her disfavor must have shown in her expression, for he added, "You do not approve." After a moment he asked, "Have you ever lived in a time of great privation, *Fräulein*? In a land that is under foreign occupation?"

"No," she answered softly.

"East Berlin was like that when I was growing up. After World War II the Americans funneled money *into* West Germany to help build it up after the ravages of war. But as for East Germany, the Russians controlled that, and they pulled what little money was left there, *out*. They said it was owed them for war reparations. There was near starvation in Berlin then—in the early fifties and for a decade afterward—for the Russian demands for reparations continued. In 1953 the situation was so bad my countrymen revolted. The Russians put down the riots with tanks and machine guns. Hundreds were killed, including my father and mother. My father, they said, was a leader of the revolt."

"Was he?" Shelby asked delicately.

"Yes."

"I'm so sorry," she said.

"I do not want your sorrow! I wish you only to understand. My sister and I, tiny children then, were orphans. There was not enough to eat. We were out on the streets—amid the rubble. Our family castle was occupied by Russian soldiers. Relatives took us in, but they, too, did not have enough to eat."

Shelby could see the deep anguish on his face as he spoke.

"By the time I was a teenage boy, years later, we were no longer starving. There were always garbage cans to rummage through. But we were badly enough off that my sister told me she might choose a way to earn more money—a very ugly way—so we could afford decent food and clothing." His face took on a harsh pained look. "It was the only time in my life I have ever slapped a woman—when she said that."

"Oh, Wolfgang, I'm so sorry." She touched his arm.

"Save your pity. I do not believe in pity. I merely wish you to understand that you, growing up in your fat well-fed land of America, have no right to pass judgment on what I had to do to make a decent life for myself and my family. If I had obeyed the system, life would have been hell. So I trod over the system, which is a bad system, a corrupt system. My relatives live well now. My sister has married and resides in Leipzig. You tell me, please, who suffers because I am a smuggler and black marketer."

Shelby didn't know what to say. "I'm not here to pass judgment," she commented quietly.

"You pass judgment whether you speak the words or not."

She said nothing. After a moment Wolfgang shuddered, as if physically shaking off the somberness that held him in its grip. "Forgive me," he began. "I did not mean to badger you with my life story, but I did want you to...understand." He looked at her, and Shelby could see in his eyes that this—this simple statement—was an intimate admission for him. He wanted her personally to understand.

"Look," he said, pointing, "Idor-Amstein."

A village appeared up ahead by several miles, visible now as they crested a high hill. It looked quaint, lovely and serene. It was quite small, with only about eighty buildings and homes situated in a natural valley between thickly forested hillsides. The buildings were gaily but not garishly painted, with dormers projecting from the slanted rooftops and shutters flanking the open windows.

Beyond the village was one of Germany's several ancient castles, which from the distance looked badly in need of repair. It was perched atop a high hill, and its foremost wall seemed to be crumbling. In between the castle and the village ran the northern border between West Berlin and East Germany, sinister and obtrusive. It appeared terribly out of place, with its concrete and barbed-wire ugliness, amid this scene of rustic tranquillity. It was a constant reminder of how close the village had come, when the postwar boundary had been decided, to being in the East.

Soon they were driving through the village, along its main street toward the public square. Shelby saw a sandstone waterwheel attached to a building and turned by a small stream. She asked Wolfgang what it was for. He told her that the main business of Idor-Amstein was cutting and polishing the jasper and amethyst gemstones originally found in the natural caves of the surrounding countryside. But for centuries gemstones had also been brought to Idor-Amstein from all over, for the small village had long been the European center for this specialized industry. Most of its citizens were skilled craftsmen in the art of stonecutting and polishing.

The village seemed strangely deserted. Shelby discovered why when they reached the main square. All the villagers were congregated there—more than two hundred, it seemed. They were dressed for the festival in brightly colored traditional costumes. The little girls looked lovely with their golden braided hair.

To Shelby's utter amazement, she found that the villagers had all been waiting for them. As Wolfgang pulled into their midst and parked, a cheer rose up from the populace. An oom-pa-pa band began playing loudly; confetti was tossed into the air, and everyone descended upon the Porsche, slapping Wolfgang on the back—and Shelby, too—smiling, laughing and shouting merrily in greeting.

CHAPTER FOURTEEN

Before Shelby knew what was happening, she was out of the car and being hustled by a crowd of villagers toward an elevated head table at the front of the square. She was separated from Wolfgang, and it was only by his holding out his hand to her across the sea of people between them that she managed to grasp it. He pulled her toward him so that they were together as they were swept along in the tide.

Wolfgang smiled at her in reassurance, but Shelby was a bit unnerved by all this—it was so sudden and intense. He put his arm around her shoulders protectively as they moved closer to the head table. The music and merrymaking was too loud for her even to ask him what this was all about.

Finally they were deposited at the elevated head table, and things quieted down a bit. The mayor of the village, a plump man named Otto Esser, shook Wolfgang's hand in greeting and welcomed him and his guest to the festival. From what Shelby could pick up, the *Oktoberfest* was the one event of the year that Wolfgang always attended here, and it was like some sort of homecoming for him. The mayor made a short speech, then hugged Wolfgang. The villagers cheered. Shelby, as Wolfgang's guest, seemed to rate a hug, also, and she tried to smile through it, though she was still a bit disconcerted.

At last she and Wolfgang were seated, along with several of Idor-Amstein's aldermen and local dignitaries. They were given the place of honor at the center. The villagers congregated in front of the table, becoming an audience to Mayor Esser, who was acting as master of ceremonies.

Glasses were filled with white Rhine wine from straw-covered flasks, and a toast was drunk to Wolfgang. Shelby found a glass thrust into her hand, and she, too, joined the toast. The wine was cool, pleasantly tart and heady. Trays of pastries and baked goods were brought forth by the children of the village and paraded in front of Wolfgang for his approval. He nodded as the procession went past. Then the trays were deposited onto banquet tables off to the side. He accepted these honors graciously, as might a medieval lord upon being feted by his subjects.

As the presentations continued, Shelby wondered what he had done to deserve such a place in the hearts of this village. Clearly these people worshipped him. The smiles and applause and toasts were in earnest. Nothing Shelby had learned from Diana's and Hans's briefing had prepared her for this.

The villagers wanted Wolfgang to make a speech, but he politely declined. All he would say when he took the podium was, "Thank you. It is good to be home again." Then he raised his glass of wine in toast to the villagers, and another wild cheer went up, and another glass, from which she took a sip, was thrust into Shelby's hand.

She was beginning to relax, now that she saw she was surrounded by goodwill. She began to let herself unwind from her tensed-up state and to enjoy the celebration. The festivities commenced after Wolfgang made his toast and downed the wine. The band started up; people began dancing in the square. Everyone welcomed the chance to celebrate, though the original reason for this major *Volksfest* was now remote—it had begun at the time of the engagement of Bavaria's Prince Ludwig to Princess Theresa in 1810. No one cared about the lack of a present official reason to celebrate, though, any more than they cared about the novel fact that the *Oktoberfest* was held in September—and always had been.

Wolfgang returned to his seat at the table next to Shelby. Now Shelby had a chance to talk to him at last.

"What are you to these people?" she asked, amazed at the reception he was being given.

"I told you this village is the center for the cutting and polishing of jasper and amethyst," he began, bending close so she could hear him above the music and partying. "During the war years, with shortages of food, clothing and everything else, you can imagine how much demand there was for jewelry and polished gemstones—none, of course. Yet the village was built around this single industry. No one knew how to do anything else, for in recent memory no one had ever needed to do anything else."

"How did they survive the war years?"

He pointed to the castle off in the distance on the far hill. "The master of that castle had a relationship with this village that went back to feudal times. Centuries ago, the village was composed of serfs beholden to the lord of the castle. Though the relationship no longer existed by this century, the tradition did, as did the sense of responsibility the master of the castle felt toward the village. He was *their* master, and they were *his* villagers, and this was the way everyone had wanted it—the villagers, as well as he—for generations."

"The master of the castle—" Shelby said, venturing a guess, "he was your father?"

Wolfgang nodded. "Baron Manfred von Heller, and that castle has been our ancestral home from the day it was built in 1612. What my father did during the war years was to finance the learning of a whole new industry from his personal savings. The only males in the village then were old men and young boys. My father brought in experts from a different field—the manufacture of agricultural implements—to teach the villagers this skill. He paid for the raw materials. He paid for their transportation here and for the machines that were needed. He underwrote bank loans for the villagers, using their buildings—which were worthless at the time—as collateral. And with the last of his savings, he himself made all payments on these loans."

"So he saved the village," Shelby said.

"He provided it with a new industry that tided it over during the lean years of the war—this way the people did not have to scatter to other parts—and he made sure they could earn their bread and meat so that here, during the war, there was no starvation.''

"They seem very fond of you personally, though," Shelby said. "You seem to be more to them than just the son of the man who did all this.''

He shrugged this off and said nothing, but then under Shelby's continuing gaze he admitted, "When I became established in my own line of work, I picked up the payments on the loans my father had underwritten. This prevented the Frankfurt banks from foreclosing on the homes and businesses of the villagers.''

"Do you still make the payments on these loans?''

He leaned back in his chair, looking displeased. "I grow weary of this subject," he said. He turned his eyes away from Shelby toward the square and watched the folkdancing.

Shelby felt she knew the truth. He did continue the payments, she thought, and like his father, she sensed that he, too, felt a responsibility to the villagers. He was their baron now, and they were his charges. Shelby knew she could be wrong in believing this, but she felt she had a strong sense of the man.

She, too, leaned back in her chair and let herself enjoy the dancing in the square before her. She felt much warmer toward Wolfgang. In fact, she felt good in general now, as well. She was enjoying herself, letting her spirits be buoyed by the music, the bright colors, the joyous townspeople. It felt strange to be so happy. She had not realized how long it had

been since she had felt like this. The tense defensive
way she had been acting in response to Donovan's
oppression had become almost second nature with
her during these past few days; she had nearly forgot
what it was like to loosen up and enjoy life.

Shelby noticed Wolfgang establish eye contact
with a very blond fair-skinned young man in khaki
trousers. At first Shelby thought some sort of signal
passed between them, but she dismissed this as silly.
However, then the young man came forward and
bowed to Shelby, asking her to dance. He was a man
about her own age.

"No," Shelby said, smiling, "I don't think so, but
thank you."

"Please," said Wolfgang, encouraging her. "I
wish you to have a good time."

"Well, you come with me, then," she replied with
impulsive high spirits, standing up and taking his
hand.

He shook his head. "My leg," he said matter-of-
factly, without self-pity. "I do not dance." He kept
encouraging her, though, and the young man was
waiting for her, smiling pleasantly. Other people saw
what was happening and also began urging Shelby to
dance.

It was tempting, and she did like dancing, having
learned German folk dances when she lived in Bonn
with her father. With an impish smile she leaned forward and kissed Wolfgang lightly on the temple—*too
much wine for me,* she thought—then took the young
man's offered hand. She followed him out onto the

square. The band struck up a waltzy tune, and they began dancing. She was not too bad and was a big hit. The villagers applauded her at the end, cheering as well as clapping. Shelby felt invigorated and happy. She bowed to her partner, then bowed playfully to the villagers who were applauding her. When she retook her seat, Wolfgang put his hand on hers and squeezed it, nodding in approval.

"You are very good," he said.

"Thank you," she replied, out of breath. "But you know, you didn't have to signal that man to make him ask me to dance. I was happy enough just sitting with you and watching it all."

"Signal him?"

"Oh, come on," she said in a friendly chiding tone. "You don't have to deny it."

But he just shrugged and turned his attention back to the square. It was then that Shelby noticed her purse leaning against the side of her chair, when she was almost sure she had left it on the chair seat itself.

The feast was served soon after that, and the exotic dishes were wonderfully rich and delicious. There were all sorts of sausage and dumpling dishes, which each German village made as its own specialty. Shelby especially liked *Kasefladel*—a pancake made with rich Allgäu cheese—and *Kuchel*—cookies made with rose petals and wild berries. There were so many dishes Shelby could eat only a forkful or so of just a few. The village square became a scene of clinking beer steins. The villagers filled their plates and retired

to the tables surrounding the square for hearty feast-
ing and good fellowship.

Afterward, though the festivities continued, Wolfgang made his farewell to the mayor and several
others. Then he and Shelby started to leave. They
made their way to the Porsche. Wolfgang turned his
key in the ignition, and the powerful motor sprang to
life. Shelby noticed something and said, "Your briefcase. It's gone. It's not behind your seat where you
put it."

He seemed unconcerned. "I left it with the
mayor."

Soon they were racing down the wooded road, the
wind in their hair. Shelby was grateful for the silence
of the open road after all the noise and commotion of
the *Oktoberfest*. She put on her coat after a bit when
the air became cooler.

Only one thing disturbed her. "We're heading
east," she realized suddenly. "Aren't we going
home?"

"Not just yet. I thought perhaps you might wish to
see my castle." He glanced at her, his expression not
quite innocent. His lean face looked very handsome
in the dappled sunlight coming through the tall trees,
but it also had a hardened aspect to it that made
Shelby wary.

"I'll look at it if you like," she said, "but I can't
stay long. And I do wish you'd asked me first, instead of just starting to take me there."

"My apologies. You have your diplomatic passport, of course? We will be crossing the border."

Shelby nodded. As an officer of the legation, she always carried it with her, as he must have known.

They drove for just a few moments more before reaching the border. Without thinking too much about it, Shelby had expected them to be passed routinely through the West Berlin checkpoint on their way to the checkpoint on the East Berlin side. This had been the case the times she had gone into the East with Donovan. She was surprised, therefore, when the uniformed West German border guards asked Wolfgang to pull off the road into the inspection area. Once he had done so, the sergeant said, "Step out of the automobile please, baron." This showed Shelby he knew who Wolfgang was and was aware of his reputation.

Wolfgang got out of the car. He seemed used to this. He lit a cigarette and looked bored as the sergeant rummaged through his pockets. Meanwhile, the other guard was inspecting Shelby's passport, which he had asked to see. He handed it back to her, satisfied, and began searching through the car, apparently looking for contraband or currency.

Shelby assumed that occasionally the guards had Wolfgang step into the shack for a more thorough personal inspection. They did not do so now, however. What the guard did do—which startled Shelby—was to ask her in a stern voice, "What do you have in your purse, *Fräulein*?"

Shelby felt a jolt of shock at the question and at the suspicious stare that accompanied it. What *did* she have, she wondered suddenly. She remembered the way Wolfgang had seemed to signal the young man to ask her onto the dance floor. Why, she had wondered then. Now a chilling possibility crept into her mind.

Wolfgang's briefcase had been left behind in the village. Could it be he had left it behind because it was empty? Because the contents had been transferred into a container less likely to be inspected?

"Your purse," said the guard more demandingly, "may I have it?"

Shelby turned to Wolfgang. She expected him to look away, as if his attention had been caught elsewhere, but instead he stared at her steadily, his clear brown eyes unflinching. He exhaled a stream of tobacco smoke. He knew what she was thinking, she could tell, and he was waiting to see how she would react.

Was *that* why he had wanted to take her on this date, she wondered with fear, why he had accepted her self-invitation? So he could use her in an attempt to smuggle contraband across the border? She knew that if there were contraband in her purse and she let the guards see it, Wolfgang would be in terrible trouble. They would know it was he, not she, who was responsible. And Diana had told her how for years the West German government had thirsted to catch him with evidence so they could put him in prison.

The guards and Wolfgang were all gazing at her now to see what she would do. Shelby stared back at Wolfgang, trying to put anger in her eyes but instead showing only keen disappointment. She had not thought he would do something like this to her.

"I will look in your purse, please," said the guard, reaching for it.

"No," she replied, pulling it back. "I'm an American State Department officer attached to our legation here. You saw my passport. You know I have diplomatic privilege. I'm sorry, but I'd rather not have you look in my purse."

The sergeant, near Wolfgang, became very displeased. "*Fräulein*, if you were traveling with anyone else, such an inspection would not be necessary. But I assume you know with whom you are traveling, and so I must ask you, please may we see your purse?"

"No, you may not. I'm sorry."

The sergeant was angry, but there was nothing he could do. He irately waved Wolfgang back into the car and ordered the second guard to raise the steel barrier arm. Wolfgang jammed the Porsche into gear and screeched away from the checkpoint in a cloud of dust. On the East German side, several yards up the road, the *Vopos* did not even bother to ask for his passport. They, too, knew him well. They raised the red-and-white barrier arm and waved him through. Wolfgang roared down the road into East Germany.

Shelby turned in her seat to face him. "What's in this purse?" she demanded angrily.

"Lipstick? Tissues? Cosmetics? I have always wondered about the mysteries of women's purses." There was no hint of remorse in his manner.

"There are illegal drugs in here maybe?"

"I hope not. I do not deal in drugs, and I scorn anyone who does."

"Or better yet," she continued acidly, "maybe there are high-denomination West German marks. That's the most profitable black-market item, isn't it?"

"Yes," he replied impassively, "in high denominations, it is."

"I don't like being used, Baron von Heller." Her voice was icily indignant.

"An admirable trait. It accompanies your other fine quality of being such an excellent judge of character, no doubt."

"You tricked me."

"Did I?"

"You used me!"

"Is that a fact? How despicable of me."

She was about to demand that he take her home at once, but first she wanted to get rid of whatever it was he had forced her to become an accomplice in smuggling. And what better way to get rid of it, she thought with satisfaction, than by throwing it into the wind? As the car raced down the road, she tore open her purse and reached for the contraband items.

But nothing was there other than her usual purse articles. She checked thoroughly. Then she looked up to find him staring at her sternly.

"You deliberately made me think you used me," she shot at him. "You made me believe you put contraband in my purse."

He didn't deny it; he didn't confirm it. He said nothing and offered no explanation.

Shelby said, "I think I'd like to go home now, please."

He cut the wheel so quickly that they careened off the road and rattled and jolted through the neighboring field, throwing up chunks of dirt and grass as the car plowed through its turning arc. Then he raced back onto the roadway in the opposite direction.

It was dark when they reached her apartment building. She opened the car door for herself and closed it after she was out. She stood there in the cool darkness, looking at him, not knowing what to say, unsure of the state of her emotions. Wolfgang said nothing, either. He nodded to her curtly, then with a screech of wheels raced away into the night.

"MAYBE HE WAS testing you," Diana suggested the next evening as they walked home after dining together at the local *gasthaus*.

"Testing me?"

"To see whether you'd act against him, thinking there was something to act against him for, or whether you'd protect him." She added with a mild reprimand, "Frankly, honey, I don't see why you didn't give your purse to the guards—I mean, if you really thought he was taking advantage of you to smuggle marks."

"I don't know why I didn't," she said honestly, in wonderment. "It wasn't a thought-out decision. I just acted on the spur of the moment. If you had asked me in advance what I would have done in a situation like that, I'd have said that I'd have given them my purse.''

''Maybe that's why von Heller didn't ask you. He tested you instead.''

Shelby's eyebrows raised in interest at this notion. She was still puzzling over her own actions as they neared her apartment building. ''I guess I just don't think he's as bad as everyone says.''

''Oh, Shelby, that's a dangerous way to think. People who know him much better than you have been treading lightly around him for years. What I don't see is why he even wanted to test you. I mean, it's not as though he's about to have some sort of deep relationship with you in which he'd really have to know if he could trust you. Von Heller never sees a girl more than once or twice. That's been his pattern ever since breaking up with his dancer.'' She looked at Shelby meaningfully. ''And from what you said about the way you parted last night, you're obviously not going to see him again.''

''Obviously not,'' Shelby agreed softly.

It was just as she said this that they passed through the fenced forecourt of her apartment building and saw the racing-green Porsche in the driveway. Wolfgang was leaning against it, wearing a black turtleneck and belted coat.

''You are late,'' he said to Shelby, his tone casual but his eyes intense. ''I expected you back from dinner much earlier.''

She frowned at him, disconcerted. ''We don't have a date, and I didn't tell you when I'd be home from dinner. Just what are you doing here, may I ask?"

"I have come to take you to the symphony. Von Karajan is conducting an all-Mozart program this evening. You have not yet heard the Berlin Philharmonic, yes?" He checked his watch. "If we hurry, we can catch the Jupiter Symphony from the beginning."

Shelby looked at Diana, showing her surprise. Diana was surprised by Wolfgang's presence, too, but there was something else in her eyes, also—a serious look of warning.

"This is my friend Diana Mercer," Shelby stated, remembering her manners.

Wolfgang bowed politely. Then he said to Shelby, "We must hurry."

She held his stare. She knew Diana was watching her worriedly. After a moment she told him, "I'll have to change," and hurried to her apartment.

CHAPTER FIFTEEN

THE CONCERT was wonderful, and so was the theater the next evening—and the dinner at Maitre, one of Berlin's finest restaurants, three nights after that.

During the next few weeks Wolfgang took her out frequently, sometimes several evenings in a row. They traveled throughout Germany for their dates—from the Hamburg Zoo to Heidelburg Castle to an excursion down the Rhine. For dinner one night he asked what she was in the mood for, and when she said seafood, he chartered a plane that took them to Marseilles, France. "If you insist on eating seafood," he said, "you might as well eat the best in the world."

He tried to give her gifts, also, including gold jewelry from Zurich and an extravagantly lovely porcelain sculpture from Barcelona. Shelby declined all gifts, though. When Wolfgang scowled in puzzlement, asking why, all she could do was say quietly, "It's too much, Wolfgang."

At first she was suspicious about why he seemed so attracted to her, thinking he must have some ulterior motive. But after several weeks of dating him and being with him in a variety of circumstances, her skepticism eroded, and she was forced to realize he really was becoming as enamored of her as he seemed. This disturbed Shelby. When she first met him at the industrialists' cocktail party, he had not wanted even to talk to her. Yet now he was falling for her in a way that grew deeper each time they met.

Shelby did not want this sort of relationship with him. As he became more and more drawn to her, she experienced more of a desire to pull away from him, to put emotional distance between them. She tried to figure out what it was about her that attracted him so. She knew his feelings for her were very unusual for him; everyone was talking behind their backs about how strange it was he should still be dating her. For years—ever since his affair with his ballerina—he had taken no more than a passing interest in women. And now this. Most people were bewildered. A few, though, said it only stood to reason. He had built such a wall around his emotions for so long, they said, it made only sense that when he found the right girl, the wall would blow apart with a vengeance.

Shelby knew he was attracted to her sensitivity and pridefulness and the way she had stood up to him after the incident at the border, but there was more to it than that. There was also, she suspected, the fact that she was constantly refusing to become amorous with him. This must be a challenge to a man who could have almost any woman he wanted and who was used to women throwing themselves shamelessly at his feet.

Another reason for his attraction was far more

disturbing. Shelby had seen a magazine photograph of the ballerina with whom he had been in love. There was a similarity between her and Shelby, a likeness in facial features and slender figure. Could it be, she wondered, that Wolfgang still carried a flame for this girl and was unconsciously transferring his emotions to Shelby?

She didn't know. She did know she didn't feel for him what he felt for her, and she knew she should stop seeing him so often—that it was giving him false encouragement. She kept telling herself over and over that she should refuse his invitations, but each time he asked her out, she found herself accepting.

It was so hard to say no! Her days as Donovan's assistant were so empty and miserable that her dates with Wolfgang were the only bright spots in her life. And they *were* bright spots. He was such a handsome dynamic man, and he treated her as if she were truly special to him. He had excellent taste in wines and restaurants and in his choice of entertainments. She enjoyed talking to him; his ideas were provocative and forced her to look at things in ways she hadn't previously.

And he seemed to be quite open with her, too—much more so than he had been on their first date. During their trip to Heidelburg, for instance, he had excused himself to go talk to a man wearing a visored hat pulled down low over his eyes. When Wolfgang came back, she asked who the man was. He could have lied, to avoid her negative feelings about his dealing with unsavory characters, but instead he said,

"He is a professional forger—the best in *Deutsch-land*. Every smuggler uses his services to obtain false papers when they are needed."

The more she was exposed to Wolfgang, the more she appreciated what a complex man he was. One particular image lingered in her mind. He had finally taken her to his castle. It was marvelously restored on the inside—luxurious and beautiful—though the exterior looked crumbling and decrepit. The image that lingered was that of him seated on the den carpet before the blazing fireplace, his arm around her. They were listening to a Dvorak symphony—one of his favorites. His brow was knitted in concentration, and his eyes were shut. She could see such power in his face as he focused on the music, immersed in each swell and ebb.

She could not deny she was strongly attracted to him. Her feelings, though, were not feelings of love, as he said his were. She knew she could never let herself fall in love with a criminal. No matter what excuses he had for his behavior, the fact remained, he did not live by the rules honest men live by. True, his explanation had sounded reasonable. But it didn't explain why he didn't just leave East Germany if he hated it so much. He had border-crossing privileges. He could start a new honest life in the West if he really wanted to.

Her feelings about his way of life caused friction between them. Several nights previously he had become disgusted by her constant refusal to let him do more than just kiss her.

"Why do you not allow me to make love to you?" he asked in anguish. "You know how I feel about you."

"Because I don't love you," she replied gently.

"And why do you not?" He became angry. "It is because I am a black marketer...am outside the law. You told me how you feel about this. Yet you have ignored my explanation."

"I'm not accusing you or passing judgment."

"What you do is worse! You close off your emotions to me. You refuse to let yourself come close."

This was true, and Shelby could not deny it. But even if it were not for that, there was a much stronger reason she would not let herself become close to him. She still loved Donovan...desperately, helplessly. And she knew he loved her. His caresses and words of love that night at the hotel had been sincere. It was his later attempt to pretend he didn't care for her that had been false, Shelby knew.

Part of the reason she continued to date Wolfgang—a dark part, which she felt very guilty about—was to make Donovan even more jealous, to force him to confront his true feelings.

It was working, too. She could see she was getting to him. He tried to pretend he didn't care, but during the time she had been going out with Wolfgang, Donovan had been more on edge than she had ever seen him. He tried to have as few dealings with her as possible, giving her busywork to keep her away from him. Shelby was aware he did this because he didn't trust himself to be near her for a long period of time, didn't trust himself to keep his emotions in check.

The moment of truth, though, was fast approaching. Up till now, Donovan had been able to schedule his investigative work locally, so that overnight travel with Shelby had not been necessary. Soon, though, the first of two important interviews in East Germany was to take place, and an overnight stay at the Schloss Tauber was impossible to avoid.

When the day arrived, Donovan seemed very uptight. He wouldn't even drive down with her. He told her to make her own travel arrangements and to meet him for the first interview at two o'clock. She finished her legation work unexpectedly early and managed to arrive hours before the scheduled interview. This pleased her, for the Schloss Tauber was on a cliff that overlooked one of the most scenic river beaches in Germany, and Shelby was greatly in need of a good swim. Though it was October, it was exceptionally warm that day, and Shelby looked forward to a dip in the bracing water.

She made her way through the spacious lobby to the registration desk. The Tauber was truly elegant and one of the few reminders in East Germany of what a grand hotel had been like in the days before the wars.

After registering and picking up her key, she went straight to her room to change. Her one-piece bathing suit was goldenrod in color and really a bit too flimsy for her taste. She preferred a more substantial swimsuit that did more to camouflage her shapely figure. She had not brought her own suit from the

States, though, and the shop she had gone into at the last minute before leaving for the Tauber had had a limited choice since it was so late in the year.

Well, she tried to reassure herself, she would be in the water most of the time anyway or wearing her robe. As she put on her white terry-cloth robe, she gazed out at the magnificent view. Her bellboy had thrown wide the hotel windows. Shelby could see the racing blue green river far below at the base of the cliff. White clouds dotted the sky, drifting in the breeze. A few sea gulls soared into view. The afternoon was amazingly warm and bright. It was perfect for swimming, so long as she was careful to stay near the shore and not drift out into the notoriously strong current.

Two stories beneath her window was the terraced patio, which led out onto the flat top of the cliff. It was paved in ceramic tiles of subdued tone and covered with a scattering of tables and chairs. Guests from the hotel often took dinner or cocktails out on the scenic terrace in the summer. Surrounding the terrace were the parapet walls where Shelby had stood silhouetted almost nakedly against the sunlight the last time she and Donovan had been there. The memory of that set her emotions churning, and she felt a tingling sensation course all through her. She forced the memory away.

As her glance shifted, she saw something disturbing. There at one of the terrace tables sat Donovan. He wore a well-tailored double-breasted suit and was conversing with two other men. One was the gray-goateed Dr. Gottfried Rinehardt, whom she had seen with Donovan at the wall, transferring that mysterious package. The other, she suspected with a flash of rising outrage, was probably Martin Kortz—the East German author *she* was supposed to help interview. He was a balding man with thick glasses. All at once it came to her—Donovan was conducting the interview without her!

She rushed out of the room and down the stairs, out through the lobby onto the terrace. As she approached their table, the balding man looked up. He became alarmed and shook Donovan's shoulder. Donovan and Dr. Rinehardt both saw her then, too.

Donovan stood up, and the others followed his lead.

"What is this, may I ask?" she said to him, reaching the table.

"We're just finishing." He turned to the balding man. "Herr Kortz, thank you for coming. I think we've gone over what we needed to."

Shelby watched, fuming, as Dr. Rinehardt translated Donovan's words into German for the author— her job. Martin Kortz nodded, looked at Shelby with obvious distress, then turned to go. Dr. Rinehardt quickly gathered up several papers from the table, put them into a folder and left with Kortz.

"What was that all about?" Shelby demanded. "It wasn't by any chance the interview we had scheduled for two o'clock, was it?"

"Two? You must be confused. The interview was scheduled for eleven."

Now Shelby was really angry. She could see from the unrepentant way he held her eyes that he didn't expect her to believe this. He didn't even pretend to believe it himself.

"You did this deliberately," she accused. "You wanted me to miss this interview so I'd feel useless and left out. Or is it just that you're afraid even to *be* with me—afraid you'll lose control of this silly game you're playing and let your true feelings come out?"

"Look," he exploded, "don't blame me if you can't get here on time because you're too tired from staying out late with that criminal you're dating."

"If you had told me the proper time to be here, I'd—"

"What do you think you're doing with him anyway? He's a hoodlum and an opportunist. He's not the kind of man you should be seeing, and I don't want you seeing him anymore."

"You don't *want*?" she repeated incredulously. "Who are you to want anything from me? You have no right telling me whom I can or can't see."

"I'm telling you for your own good, damn it!"

"Why should you care?"

"Because I. . . ." He stopped. His anger and jealousy had carried him this far. It was the first time he had vented his rage over her dating Wolfgang. But now he seemed to realize he was on the verge of saying something he didn't want to say, and though Shelby wanted dearly to hear it, he shut his mouth firmly. "I don't care," he said finally.

"Good, then it's none of your business, is it?"

He held her stare. "No, what you do with your life is none of my business."

"Then I'll thank you to stay out of my life, since you obviously don't want to take any part in it!" She was so filled with emotion she thought she would explode—or maybe cry.

For a long moment neither of them spoke. Then Shelby thought dismally, *oh, the heck with it.* "I'm going swimming," she said. She took off her terry-cloth robe and draped it over the back of a patio chair.

When she turned back to him, she saw he was helplessly staring at her body. Her swimsuit—that thin wisp of material—hid nothing. His face was tortured, filled with a burning hunger. Shelby felt sharply embarrassed at her exposure, and her first instinct was to hurry down the stone steps of the cliff, away from his stare. But she forced herself to stay put. Her hands dangled at her sides.

No convenient excuses sprang to her lips to justify why she was standing almost naked before him. The situation was clear to them both. She was doing this to torment him, to tantalize him with the body he would never have, would never touch. This was Shelby's only way of striking back at him, and she took it. But it struck at her, too. Under his hungering gaze her nipples became hard, and the thin fabric of the swimsuit did nothing to hide them. She began blushing, but still she remained.

Donovan's brow was sweating, his eyes anguished. Shelby was filled with embarrassment. She knew he wanted her. It was only when she began fantasizing about his hands and lips moving possessively upon her body that she could take no more. Her body was burning up with heat. It was she who turned away first. She hurried past him and started down the stone steps built into the face of the cliff.

"Stay out of the current," he called after her in a throaty voice.

"Mind your own business," she answered.

She was still sensuously burning from her own brazenness as she reached the hard-packed sand at the bottom of the cliff. The beach was nearly deserted, but one or two other hardy souls were in the water, hugging the shore. Shelby moved farther out. She didn't want to be near anyone now. She plunged into the deep water, hoping to cool her raging emotions.

The water was cool but not cold; the air was warm. She began swimming hard, feeling the need to exert herself, to work out her hostility. She swam in an elongated loop, remaining roughly in the same part of the river. She considered herself a good swimmer and felt she didn't have to stick too closely to the shore. She proved she was right when she began tiring after a while and started to swim back in, with no trouble at all. She looked up at the clifftop terrace, though, and saw Donovan at the parapet, gazing at another part of the river, pretending to ignore her. This made her angry, and she decided to stay in the water a bit longer. She knew he was secretly stealing glances at her, worried about her safety. Well, she'd show him. She'd stay out here until he looked at her openly, admitting his concern.

It only took a few minutes more. Finally he did look at her openly, with a worried expression. Shelby felt satisfied now, as if she had won some small victory. She began to swim back to shore.

It was then that she knew she was in trouble. She had begun drifting with the current and now had to swim hard to make any kind of headway back toward the shore. When she had started to come in earlier, this had been no problem; she had had plenty of strength. Now, though, she had stayed out too long. Each extra moment had drained her strength and weakened her muscles, and she was getting colder by the second. She had let her judgment be warped by her anger.

Shelby became frightened. The harder she swam toward shore, the weaker she became—without making any progress. The deadly current had her in its grip now, and she was being swept helplessly downstream. She passed a lone swimmer who was close to the beach. She did not call out to him, but she didn't have to. Anyone could see she was struggling to stay afloat. The swimmer started toward her but had to turn back, no match for the current.

Water splashed into her mouth, and she began to choke. All her energy was spent in barely managing to stay afloat. For the first time in her life she realized she was on the verge of death. She glanced up at the cliff for a final look at the man she loved. She could not see him, though. Then she looked farther forward on the cliff and saw him flinging off his coat and shirt, running parallel to her course downstream.

She knew what he was going to do, and she wanted to warn him away. He could do her no good! It was suicide to dive off that cliff into this current. Only a powerful practiced swimmer would have even a chance of survival, and he told her he could barely swim.

He finally got to a point on the promontory that was ahead of her downstream journey. He leaped onto the parapet wall and dived off of it. For an instant he was suspended in midair—a bold bare-chested form, arms extended. Then he soared downward.

Shelby tried to watch him as he hit the water, but she lost her strength and submerged, her mouth filling with water. When she finally fought her way back up, coughing and gasping for air, Donovan was gone from view. She looked everywhere. He was nowhere in sight. Drowned, she thought. She cried out in anguish and went under once more. This time she had no strength left to fight her way back up.

The silence of the sea...water in her open eyes three feet under.

Suddenly a powerful arm grasped her from behind, encircling her chest. She was dragged back up to the surface, coughing and sputtering for air. With his free arm Donovan stroked steadily, mightily, back toward the shoreline. Shelby breathed the sweet, sweet air in gasps. She tried to kick with her legs to help him, but was completely exhausted. The shoreline drew nearer and nearer. Then—thank God!—she felt hard ground under the soles of her feet.

He picked her up in his arms and carried her onto the narrow strip of beach, but the swim had been too much for him, and he collapsed. They both fell onto the sand. His body was half covering hers, an arm across her bosom, one leg between her thighs. Both of them were panting, shivering violently.

"You damn fool!" he raged, coughing and gasping. He was overcome with emotion, completely out of control. "You damn little fool! Don't you know I love you? Don't you know I can't live without you?"

He coughed some more. Shelby was gasping for breath too much to speak. He lowered his head, and his tousled black hair brushed against her cheek. Then he looked up again, and she could see from the fire burning in his eyes how overwhelmed he had been at the realization that he was about to lose her forever. He put his arms around her and hugged her for dear life.

Shelby's cheek was against him. She could feel the bristles from his morning's shave. She saw other hotel guests off in the distance, running toward them along the sand. Her hands were on his powerful broad back, clutching him to her, feeling his skin beneath her palms. His hand was in her hair, holding her head against him.

"Oh, Lord, Shelby," he said with profound emotion. "Oh, Shelby...Shelby...Shelby...."

HE CAME FOR HER that night in her hotel room. This time there was none of the denial that had followed his words of love several weeks earlier. The realization that he had almost lost her forever had affected him too deeply for that. The time for game playing was over. Whatever reasons he had had for trying to hide his love, they were no longer important.

He stood before her in his dinner clothes. His jaw was firm; his handsome face looked sternly resolute. "I can't pretend anymore," he said, his voice even deeper than usual. "I tried to hide my love, but I'm not strong enough for that now. I want you, Shelby. I want you so badly I can't go another day without having you...not another hour. I can't live my life without you. You've got to be mine."

"Yes," she said softly.

"Marry me."

"Yes, Donovan." She shut her eyes for an instant. Then she looked at him again.

"I love you," he said. He came forward across the few steps that separated them. His hands went to the buttons of the blouse she wore and slowly began undoing them. She stood still, her hands at her sides, her fingers rigidly clutching the empty air. Their eyes were locked in a gaze of love and sensuousness. When he had her blouse unbuttoned, he peeled it open and pushed it down her shoulders. His hands went to the front closure of her brassiere. She couldn't help gasping audibly as he unhooked it.

Her breasts were bare before him. He kissed her lightly on the mouth, scarcely brushing his lips against hers. Then his hands went to her slender waist, and he bent forward. The sensation of his warm mouth upon her naked nipple was like an electric shock of pure pleasure. She couldn't stop herself from moaning out loud. . . .

CHAPTER SIXTEEN

HE SANK DOWN on one knee before her, the side of his face pressing against her midriff. She felt the flutter of his eyelids against her skin. His arms were around her waist, one hand on her derriere, pressing her against him. She heard a moan deep in his throat—a surrender to longing and passion. Then she felt his lips and tongue on her stomach, hot against her tender flesh. One hand moved up to caress her breast. She gazed down at him, and the sight of his handsome face against her nearly made her swoon. Her hands found their way into his thick black hair and became lost there.

He tugged at the top of her skirt, then yanked at it, so lost to his passion he did not know his own strength. The material ripped, leaving her standing there in only her panty hose and panties, her blouse fully open and halfway down her arms. Donovan slowly skimmed her panty hose down her legs until they bunched up around her ankles. She had to put her hands on his hard shoulders to keep her balance or she would have fallen.

She began to panic when his hand went to her white panties and slowly began peeling them down her hips. She would have pulled away from him then for sure—involuntarily in reaction—but she couldn't move because her ankles were trapped together by her bunched-up panty hose. So she had to stand there, breathing heavily, her heart racing, as he lowered her panties.

He buried his face against her belly, beneath her navel, while clutching her to him. He cried out in loving torment, from deep in his throat, "Oh, Shelby."

She moaned and threw her head back, her mouth and eyes wide open. After a moment he stood up. He lifted her in his arms and carried her to the bed. He yanked the panty hose and panties completely off of her. Then, standing tall by the side of the bed, he began undressing.

She could not bear feeling so burningly exposed, laying here naked on her back under his gaze. She reached for the edge of the *Federbett* she lay on—the thick down comforter found in all German hotels in place of blankets. She pulled it up over her from the side of the bed. Then she turned her eyes back to him, and what she saw made her gasp.

She knew she sometimes gave the impression of being a worldly sophisticated woman. The truth, though, was that she was quite modest and shy—not worldly at all. She had never fallen in love previously, and so she had never let a man make love to her. And the fact of the matter was, she had never seen a naked male body. Now Donovan was bare-chested before her, and his hands were at his belt, unbuckling it. He stepped out of his trousers. The sight of his shorts riding low on his hips, his overpowering virility, made Shelby turn her eyes away quickly just as he began stepping out of the shorts.

She was on her side, facing away from him, clutching the thick comforter up to her chin. He came down onto the bed beside her. Her heart was racing, and her breathing was shallow. She felt his hand upon her bare arm and then his lips nuzzling against her shoulder. He kissed her shoulder. He pushed aside her long hair and kissed the nape of her neck. He kissed her ear, his tongue touching lightly there with startling effect. Shelby heard his rapid breathing in her ear and felt the warmth of his breath upon her skin. Then she heard his voice, throaty with sensuousness.

"I love you, Shelby. I've loved you almost from the day you arrived. It was so hard pretending not to, so hard feeling I had to send you away from me. What torture to think I had to give you up!"

His hands moved under the thick *Federbett* and went around her from behind, caressing her breasts. He gently squeezed and kneaded, his fingers teasing her excited nipples.

"Why did you have to pretend?" she asked, her voice a stranger to her now, sounding like that of a little girl.

"Not now." He could barely speak, he was so lost to his passion. "But I'll tell you this. I'll never pretend again. I'll love you always. Nothing will change that, and I'll always have you near me."

He stopped speaking, overwhelmed with love and

desire. He kissed her shoulders and her back. Then he turned her toward him, she still clutching the *Federbett* about her. He was completely naked, and the sight of him took her breath away. He had powerful thighs and a firm flat stomach. His body was lean and strong and extremely masculine.

He began tugging at the comforter. She was reluctant to give it up. She knew she wanted him. She knew she loved him dearly, desperately, that he was the love of her life. But still, she was timid and a bit frightened. She had been so modest for so long it was hard to give herself up to her passion and his. It was hard to surrender...

He kissed her on the forehead tenderly. His lips moved down to kiss her eyelids. They moved over her cheeks and her throat. He grasped the comforter and pulled it away from her. She was naked before him, scant inches from his own naked body. The heat radiating between them was like that of an inferno. His lips descended on hers in a passionate kiss of overwhelming eroticism. He couldn't take any more delay. He pulled her to him as they lay side by side. Her breasts and belly and legs pressed against him, seared with the heat of his skin, the muscular hardness of his body.

All the weeks of frustrated longing; all the tortured nights of secretly dreaming about his body upon hers, his handsome face revealing his love for her; all the agony of anticipation and frustration; it had all heightened her senses. Everything came together now in an explosive moment of raw sensuous surrender.

"Oh, Donovan," she cried, "I love you so much." Her arms opened and went around him. His weight forced her onto her back. Then, purposefully, she spread her arms and ankles out toward the corners of the bed as she gazed up at him lovingly in total surrender. She wanted it this way; she wanted to give herself to him, not be taken by him. His body covered hers, and his lips crushed down upon her mouth. There was a flash of pain and ecstasy. Then the world dissolved into a throbbing inferno of erotic rapture as their bodies fused lovingly. The intensity of his love for her surrounded her, pervaded her, engulfed her in its fullness and richness. The sensations went on and on....

AFTERWARD HE LAY by her side, gently stroking her hair and gazing at her. It was a simple gesture, stroking her hair, but Shelby loved it. It was such a tender sign of affection.

She took his hand and put it to her lips and kissed his fingers. He smiled at her. Then he hugged her. "I'll leave the date of the wedding up to you," he said, "but make it soon."

"Yes," she replied. The thought of the wedding made her smile. She and he together, marching down the aisle in bridal gown and tuxedo. She had never thought it would happen to her. The feeling she had taken to heart during her childhood that she was somehow "unlovable" had made her believe it would never happen. Now, for the first time, that horrible belief left her.

Donovan got up and went to her closet, looking for a robe or something to put on. There was nothing, of course, that would fit him—or look anything less than ridiculous on him. He went into the washroom and grabbed a bath towel, wrapping it around his waist. Shelby felt a sense of loss seeing part of his beautiful body disappear from view. She felt very possessive about it now. It was *her* body.

When he came back, he took a seat on the chair next to the bed. Shelby noticed something that made her blush pinkly. On his neck there was a visible love bite, which she had given him during the height of their passion. She had always been timid about sex. Tonight, though, her passion and her love for him had turned her into a tiger for several uninhibited moments.

Donovan saw her blushing, and he laughed.

Shelby was glad he wasn't getting dressed. She wanted him to spend the night with her here in her room, as she saw he was going to do. Who cared what people would think if they saw him leaving from here in the morning? She didn't. Not now.

"Donovan," she began, "why did you pretend for so long not to care for me? Why did we have to go on hiding our love? If I hadn't almost drowned, we never would have found each other."

She could see the question distressed him, but he answered it anyway.

"I'm involved in something that's very important to me, Shelby, and I can't let you get in the way of it. I knew if you stayed with me as my assistant, working so close to me, you'd find out about it sooner or later. Either that or you'd force me to spend so much time *preventing* you from finding out that I couldn't get my work done—which is just what's been happening.''

"That's why you tried to send me home?''

"And it's why I couldn't tell you I loved you. You would never have agreed to leave me if you'd realized how much I love you. You would have insisted on staying here with me, hampering my movements. You would have become suspicious about why I'd want to send you home, would have asked questions I'd have had to refuse to answer.''

"What *is* this thing you're so afraid I'll find out about? You make it sound like such a deep dark secret.''

"It is a deep dark secret. Make no mistake about it.'' He leaned forward in the chair and took her hands in his. He looked her in the eye. "And as much as I love you, I can't talk about it. Not even to you.''

"Donovan, we're engaged to be married!''

"You've got a right to know; I don't deny it, but I still can't tell you.''

She didn't know how to deal with this. She had always felt that a husband and wife should have no secrets between them. She got up from the bed and put on her white terry-cloth robe.

"Remember Nancy Nash,'' he said, "the girl you replaced?''

"Yes?''

"She knows about this thing I'm involved in, and

she accepts it. That's why I wanted her here instead of you—so I wouldn't have to hinder my movements to stop you from finding out about it. I'm afraid you'll take it badly if you find out."

Now she was not only curious but deeply concerned. What was this shameful thing he was involved in that would make her react badly if she were to discover it? Her memory wandered unbidden to that day she had first visited him in his legation office. He had been on the phone, speaking about the delivery of a package of drugs.

"Donovan, what are you involved in?" Her words had an undertone of panic.

He came around the bed to where she stood and put his hands on her arms. His expression was sincere and reassuring—but it was also unyielding. "I can't tell you. All I can do is ask you to trust me and tell you it's nothing bad or dishonorable. I promise you that."

She didn't know what to say. Donovan frowned at her silence, and his voice took on a hint of harshness. "This is exactly why I couldn't let you know I loved you. You'd ask about this. You'd feel you had a right to know about it, as you're feeling right now. You'd insist I tell you about it, as you're insisting right now. And I can't tell you. I've already told you more than I should have."

"I'm not insisting, Donovan," she said gently. She put her head against his dark-haired chest and her hands on his broad shoulders. She made a decision then and there. "I love you. I think you're a good man. I'd rather know all there is to know. But if you ask me to trust you, I will."

After a moment's hesitation his arms went around her. Then his hand began stroking her long hair again, so gently and lovingly. "You're a wonderful girl. You're better than a man like me deserves."

"But you'll have to tell me just one thing," she said softly. "Is it related to these rumors I keep hearing about your being such a playboy?"

"I'm not a playboy. Those rumors are lies." He raised her chin to make her look at him. "There's only one woman in my life, and there will never be any other." He lowered his head and kissed her on the lips.

Her hands went around him and locked together at the small of his back, where his towel was tucked into itself, riding low on his hips. His lips on hers were erotic and lingering. She kissed him back, savoring the sensation. And then, because she was in love and feeling very brazen, she tugged at the towel where it was tucked in. It fell away from him in a heap.

It took only a few seconds more before her robe joined the towel on the carpet, done in by Donovan's hands.

CHAPTER SEVENTEEN

IN THE MORNING Donovan told her he wanted her to go back to the legation. He said this as they were finishing a late breakfast of *Bokwurst*—a type of sausage—sweet red cabbage and toast.

"But what about today's interview?" she asked.

"There isn't any interview. I just said there was so I could account for the time I'll be spending doing something else here today." He looked at her pointedly. "I was going to invent some false excuse to send you away this morning, but now I'll just tell you the truth. What I have to do, I can't do with you around, so I want you to go."

Shelby remembered the way the bald-headed Professor Kortz had hurried away yesterday when she had approached. She felt then that she had interrupted Donovan and him in business that had not really been finished. "Does it have to do with Professor Kortz?" she asked.

He looked at her but said nothing.

She disliked the feeling of being left out, but she did want to show him he was right to be truthful with her, instead of inventing some false reason to give her. She also wanted to show that she trusted him.

"All right," she said, sipping her coffee, "I'll go back to the legation. I should spend more time trying to reconcile that vague description of the Lion—the one we got from the *Vopo*—with the others we have. None of them seems to match."

"Good girl." He saw her pouting expression and added in a cheerier tone, "Hey, things aren't that bad. You're about to become my wife. Look, why don't you call your father and tell him about our engagement? That should be good for stirring up a little excitement. If my memory is accurate, Mr. Charles Porterfield Everest can't stand me."

Shelby saw he was grinning, and that made her feel a little better. She smiled back. He was right about one thing: her father would not take her choice of husbands well.

Donovan drove her to the *Bahnhof* and kissed her before she boarded her train. Then, from her window seat, she watched him leave the platform just as her train was pulling out. His expression when he turned away from her was no longer cheery. It was grim as he prepared to embark on whatever secret task he had set for himself today.

Instead of getting off at the station near the Clayallee, close to the legation, Shelby decided she would disembark at Schwanheide. This was the station nearest Wolfgang's castle.

Her father could be told about the engagement later. Though he wouldn't like it, she believed he would accept it. Shelby thought that perhaps he was aware of his shortcomings as a parent, that he felt badly about the way she had been forced to grow up with no show of affection from him. Maybe he knew that as a child her heart had been crying out for just a little of his time, of his attention. Perhaps, because of this, he would accept whatever husband she chose, so long as this man would make her happy and give her the love she had never known.

Besides, Shelby knew her father felt she should have married years ago. Many bright handsome young men of whom her father had approved had courted her. Some had proposed to her. When she had turned each of them down in turn, Charles Everest seemed to have become worried she might never find the man she was looking for.

The train slowed as it approached the *Bahnhof*, and steam from its brakes rose outside Shelby's window. She left the train and hailed a taxi stationed in front of the *Bahnhof*.

"Baron von Heller's castle, please, outside of Idor-Amstein."

As the taxi wound its way through the forested hills, Shelby reflected on how hard this was going to be. She knew how much Wolfgang cared for her. He would not take it lightly when she told him she couldn't see him anymore.

She gazed out at the scenery. Dappled sunlight filtered down through the treetops. The forest fragrance wafted into her open window on the cool air. The small village of Idor-Amstein appeared far off, on the western side of the border. A bit nearer, on this side, was Wolfgang's castle.

Shelby felt terrible. This was going to be so hard! She did care for Wolfgang; she couldn't deny it. If it weren't for his being a criminal and for her love of Donovan, she could easily see herself falling for him; he was such a desirable man. But—he *was* a criminal, and she *was* in love with Donovan.

The thing that made telling him so hard was not just that she would hurt him but that she knew it was her fault he would feel this pain. She was responsible for bringing about his courtship of her; he wasn't. *She* was the one who had approached *him* at the party. She was the one who had struck up a conversation when he had wanted only to be left alone. Their first date had been at her instigation, not his.

True, she had never intended things to go as far as they had. But that offered her little comfort, for her intention had been purely selfish, with no thought as to how Wolfgang would feel. She had wanted to make Donovan jealous, and she had succeeded. But along the way, Wolfgang had fallen in love with her, and now she was going to have to crush that love.

Oh, what guilt she felt! How could she even break the news to him? She had no idea. All she knew was that she had to do it soon, because the longer she put it off, the harder it would be. Besides, he had a right to know now.

As they crested a hill, the castle loomed closer, its crumbling southern wall looking jagged and ancient. Finally they reached the castle. Shelby paid the taxi driver and asked him to wait. She thought it very likely that Wolfgang would not be driving her back after this particular visit. At the door, though, she learned from his butler that Wolfgang was out and was not expected back for two hours. She was welcome to wait.

What she really wanted to do was rush back to her taxi and be driven far away—to run from her problem, instead of facing it. But that would be cowardly, and Shelby had never been a coward. She knew she owed Wolfgang the respect of telling him her decision to his face, without delay. And if his reaction was to vent his wrath on her, she would not shrink from it. She sent her taxi away, telling the driver when to return for her.

She waited in the huge den—one of the five chambers of the castle that Wolfgang had restored. The nine unrestored rooms were cold stone and rotting wood, whereas the restored rooms were spacious, opulent, luxuriously appointed and warm. The den had a thick area rug over a rich hardwood floor. His family crest hung above the large fireplace. Tapestries adorned the white mortared walls, except the far wall, which sported glass-enclosed shelves filled with books and ancient artifacts. Shelby sank down in the overstuffed sofa across from his work area. She thought of the times the two of them had reclined on this sofa in front of the blazing fireplace, while Wolfgang had kissed her and held her.

She stood up quickly and shook her head to clear it of the memory. Then she poured herself a small cognac.

Finally he arrived, preceded by the roar of the Porsche's motor. He burst into the room, grinning at her. He was wearing boots, jeans and an old leather jacket with a fur collar. The brown boots made him appear even taller than his usual commanding height. His grin and his shock of blond hair made him look charmingly boyish.

"How nice a surprise," he said, striding toward her. "An unexpected visit. I knew you would be returning early from your trip, but I did not know you would come here." He opened his arms and embraced her. When she did not respond but simply remained limp in his arms, he pulled back his head and frowned at her in puzzlement. "What's this? Something is wrong?"

She didn't know how to say it. She didn't; she didn't! The last few minutes of anticipation had whipped her emotions into a frenzy. Before she could even think how to begin, the words blurted forth of their own power. "Wolfgang, it's over between us!"

He scowled at her. "What is this you say? You are joking me, yes?"

"I'm not. I'm sorry. I'm so very sorry. But you know it was never as strong on my part as it was on yours. And—"

"Do not joke me! You know how I feel about you."

"I'm not joking! Wolfgang, it's over."

He continued to stare. He seemed stunned. Slowly her words began sinking in, though he resisted them mightily.

Shelby knew her tone had been too harsh and biting, but she couldn't help it. She had reacted out of
her own defensiveness. The result was that she was
being unnecessarily cruel to him, hurtful. She didn't
want that. She put her hand on his arm and forced
herself to speak more softly, to try to make him
understand.

"Wolfgang, it's not that I don't care for you; I do.
It's just—"

"Enough!" he declared savagely, shoving her
away from him with unintended force. "Do you
think I need your caring? Do you think that maybe
Wolfgang Friedrich Manfred von Heller needs it as a
'consolation prize' because I cannot have your love?
I need nothing from you. Nothing!"

She had handled it terribly and felt awful about it.
He turned away from her so she could not see his
face, and he clenched his fists at his sides in reaction
to his agony. For a moment he could not speak at all.
When he did finally speak, his voice was lower, more
tightly controlled.

"Tell me this. It is because I am a lawbreaker, is it
not—a criminal in your eyes?"

Her voice was soft. "That's part of it," she said
honestly. "I could never let myself fall in love with
a—a man who does what you do. But that's not the
main reason." She lowered her eyes. "I'm in love
with Donovan. He asked me to marry him...and I
accepted."

His reaction startled her. He threw his head back
and laughed. It was a harsh laugh of bitterness and

torment. "You naive woman! Are you really so gullible as all that?" He looked at her. "So you turn down my love, do you, because I am a lawbreaker, and then you accept the marriage proposal of Donovan Hawkes?" He laughed again—savagely. "Do you truly believe he is so pure and pristine? That he is only the diplomat he pretends to be and nothing more?"

Her voice became quieter, and she felt a sudden hollowness in her stomach. "What are you saying?"

He practically spat the words at her. "Your 'law-abiding' Donovan Hawkes—he is Berlin's leading figure in the smuggling of—"

"No!" she screamed. "Stop it!" She couldn't bear to hear it. All along, at the back of her mind, she had feared that Donovan's secret was something like this.

Wolfgang was looking at her. They both knew her reaction was too vehement to be caused by anything less than her own suspicions about Donovan. "Why do you think he tried to get rid of you as his assistant?" he demanded. "It is because he knew you might find out about his other activities."

"No," cried Shelby, backing away from him. "It's not true! It's because...because...there's some other reason. There has to be."

She wanted him to stop, but Wolfgang continued on relentlessly, pursuing her across the room. She had hurt him so deeply by rejecting him in favor of Donovan that he could not help but lash out at her this way. She sensed he hated treating her like this but was out of control of his emotions.

"You are back early from your trip," he remarked. "I knew you would be. You told me the trip would last two days, but I knew Hawkes would create some pretext for sending you away, that he would not let you remain with him past this morning."

"How could you have known that?"

"I know all that goes on in the Berlin underworld. Nothing escapes my notice. I know what Hawkes is doing today, is doing at this very moment, in fact, and I knew he could never allow you to be there with him to witness it." He glared at her. "Do you know what he does when he is not playing at being a diplomat, what he has been doing for years?"

Shelby shook her head vigorously. Her expression said, "Please. . . I don't want to know."

Wolfgang grabbed her wrist. "Come, I will show you."

She tried to pull away, but not very forcefully. She let herself be led outside. She knew that if she resisted more strongly, he would release her, but she let herself be put into the car and remained there as he jammed the motor into gear and roared away down the road.

The afternoon had become a bit windy. Shelby prayed silently as they raced down the hill. *Please, God, don't let him be a criminal. Don't take him away from me like that. I haven't asked much. Please don't make me give him up!*

When they reached the Alexanderplatz section of East Berlin, Wolfgang parked near a sidewalk café.

He guided her along the busy boulevard to the ring of bushes surrounding the café. He held her there with him, screened by foliage. They could see the patrons at the round outdoor tables beneath the Cinzano umbrellas, but they themselves could not easily be seen. Wolfgang gestured for her to look.

Apprehensively Shelby scanned the people seated at the tables. They were eating, drinking, engaged in conversation. Donovan was not there. Whatever sinister activity Wolfgang thought she would see him engaged in, he was wrong.

"I told you," she said with vast relief. "You're mistaken."

"Am I?" he replied coldly.

She didn't understand. What did he mean? She turned her eyes back to the patio. But no, Donovan was definitely not there. Only a dozen or so customers were present at this time of day: a sharp-nosed man in a gray homburg reading the paper, a teenage boy and girl, two old men playing chess, a man wearing a visored hat pulled down low over his eyes....

Shelby frowned. The man in the visored hat—she had seen him previously. He was the forger Wolfgang had dealt with in Heidelberg—the one Wolfgang had said a smuggling operation could not do without. At the moment he was laying a package on the table next to his coffee. It was picked up casually by the tall man seated beside him. Now Shelby looked more closely at the tall man, who was turned partly away from her. No! She didn't believe it!

Could it be? The resemblance was so startling.

It was Donovan. But no wonder she hadn't recognized him right away. She was used to seeing him in dignified diplomatic attire or conservative business suits. Now he looked so different that it was obvious he had dressed this way as a deliberate disguise. His black hair, usually so carefully groomed, was slightly disheveled; it was combed down across his forehead and half covered his eyes. A stubbly shadow of beard was visible on his strong jaw. Shelby remembered she had not seen him shave that morning. Green aviator sunglasses hid his eyes. He wore old khaki trousers and a turtleneck covered by a black trench coat. He looked more dashing and rakish than Shelby had ever seen him. As she watched, he glanced into the package taken from the forger, nodded, then slipped it into the pocket of his coat.

Shelby felt her heart break. "Trust me," he had said. "My secret isn't anything shameful or dishonorable." Oh, no, she thought, of course not! It was only that he was an international smuggler, using the privileges of his diplomatic office for his personal gain. No wonder he had refused to tell her. He knew she would never have let herself get close to him if she had realized what he was, and she would certainly never have accepted his proposal.

Donovan removed a white envelope from his pocket and passed it to the forger. The man accepted it, stood up and quickly left the café.

Wolfgang took Shelby's arm and began to lead her away. "Come," he said, "we will go back now. I will tell you the significance of what you have just seen. Hawkes is a...."

Shelby stopped in her tracks. Wolfgang looked to see what had made her stop. He saw she was watching Donovan again—and an attractive redhead who was approaching his table, smiling gaily. *"Liebling,"* said the girl.

Shelby's eyes went wide as she saw Donovan smile at the girl, stand and embrace her as she came into his arms. They kissed passionately for a long moment.

Shelby felt crushed—and very, very alone. Oh, what a fool he had played her for! He had admitted he had a deep secret but had promised her it was nothing shameful or bad. He had acted so sincere. The truth was, he *was* a playboy—and a smuggler—and he had sent her away this morning so he could be free for this rendezvous with his lovely redhead.

He had used Shelby cruelly and selfishly. Maybe he did love her; she thought that he did, even now. But what did that matter? He certainly didn't have a shred of respect for her. What he wanted most was to have his cake and eat it, too, and so he had taken from her her most precious gift, which she had hoped to give to the man she loved—her future husband. He had taken it from her and given her lies in return. And now he was standing here, passionately kissing another woman. He was doing it so publicly, flaunting it, as if he wanted people to watch and notice.

"We must go," Wolfgang said urgently, tugging at Shelby's arm. "You have no idea what you are seeing here. Come, we leave now, and I will explain it to you.''

"No!'' she cried, wrenching free of him. She hurried to the patio entranceway and marched up to Donovan's table. Wolfgang started after her, clearly distressed. He had not intended this turn of events.

Donovan saw her coming and looked stunned by her presence here.

When she reached him, she stared helplessly. She wanted to vent her anger, to rage at him and curse. But all she could do was ask, from the agonized depths of her soul, "Oh, Donovan, how could you?'' The words were like a sob.

For a moment he said nothing. When he did speak, it was to deny sternly he even knew her—and in flawless fluent German. "Donovan?'' he said. "*Ich bin nicht dieser mann*—I am not the man you want. *Ich bin Rutger Schmidt*—my name is Rutger Schmidt.''

Shelby was startled. Could she have made an error? The resemblance was striking, but could this really be a man who simply looked very much like Donovan?

"Do not bother to apologize,'' he said, also in German. "I forgive you your mistake.''

For a moment she really believed she had made a mistake. But when he turned away, she saw the love bite on the side of his neck, the one she had given him during their passionate lovemaking.

"You bastard!'' she cried. "Oh, you horrid bastard!'' Shame and humiliation overcame her as she remembered how uninhibitedly she had given herself to him, letting her lovemaking be the flowering expression of her heartfelt love. Now, looking back, she wondered if he had been laughing at her all the while—laughing at the way she had become a tiger in bed. Maybe he was even secretly laughing at her now.

She reached up and yanked off his aviator sunglasses so she could see his eyes. She was causing a commotion, she noticed, but she didn't care. Everyone in the café was staring at her and Donovan. Wolfgang was beside her now, seizing her arm, trying to pull her away. Donovan was glaring at her, angry and upset, his eyes commanding her to leave. It was this that bothered her most. How dare he be angry with her? Then Shelby glanced at the redheaded girl, who seemed shocked and nervous, and she understood why Donovan was angry—and why he was pretending not to know Shelby. Oh, it was so obvious. The girl would never let herself be seduced if she knew Donovan had a fiancée, so Donovan was pretending that Shelby meant nothing to him, that he didn't even recognize her.

This made Shelby furious, and, reeling with agony, she did the first thing that came to mind to strike back at him. She put her hand over Wolfgang's hand, which was grasping her arm.

"This is the man I really love," she lashed out at Donovan. "I never loved you! It was only a moment of weakness that made me. . leave myself vulnerable to you and accept your proposal. Wolfgang is the man I truly love and want to marry. I've been trying to find a way out of my engagement to you ever since I accepted it!''

This hit Donovan hard; she could see that in his eyes. It hit him very hard.

"Enough!" declared Wolfgang. "You do not know what you are doing. You have no idea what is involved here." Then, for the benefit of the café patrons who were staring at Donovan, he added, "You are mistaken. This is not the man you think it is." He began forcibly pulling her away.

"Oh, you're both alike!" she declared, swiveling on him. "Brothers in crime! Now you're trying to protect him." When she turned back to Donovan, he was hurrying away, hustling the redheaded girl along beside him.

Shelby thought of following, but was surprised to see someone else leap to his feet and begin doing so first—the needle-nosed man in the gray homburg.

Wolfgang pulled her roughly out of the café, back toward his car. She tore free of him. She couldn't bear to be with him now—or with anyone. She fled down the street, a frantic wounded animal flooded with pain.

"Shelby!" he shouted after her. She didn't respond. She heard his footsteps hurrying near, but before he could reach her, she had climbed into a taxi and ordered it away. She sat in the back seat sobbing, leaving him far behind.

CHAPTER EIGHTEEN

SOON SHE LEFT THE TAXI and began to wander through the cold damp streets of East Berlin. She was in a daze and couldn't have made herself think even if she had wanted to. Her whole body throbbed with the pain of betrayal. She walked the streets, her heels clicking against the pavement.

She passed the town hall, which, as usual, was festooned with Communist slogans emblazoned in white letters against a red background on enormous banners that could be seen from a mile away. She walked down Karl Marx Allee, which was the street on which the riots against the Russians had first begun in 1953—the ones Wolfgang's father had helped to incite. She passed the Russian memorial at Treptow—a monolithic construction built with marble taken from Germany's destroyed Reich Chancellery. A massive bronze statue of a Russian soldier rose up, flanked by huge white stones.

Before she knew it, it had grown dark and her legs and body were very weary. She had been walking for hours. Dejected, she crossed back into the West. She went to her apartment and began packing. She didn't want to take the time to pack everything, so she filled just two bags and decided she would ask Diana to send the rest to the States after her. She was very tired, but she forced herself to sit at her desk and write a brief formal letter of resignation. This was required by protocol. She addressed it to Mr. Stanton, said she was resigning her post for "personal" reasons and asked for reassignment once she was back in the States. If this would be bad for her career, she thought, the hell with it. She wouldn't stay here even another day. She didn't want to see Donovan, not ever again.

She put the letter into an envelope. She wanted to deliver it right now, then leave for Tegel Airport. She was far too tired, though. She had got almost no sleep the previous night—the night she had spent with Donovan, and today's confrontation had left her emotionally exhausted. She barely managed to shower and change into her nightgown before collapsing onto her bed and drifting into a deep black sleep.

In the morning she dressed, put her bags by the door and took her sealed letter of resignation to the legation. She was on her way to Mr. Stanton's office, walking down a corridor bordered by a long wall of windows, when one of her colleagues came up to her. "Have you seen the deputy minister?" the man asked with concern. "He has an important meeting in a few minutes, and nobody can find him."

"I don't know where he is," Shelby answered tonelessly, "and I don't care."

The man narrowed an eye at her but said nothing

further. He hurried off on his mission. A minute
later, Donovan's secretary, Mary, came up to Shelby
and asked the same question. Shelby said no, she
didn't know where Donovan was. Mary seemed to
sense that something was wrong from Shelby's expression—or rather, from the lack of it. "Hey, are
you all right?" she asked. Shelby said she was fine
and let it go at that.

James Stanton's office was at the end of the hall,
and just before it was the room sometimes used to
process incoming refugees who were requesting
asylum. Shelby glanced into the room as she passed
and was so startled by what she saw that she had to
back up again to make sure her eyes were not deceiv-
ing her.

Martin Kortz was in there—the balding East German author whom Donovan had interviewed two
days earlier. But that was impossible. How did he get
here—into the West? He was seated on the sofa,
agitatedly speaking to Diana, who was taking notes.
Someone else was in the room, too, someone seated
outside of Shelby's view by the door. When Diana
turned to ask that person a question, she saw Shelby
looking in. Shelby's feelings must have shown on her
face, for Diana excused herself and left the room.

"What's wrong, honey?" asked Diana, joining
Shelby a few paces away from the door. She looked
concerned and compassionate.

"It's...I'll tell you about it later," Shelby said.
She couldn't bear to discuss matters now, not even
with Diana. She was still too shaky over what had

happened. She nodded in the direction of the processing room. "What's Martin Kortz doing here? The East Germans never let their literary figures into the West. They know there's a good chance they won't come back."

"Haven't you read the morning paper?"

Shelby shook her head.

"He defected last night, along with his granddaughter. A people smuggler arranged their crossing."

"But that's impossible. Two days ago he was giving information to Donovan to help track down the Lion. Only a dedicated East German would do that, and dedicated East Germans don't defect."

"You're wrong, Shelby," Diana said, shaking her head. "Herr Kortz would never do anything to hurt the Lion. He's violently opposed to the East German government. In fact, we all knew it would be just a matter of time before they came to arrest him for the ideas expressed in his writing. Our intelligence sources told us the *Vopos* would come for him today. If he hadn't got out last night, he'd be in jail right now."

Shelby was puzzled. If Herr Kortz hadn't been giving information to Donovan to help him track down the Lion, what *had* they been talking about? She had an uneasy feeling suddenly. She walked back to the room to see who the person seated against the door was. She prepared to enter the room, but it turned out not to be necessary. The person had joined Herr Kortz on the couch and was quietly conversing with him.

Shelby felt jolted. It was the red-haired girl who had been with Donovan at the café.

Shelby returned to Diana. "That girl is his grand-daughter?"

Diana nodded. "She played a major role in their original escape plan. The people smuggler who helped them had arranged an elaborate ruse in which she was supposed to be the people smuggler's lover. Herr Kortz was supposed to be a West Berlin clergy-man who would marry them. The people smuggler even managed to get the forged documents they need-ed. But then at the last minute, just before they were to leave for the checkpoint, something went wrong."

Shelby felt weak and queasy. "What?" she asked.

"Some woman showed up at the café where they were—a woman who knew the people smuggler was going under a false identity. She made a scene. Well, you know the undercover *Vopos* hang out at all those places along the wall, just hoping to overhear some-thing like that. One followed them from the café. The people smuggler sent Kortz's granddaughter away and managed to lead the *Vopo* after himself instead of her. The girl and Herr Kortz later crossed at the wall, using an emergency plan the people smuggler and his ac-complice had arranged as a last resort."

Shelby asked in a deathlessly quiet voice, "What happened to . . . ?"

"He was captured. The paper says his name is Rutger Schmidt. He's in an East Berlin prison right now, awaiting trial—and about twelve years at hard labor."

Shelby sank against the wall, suddenly too weak to support herself.

"Hey, are you all right?" asked Diana with alarm.

Shelby shook her head.

"Do you want me to go get the nurse?"

"No, please. I'll be okay in a minute."

Just at that moment James Stanton came barging out of his office, exclaiming, "Where the heck is Donovan? The man seems to have disappeared off the face of the earth." He noticed Shelby's queasy look. "What's the matter with you, young lady? You don't look well at all."

"I'm fine, Mr. Stanton. I just need...a minute to rest."

He looked skeptical. "Well, you're in good hands with Diana. She'll take you to the infirmary if you need to go there." He started brusquely away, intent upon his search for Donovan. He stopped for an instant and turned back. "What's that in your hand?" he asked Shelby.

She glanced down at her letter of resignation. "Nothing," she said.

He started away.

Diana said in a serious tone, "Shelby, are you going to tell me what's wrong, or aren't I a good enough friend to share it with?"

"I'll tell you," she said, squeezing Diana's hand. "But first I need you to get something for me— Donovan's five-year travel record."

"That's restricted data," she replied warily.

"But you can get it; your cone has access."

After a moment's reflection Diana said, "Okay. It's obviously important to you. You go sit down, though. You don't look well at all."

Ten minutes later Diana brought the folder to Shelby's office. The office had only one small window, but the indoor plants Shelby had hung from all the corners gave it a bright look. Shelby's old Washington, D.C. license plate hung on the wall behind her desk, a souvenir that added a unique touch. Diana sat opposite the desk as Shelby began comparing Donovan's travel folder against a second folder. "What's in that one?" asked Diana, referring to the second folder.

"The dates of the crossings arranged by the Lion."

"Shelby! You're kidding! Either that or you're crazy."

The match was almost perfect. There had been many crossings attributed to the Lion during the past five years, and on every occasion except for four, Donovan had been in Germany on either a courier run or a trouble-shooting mission. The other four times coincided with "vacations" he had taken, supposedly in nearby Austria.

Shelby leaned back in her chair and took a deep breath to steady herself. It was shocking enough to learn he was a people smuggler. But now she knew even more. Donovan wasn't just any people smuggler. He was the most dedicated, skilled and notorious of them all: the Lion of Berlin—the very man he and she were supposed to be tracking down.

Diana saw Shelby's expression and quickly turned

the two folders around and began comparing them herself.

So many things were suddenly clear to Shelby now—why Donovan had pretended to be a cold-blooded mercenary, why he'd pretended he couldn't speak German, why he'd hidden the fact he was such a powerful swimmer. Everything had been directed toward giving the wrong impression so no one would suspect he was the Lion. If people knew his true sympathies—that he was dedicated to helping refugees cross to freedom—they would suspect him. So he pretended the exact opposite. If they knew he was a strong swimmer—and that he evidently exercised vigorously to keep up his strength and stamina—they might realize he was the organizer of that scuba crossing under the Baltic Sea. So he denied his physical prowess and tried to hide that trim athletic body beneath three-piece suits.

He had been forced to create the deception, Shelby realized, because he knew that if anyone suspected him, they could easily compare the dates of his visits to Berlin against the dates of the Lion's crossings—just as she had done. So he had to avoid suspicion at all costs.

Now Shelby realized, too, why he had tried so hard to get rid of her, to get her out of her position as his assistant. It was just as Donovan had said. He was afraid she would learn his secret. And *why* was he afraid? Because she had told him she would turn in the Lion if she discovered his identity. He had asked her about this not once but twice—once in Washington when she had criticized his "mercenary" attitude and then again when she had first been assigned to the legation as his assistant. No wonder he had treated her badly, trying to make her quit and go home! How could he risk letting her discover his identity when he was sure she felt duty bound to have him arrested?

"I don't believe it," said Diana in amazement, looking up from the folders. "It could be coincidence?"

"Try this 'coincidence' on for size," said Shelby as she began telling her about the incident at the café the previous afternoon.

By the time she had finished, Diana was looking dumbfounded—which was exactly the way Shelby herself had felt when she had first realized the truth. "Well," said Diana, "at least that explains his playboy reputation—which I always had a hard time believing of him anyway."

"How so?"

"If Mr. Hawkes is the Lion, he needed an excuse for not being at home on the nights he was bringing refugees across the wall or making arrangements to do so. Otherwise people would wonder where he was all night. What better excuse than to have everyone think he's a playboy who spends his nights with his girl friends?"

Hearing this, Shelby instinctively knew it was right. Now she felt better about Donovan than ever before. That gnawing concern about his being a playboy had bothered her more than she cared to admit.

Of course, realizing how virtuous he was—under the circumstances—seemed tragically absurd. She probably would not see him or be with him again for twelve long years, twelve years during which she would have to bear the guilt of knowing that his capture had been mostly her fault.

"Oh, Diana," she moaned, "what am I going to do? I've got to help him."

Diana tried to comfort her, but her efforts were in vain. Shelby was beyond being comforted. However, she was not beyond pulling herself together and getting a grip on her emotions. *Donovan needs me now,* she told herself. *This isn't the time to fall apart. This is the time to think clearly and figure out what has to be done—and to do it.* She knew one reason Donovan loved her was that she had spirit and spunk and resourcefulness. Well, she wouldn't let him down now. She stood up and began pacing across her office, her brow furrowed in concentration.

"There has to be something we can do," she said.

"I don't mean to be pessimistic, honey, but I don't see what. He's in an East German prison right now. They caught him with the forged papers right on him."

"But they don't know he's the Lion, do they?" she asked hopefully.

Diana looked reluctant to dash Shelby's hopes, but there seemed no way not to, if she was to tell the truth. "They don't know yet, but they will soon. That *Vopo* who was in the tractor with him—the one he wounded—will be brought down to look at Donovan. They bring him in to look at every suspected people smuggler to see if he can identify him as the Lion. Once that happens...." She hesitated.

"What?" asked Shelby, urging her on, though she dreaded what she might say.

"When they identify him as the Lion, it won't be just twelve years he'll be sentenced to. It'll be more like twenty. Remember, they're calling the wounding of that *Vopo* 'attempted murder.'"

Shelby bit her lip, grimacing. Everything she heard seemed to make the situation worse! What could she *do*? She had to have help. There was no way she could figure out what do alone; she didn't have enough information. "Is there anyone we can turn to for aid on this?"

"Certainly not the State Department. Mr. Hawkes's actions as the Lion were strictly illegal. We'd probably find some sympathizers within the department, but that wouldn't stop the top brass from putting him in Leavenworth. They'd *have* to— for the wounding of that *Vopo*, if nothing else, no matter how good his reason for doing so. These are major international crimes. The State Department could never condone a diplomat doing the things he's done as the Lion. It would cause an international uproar."

Shelby knew this was true, but hearing it only made her feel more wretched. She continued pacing, determined to find some way to save Donovan.

Finally Diana came up with the solution without even realizing it.

"I hate to say it," she said glumly, "but the only sort of person who could save Mr. Hawkes is the sort who would never do it. You need a man with strong political connections in East Berlin... someone who's got the power and the guts to call in favors, bribe people, threaten them if necessary. Even if you found a man like that, he'd never risk everything to save Mr. Hawkes. And that's just what he'd be risking—everything—if he tried to free the Lion of Berlin once the East Germans had finally caught him after all these years."

Shelby shut her eyes in anguish. She knew what she had to do now—to whom she had to go. She felt she had known all along, at the back of her mind, but had not wanted to face it. She would have forced herself to face it eventually, but now there was no putting it off. She stood up straight and squared her shoulders. She felt like a sacrificial lamb about to be thrown to a dragon. There was a possible way to save Donovan, she knew, but the price would be very high, and it would be she who would have to pay it.

"Diana, I want you to do something for me, please," she said in a quiet voice, more firmly in control of herself now that the decision had been made. "Go to Mr. Stanton and tell him I told you Donovan just called me. Tell him Donovan said he's busy tracking down a lead on his investigation. Say he's looking into the arrest of this people smuggler named Rutger Schmidt on the off chance Schmidt has dealt with the Lion. He won't be back for several days."

Diana raised her eyebrows in appreciation of the

idea. "That'll get him off the hook for the moment. They won't launch a search for him if they think that. But it won't work for too long, honey. Mr. Hawkes will have to call or show up soon." She looked inquisitive. "What is it you've got running through that devious mind of yours?"

"I'll have to tell you later." She picked up her purse and started for the door. Now that she knew what she had to do, there wasn't a moment to lose.

"Hey, where are you going?" asked Diana.

"To Wolfgang."

CHAPTER NINETEEN

HER TIMING was good. Wolfgang pulled up to the castle just a moment after she arrived, as she was approaching the doorstep. He leaped out of the car, as usual not bothering with the door. He was dressed just as he had been a day earlier, in boots, jeans and that old unzippered jacket with the fur collar. In fact, Shelby could see from his look of weariness that he had not slept, probably had not returned to the castle, since the incident at the café the previous afternoon.

"What is it you want?" he asked in a not very friendly tone as he strode forward. He pulled off his driving gloves and ran his hand through his thick mop of blond hair, brushing it out of his eyes.

She wasn't surprised at his anger. The last time she had seen him, after all, was to tell him she was rejecting his love so she could marry another man. And then at the café she had "used" him yet again, striking back at Donovan by telling him it was Wolfgang she really loved—while Wolfgang knew this was only a cruel lie.

"Donovan is in jail," she said. "Did you know that?"

"Of course I know it," he snapped. "I knew it would happen before it ever happened. I knew it the moment you began making that noisy scene at the café. Did you not realize *Vopos* frequent cafés that close to the wall?''

"I know this is my fault," she said sadly, "but you're not totally innocent." She followed him inside the castle and up the stairs to his living chambers. "You're the one who took me there," she continued, "the one who made me believe he was a smuggler and a—a playboy!"

"Made you believe?" he said cynically as he shucked off his jacket and sat on the bed to pull off his boots.

"If you had told me what he was doing there, I wouldn't have jumped to the wrong conclusion!"

"Is your memory really so short? I tried telling you. I tried to pull you away from there so I could explain what it was you had seen. But did you let me? You saw him with the Kortz girl, and you became like a crazy woman."

Shelby's tone was full of fiery accusation. "You had to know what impression I'd get from seeing the two of them together like that!"

"Did I? How was I to know your faith in the man you supposedly love is so shallow that you would distrust him so quickly, that you would instantly jump to exactly the wrong conclusion?"

He was standing now, barefoot, unbuttoning his shirt and tossing it off. He continued speaking as he went across the large sleeping chambers to the elegantly appointed bathroom, where he turned on the shower water to let it get hot. Shelby followed him absently, intent on stating her case. "Besides,"

Wolfgang continued, "I never expected you to stay long enough to see that girl there. I tried to hustle you away so I could explain to you what Hawkes was doing with the forger. You, however, had your own ideas about when to leave."

Shelby was watching his lean flanks as he stretched forward to test the temperature of the shower water with his hand. She had never seen him shirtless. He had a hairless well-shaped chest and very smooth skin. He was quite lean, and his tall body seemed hard and tightly compacted.

He turned to see her looking at him. She glanced away quickly.

"Pardon me for attending to other matters while we speak," he said, "but I haven't had a shower since yesterday morning—or any sleep for that matter." He unbuckled his belt, and Shelby heard the sound of his zipper opening. She turned, facing completely away from him. She saw his jeans fly through the air onto the top of a hamper. Then she heard the sound of water spraying on his body. "Besides," he said from the shower, "if you follow a man into his bedroom, you forfeit the right to be shocked at anything you might see."

"I have to talk to you," she said. "That's why I followed you in here."

"So talk."

"And there isn't any time to lose. Donovan is in serious trouble now, but he'll be in even worse trouble soon if the *Vopo* guard from the tractor has a chance to identify him."

He said nothing to this. She was sure he heard her, even though there was the sound of the water to contend with. Warm steam was billowing out from the enclosed shower stall. She spoke more loudly this time as she said, "Wolfgang, I didn't mean to be angry with you a moment earlier. I intended to be calm and reasonable. But when you made it sound as if that scene at the café was entirely my fault...."

"It was entirely your fault," he called out, not giving an inch.

"It most certainly was not," she declared, her anger getting the best of her again. She was still facing away from him. She wished she could look him in the eye, but to turn around now was, of course, unthinkable. "Listen, you," she began, "you shouldn't even have taken me there in the first place. Why did you?"

"You know exactly why I did. It was so you could see that your precious Donovan Hawkes, whom you are leaving me to marry, is no less of an outlaw than I. He is no better a man than I."

"He is a better man!" she shot back at him emotionally, knowing even as she said it that she shouldn't have. "He breaks the law so he can help smuggle refugees to freedom. You do it for your own personal gain!"

Suddenly a wet hand descended on her shoulder, soaking her blouse. He swiveled her forcefully to face him. He was stark naked and dripping wet. She tried to turn away, but he stopped her. His face was raging.

"Get this straight," he said in a growl, his accent stronger than usual. "I smuggle goods. He smuggles people. I do not recognize a distinction. You—you come from your land where every man can be king, where there are such wonderful freedoms as are found nowhere else on earth, and you pass judgment upon my morality? Listen to me, Shelby. What I do is, to me and to the villagers of Idor-Amstein, very moral. What would be incredibly *immoral* would be to submit to the Communist tyranny, to condemn myself to the same deadening low-level life as their fabled 'masses.'"

She did feel chastened by his words. She was wrong to condemn him and to compare him to another man. She wanted to tell him so, but she was so tense she could not speak. He was holding her there, only inches away from him.

He released her and turned away angrily. "Bah! Why do I waste my time justifying my life to you." He grabbed a towel and began drying himself. Shelby left the bathroom and waited for him in the other room. When he came out a moment later, he was wearing a bathrobe, his wet hair combed straight back from his forehead.

"Wolfgang," she said in a subdued voice, "I'm sorry. You're right. I have no right to pass judgment."

"What do you want from me?" he asked frustratedly, lighting a cigarette and inhaling deeply. He was very agitated. "I can't even be sane around you. You force my emotions to explode out of me. I love you. This is so hard for me, having you here, seeing you, talking to you. Why do you not leave me alone, for God's sake?"

"Wolfgang, truly I—I don't mean to torture you."

"What is it you want? Tell me and we can get this over with."

"I need your help. I want you to help me get Donovan free."

"It is almost impossible. I know because I have just come from the prison, where I spoke to a contact about doing just that. In fact, I have spent all yesterday and today, ever since Hawkes's arrest, trying to find some way to get him released."

So he does feel guilty about taking me to the café, Shelby thought, *and bringing about the scene I caused.*

He seemed to read her mind. "Yes," he said, waving his cigarette, "I admit some responsibility. I was wrong to pretend otherwise. I should never have taken you there." He shook his head in angry wonderment over his actions. "Normally I never would have done such a thing, never would have revealed his identity to you. But... I was too angry. I was not in control of myself. That you should choose him over me—it was too much. And that you should do so because *I* am a *lawbreaker*?" He threw up his hands in despair.

Shelby's voice was quiet and subdued. "You say it's 'almost' impossible. Does that mean there is some chance, no matter how small?"

He shrugged. "Half steps will not work. If he were a common criminal—say a burglar—I could lean on people, insist that past favors be repaid. But with a people smuggler it is different. His is a political criminal, and to the East Germans, one of the most hated kind. It would take a bribe to free him under these conditions—a very major bribe.''

Hopefulness sprang up within her. "Is that all?" she asked in amazement.

"You do not understand," he said as he moved to his closet and began pulling out a shirt and slacks. "It is not the money itself that is the difficulty. If it were only a question of paying money to free him, I would do it. We have worked together on occasion, and I feel that I owe him this much.''

"On what occasion?''

He looked at her. "Twice he needed special equipment for his crossings. Scuba tanks, for instance, on one. I secured these and smuggled them across for him.''

"You said it's not just a question of the money...?''

"It is a question of the risk, Shelby. To accomplish this sort of bribe I would have to approach a guard or bureaucrat at the prison and make my offer. Even to make the offer is highly illegal and could get me thrown into prison alongside Hawkes. But the true danger comes later, if the offer is accepted. For then I must transfer the money to the man I bribe. If he has only pretended to go along—if he has meanwhile reported me to his superiors—I will be caught with the bribe in my possession. The prison term would be very long and severe then, and it is not unlikely that my bank accounts and property would be confiscated, also, while I was in prison, unable to protest.''

The magnitude of the risk was staggering, and Shelby felt it deeply. "Isn't there someone else you can send to approach the guard or deliver the money?"

He snapped at her, "I do not send others to take risks I fear taking myself." He realized his tone had become harsh, and he added more even temperedly, "Besides, it would do no good. The man who is to be bribed must have no doubts that the money will be paid as promised. Everyone knows I have the money and will stand by my word. As for some underling I might send...." He shrugged. "He would be a stranger. He might even be suspected of being an undercover *Vopo*, out to test the man's loyalty."

Shelby felt unbearably frustrated after coming so close, after having her hopes raised, only to be dashed. She knew she had no right to ask this of Wolfgang, but she was so desperate she couldn't stop herself. She found herself rushing to him and clutching the front of his robe. "Please, Wolfgang," she begged, "please save him."

"Good Lord, what a thing you ask of me! Do you not realize what he is to me? He is the man who keeps you from me. He is an obstacle preventing me from having the woman I love!" He unclasped her hands and moved away from her, his expression reproachful.

Shelby sank down on the edge of the bed despondently. Wolfgang left to go into the bathroom to dress. Moments later he came out wearing gray slacks and a chocolate brown shirt. His hair was drier but still combed straight back.

Shelby knew what she had to do. It was the price she had known all along might have to be paid to save Donovan. She had tried to avoid paying it by pleading with Wolfgang instead, but now she knew that that had been dishonorable of her—asking him to risk sacrificing everything while she sacrificed nothing. No, there was only one fair way to ask him to do what she needed him to do. But it was so hard....

"Wolfgang?"

He looked at her.

Her voice was soft. "You know you're wrong in thinking it's Donovan who stands between you and me. Even if he were out of the picture entirely, I feel I still couldn't marry you."

He said nothing, just watched her intently.

"But there is a way you could change that...."

He narrowed his eyes and regarded her through thin slits.

Her voice had been low. Now, though, in reaction to his infuriating silence, she glared up at him and exclaimed in agony, "Are you going to make me spell it out to you?"

He held her eyes, not quite knowing how to react. Conflicting emotions seemed to be battling within him. Finally he came to her, took her hand and raised it to his lips. He kissed it gently and returned it to her lap.

Shelby felt nothing.

When he spoke his voice was solemn. "You will probably hate me for it, but I will accept your offer. I want you so badly, I will endure anything to have you, even your hatred. In time, perhaps, it will go away."

"I don't hate you," she said, looking down at her lap. "I feel. . .nothing for you. Now."

He transferred his wallet and keys to his pockets and grabbed a coat. "Stay here in the castle," he said, his manner brusque. "I'll be back in a few hours to tell you what I discover. It may be that your 'sacrifice' is not necessary. It may be that I will find no one willing to accept my bribe. If I do, though, and if I succeed in rescuing Hawkes—you will marry me."

"Yes." Her voice was a whisper.

He went down the stairs out to his car and left on his mission. After a moment Shelby walked over to the window and looked out. She did not peer down at the road, though, or even out at the magnificent forested hillside. She gazed off into space. No matter what happened now, she reflected, her life was over—whether Donovan remained in prison for twenty years or was freed to watch her become Baroness Wolfgang von Heller.

Her life was over.

CHAPTER TWENTY

WHEN WOLFGANG RETURNED hours later, he had a black briefcase with him that seemed quite heavy. He met her in the den, setting the briefcase on his large desk. His face was grim.

"Is it arranged?" Shelby asked.

He held up his hand. He pulled the telephone toward him and dialed a number. "I have the money," he said into the phone. "Now you and that other one will do as I told you?" He scowled angrily and his voice became like molten lava. "What do you mean he has not decided? Do you think I have time for games? Listen, I'm coming down. Now, with the money. You convince your friend. If you do as I tell you, you'll be rich. If you do not, you will regret the day you were born." He hung up.

"Trouble?" asked Shelby.

"Two men are involved instead of one." He bent over his desk and wrote something on a sheet of paper. "The guard in charge of Hawkes's cell refused to release him without orders to do so. This means I must also bribe the duty officer to give the false orders. I want him to 'accidentally' order his release, instead of that of another prisoner who is due. Later it can be explained as a paperwork mix-up."

Shelby was staring at the black briefcase. Wolfgang noticed this and opened it for her. It was filled with stacks of one-hundred-mark bills. Shelby was astounded. "So much?"

"There are two men, remember, and the risk they take is very great."

He shut the briefcase and handed Shelby the notepaper on which he had written a phone number. "This is the number of Hawkes's accomplice. I cannot call him from the East without complications. If I am successful in arranging the escape, I will phone you at your apartment in the West. You will then dial this number. Tell the accomplice to drive to the street north of the prison gates, just around the corner. I will make sure the guard lets Hawkes know he is there. There will be little time before the paperwork 'error' is discovered and a search begun. Have the accomplice immediately take Hawkes to their safehouse for the night. I will arrange false papers to be delivered to them there before morning."

"Does this accomplice know what safehouse you're talking about?"

"There is only one—an apartment they hold under a false registration. They keep refugees there sometimes the night before they smuggle them across the wall."

"This accomplice," Shelby said, "it's Doctor Rinehardt, isn't it?"

Wolfgang was surprised. "How do you know this?"

"He was with Donovan and Herr Kortz during that 'interview' the day before the crossing. I thought he was there as a translator, but now that I know Donovan speaks German, I know Rinehardt was present for some other reason. And since it wasn't an interview at all but probably a planning session for their crossing, Dr. Rinehardt must have been involved.''

"You are a bright girl...perceptive. Yes, Gottfried Rinehardt is his accomplice, and lucky for Hawkes that he is. Without him he would have been captured long ago. Hawkes was very reckless and passionate in his early career as the Lion, completely without caution. Gottfried taught him to be less passionate, more professional. So long as Hawkes listens to him.''

"You seem to know a lot about their relationship.''

"I told you once—there is nothing that happens in Berlin I do not know of.''

Shelby remembered the way Wolfgang had grinned at her in amusement the day of the *Oktoberfest* when she had told him her job was to help Donovan track down the Lion. He'd known how ridiculous that was—helping Donovan in his pretense of tracking down himself.

Wolfgang went to a locked hardwood cabinet and unlocked it. Before he opened the doors, he said to Shelby, "Turn around.''

"Why?''

"Do as I tell you.''

She turned away from him. She heard him taking something from the cabinet, then relocking the doors. When he told her it was all right to look again, there was no indication of what he had removed. The only difference was that his coat was on now, whereas earlier it had been draped over a chair. He came to the desk and picked up the briefcase, preparing to leave.

"A taxi will be arriving for you shortly. I summoned it before I came." He had only one other thing to tell her. "When you call Gottfried, do not let him know it was I who arranged the release. Tell him only that I learned from my sources about the mix-up in release papers and I told you so you could tell him."

"I don't understand. You're taking such a risk; why don't you want to be given credit for it?"

There was a sudden flash of anger. "Do you think I want the world to know that the only way I can get the woman I love to marry me is by making a 'deal' with her? If he knows I am the one who freed Hawkes, then you and I marry afterward, it will be only too obvious."

He started for the door.

"Wolfgang?"

He turned back to her.

"You said there's a chance they'll set a trap for you to catch you in the act of bribery. How good a chance?"

"From the guard, very little. It is the duty officer I worry over. He knows the hard-liners of the party have hated me for years, though the government tolerates me. He knows the hard-liners might reward him if he were to aid in trapping me. From him the danger of entrapment is. . . perhaps fifty percent.''

Shelby's eyes went wide.

"If, by four-thirty, you receive my call telling you to contact Rinehardt, you will know I have succeeded. If you do not hear from me—'' he shrugged ''— you will undoubtedly read about me in tomorrow's papers.''

He pulled open the door and left the room.

"Wait!'' she called after him, rushing to him. He looked at her quizzically. She flung her arms about him and hugged him, her brow creasing with worry. She did care for him. He was a good man, and now he was risking everything—maybe even his life—for her benefit. She knew there was the chance she might never seen him again.

When she released him, he looked at her hard, refusing to show his emotions. Then he left.

SHE DIDN'T HEAR from him by four-thirty—or fourforty—or five. She was on the verge of slamming her phone against the wall. An instant later it rang, and she lunged for the receiver.

"Yes?''

"It is arranged,'' said Wolfgang. "Make the call.''

Before she could ask any questions, he hung up. Shelby quickly dialed the number he had given her. When Dr. Rinehardt answered, she told him what Wolfgang had told her to say. Dr. Rinehardt was surprised she knew not only about the Lion but also that he himself was the Lion's accomplice. His surprise, though, did not stop him from quickly agreeing to meet Donovan around the corner from the prison.

Shelby deviated from Wolfgang's instructions in only one way—she asked Dr. Rinehardt for the location of the safehouse in return for the information she had given him. She knew Wolfgang would have objected to this, but she did it anyway. She intended to be there when Donovan arrived, and nothing would stop her.

She took a taxi to within a few blocks of the safehouse, then walked the rest of the way—for security reasons. It was an upper-floor apartment in an old two-story prewar building. She let herself in with the key Dr. Rinehardt had told her was hidden above the doorframe. The apartment was cozy, sparse and a bit musty from disuse. She turned on music from the radio to calm her frayed nerves and began inspecting the pleasant old one-room apartment.

She found canned goods and nonperishable foods in the cabinet over the sink. A small gas stove and refrigerator near a table in one corner of the room comprised the kitchen. The rest of the room was taken up by an old overstuffed sofa of fading floral-print design and a few pieces of simple wooden furniture. There was also an armchair and a single bed with a quilted covering and thick pillows. There wasn't room for much else. Even the bookcase near the armchair was of narrower than normal width, with a few dusty old books held in place by brick bookends.

The attached bathroom had a shower but no bath.

A chest of drawers had been put in here, since there was no room for it in the main room. Shelby found it stocked with a few articles of clothing for both men and women. Apparently refugees who stayed here did not always have a chance to return to their homes for their own clothing before a crossing and did not always know how long they would have to stay.

Shelby tried to concentrate on the soothing radio music to calm herself, but her thoughts kept wandering to fears about all the things that could go wrong. She went to the curtained windows and opened them so that fresh air could breeze in to dispel the mustiness. Beneath her, she saw, was a narrow street with a few cars parked along one side. Children were playing a loud merry game of kick the can. As Shelby watched, one of the children's mothers called out that dinner was ready, and the children ran inside.

The music was suddenly interrupted by an urgent announcement. Shelby tensed and was drawn over to the radio as if by magnetic attraction. She stared at the old brown box as the newscaster began speaking.

"A suspected people smuggler named Rutger Schmidt was shot while trying to escape from prison. He had been released due to an administrative error. The error was discovered an instant after the suspect walked out through the prison gates. He was immediately called back, but instead of returning, he attempted to run. Shots were fired, and the suspect was seriously wounded...."

Shelby was in shock. She slumped against the wall, unable to move. The broadcast droned on. Shelby's lips were slightly parted, her eyes staring vacantly.

A sudden banging sounded at the apartment's front door. She didn't answer it. *The Vopos,* she thought blankly, nonsensically. *They've found out I was involved, and they've come for me. I don't care.*

The banging came again, and this time the door burst open, as if violently kicked. Donovan stood there on the threshold, looking at her, tottering and wincing against the pain. His black jacket was draped over his shoulders rather than fully on, revealing a partially bloodstained shirt.

Shelby gasped and ran to him. Before she could reach him, he collapsed to the floor, still and unmoving.

CHAPTER TWENTY-ONE

"DONOVAN!" SHE CRIED, going down to the floor beside him. She lifted his head and upper torso and cradled him in her arms. "Donovan?"

There was the sound of running footsteps on the stairway. She looked up and raised her hand instinctively, as if to ward off anyone who was coming after Donovan. But it was Dr. Rinehardt who appeared, looking harried and out of breath. His goatee and hair looked grayer than usual against the contrast of his face, which was now reddened from his exertions. He glanced at Shelby. His expression was both a welcome and an acceptance, as if he recognized her as a partner in mutual purpose. He looked at the other apartments on both sides of the hall to see if anyone, alerted by the commotion, was peeking out their doors. No one was.

Donovan moaned in his unconsciousness.

"Quickly," Dr. Rinehardt said to Shelby. "Inside." He grasped Donovan beneath the arms and began tugging him along the carpet into the room. Shelby grabbed Donovan's ankles and helped move him onto the couch.

"The door," said Dr. Rinehardt urgently.

She shut it from the outside. She quickly walked along the hall and down the stairs, checking to find out if Donovan had stained the carpet with blood, which could be traced to the safehouse apartment. With relief she saw that he had not. She returned to the apartment, glancing at the other doorways as Rinehardt had done to see if anyone was watching.

The safehouse door closed but would not lock. Donovan had smashed the lock mechanism when he kicked the door open. "Let it go," Dr. Rinehardt said to her as she tried to make it lock. "Please, come here. I need you."

He had Donovan's black jacket off and was busy cutting away his shirt to expose his wound. "How badly hurt is he?" Shelby asked.

Dr. Rinehardt inspected the wound. "It is his shoulder. A few inches lower into his chest, and he would probably be dead. Fetch me a clean towel and hot water. Don't take time to boil it. Just hot from the tap for now." He continued examining the wound as Shelby did as he asked. When she came back with a pot of hot water, he took a plastic bottle of antiseptic soap from his pocket and began to cleanse the wound. Then he took other items from his pockets and put them on the old coffee table near the couch.

"I never bring my medical bag when I come here," he explained, absorbed in attending to Donovan. "If people knew a doctor visited this apartment, even a retired doctor such as me, they'd become suspicious."

Shelby was looking at Donovan's face. Although unconscious, he was still grimacing. She kept her eyes averted from his wound, though, as Dr. Rinehardt began to talk about it. "See here," he said, "the bullet entered at the top of his shoulder from behind and exited here a bit lower down near his chest. It is good that it has exited. I am not a surgeon. To remove it would have been difficult."

"Will he be all right?" she asked anxiously.

He hesitated. "He is unconscious from weakness and shock. He kept running even after he was hit—until he reached the car, which was out of sight around the corner. The wound itself—I think it is not so critically bad. I need X rays to be sure, but there is no way we can get them. His collarbone might be damaged—" he sighed dismally "—but it is the shock to his body I am more concerned over. There lies the danger. And he is running a fever."

Shelby put her hand to Donovan's forehead. He was burning up. She felt so helpless. "Isn't there anything I can do?"

"Go to the cabinet above the sink," he said as he began bandaging Donovan's wounded shoulder in white gauze. "There is a package of antibiotics. Bring it to me."

Shelby found the package and was surprised by its familiarity. She had seen it previously. This was the small brown-paper-wrapped parcel Dr. Rinehardt had handed to Donovan that day at the wall, looking nervous as he did so, due to Shelby's presence.

When she gave it to him, he tore off the wrapping.

Inside was a small vial of liquid, a bottle of capsules and three small disposable needles. Dr. Rinehardt proceeded to prepare and give Donovan an injection of antibiotics. Shelby looked away. She had never been able to stand needles.

"This was a wise precaution—having these drugs here," he said as he worked. "It was Donovan's idea. On one of his previous crossings a man was wounded in the leg. We did not have antibiotics ready then, and I could not smuggle them to the safehouse. The East Germans keep very tight control on antibiotics to make sure they are not used on failed crossers. It is a good thing the man's leg did not get infected."

He finished. Shelby had been busy gathering up the pieces of Donovan's shirt. She glanced at Donovan, bare-chested, the white gauze wrapped diagonally across his chest and under his left arm. The injured arm was taped across his stomach to prevent it from moving.

Dr. Rinehardt stood up. "I must go; the car has to be moved. I parked only a block away after letting Donovan out in front of the building. I do not think they saw the make of the car, but I am not sure. Now I must reappear at my home, to be visible so the *Vopos* do not know for certain I was involved in this."

Shelby nodded.

"Donovan must remain here for at least three weeks. Even when he regains consciousness, we cannot take him across the border in this condition. The

Vopos will be looking for a weakened wounded man. Already they are searching." He glanced at Donovan. Shelby could see deep affection and concern in his eyes. "I will see if I can perhaps find someone to stay with him."

"Don't be ridiculous. I'll stay."

"The danger—it is very great, *Fräulein*. If they catch you with him, it is harboring a known fugitive. Even though you have diplomatic immunity, 'accidents' have been known to happen. Guns have gone off...."

"I said I'll stay," she retorted testily.

He nodded. "You are a courageous woman. No wonder Donovan is in love with you."

Shelby was surprised he should know about that, and she showed it.

"Of course I know," said Rinehardt. "Why do you think I gave you the safehouse address when you asked and allowed you to come? I have known Donovan for years now, from shortly after his very first crossing. He is like a son. There is little he keeps from me."

"I wish I could say the same about me." She looked at Donovan, lying wounded and unconscious. "If he'd told me the truth about himself, none of this would have happened."

"He *desired* to. He desired to greatly. But he told me you had stated you would feel duty bound to turn in the Lion if you discovered his identity."

Shelby lowered her eyes and said nothing.

Rinehardt picked up the bottle of capsules. "When

he regains consciousness," he said, "give him one of these every six hours."

Shelby asked hesitantly, "What if he doesn't...." Her words petered out.

"Then there will be no need for antibiotics one way or another." He gave her further instructions on what she must do to attend to Donovan. Afterward he turned to go.

"Goodbye," Shelby said, "and thank you."

"Do not thank me. It is I who thank you. I am a *Deutschlander*. I aid the Lion because it is for my country, and I take these risks for the freedom of my countrymen. But you, you are not German. Yet you now endanger yourself so greatly."

"For the man I love," she said proudly. "I'm not a saint. My reason is every bit as strong as yours."

He smiled at her grimly and squeezed her hand. "I approve of you. Donovan has chosen wisely. To me you are family now." He turned and left.

Shelby shut the door after him and again tried to lock it. It refused to lock. Finally she tried something she had seen in a movie once and was amazed that it actually worked. She took a tall chair and wedged its back up against the door handle. The door was firmly locked in place.

Then she went to the man she loved....

HE TOSSED AND TURNED in delirium for most of the night. Shelby sat by his side, washing his face and neck and chest with a cool washcloth. Occasionally he mumbled unintelligibly.

Finally, at about two in the morning, he jerked upright, frowning, glancing about him with a look of disorientation. Shelby was startled by the suddenness of his awakening. Watching him, she thought he looked like an angry bull—strong and dangerous because he was uncertain of his situation. She came forward to reassure him.

"Donovan," she said softly, "I'm here."

He looked at her sharply, as if not recognizing her. He glanced about the room, his expression savage. The curtains were closed, and the room was dimly illuminated by a bedside lamp. After a moment his expression relaxed slightly. He tried to rise up off the couch but fell back, wincing in pain.

"Careful!" Shelby said. "You're hurt badly."

He sat up on the couch slowly. "Where am I?" he asked, his voice gravelly. But then he regained his bearings more fully and recognized the room. "This is the safehouse," he said. "How did I get here?"

"Dr. Rinehardt brought you."

He put his hand to his temples and squeezed. He had been breathing rapidly to catch his breath, but now his breathing became more normal. He still seemed in pain and looked as if concentration were an effort. "The last thing I remember is that I kept walking after the *Vopos* called my name. I was out of the prison gates, and they kept calling me, and I kept walking, pretending not to hear. Then, when I neared the corner, they started firing."

"Don't talk now," she said. She feared he was too weak for the shock of the memory.

"I remember staggering around the corner to Gottfried's car...." He had been squinting in concentration. Now he sighed and leaned back. "That's all I remember."

"He brought you here," Shelby said. "You were carrying your black jacket, and he put it over your shoulders so no one would see your wound. You walked up here to the apartment under your own power, but you collapsed when I opened the door." She paused. "Donovan, I know all about your being the Lion."

He looked at her more pointedly as the last vestiges of his woozy disorientation left him. He seemed truly to recognize her for the first time. His gaze was one of tenderness, but then he remembered something, and his expression turned harsh. "What are you doing here?" he said.

"I came—to help you."

He seemed about to say something, but instead he shook his head and changed the subject. "How is Herr Kortz and his granddaughter? Did they make it all right? They wouldn't give me any news in prison."

"They crossed safely, using the emergency plan you told the girl about. Dr. Rinehardt helped them, I think."

He nodded, satisfied. He noticed the bandages wrapped around his shoulder and chest. "How badly am I wounded?"

She told him. Then she felt his forehead. "You still have a fever, and you're probably a lot weaker than you realize."

He reached for the tumbler of water on the coffee table, seemingly forgetting that his arm was taped to his body. The movement almost made him keel over. Shelby held out her hands to stop him, but he managed to stop himself first. "Can I have some of that?" he asked, nodding toward the water.

She poured him a glass. He drank it down thirstily. She poured him more and gave him an orange capsule from the bottle. "Antibiotics," she said. He swallowed the pill.

He stood up slowly, unsteady on his feet. Shelby became alert, ready to help. He walked over to the bed, then back to the couch, apparently just to prove to himself he could still move under his own power. "How long do I have to stay here? Did Gottfried say anything about that?"

"Three weeks at the very least."

He looked grim and thoughtful. "I'll want you to stay with me for the next couple of days. I'll need you to get me food and some supplies and to help prepare the room for my stay. Then you can go."

She was startled. "Go? I don't want to go."

"And I don't want you to stay," he said with sudden harshness, looking at her coldly.

She was stung. It took a long painful moment before she realized the reason for his attitude. The last time he had seen her was in the café, as she was venting her agony by telling him she didn't really love him, that she loved Wolfgang instead, that she had been trying to get out of her acceptance of Donovan's proposal ever since she had agreed to it so she could marry Wolfgang.

"Donovan, those things I said in the café weren't true! I felt betrayed by you and hurt. You must know that. I only said those things out of blind emotion, wanting to hurt you back and to save my pride."

"Uh-huh," he replied cynically. "Sure."

"Can't you imagine what I was feeling?" Her voice was becoming charged with emotion. "I saw you there with that girl, kissing her and acting as if you were secret lovers, right after you had—" she lowered her eyes "—after you had just made love to me. Can't you understand what I was feeling when I went there and saw that?"

"You mean when you went there with von Heller at your side?" he flung at her savagely. "With your hand on his arm."

"My hand *wasn't* on—"

"When you came there to check up on me after I asked you to trust me, after I told you how important it was that you trust me? Is that the time you're talking about?"

She couldn't bear his sarcasm. She turned away from him and went to the table. One reason his words touched her so deeply was that she knew they were true. She *had* betrayed him when she let Wolfgang take her to the café to check up on him. Donovan had asked her to trust him, and she had promised she would. Then she had thrown her promise to the wind.

"Maybe you were just looking for an excuse to call off the engagement, as you said."

"That's not true, Donovan. I told you."

"Yes," he said sarcastically, "you told me."

She wondered why he was persisting in his accusation, refusing to believe her. As she looked in his eyes and saw the suppressed longing and caring that was dammed up there, she understood. He was deliberately holding back his feelings because he was waiting for something.

Shelby knew what it was. He was waiting for her to say she loved him. It was that simple. She had not said it. She had given him an "explanation" for her earlier denial of love, but she had not reaffirmed that she still did love him. He was waiting—wanting, needing, to hear those words from her lips.

But Shelby could not say them. She wanted desperately to say them, but how could she, when in about three weeks she would be saying something completely different? She would be telling him she was leaving him to marry Wolfgang. How would he feel then, looking back at this moment, if she were to reaffirm her love now and let him take her in his arms, only to have his love forsaken when their time together in this old apartment was over?

She felt tormented as she gazed at him. She couldn't think clearly. She didn't know what to say.

Donovan was beginning to weaken, his stamina still very low. His face and body were sweating from his continuing fever. He went to the bed and sat on it, then lay back. "God, I'm tired," he said, his voice weary. "Forget about it, Shelby. I don't need your love. I don't need anything from you." He shut his eyes and tried to fall asleep.

HIS BITTERNESS didn't last. Something happened to change his attitude—something that Shelby had never intended. It happened late the next night. Before it happened, though, during the morning, afternoon and evening of that day, Shelby went through hell. His bitterness toward her intensified. He kept hoping she would say she loved him, and Shelby kept forcing herself to choke back the words, convinced that nothing good could come of them— only more pain and recrimination further down the line.

He had her go shopping for the supplies he would need and then place them on the end table near his bed. He had her arrange the room so he could get along by himself, moving around as little as possible. She didn't like doing this, but she did it anyway. She had decided, however, that she would not leave even when he ordered her to—which he intended to do the next morning. He was in no shape to be alone. His fever was worse than ever, not yet having broken. His face and body were sweating, and he could barely walk without collapsing. Shelby had to change his bandage every few hours to keep it fresh.

He tried to refuse her efforts to help him. Shelby saw a self-destructive side of him she had never been exposed to previously. Instead of letting her bathe him with a cloth, he went into the bathroom and tried to shower by himself. He succeeded, but when he returned to the room, he was ashen from the strain, and he collapsed to the floor before he could reach the bed. He wouldn't eat the light dinner she cooked for him, either, insisting he'd rather eat cold food. He undid the bandage she had fashioned that held his arm tightly to his body and replaced it with a sling.

Shelby attributed his behavior partly to his feverishness and partly to his desire to reject her completely. This hurt her deeply. She was convinced he was trying hard to stop loving her, to ruthlessly suppress his feelings for her, as if cutting them from his very soul.

The incident that changed all this happened late that night. Donovan had fallen into a natural sleep when he went to bed. Sometime during the night, though, his sleep had turned into a state of delirium. He began tossing and turning so recklessly that Shelby feared he would open his wound. She tried to awaken him to make him stop, but he was lost to his wild dreams. She felt his forehead and saw that he was burning up.

He was wearing flannel pajama bottoms. Shelby, wearing a long cotton nightgown, had been sleeping on the couch. Now, as his tossing and turning became even more wild, she saw that he was trying to rise up from the bed. She had no idea where he would attempt to go, but she knew she had to stop him. When words proved useless, she climbed onto the bed on top of him, covering his body with her own, forcibly trying to hold him down. Even in his weakened state he was almost too strong for her. She did manage to keep him down, though, by using all her strength.

He was rocking and jerking beneath her, trying to

sit up. His eyes were shut and his teeth gritted, his lips peeled back. His body was so feverish that Shelby felt the heat all along the front of her, from her breasts to her thighs. He had been mumbling incoherently all along, but now his words became clear enough to be understood.

"Shelby," he called out in delirium.

"I'm here, Donovan."

"Shelby!"

"I'm here, darling. I'm here."

He couldn't hear her. He continued muttering, lost to his fever. "Why did you pretend to love me? You mean so much to me! Why did you pretend...why did you let me believe we really had a chance?"

"I didn't pretend, Donovan." Tears welled up in her eyes and streamed down her face. "I do love you," she cried, knowing he could not hear her. "I do! I've always loved you, and I'll never love anyone but you as long as I live."

She continued holding him down with the weight of her slight body, sobbing, speaking these words to him. It was only after a few moments that she realized he was no longer mumbling or tossing about. When she looked at him, she saw that his eyes were open and he was gazing at her. He had come out of his delirium and had heard what she was saying. A expression of tenderness was on his face. He put his hand to the back of her neck and gently pulled her head down so her cheek was against his own. His good arm went around her back.

His fever had broken—she could tell from the nor-

mal heat of his cheek against hers. She became aware
that she was lying fully atop him and tried to get off,
but he held her there gently. It took a moment for
him to catch his breath. When he was breathing normally again, he sighed and said in a low raw voice,
"Oh, how I love you. You don't know how it hurt to
think you loved von Heller instead of me."

She didn't respond. Her lips were against his hard
cheekbone. She kissed him there. She felt his hand go
up to her long hair and begin gently stroking it the
way she liked so much. She noticed that she had not
stopped crying. Her eyes were still wet with tears. She
tried to shift so she could wipe her eyes, but he held
her in place. He seemed unwilling to let her go, to let
her move away from him even for an instant.

She snuggled against his chest, feeling warm and
loved and cared for.

CHAPTER TWENTY-TWO

THE FOLLOWING DAYS were the happiest of her life. They were filled with love and tenderness and sharing. Shelby had never felt more like a whole woman or been so emotionally fulfilled. It wasn't that they did anything special. What was there special to do in a small bachelor apartment? But the time they spent together—talking, touching, exchanging tender looks—seemed very precious and wonderful to her. It made her so happy that at times she thought she would burst with joy.

She knew she was blocking something from her mind, some terrible future possibility that might turn her happiness into horror, but she continued to block it ruthlessly, because if she didn't, she knew she wouldn't be able to function. And besides, after living in the almost dreamlike world of Donovan's constant love and affection, she began to convince herself that maybe there would be some way out of the marriage to Wolfgang...maybe it wasn't as certain as it seemed. If he loved her as much as he said, wouldn't he want her to be happy? Shelby didn't dwell on these thoughts for fear they might turn out to be fantasy. She just decided instead that sometime later she would ask if he would release her from her promise. For now, though, she lived each day for its own simple pleasures, one day at a time, and thought wistfully, *if only time could stand still. . . .*

Their days were filled with small odds and ends of activities. Sometimes she would sit at the kitchen table and concoct glowing, completely fictitious reports about their ongoing investigation of the Lion. Donovan would smile as he read these and tell her she should have been a novelist. Then he would sign them. Shelby took them to the legation every few days to keep up the appearance that Donovan was still on the job and sending in reports from the field. She also used these occasions to pick up clothing from her apartment, as well as other supplies they needed.

Sometimes she and Donovan would sit on the couch and listen together to the news broadcasts about the continuing manhunt to track him down. Now that he had been identified as the Lion, after the *Vopo* from the tractor crossing had seen the mugshot photo taken of him in prison, the manhunt had broadened into an intense door-to-door search. Fortunately, though, the *Vopos* made the mistake of concentrating on the immediate vicinity of the prison. It was fortunate also that no one had yet made the connection between the man in the photo and Deputy Minister Donovan Hawkes.

Often Donovan would sit propped up at the table and work on his own project. He was devising a way to find and train someone to replace him as a people

smuggler, a person—or perhaps more than one—
who could continue his work. Now that the *Vopos*
knew what he looked like, it would be suicide for him
to go on crossing into the East to bring out refugees.
There was no reason, though, why he could not
mastermind the crossings from the West and super-
vise others who would work under him.

Shelby helped him in his project. She served as his
legs, getting information he needed to plan the crossings that others would carry out. He had her obtain
train timetables, subway maps, even charts of the
tides and the moon in case another crossing under the
Baltic was necessary. Once he had her search out a
company that made grappling-hook launchers, for
God knew what purpose.

Shelby liked the evenings best. Often they would
sit together on the couch, her head against his
shoulder, his arm around her, and just talk softly.
She felt warm and sharing and protected during these
moments. Sometimes Donovan told her about his life
as the Lion, which Shelby found fascinating.

"You can't imagine," he once said as they sat by
the light of flickering candles, "how rough it was for
me when you just arrived, when I thought I had to
send you back to the States. I knew I was falling in
love with you even then. Even that first night in
Washington, at that ball, I felt there was something
powerful between us."

Shelby remembered him mentioning this on the
night of the ball.

"And when you showed up here and I knew I had

to send you away from me...." He shook his head grimly. "It was hard. Then, making your life miserable while I tried to force you to quit.... That was almost impossible for me—having to hurt you like that."

He looked at her seriously as he tried to explain himself. "I believe in what I'm doing, Shelby. I hate that damn wall and what it stands for, and I believe it's the duty of one free man to help others gain freedom. So even though I was willing to risk my own neck by telling you I was the Lion, I couldn't risk the chance that you'd put me out of business. It wasn't just my own happiness I had to think about; it was the freedom of a lot of people I could help if I managed to keep up my activities."

"I understand," she said softly, putting her hand to his cheek, "and I respect you for it." She added with a hint of a smile, "But I admit I hated all those darn interview reports you made me do when you were trying to get rid of me. They were false, weren't they—all those interviews of refugees?"

"Completely. Everyone from Furth on down knew I was the Lion. They were playacting for your benefit—telling us just what I told them to tell us."

"That's why the few descriptions we got from the crossers and the so-called witnesses never jibed with the description of that *Vopo* who saw you in the tractor cab?"

"That's right. It was the only way I could get the police to discount the *Vopo*'s description. I made sure there were other descriptions that didn't match

it. It also helped that the *Vopo*'s description was so
hazy.'' He looked serious as he said, ''You know, I
had to go to a lot of trouble to pretend I was tracking
down the Lion, and all of it was for your benefit. All
that time I spent on the false investigations and false
interviews could have been spent planning the Kortz
crossing, instead of waiting until the very last minute.''

He saw that his words had made her feel bad, and
he added quickly, ''I'm not blaming you. I just want
you to know why I was trying so hard to get rid of
you. I wouldn't have had the same problem with
Nancy Nash. She knows I'm the Lion and would
have faked the reports without my having to do the
actual investigating.''

Just as I'm doing now, Shelby thought.

Sometimes when they talked, Donovan asked her
to tell him about herself. He was interested in knowing everything about her. He had to prod her,
though, because Shelby was a very private person
and didn't open up easily. But the closeness and the
warmth she felt for him with just the two of them in
the candlelit room helped her tell him things she had
never mentioned to anyone—such as her feelings
about her childhood in the foreign service.

''It wasn't just that my father didn't know how to
show affection,'' she said a bit timidly, because it
was so personal. ''It was the nature of the service that
made things so hard. I never had any really close
friends, because as soon as I'd make friends, we'd
pick up and move to father's new post. As a foreign-

service brat you learn very quickly to be wary of friendships—not to invest any feelings in them since you know they won't last."

She told him also about the succession of nannies she had had after her mother had died and how they had never really filled the deep void that yearned to be filled. He hugged her then when she uttered that, and he said in an emotional voice, "I'll fill it. You'll never be without love again."

Twice during the first two weeks of their stay at the safehouse they had visitors. First it was Dr. Rinehardt, who found he could safely risk coming at least once without being followed by *Vopos* or arousing too much suspicion. He had to be careful, because doctors were watched whenever a wounded fugitive was known to be about. He brought some of Donovan's papers when he came, including his personal passport. He also checked Donovan's wound thoroughly.

Donovan was improving, he told the two of them, but he was still very weak. He couldn't risk crossing for at least two more weeks, since the *Vopos*, especially at the checkpoints, were sharply on the lookout for a weakened wounded man. Aside from the weakness, though, he said that Donovan seemed to be coming along nicely, and his wound was healing.

Dr. Rinehardt stayed for the rest of the evening. Shelby cooked a special dinner for him of paprika chicken with onions and potatoes au gratin. Donovan loved her cooking, and Dr. Rinehardt, having his first taste of it, did, too. He was particularly amazed she could do so well with limited facilities. After dinner they sat around the table, and Rinehardt reminisced fondly about some of Donovan's past crossings, about how they had remained together through thick and thin. Shelby could see the warmth Rinehardt felt for Donovan and—surprisingly—for her, as well. Donovan grinned in mild embarrassment as Rinehardt related some of the tales.

Several days after that Diana came to visit, and Hans came with her. The two of them brought schnitzel, sauerkraut and spicy-hot German potato salad, and they had a nice dinner together. Plenty of white Rhine wine flowed, and Shelby felt wonderful about being in the midst of such friendship and affection. Donovan's arm was around her almost the entire time.

Hans knew Donovan was the Lion. Shelby had told Diana she could tell him because she knew Hans could be trusted. When the East Berliner started to question Donovan about ways to cross, though, Diana became upset. She didn't want to think about Hans trying to escape, knowing how dangerous it was. Donovan looked somber himself and told him he couldn't give him any advice, because an amateur like Hans, crossing without professional help, would likely get himself killed. The only encouragement he could give was to tell him to wait, that he was trying to recruit someone to replace him, and when he succeeded, he would plan a crossing for Hans.

So, though the visit had started out pleasantly, toward the end it turned more downbeat. Hans was feeling frustrated and impatient. Donovan was understanding of his feelings and a bit angry at himself for being in this situation, unable to take Hans across personally. Diana was scared that Hans would risk a crossing despite Donovan's warning. She had even further reason to be upset later, when her suspicions were confirmed about the deal Shelby had made with Wolfgang. This happened as she and Shelby left the apartment for a talk, leaving Donovan and Hans alone together.

The night was cool and a bit foggy. The aroma of cooking from the neighboring apartments hung in the air. The heels of the two women clicked upon the pavement as they strode along briskly, walking off their emotions.

"Oh, Shelby," chastised Diana, "how *could* you? You actually agreed to marry him?"

"I felt I didn't have any choice. You remember how hopeless the situation was. There wasn't anyone else to turn to but Wolfgang."

"But, honey—to *marry* him? You don't love him. You love Mr. Hawkes. What a life you're condemning yourself to!"

Shelby didn't want to hear her say this. All these past days she had been trying hard not even to think about it, to block it from her memory. Now, hearing Diana mention it so insistently, she knew she could no longer hide from her fears.

"You obviously haven't told him yet," Diana said. She saw how hurt Shelby was and tried to be more sympathetic. Her voice was softer, now that she had got over the initial shock. "How are you going to break it to him that you're marrying someone else?"

"Oh, I don't know," Shelby exclaimed in anguish. She felt like crying but knew she would not. "I was hoping I might be able to get out of the deal—that there might be some way to make Wolfgang see it won't work. But I know now I was kidding myself. I saw him yesterday at his castle."

"Why did you go there?"

"I wanted to find out why he hadn't brought the false papers he'd said he'd bring. He told me he still intended to bring them, but that they'd be useless while Donovan was still weak from his wound. The *Vopos* are looking for a wounded man, as Dr. Rinehardt said. Donovan will have to wait until he heals before he can cross, so there's no need for the papers yet."

"Did you ask him to let you out of the agreement?"

Shelby shook her head in sadness. "I didn't have to. I could see it would be useless. He'll never let me out of the deal—I can see that. It was just fantasy that made me think he would. I still plan to ask him sometime, but not just yet. I don't want to have him tell me no right now. Because...you see, I have to keep blocking it from my mind, have to keep pretending it might not happen." She was becoming so distraught talking about this that it almost seemed she might become hysterical.

"Steady," said Diana, putting a hand on her arm, looking distressed at Shelby's emotional state.

"Don't you understand?" Shelby asked. "I have to block out the thought of how this is all going to end, because if I don't, he'll see in my face that something is terribly wrong. He'll wring it out of me then, make me tell him about how I'm going to marry Wolfgang. Once that happens, he'll know about the deal. He'll figure it out for sure."

"He'll have to find out sooner or later anyway."

"Yes, but don't you see? If he finds out while he's still here in the East, he'll refuse to be a party to the deal. He'll leave the safehouse, no matter how weak he is, no matter how much danger he's in from the manhunt. He'll do it thinking it will free me from the deal. He'll figure I made the deal to gain his safety and that he can free me from it by rejecting safety on those terms. So he'll walk out of here—into almost certain capture!"

Diana looked thoughtful. "Yes," she agreed, "that sounds like something he'll do if he thinks it will free you from the agreement. He certainly won't voluntarily go along with it."

"So I can't tell him yet, don't you see? I have to wait until this is over with, when he's safely back in the West. That's why I haven't told him so far, why I've blocked it from my mind."

"Oh, you poor girl," said Diana sympathetically. "The pain you must be going through!"

"Diana, you have to promise not to tell him about this. I don't want him to know until I decide the time is right. Promise?"

"All right, honey, whatever you say." She shook

her head in dismay. "Lord, what a situation you've got yourself into, and all of it out of nothing but good intentions, too."

They stopped walking as they reached the edge of a huge open plaza area. Shelby realized where they were. How fitting, she thought ruefully. What a perfect symbol of the thing that was happening to her relationship with Donovan.

"Marx-Engels-Platz," said Diana, naming the square.

They gazed out at it as it lay surrounded by streetlamps in the cold foggy night. Shelby remembered the story of this square from her orientation course. Originally it had been the site of one of Berlin's most prized architectural splendors, the old Imperial Palace. When the Russians took over East Berlin, though, they completely obliterated the palace, razing it to the very ground, leaving not a single brick standing. In its place they paved over the earth and created this bare desolate square. Many Berliners had wept openly as they watched their beloved national monument destroyed so callously and completely.

What had started out as something lovely and worthwhile had ended up as something bleak and empty. It was just like what was happening to her relationship with Donovan, Shelby thought.

They started back. Shelby felt terrible. Earlier she had been able to temporarily erase from her mind the fate that awaited her at the end of Donovan's stay at the safehouse. Now she could do so no longer. She could no longer pretend there might be some way out. Now she knew that the happiness she was experiencing with Donovan was the last she would ever have.

Diana wanted to ask something, but it was a delicate matter, and she seemed to have a hard time getting it out. Finally she said, "What do you do about. . . you know." She looked awkward.

"So far he's been too weak and in too much pain to think very much about romance. Any movement that jiggles his shoulder makes him wince. I'm hoping there won't be too much of a problem with that."

Her hope turned out to be in vain, though, and by coincidence she realized it that very night. After Diana and Hans left, Shelby showered, then sat down at the table to write another fake report while listening to background music on the radio. Her hair was swept up and piled atop her head after her shower. She had a long, fluffy, floral-print towel wrapped all around her, which was really quite discreet. The only part of her left bare was her shoulders. Donovan came up behind her and bent down and kissed her shoulder. He began nuzzling the nape of her neck and then kissing her ear. Shelby tensed. She tried hard not to react to this, to fight down the yearning sensations that suddenly began sweeping all through her. But when his hand crept around to the front of her and gently caressed her breast through the towel, she jerked away from him and quickly stood up. She faced him, her hands across her breasts, her eyes fearful.

"What is it?" he wanted to know.

"Nothing." She said it too quickly, her voice a shade too high.

He grinned. "If you're wondering about my intentions, I'll save you the wonder. They're strictly dishonorable." When she didn't smile at this but continued to look uneasy, he frowned. "Hey, babe," he said gently, "is anything wrong?"

She shook her head, but this, also, was too stiff a gesture. It looked defensive. "I'm just... tense is all. I don't want to think about romance right now, if you don't mind."

He shrugged. She could tell he was disappointed—and concerned. He let it go, though, not wanting to push her. Shelby went into the bathroom to get her robe. She felt very vulnerable and sensitive to him now—and panicky at this new development. How could she handle it? Tomorrow he wouldn't be so quick to accept her excuse about tension. And even if she came up with another excuse, what about the days after that?

She knew Donovan wanted to make love to her for more than just sexual reasons. She knew him well enough to know he felt that sex was an expression of his love, a physical sensuous way of showing how much he cared for her. And he saw no reason not to make love to her, now that he was becoming well again. As far as he knew, they were soon to be married. He had no idea of the terrible truth, which Shelby carried around with her like a nail in her heart.

Shelby looked at herself in the medicine-cabinet

mirror and saw a frightened vulnerable girl. She had always prided herself on being strong and capable enough to handle crises, but now she was facing a crisis that made her quake with self-doubt. How could she possibly make love to him? It would be such a lie—pretending to give herself to him fully, heart and soul, when in only a few weeks she would be in another man's bed as another man's wife. In the mirror Shelby saw herself frowning.

She was a one-man woman, and she knew it. She would have given anything in the world to have Donovan be that man, but that was impossible now. She had made her deal and would have to live with it. So the man who would share her bed for the rest of her life would be Wolfgang, and no matter how much it hurt, she would be faithful to him.

She hung her head. Not only would it be dishonest to go to bed with Donovan at present, she knew, but it would also cheapen them both. He himself would feel dirty about it later if he learned she had known, all the while she was making love to him, that she would leave him for another man.

"Shelby," Donovan called through the bathroom door, "are you all right? Babe, I'm worried about you."

"I—I'm fine. I'm just . . . drying my hair. I'll only be a moment." She shut her eyes tightly and prayed she would find an answer.

No answer came, though. During the next two days Donovan became more aggressive. He loved her, but he also wanted to possess her, for no other reason than he was a virile masculine man and she was the feminine sensuous woman he expected would soon be his wife. His kisses became more impassioned, his embraces more demanding. Shelby had to struggle to break away from him on more than one occasion.

A tension sprang up between them. Donovan was frustrated and confused. He couldn't understand why she didn't want to make love with him. It was not as if they were giddy teenagers out on a first date. They were adults; they were in love, and they had physically expressed that love once already. So why was she avoiding him? He was clearly skeptical of the excuses she gave—that she was fearful of hurting his shoulder, that she was too tense with worry over the continuing East German manhunt.

She *was* nervous about that manhunt. If it had not been for that, she would have told him the truth about her upcoming marriage. She desperately longed to do so. She hated lying to him, even by omission. But there was nothing she could do while he was still weak and convalescing and the East Germans were scouring their city in an attempt to find him.

The sexual situation couldn't go on like this, Shelby knew. Something awful was happening. She realized Donovan was beginning to believe that maybe she really didn't love him anymore, that possibly—just possibly—those words she had uttered in the café were true. She could see the simmering resentment in his brooding eyes as he flirted with these thoughts, trying hard to fight them down.

There was another reason, too, that the situation couldn't continue without exploding. Shelby was not made of stone. Seeing his bare broad-shouldered physique each day, day after day; his flat hard stomach above his low-slung pants—this was having an undeniable effect on her. At night they slept in the same single bed, often with his arms around her, her covered breasts brushing against his muscular chest. She had borrowed one of Diana's nightgowns for her stay here because it was thick and absolutely unsexy; in fact, it was downright frumpy. But this didn't lessen the tingling yearning she felt when she lay against Donovan's sleeping form at night, his face at the crook of her neck, his breath warm against her tender skin.

At times like these she felt as if a low-voltage charge of sensuality were surging all through her. Hearing him speak about how much he cared for her only made matters worse. It weakened Shelby's will and tormented her with a passion she knew she had to suppress.

The situation came to a head on a Wednesday morning. Donovan rejected her latest excuses about concern for his shoulder.

"My shoulder be damned!" he said. "I want you, and I want you before this day is through." She had to leave for the legation on prearranged business, but she knew that when she returned that evening, he intended to make love to her, and nothing was going to stop him.

What could she do? She was tense all day, wondering how she would handle his move when he made it. But then, just before nightfall, hurrying footsteps echoed in the hall and a banging sounded at their door, jarring them with shock and interrupting everything.

CHAPTER TWENTY-THREE

THEY BOTH STARED at the door. When the knock came again, Donovan grabbed a brick from the bookcase and took up a position at the side of the doorframe, holding the brick aloft.

"Who is it?" Shelby asked through the door, trying to keep her voice calm.

"It's Wolfgang."

She breathed a sigh of relief. She removed the chair that was braced against the knob and opened the door. Wolfgang shot into the room, his expression stern. He glanced at Donovan standing with the brick poised for action.

"Good," Wolfgang said. "I see at least you are not so sickly that you cannot clobber your friends."

"You're lucky I'm as sickly as I am," said Donovan, lowering the makeshift weapon, "or I would clobber you. You're no friend of mine. You're the one who took Shelby to the café to let her see me as the Lion. If it hadn't been for you, none of this would be happening."

"Donovan," Shelby interceded delicately, "he's also the one who...arranged the mix-up of release papers."

"And I am also the one," said Wolfgang urgently, "who has come here now to tell you that you must leave. How badly are you hurt? Can you walk down to my car?"

"He can't leave," protested Shelby. "He's still very weak."

"What's the situation?" Donovan asked Wolfgang, realizing that it must be urgent or Wolfgang would not be there.

"The *Vopos* have shifted their door-to-door search to this area. I found out only recently. The platoon assigned to this sector has searched the four blocks north of here. They are on the way here now. Quickly, there is no time."

Donovan was bare-chested, his arm in his sling. He went to the closet for his black leather jacket.

"But he can't go out in his condition," Shelby protested worriedly. "If they stop your car and find him, they'll know he's been wounded. He can barely walk or sit up straight without leaning slightly, favoring his hurt shoulder."

Wolfgang looked her directly in the eyes. "There is no choice."

"He's right," said Donovan. He handed her the jacket. "Here, put this on over my shoulders."

"Not that," said Wolfgang. "That will give you away for sure. They are looking for the man wearing that jacket."

Before anyone had the chance to return to the closet for another garment, the sound of vehicles came up from the street below, followed by a commotion as the vehicles stopped and people jumped out. "The lights," Donovan said to Shelby. She shut them off. Then the three of them went to the window and looked out past the curtain at the scene below. Two personnel carriers had arrived, and gray-uniformed *Vopos* had unloaded from them. The *Vopos* were fanning out now, entering the buildings on both sides of the street.

"Too late," said Wolfgang. He quickly glanced around the small room. "There is no place to hide you?"

"No," moaned Shelby. She had already looked at every possibility during the first few days of Donovan's stay there.

The sound of boots tromping around on the bottom floor filtered up the stairway. "What can we do?" Shelby asked in near panic.

"This," said Donovan. His expression was grim—and also saddened and very loving. He drew Shelby near and gazed into her eyes. Then he kissed her tenderly. It was a farewell kiss, and it frightened her. Afterward he pulled open the door and started out.

"No!" she cried.

He turned to face her. "I can't implicate you. I'm lost already. There's no sense in dragging you down with me."

Shelby saw he was determined to go. She turned to Wolfgang. Silently, with her eyes, she pleaded with him to do something. At the back of her mind she knew that anything he might do would be a desperate act and that she had no right to ask such a thing of him. But she asked it anyway. Wolfgang held her eyes for the briefest second as the sound of a man's heavy boots came up the stairway toward their floor. Then he sprang into action. He grasped Donovan by his good arm and pulled him back into the room.

Donovan was caught off guard. "What do you think you're doing?" he demanded as Wolfgang shoved him into the armchair. He was too weakened to rise up quickly enough. Before he could respond, Wolfgang grasped the black jacket from Shelby and started out the door. He quickly put it on—just as the *Vopo* who had been sent to search the rooms on this upper floor reached the top of the stairs. Wolfgang rushed past him.

"Hey!" shouted the *Vopo*, surprised by the flash of motion and the sight of the black leather coat. "*Warten Sie!* Halt!"

Wolfgang bounded down the stairs, unheeding. The *Vopo* turned and rushed after him, drawing his pistol from its holster at his waist.

Shelby gasped, and her hand went to her throat. She closed the door. She and Donovan both went to the window and watched as Wolfgang ran out the front of the building into the cold darkened street. An instant later the *Vopo* appeared, shouting for him to halt. Wolfgang continued running. He was almost to the corner of the building across the street when the *Vopo* fired two shots in rapid succession. Part of the masonry from the building near Wolfgang chipped off, only inches from his skull.

Wolfgang halted. He raised his arms up high to

show he was not armed. He turned to face that *Vopo* and the other *Vopos* who had rushed out into the street, alerted by the gunshots. Shelby's heart was in her throat. *He's finished now,* she thought. *There's no way he can escape. They'll look inside the coat, see the dried blood staining the lining. They'll know he's not the Lion, but they'll know, too, that he was involved in Donovan's escape.*

But then Wolfgang did something startlingly unexpected. He started stalking briskly toward the *Vopo* who had shot at him, cursing angrily. The *Vopo* looked dumbfounded and shouted for him to halt. Wolfgang kept coming forward, though, declaring, "What kind of fool are you to shoot at me like this? What kind of moron!"

The *Vopo*'s eyes went wide. He held the pistol aimed at Wolfgang, not knowing what to do. Other *Vopos* were near him now, including the grizzled old sergeant of the detail. "Halt!" tried the *Vopo* one last time.

"Shut up, you fool," said Wolfgang, reaching him. "And get that blasted thing out of my face." He slapped the gun aside. The *Vopo*'s face went red. Wolfgang stood there glaring at him, his fists on his hips.

The *Vopo* turned his pistol back toward Wolfgang, but the sergeant pushed the muzzle of the gun down so that it was facing the street. The sergeant looked at Wolfgang harshly, then looked at his *Vopo*. When he asked what had happened, the *Vopo* told him that Wolfgang had started running from him when he ordered him to halt.

"Of course I ran, you blithering idiot!" declared Wolfgang. "What do you expect me to do when you pull a gun on me like some trigger-happy hoodlum?" He turned the force of his rage on the sergeant now. "Do you have no better sense than to train your men to draw weapons and fire without asking a single question first?"

The sergeant was not cowed by Wolfgang's aggressive tactics. He regarded Wolfgang with a cold look. "Who are you?" he demanded.

"Wolfgang Friedrich Manfred von Heller."

The name was not lost on the sergeant, nor was the reputation that went along with it. This was shown in his expression. His tone was only slightly less severe, though, when he said, "Baron, we are searching for an escaped fugitive. You must have heard about it on the newscasts. He was last seen with a black coat exactly like that."

"Oh, well that explains it," said Wolfgang with biting sarcasm. "There must be no more than a hundred men in Germany wearing a coat like mine. So naturally it makes only sense that you will have your *Vopos* fire upon every one of them. What could be more reasonable?"

A crowd had gathered in the chilly street, watching the exchange. People were leaning out of windows from the upper stories of the bordering buildings. The sergeant and Wolfgang were staring at each other as the *Vopos* stood around wondering at the outcome. Tension was in the air. The sergeant seemed undecided about whether to let Wolfgang go on his way—possibly with an apology—or to search the coat thoroughly and take him down to headquarters for interrogation.

"Tell me," said Wolfgang, pretending boredom with the subject, "is there any reason you can think of why I might run from a *Vopo*—other than fear that the man is a trigger-happy dolt who might blow my head off out of sheer incompetence?"

The sergeant considered this. The *Vopo* in question was burning with frustrated anger at having to take such abuse. The sergeant asked Wolfgang, "What are you doing in this area?"

"None of your business."

"If you do not tell me, I will arrest you for questioning."

"I was visiting my fiancée. Up there." He pointed to the slightly opened window of the safehouse. Donovan leaped to the side, out of sight. Shelby had been partly hidden by the curtains. Now she parted them and stood clearly before the window. A flashlight was turned on her. She squinted against the bright beam.

"Very nice," said the sergeant, trying to defuse the situation. "I congratulate you."

"Thank you," said Wolfgang stiffly.

The sergeant turned to his *Vopos*. "Get on with it! We're behind schedule already. Move, move on to the next building."

The *Vopos* dispersed, continuing on down the block. The sergeant left with them. Wolfgang strode down the street to his Porsche and roared off.

Shelby closed the curtains and moved back into the

room. She lowered herself into a chair, weak and deflated. She felt relief that Wolfgang was safe and that
the *Vopos* were no longer searching this building, but
she felt a sinking sensation, too, as she realized that
now there was not even the slightest chance she could
ask him to free her from their agreement. The image
flashed into her mind of the way the mortar of the
wall had churned up as the bullets struck inches from
his head. He had risked so much for her—more than
she had any right to expect.

She glanced up. Donovan was standing over her,
eyes narrowed. "What did he mean," he asked warily, "when he called you 'my fiancée'?"

CHAPTER TWENTY-FOUR

THE MOMENT of truth. Shelby knew she could pretend no longer. She had hated lying to him all these past days, though it had been for his own good. Now she no longer had the strength to continue the lie. She saw how suspicious he was, and now he was oversensitive, too, for he was a proud man, and his pride had been hurt by his being forced to stay inside while another man risked his life to save him.

Donovan ran his hand through his hair, trying to reason out the situation. He clearly did not want to believe the thoughts coming into his mind.

"It's not like von Heller to do something like that—risk his life for me. He's capable of doing it, but not for me." He looked at her. "That means he did it for you. I want to know why he'd do that. Unless you and he mean one hell of a lot to each other."

She wanted to tell him the truth now, this instant, but the words would not come. Her voice refused to speak.

"The reason you've been so standoffish about making love to me..." he said. "It doesn't have anything to do with him, does it?"

"I don't love him," she replied helplessly. "I do love you."

Suddenly he grasped her arm and pulled her up to face him. His eyes were tormented. "What the hell did he mean when he called you his fiancée?"

She couldn't hold it in any longer. "I'm going to marry him."

The silence that greeted this was electric. Their stares locked. Shelby felt she was hardly breathing. *Now he'll realize the truth,* she thought. *He'll put two and two together and see that I made a deal to free him from prison. He'll know there's no other reason on earth that could have made me sacrifice myself this way, giving up his precious love. Now he'll say he understands....*

"So you do love him after all," he accused.

"No! That's not it at all!"

"And those words you said to me at the café—they were all true."

"Donovan, they were lies!" How could he be thinking this? She had been so sure that when she told him she was marrying Wolfgang, he'd understand the real reason she had made the deal—that it was a sign of how deeply she did love him.

But he wasn't thinking this at all. Instead he was quick to believe the worst thing possible about her— that in her heart she had been unfaithful to him.

Donovan laughed, a harsh laugh of pain and anger. "I see it all now. I must have been blind not to see it earlier. You don't love me. That's why you wouldn't go to bed with me. And those words you said at the café—they were true. You never would have denied them afterward if I hadn't got captured and wounded as a result of your actions."

"Donovan," she pleaded, "it's not true."

"Of course it's true! I know why you took back those words. It's because you knew I'd never stay here with you if I realized you love von Heller instead of me. So you lied to me. You told me the words were said in anger and weren't true."

"They weren't true!"

"But the fact is," he continued on heatedly, ignoring her protests, "you had to take back the words, to say they weren't true, because you knew that that was the only way you'd get me to stay in the same room with you. And you didn't want me walking out that door. Oh, no, because then your guilt would be even worse. Then you wouldn't be responsible just for getting me captured but maybe killed, as well."

She went to him and touched him, trying to make him listen, to make him understand, but he pushed away her hands, so upset that he couldn't even stand to be touched by her.

Now Shelby was becoming upset, too. She knew he was hurt; still, she felt he should have more faith in her than *that*. Here she was, sacrificing her happiness because of her love for him, and he was accusing her of being shallow and unprincipled, of worrying only about her own selfish desires. What had she ever done to deserve such a low opinion of her integrity?

He went to the closet and pulled out a flannel shirt.

"What are you doing?" she asked in alarm, afraid that she already knew.

He removed his arm from the sling and let it hang by his side. He began putting on the shirt, trying to slip the sleeve over his arm. "Help me with this," he said, wincing.

"No! You can't go out there now. They'll kill you."

He continued putting on the shirt without her help. Sweat covered his face. When he finished, he donned an overcoat.

"Donovan, please," she begged, "don't go out there. Here, I'll tell you why I'm marrying Wolfgang if you're so distrustful of me that you won't figure it out for yourself. It's because he and I made a—"

"Shut up." His eyes were on fire. "No more lies, Shelby. I couldn't bear any more lies from you."

He had never spoken to her like this. It was a measure of how deeply she had hurt him. He stuffed his papers and other articles into his pockets, then started for the door. She tried to stop him, but he held up his hand, ordering her away. He seemed like a wild man. She tried to reason with him, but it was useless. He jerked open the door so hard it slammed back against the wall. Then he stalked out.

She couldn't let him go out into the night alone. The *Vopos* were only a block away, and even if he avoided them, he'd probably be stopped and recognized at the border checkpoint—if he made it that far. It would take a major effort for him to hide the fact he was still weak and in pain from his wound.

She put on a jacket and went after him. She saw him hailing a taxi when he reached the intersection. His eyes warned her away from trying to share it with him. Helplessly she watched him get into it and drive off. It took a moment for her to find another cab. When she did, she ordered it to take her to the Freidrichstrasse checkpoint. She remembered what he had told her of the way he operated as the Lion. Two different checkpoints: one for the Lion, the other for Donovan Hawkes. He couldn't go out as the Lion now, under the false identity of Rutger Schmidt. That meant he would have to risk crossing under his own name, using his own papers.

When she arrived at the checkpoint, he was already there, inside the lighted guardhouse, processing through. She stood outside in the darkness, watching through the windows, listening to the electric hum of the overhead high-power lines. Even from here she could see the intense strain on his face from the effort of standing up straight, pretending he was healthy and whole. She was aware of the lifeless way his left arm dangled at his side, but neither of the guards seemed to be. Donovan said something and grinned at one of the men. What strength that must have taken, Shelby thought—to force that grin through the pain and physical weakness that must be racking him.

The guard looked suspicious for a moment. Shelby tensed. Maybe it was because Donovan was not wearing a suit. In his persona of the diplomat he always wore one, and they were used to seeing him like that at this checkpoint. But if that disturbed the guard, it didn't seem to disturb him for long. As Shelby watched, Donovan's passport was handed back to him, and he was nodded through the far end of the shack. All that remained now was the customs and currency shed—more formalities. She watched as he was passed through these, too.

A moment later he crossed the broad white line that marked the boundary between East and West Berlin, and five seconds after that he staggered a few feet to the side, looking as if he would collapse at any moment onto the black concrete. Shelby entered the checkpoint shack and processed through as quickly as she could. By the time she had got out into the cold night and had scanned the area, desperate for some sign of him, Donovan was gone.

She went to his apartment. She saw his silhouette against the curtains of the illuminated front room. When she knocked on the door and called to him, though, he refused to answer or let her inside. She went to the nearest telephone and summoned Dr. Rinehardt, who arrived quickly. Donovan opened the door to Rinehardt and let him in, but then he stood in the doorway, blocking entrance to Shelby. She had not been trying to enter; she knew she was not welcome there. She only wanted to see him, to know that he was all right.

He was not all right. He stood in the doorway looking at her, leaning partly against the frame to support his weight. His face and his flannel shirt were drenched in sweat from the strain of the past hour.

He was trying hard not to show his fatigue and pain, but the rigidity of his features and the way his teeth clenched gave him away. He looked as though he would collapse at any moment.

They stared at each other, Shelby feeling great anguish. Donovan's eyes were fiercely accusing and filled with the bitterness of betrayal. He staggered back into the room and shut the door.

She knew then that it was over between them.

There was no hope they could ever be together again. She knew him well enough to know he would refuse ever to see her now. It was not just that he had been hurt badly and felt betrayed. Mostly it was that he was sure she didn't love him, that she loved Wolfgang instead. She had told him differently, but he refused to believe her. If he didn't believe her now, what were the chances that he would believe her later, once she was married to Wolfgang? And even if he did, what would it matter? She would be the Baroness Wolfgang von Heller then, the wife of another man.

Oh, damn him, she thought with sudden pain, turning away from the door. How dare he not believe her? How dare he not realize the deal she had made with Wolfgang? What an insulting low opinion of her he must have! *Oh Donovan,* she thought, *I deserve better from you. Couldn't you have just a tiny bit of faith in me?*

She went to her apartment and packed a single bag. Then she went to Wolfgang.

He was happy to see her, but surprised. When the

butler announced her, he came out from his den, looking strong and fresh and untroubled. He wore a chocolate brown shirt and corduroys, his shirt sleeves rolled up. "I did not expect you to come to me," he said, "until after Hawkes was healed and smuggled safely back into the West."

"He's back," she said impassively. "He left the safehouse right after your brush with the *Vopos*."

Wolfgang was amazed. "But that is absurd! He was safe there. They wouldn't have returned to search that sector again once they had left it."

"Wolfgang...I'm very tired."

"Tell me. He crossed back safely?"

"Yes. He risked everything on a reckless bold gamble. He went right up to the checkpoint and presented his own passport. He tried to hide the fact that he was wounded and on the verge of fainting—and he succeeded."

Wolfgang looked thoughtful. "That is just like him—foolhardy and brave." Turning his attention to her, he saw how emotionally drained she looked, how nearly traumatized. "Forgive me," he said gently, taking her arm. "Of course you are tired and distressed. I will take you to our room. You can bathe and rest." His hand on her arm was firm and supportive. "Werner," he called out to his butler, "bring a glass of wine."

She let him lead her up the winding stairs. She felt as if she had no will of her own now, no power. She was depending on his strength to carry her through.

"You are staying with me now, yes? I do not mean

only for tonight. You are moving in to live with me?''

"Yes," she answered wearily, the fatigue and emotional drain of the past hours catching up to her. It was barely ten o'clock; yet she felt exhausted. "I'll get the rest of my things in the morning from my apartment and the safehouse.''

She didn't protest as he led her into the large bedroom of his suite, instead of taking her to the guest bedroom. Shelby surveyed the room. The huge bed had a covering of plush white fur and a headboard of elaborately hand-carved oak. Its four pedestals were also of hand-carved oak. The room's furniture was sturdy and traditional in design. A rich Persian rug covered part of the floor, and the white masonry walls were hung with paintings and artifacts from feudal days. An enclosed fireplace—an addition of just this past century—kept the room cozy and warm. Adjoining this chamber was the modern bathroom, with its gleaming silver fixtures.

Werner appeared with a glass of wine on a silver platter, and Shelby accepted it gratefully. Wolfgang nodded to the butler, who bowed and departed. Then he turned to Shelby, longing in his eyes.

"If I could just be alone for a while. . . ?" she said.

"Of course." Wolfgang went to her and put his arms round her. He looked at her with intensity. When he tried to kiss her, she turned her head to the side.

He scowled. For a moment he didn't speak. Then he said tightly, "You are tired.''

"Yes, Wolfgang, I am."

He released her. "Get some rest. This is the best thing for you." He looked at her once more, then left the room, shutting the double doors after himself.

Soon Shelby was in her nightgown, in Wolfgang's bed, under the heavy covers. She wanted the welcome blackness of sleep, but before she could allow herself that luxury, there were things she had to get straight in her mind, had to make herself accept.

The first was that since she would be Wolfgang's wife, she would do everything she could to make him a good mate. It wouldn't do to deliberately make life miserable for him. He had done nothing to deserve such treatment. No, he had upheld his part of the deal in good faith, and now she would uphold hers. In the months and years to come, she would work hard to make him happy; she would try to make him proud to have her as his wife.

The second thing Shelby had to accept was a lot harder, but she knew she had to do it. To give added weight to it—to make herself fully realize that there would be no escape—she forced herself to state the facts out loud.

"I will never see Donovan again. I'll never be held by him again. I'll never kiss him. I'll...." She had to stop for a moment to choke back the sob that threatened to burst from her throat. "I'll never be his wife...or make love to him...or bear his children. He's no longer part of my life and never will be again, not ever."

She had tried to be strong while forcing herself to

say this. Now, satisfied, she allowed herself to lay her head upon the pillow, ready for sleep. *I'm strong,* she thought to herself. *I can take it. I'm really... very...strong....*

She had to stop thinking. Because the more she thought, the more she realized that her white silk pillowcase was becoming soaking wet from her silently flowing tears.

CHAPTER TWENTY-FIVE

WHEN SHE AWOKE in the morning, she was still groggy with sleep, not yet fully alert. She was so used to waking up in bed with Donovan that she instinctively moved over on the bed, her eyes still shut, and put her arms around the male figure beside her. She snuggled her head against his chest. A small smile played upon her lips, for her mind was still on the dream she had had of Donovan. It was her hands that first noticed something was wrong. The back she was touching was not quite so broad, and the flanks were leaner and firmer.

She opened her eyes to see Wolfgang looking at her. She jerked away from him and moved to the opposite side of the bed. Wolfgang looked disappointed but said nothing. He seemed to be willing to give her the time she needed to adjust. He was clearly anxious, though, to have that time to be as short as possible. Shelby could tell he wanted to make love to her—and wanted it badly.

She got out of bed and put on a robe, then went to a chair and began brushing out her long chestnut hair. There was no vanity in the bedroom. That was something that would have to change. The tall windows were open, and a gentle breeze fluttered the wispy curtains. Rays of sunlight filtered in, brightening the room. Beneath their windowsill was the rooftop of one of the archer's turrets of the castle and beyond that was a magnificent view.

"You are afraid to be in the same bed with me?" Wolfgang asked with a slight grin, teasingly.

"For now I am. But I won't be tonight."

"And why is there so much difference between now and tonight?"

"Tonight we'll be man and wife," she said, brushing her hair more forcefully as she uttered the words.

He looked surprised. "You expect we will be married by this evening?" He propped himself up in the bed, his back against the headboard, the fur bedcover slipping down to below his navel. Shelby saw his well-developed chest and flat hard stomach before quickly looking away. Wolfgang grabbed a cigarette from the night table and lit it. "*Liebling*, such a thing is not possible."

"We don't need a big ceremony, do we?" she said entreatingly. She came over to the bed and sat on the edge beside him. "I just want a simple ceremony, just you and me and a minister, and I'd like it right away."

Wolfgang gazed at her fondly, completely misinterpreting her motives. He didn't realize she wanted to be married soon so she could get the terrible thing over with, so she could have it behind her, where she could stop dreading it, stop hoping forlornly for some last-minute reprieve.

He reached out and covered her hand with his. "I, too, want you as my wife right away," he said, "but such a thing is impossible. There are traditions regarding my family that have evolved through the centuries that must be respected. The mayor of Idor-Amstein must be told of the coming marriage by me personally. He must have time to arrange for the festivities and for the ceremony itself. The village will throw a celebration for the wedding that will last two days. On the morning of the second day we will be married."

Shelby felt gloomy at this news. She felt so bad already about marrying a man she didn't love. The last thing she wanted was a big, joyous, public ceremony to celebrate it. She would certainly feel no joy. What she wanted most was to skulk away into a corner and have a quiet guilt-ridden little civil rite.

"If we have to let the villagers have a celebration for the wedding," she asked, "how long must we wait before they can stage it?"

He shrugged. "A month at the earliest."

"That long?" she commented with keen disappointment.

"There are invitations to be sent out, plans to be made. My darling, you do not understand my position. I cannot hurry this. The tradition dates back to feudal days. The villagers consider it an honor to stage the ceremony and festivities for the marriage of the first-born son of each generation of von Hellers. It is the social event of each generation. They must be permitted to honor me this way, as their fathers honored my father and their grandfathers honored my grandfather. To refuse them such a thing would be a great insult.''

"I understand," she said quietly. She understood, but she still hated the idea. To wait a month would only prolong the torture. She needed that gold ring on her finger now, so she could stop resisting the situation emotionally.

Wolfgang pulled her toward him. When her face was very near, he grinned, a taunting sensual grin, and said in a deeper tone, "Just because we must wait for the ceremony does not mean we must wait for the rights of marriage." He put a hand to her cheek and brushed it softly, then moved down her throat, then—

She pulled away from him. He scowled in bewilderment.

"We'll wait," she said.

"But *why*? Surely you don't believe in the petty rules of conventional morality?"

"I believe in two people sharing the same bed after they're married and not before. That's one 'petty rule' I'm quite comfortable with, thank you." She didn't mention that that rule had been broken regarding Donovan. So many rules had been broken regarding him, so many beliefs and ways of thinking had been overwhelmed by the force of her love for him—and his for her. With Donovan she had known instinctively that it was right. But with Wolfgang....
"No," she said, shaking her head. "When I'm your wife, I'll be the best wife I can be, in...every respect. We're not married yet."

She saw how disappointed he was. She was sure he was thinking about violating that revered centuries-old tradition he had told her about. That would be fine with Shelby. Let him violate it! Let them be married now, right away, without any ceremony other than a civil one. But no, she saw him shake his head and realized that his sense of duty had won out over his love and lust.

He got out of bed and stretched. She saw with relief that he wore pajama bottoms. He pressed the button of the intercom set in the wall opposite the windows. "We'll be down for breakfast shortly," he said.

"Wolfgang?" asked Shelby.

He looked at her.

"I—I can't stay here. Not for a month. I couldn't bear just sitting around, waiting. I'll go crazy if I have to do that. Isn't there any place we can go until the ceremony?"

A thought seemed to strike him, but then a hesitant look came over his face, as if he were reluctant to mention it. "I do have a business trip I must make." He looked away from her, out the window. "I had planned to make it alone."

"Take me," she said eagerly. "Please."

"It is business," he repeated in an ominous tone.

"I won't get in your way, and there's nothing for me here. I won't go back to the legation. They'll have my request for an indefinite leave of absence by the end of the day."

He considered this as he stood gazing out at the panoramic view. He took a deep draw of smoke from his cigarette and exhaled it into the morning air. "All right," he said, "I will take you." He ventured a smile. "It can be quite nice, really, if we arrange it properly. I must hit Amsterdam, Hamburg and Paris, as well as other cities. It is a buying trip for me. During the days I will attend to my business matters. In the evenings we can be together, for dinner, for the theaters, the operas. There is much to see in these cities."

"Thank you," she said, going over to join him at the windows. "And...thank you for being so understanding about my wanting to wait until after the ceremony." She really was grateful to him for that. She went up on her tiptoes and kissed him chastely, platonically on the cheek.

Wolfgang's eyes began smoldering. He pulled her against him suddenly, embracing her. His lips descended passionately on hers. Shelby did not fight him; she let her body react honestly on its own. But the reaction was one that made Wolfgang thrust her away from him in disgust after only a moment. She had gone cold and unresponsive in his arms. To Wolfgang it must have been like kissing a lifeless mannequin.

Wolfgang glared out the window, breathing tightly through gritted teeth. Shelby had not meant to hurt him. That was the last thing she wanted to do.

"Wolfgang," she said gently, "I didn't act that way on purpose. My body just responded like that on its own."

He glared at her. "You think that makes it better?

That makes it a thousand times worse!'' He stalked away from her to shower and dress.

THE TRIP LASTED almost an entire month—through the end of November and into December. If Shelby had been a different sort of person—the sort who could shut out her feelings—she would have had a wonderful time. They traveled to eight cities in all, and in each they stayed at the finest hotels and dined at the most elegant restaurants. In Frankfurt it was accommodations at the Hessischer Hof and dinner at the famous Bruckenkeller; in Paris, the Ritz and Le Sanglier; at Lake Constance they resided at Langenargen, situated directly on the lakefront, and dined at Chalet Suisse Coralle.

The trip was first class all the way. Wolfgang, Shelby learned, was accustomed to the very best. Their boxes at the symphonies were always the finest, as were their tables in the restaurants. Shelby learned something else surprising, too. Everywhere Wolfgang went, he was greeted with respect and esteem. Concierges went out of their way to please him. Dining-room captains delivered complimentary bottles of their finest wines to his table. Each time they arrived at a new hotel, elaborate bouquets of flowers awaited them.

This was not just because Wolfgang was wealthy, Shelby realized, but more because he was recognized as a man of excitement, flair and style. Shelby was surprised to find that his reputation extended far beyond the boundaries of Berlin and even of Germany. He seemed to be known throughout Europe.

Shelby liked the way he was so casual about accepting the reverence bestowed upon him. He was completely unpretentious and shunned any notion of self-importance. If Shelby had not seen him treated this way with her own eyes, she never would have known about it. Wolfgang had never said anything about it—and probably never would. When she mentioned to him the awe with which people seemed to regard him, he just shrugged it off. It was like his manner of dress, which was casual and not particularly stylish; he didn't care for the outward expressions of wealth. He did, though, care for the luxuries his wealth could buy.

In each major city they visited, Wolfgang made sure they caught a performance of that city's symphony. Shelby had known all along he was a lover of classical music. Now her knowledge was reaffirmed as she watched him listening to certain passages being performed, his face locked with intensity. Afterward they sometimes went to congratulate the conductor, and Shelby was surprised to find that the conductors all knew him and welcomed his appreciation, since they respected his discernment.

Though Shelby had previously refused gifts from him, on this trip she made an exception in one area: clothing. The evening entertainments he took her to demanded fashionable expensive apparel that Shelby herself could not afford, so she agreed to buy the gowns and accessories she needed and have the clothiers send the bills to Wolfgang.

Shelby forced herself to go out with Wolfgang nearly every evening, though she was not at all in the mood. She made herself go because she knew that if she did not keep busy, her mind would start wandering to thoughts of Donovan and how things might have been. There was nothing but pain in these thoughts, and she tried to ruthlessly suppress them whenever they came up. She knew she would never see him again. This was not just her intention, but his, as well. He had left word with Mary that Shelby was not to be admitted to his office and her calls were not to be put through. Diana told Shelby he was so bitter about her that she was sure he'd slam the door in her face if she ever tried to visit him at home.

Shelby had no intention of visiting him or calling.

DURING THE MIDDLE of their trip, Shelby saw a side of Wolfgang she had seen only once previously. It happened when she returned to their hotel suite earlier than she had expected after a morning's visit to a famous art museum. Wolfgang was in the midst of a meeting with two men from whom he planned to buy black-market goods. Shelby asked if he wanted her to leave after seeing his look of displeasure, but he said no, he was almost finished.

She took a seat in the living room of their two-bedroom hotel suite and pretended to read. Actually she was watching the discussion. As Wolfgang dealt with the men, he was unsmiling and cold, hostile and quite frightening-looking. He seemed every bit the tough underworld figure his reputation made him out to be. The men seated opposite him at the table were seedy disreputable-looking thugs—the mean-eyed sort whom Shelby would hate to meet in a dark alley. Now she understood why Wolfgang was so careful to arrange his meetings so she would not be there to witness them and why he went to such great lengths to keep his life with her separate from his business affairs. He must have been aware that Shelby would shudder at knowing he was involved with such people.

After the men left, Shelby asked what his dealings with them were.

"They are not my preferred type of contacts," he said as he poured himself a Steinhager from the bar. "They do serve a purpose, though."

"What purpose?"

"They smuggle in the goods that I market illegally. In the early days of my business I myself did the smuggling. As I grew, though, this became too dangerous. These days the large volume I handle makes such personal transport impossible."

"So what you do is just...market the smuggled goods?"

He nodded and took a swallow of his drink. He clearly did not like discussing his business with her. He did answer her, however. "I buy the goods outside East Berlin. They are then brought in to me by a variety of people. I in turn sell them inside East Berlin through a variety of other people. There are many men in my organization."

And do they all look like those last two, she wondered, trying hard not to show how appalled she was by his dealing with them.

That night she had a dream. It was the same dream she often had, in which she imagined herself with a loving husband and happy children. Tonight, though, something was different, and this difference turned her dream into a nightmare.

She envisioned herself watching her young children being bounced on the knees of family friends. The children were laughing and loving every minute of it. When Shelby's eyes focused on these friends, she saw they were the mean-eyed hoodlums Wolfgang had dealt with earlier. Shoulder holsters bulged from under their arms. Shelby knew the men were no threat to her children, though. In fact, there seemed to be genuine warmth between them and her children. Shelby could even see the growing respect and admiration for these men in her children's eyes as they gazed up at the men fondly. . . .

She sat bolt upright in the bed, a cold chill working down her spine. Her face was sweating. It took a long time before she could fall asleep again.

There was only one other time she saw the type of men Wolfgang dealt with. It was in Amsterdam, a week later. He had to meet some men in a bar very briefly, and Shelby happened to be with him, after an evening together at the theater. Amsterdam had a reputation as one of Europe's most dangerous cities, and he didn't trust sending her back to the hotel alone in a taxi, so he took her with him.

The bar was dark, with seminude girls dancing on

a lighted stage. Shelby and Wolfgang were glaringly out of place in their fashionable attire. Wolfgang seemed as coolly untroubled and as at home there, however, as if he had been in an elegant nightclub. The men he dealt with were as disreputable-looking as the others Shelby had seen. They conducted their business in low voices, the men's beady eyes darting about nervously. It took only a moment, then Wolfgang stood up to leave.

"I hear you're getting married," said one of the men, nodding briefly at Shelby. "Who would have guessed it, huh? I mean, you always seemed too hard a chap ever to be the marrying kind."

Another man growled his agreement with this observation.

Wolfgang said nothing. He nodded curtly in parting, then guided Shelby out of the dank dismal bar.

On the way back to their hotel, as they were being driven through the gawdy neon-lit nightlife district, Shelby asked him about this. Surprisingly, Wolfgang admitted it was not just others who thought of him as too hardened ever to fall in love or marry. He himself had always thought this. He had never believed that a tough violent man like him could ever be tamed enough to become a husband to the woman he loved. "I never believed it," he added, "until I met you."

Shelby could see in his eyes how strongly he felt toward her, and it hurt her that he cared so much. She felt guilty she could not feel anything back. She didn't love him now, and she knew in her heart she never would. Oh, if only he were a bad or cruel man, she thought, then at least she could have the satisfaction of hating him. But he was neither of these things.

From the way Wolfgang gazed at her during the ride back, Shelby could tell that once they reached their hotel, he was going to try to make love to her again. He had not made a move in this direction since that night at his castle three weeks earlier, when her limp cold reaction to his passion had disgusted him.

Shelby made a decision. She would not resist. She was no longer opposed to making love to him now, as she had been that night. What she really wanted now was just to get it over with. If he made love to her, it would be a milestone. She would be his then; she could stop torturing herself by pretending there might be some way out of the marriage.

The cab pulled into the well-lit circular driveway fronting their hotel. Wolfgang guided her through the lobby, then up to their suite. The suite was spacious and done almost entirely in white—plush white carpet, overstuffed white sofa and armchairs. The rest of the furniture was chrome-and-glass modern. One wall was composed of large windows that looked out onto the rooftops and neon lights of the bustling city.

Shelby removed her wrap and draped it over the sofa. She wore a strapless sequined gown. Wolfgang removed his overcoat and jacket and then approached her. She stood straight, not backing away, her gaze meeting his. He came directly up to her, his brown eyes smoldering with passion. Shelby felt his lips slowly pressing against hers, his strong arms tightening around her, pulling her slender body against him. She put her hands on the back of his waist, trying to do her part. She felt...absolutely nothing. Her body was limp and unresponsive in his arms, her lips cold beneath his. Though her mind was willing, her body rejected him, refusing to respond to any lips but Donovan's, no matter how overpoweringly handsome Wolfgang was. Her body, at least, was faithful to Donovan.

Wolfgang recoiled from her and stood glaring at her, fire in his eyes. Shelby remained just as he had left her, her arms slightly behind her, her head tilted back and lips parted. It was as if she were some plastic doll, to be manipulated into any position he desired—but only as responsive as a doll, also.

"Bah!" he declared. "Is this the way you uphold our bargain?"

"Wolfgang," she said softly, "I'm sorry. I—maybe it'll get better when we're married. Maybe I just need time."

"You scorn me! Is that supposed to get better in time?"

"That's not true. I don't scorn you."

"Your body does," he raged.

There was nothing she could say to that. It was true and obvious, and they both knew it.

"Do you think you can get out of the marriage this way? Never! I'll never release you from your vow—not even if I must make love to an icicle every night!"

She was so hurt he would think she was doing this

on purpose that she turned and ran from him into her bedroom.

Several moments later, after his emotions had cooled down he came in. "I apologize," he said stiffly. "I know you would not do such a thing for such a reason. You are a woman of integrity. I never should have accused you. It is only that—" his pain showed "—I love you so much that it hurts me you do not love me back." He turned and left her room. Shelby knew he would not try to make love to her again until they were married.

Which would be in less than two weeks.

CHAPTER TWENTY-SIX

THE NEXT DAY they flew back to West Germany for a meeting Wolfgang had scheduled in Hamburg, the nation's great port city on the Elbe River. While he met his contacts, Shelby went to visit the city's many canals, which she had fallen in love with years earlier when she had lived in Germany.

Shortly after she left her hotel she noticed someone was following her. All she saw of him was a momentary flash of a dark overcoat and hat; he disappeared when she turned to face him. She thought perhaps it was her imagination. Knowing the sort of men Wolfgang dealt with did make her jumpier than usual. As she walked along the Niederbaum, which crossed several of the canals, she kept glancing over her shoulder, worrying about being kidnapped, or something equally melodramatic. But no one was there. *No,* she thought, *it must have been my imagination.*

She boarded a sight-seeing boat at the St. Paul wharf for a tour around the picturesque harbor. As one of Europe's largest seaports, Hamburg had more than fifty separate docks. Shelby passed dozens of ships flying the flags of various nations. They were many luxury yachts among them, since this was a favored port for the very rich.

The water was clear blue and placid, and the crisp air was invigorating. Off in the distance she could see the steeple of the *Rathaus*—the town hall. The *Rathaus* was one of the marvels of Hamburg. The marvel was that it did not sink straight into the ground—which was extremely swampy. The condition that caused all the canals to crisscross the city also caused water to permeate the ground. The reason the *Rathaus* did not sink, even though it was a massive concrete-and-steel building with many pillars and arches, was simple: Its foundation was built upon enormous wooden stilts hammered deep into the soggy earth—eight thousand of them! Most of the major buildings in Hamburg were built upon stilts in this way.

When Shelby looked around to catch the view on the other side of the harbor, she saw from the corner of her eye a man in a dark overcoat. Suddenly a hand descended upon her shoulder. Her breath caught as she turned to face the man.

"Dr. Rinehardt," she exclaimed in surprise. She had not seen or spoken to him since that day she had summoned him to Donovan's apartment three weeks earlier, after Donovan's risky crossing back into the West.

"I must speak to you," said Rinehardt, looking grim.

"What's wrong?" she asked quickly. "What's happened to him?" She knew something terrible must have befallen Donovan. Why else would Rinehardt be here? At the back of her mind she had been anticipating for weeks that something would occur;

she knew how self-destructively Donovan was reacting to her upcoming marriage.

"He staged another crossing," said Rinehardt in a hushed voice, glancing left and right to make sure none of the other sightseers could overhear.

"Oh, no! Did they catch him?"

"Almost. He managed to bring it off, but it was very nearly disastrous." He became animated as he declared, "He *never* should have crossed back into the East to do this thing. They know what he looks like now. The search is still on. And his shoulder—it is stronger, but by no means fully healed."

A steam whistle blew nearby as a large freighter approached the harbor. The captain of the boat Shelby was on answered with a blast from his own steam whistle. The freighter passed very close to them, churning up the blue water between the two vessels.

"How did he accomplish the crossing this time?" she asked.

"In an inexcusably reckless way. I do not know what has come over him. He crossed into the East on a forged passport with no disguise whatever but a paste-on mustache and clear-lens glasses. Then he rendezvoused with the crosser at the top of one of the tallest buildings near the wall. You know him, I believe. Hans Dietrich is his name."

Oh, God, thought Shelby. She hoped he was all right. Rinehardt had said the crossing was nearly disastrous. How nearly, she wondered.

"They had an accomplice on the street, on the Western side of the wall. It was not I. When Donovan told me his plan, I refused. I told him to abandon it; the risk of his being killed was far too great." Rinehardt shrugged, looking pained and grim. "He ignored my warning. For the first time in all these years he proceeded without me."

Shelby touched his arm in sympathy. She could see how affected he was that his deep-feeling fatherly relationship with Donovan had come to an end. "How did he cross?"

"His new accomplice in the West—a boy named Christian—shot him a line with a grappling-hook launcher—the kind commandos use for scaling cliffs. The line shot out right over the wall, onto the top of the building where Donovan and his refugee waited. Donovan secured the line to the roof while his accomplice tied his end to the base of a lamppost. Donovan and Hans Dietrich clipped eyelet hooks onto the line—they had already attached the hooks to harness belts around their chests. Then they slid down the line, one after the other, right over the wall."

Shelby could see how dangerous this was. They would be helpless as they raced down the sloping line, suspended in the air.

"The only precaution he took," Rinehardt said, "was to make the crossing at night, so the line would be less visible. Still, the *Vopos* saw them and began firing. But by the time they sighted their weapons in the darkness, Donovan and Dietrich were safely across the wall."

What a brilliant idea it was, Shelby thought. She

knew the "death strip" on the East Berlin side of the wall was brightly lit up at night, but the floodlights were directed down toward the ground, where crossings were anticipated. No one expected a people smuggler to go sailing over the death strip from above and then right across the wall.

"They're both unhurt, you say?" she asked with concern.

"This time, yes, but they came as close as one can to disaster. Listen, you will be amazed at this. The bullets from one of the *Vopos'* submachine guns hit so near to them the heel of Hans Dietrich's left boot was shot off. Three inches higher, it would have been his ankle. Three feet higher, he would be a dead man."

Shelby shuddered.

"It was reckless...reckless!" declared Rinehardt. "Not so much the crossing, but the fact that the Lion went back into the East to bring it off. He must never do this again! But he will; I know he will, and his schemes will become more and more daring until. .." He paused. His lined old face became intense. "*Fräulein*, he must be stopped before it is too late. You must stop him."

"Me?" she said, astounded.

"No one else can talk to him. He no longer listens to me."

"He won't listen to me, either," she protested. "He won't even see me."

His eyes became imploring. "*Fräulein*, you are the cause of his self-destructive behavior. I do not say blame, I say 'cause.' Whatever it is that happened between you and him, it's the reason he is this way now, the reason life suddenly means so little to him. Only you can save him. Only you can talk sense into him.''

She felt helpless. "But he won't even see me."

"I can arrange that. I can tell him to be at a certain place at a certain time. I will have to lie to him about the reason, and I hate doing so—I have never lied to him previously—but I will do it if you will be there when he arrives, to try to reason with him. You will do this thing, yes?''

Turbulent emotions roiled inside her. Her expression became agonized. Finally the answer welled up from deep within and burst forth. "No!" Her voice became pleading. "Dr. Rinehardt, don't you see? It wouldn't do any good. He wouldn't talk to me even if you did manage to get us together. He...he hates me.''

Rinehardt looked at her with wise aged eyes that said, "You are not fooling either of us."

This only made Shelby more flustered. "Well, he won't speak to me, that's for sure, no matter what he thinks of me.''

"He will not speak to anyone else about this; that is for sure. He is so crazy with grief that he seems determined to get himself captured or killed. Already he is planning a new crossing.''

"Oh, no," she said despairingly.

"It is more reckless even than the last. *Fräulein*, someone must break through his wall of self-destructiveness to make him see what he is doing to himself. You must try. Even if you feel the effort is doomed, you must try. Do you not owe him this at least?''

She shut her eyes. The sea breeze ruffled through her hair. ''Oh, why do you do this to me?'' she asked tormentedly. She had tried so hard for so long now to resign herself to never seeing Donovan again; to force herself to accept that he was part of her past, that there would be no further contact at all. It had taken great effort, but finally she had convinced herself, and now this man was asking her to throw all of that away.

She knew what would happen if she agreed to see him again. Her heart would begin grasping at straws, pretending their meeting might somehow change her fate so that she and he could be together again, forever this time. She would be tantalized once more by impossible hopes and dreams, and then she would meet with him and be subjected to his bitterness and scorn. She couldn't bear to have him look at her that way.

''No! I won't do it. I can't. Don't you understand? It wouldn't help anyway. He wouldn't listen to anything I have to say. Don't you see that? All it would do would be to make my life more terribly painful than it already is.'

Dr. Rinehardt became skittish at her raised tone of voice. He seemed disappointed, too. He tipped his hat to her and said, *''Auf wiedersehen,''* then moved away quickly. He stayed clear across the deck from her until the boat docked a few moments later. Then he left, hurrying down the plank and onto the wharf.

When Shelby disembarked, she immediately began looking for a phone kiosk so she could call Diana to ask about Hans's escape. On the way she picked up a copy of the morning *Zeitung* from a street vendor. One of the secondary headlines on the front page read: "Lion Stages Daring New Crossing," and there was a photograph of Hans looking joyous but disoriented only seconds after crossing the wall. The article told of the extreme danger of the crossing and how the Lion had rushed away right afterward, as he always did. And Hans, naturally, would give no information to help identify the Lion. One part of the article made Shelby want to laugh, though not in amusement.

A search for the Lion is being conducted by the U.S. State Department in the belief that he may be an American citizen. Deputy Minister Donovan Hawkes is heading the investigation. A photograph of the Lion taken during his recent confinement in an East German prison should prove useful to Herr Hawkes. As he is chief investigator, the photograph was sent directly to him.

That at least answered for Shelby the question of how Donovan could continue to hold his post, now that a photograph of him as the Lion existed. The answer was that *he* was the one who had received the photograph, and naturally he had passed along a doctored-up or completely false copy to the West Berlin police, who were working with him on the case. The East Berlin *Vopos* had a true copy. Who was to know that the two pictures were completely different, other than Donovan himself?

Shelby found a red-painted phone kiosk. With the sound of whizzing honking traffic outside the glass door, she called Diana. Diana was in high spirits when she answered and glad to hear from her. "Have you heard about the crossing?" she asked.

"I just heard about it now," Shelby said. "Diana, I'm so happy for you."

"Oh, thank you." She sounded as if she would cry with joy. "I—I never really thought it would happen. I never thought he'd end up here and that we could be together. He's at my apartment now. We're going to be married right away. He sends his love."

"My love to him, too."

"Honey, will you be my bridesmaid?"

"Of course I will." She was happy for Diana, despite her sullenness over her own situation. "How is he?" she wanted to know. She was asking about Hans, but Diana immediately assumed she was inquiring about Donovan.

"He's just awful," Diana informed her in a voice filled with dismay. "Have you seen him lately? He's like a wild man. He never smiles. He doesn't care about his appearance and sometimes doesn't even shave. He won't talk to you unless you speak to him first. Shelby, he doesn't seem to care about anyone or anything. And he's reckless now, too, as though he's got a death wish or something. Hans said Mr. Hawkes waited until the very last second before following him on their slide down that rope, almost as if he were daring fate to step in and stop him.'' She paused. ''We're so grateful to him, both of us; we just wish there were something we could do.''

''Diana, I have to go.''

Diana instantly became regretful and guilty. ''I'm sorry. How stupid of me. I shouldn't be talking to you about this.''

''No, it's all right. I just...I have to go now. Goodbye.'' After she hung up, she stepped from the booth and stared out at the traffic moving noisily by. She wished she could blank out her mind and not think at all.

Two nights later she and Wolfgang were in their hotel suite, dressing for dinner. Wolfgang had already made reservations, and afterward they were to take in a performance of Hamburg's leading modern-dance troupe. By now Shelby was merely going through the motions. She took no pleasure from the glamorous restaurants they dined in or the exciting nightlife of the cities they visited. Her attempts at distracting herself from her sullen mood and thoughts of Donovan had failed utterly. And the previous night she had again had that nightmare regarding her children and Wolfgang's hoodlum associates.

She finished dressing in her bedroom of the suite, then came out to join Wolfgang, who was standing at the bar in the living room. She wore a one-shouldered slim-fitting gown of cream-colored chiffon, her long hair in a sleek chignon. Wolfgang was watching the financial news on television. He was dressed in a dark jacket, with a coarse gabardine blue shirt underneath. The sartorial combination shouldn't have worked, but on him, with his indomitable will reflected in his hard face, it did; he made it work.

"You are ready, then?" he asked, sipping his usual predinner cocktail—a glass of Steinhager liquor.

Shelby nodded.

Wolfgang reached for the remote-control unit to shut off the television just as a picture of the Berlin Wall flashed on the screen. "A fugitive people smuggler was killed today—" said the newsman.

"Wait!" called Shelby.

"—during an unsuccessful crossing of the Berlin Wall."

Wolfgang himself had stopped the moment the announcement had come on. They both watched in rapt attention as the camera scanned the section of the wall where the crossing had been thwarted. The crossing attempt was described as reckless and hastily conceived. There was no picture of the people smuggler.

"They do not say it is him," Wolfgang said quietly, knowing what Shelby was thinking. "The man they killed is named Shoup, they say."

"That doesn't matter," she cried out, almost in hysterics. "You know he uses false papers when he crosses."

The newscast returned to financial news, with a

promise of further details about the failed crossing later in the evening. Shelby rushed to the telephone and started to call. She had to find out if it was Donovan. Her fingers were shaking too much, though, to push the right buttons.

"Give me that," commanded Wolfgang gently, taking the phone from her hand. "I can find out more quickly than you." He began calling members of his organization in East Berlin—men who were paid to know everything of importance that happened there.

Shelby was too tense and distraught just to stand there. She had to do something. She grabbed her purse and rushed out the door to the elevator. "The lobby," she said to the old operator as he closed the gate. Shelby was sure it was Donovan. He was dead now, and he had died thinking she didn't love him.

She crossed the lobby to the telephones, went into a booth and shut the door. She placed a call to Donovan's apartment. There was no answer. She called the legation and asked if he was working late in his office. The night-duty operator told her no, he wasn't in the legation. With growing frustration she called Dr. Rinehardt, but this call, too, went unanswered.

Donovan's dead, she thought in a frenzy of despair, listening to Rinehardt's phone ringing in her ear. *He's dead; he's dead. Oh, if only I'd agreed to talk to him! If only I did as Rinehardt wanted, tried to talk him out of his self-destructive ways. It might have made a difference; it might have!*

She was about to hang up when suddenly the phone was answered, and Rinehardt's voice came through clearly. *"Ja? Wer ist es?"*

"Dr. Rinehardt, it's me, Shelby Everest. Is it... is it...?"

"No, the man involved is not the one you speak of. Another has been killed." He had to be careful about names, in case the line was tapped.

Shelby let out a sigh of relief, and her body, which had been so tense, now seemed to deflate. She sank down onto the seat of the phone booth. "Thank God," she breathed.

"That is a strange sentiment," said Dr. Rinehardt. "This man had a wife and small child."

"I didn't mean it that way. I... You know what I meant." But she did feel embarrassed by her comment.

"Yes, I know."

Silence filled the line. Shelby knew what he was thinking, though he did not say it. They were both thinking the same thing—that it was only a matter of time before the people smuggler on a future newscast of this kind did turn out to be Donovan. It took a moment for Shelby to bolster her spirit enough to make the decision. Once she had made it, she said with resignation, "All right, Dr. Rinehardt. I'll meet him. I honestly don't think it'll do any good, but if you can arrange for him to see me, I'll talk to him. I'll *try* to make him change."

Rinehardt knew what this cost her emotionally, and there was admiration in his voice. "You are an unusual woman, Shelby Everest. I do not know what is behind this upcoming marriage of yours to the baron. I suspect, though, that there is a more noble purpose than meets the eye.''

Shelby said nothing.

"I will begin making arrangements immediately. I do not know if I will succeed. He is perceptive; he is difficult to trick. But this is for his own good, and I will do my best to trick him into this rendezvous.''

"How will I know where and when to meet him?"

"I will contact you. Your marriage celebration in Idor-Amstein begins on the fifteenth, yes? If you do not hear from me before then," he said, his voice somber, "it means I have failed. I could not arrange the meeting.''

After they had exchanged goodbyes, Shelby returned to her suite. "Where have you been?" Wolfgang asked.

"The telephone in the lobby. I called Dr. Rinehardt.''

"You know, then. It was not the Lion. It was another man. Your Hawkes was not involved at all.''

Shelby nodded. She felt dull and drained. Wolfgang seemed to be feeling mixed emotions. On the one hand he was sensitive to her mood and wanted to be sympathetic; on the other hand, though, he felt angry that her feelings for Donovan were still so strong. He seemed to be wondering whether she would become so emotional if it were *he* she thought was involved in a fatal disaster.

He draped a plaid wool muffler around his neck

over his coat. "You are coming to dinner, or you are not?"

"Not now," she said. "Please, Wolfgang, I just want to. . . be alone for a few minutes."

He nodded curtly, suppressed anger smoldering in his eyes. Then he left without her.

CHAPTER TWENTY-SEVEN

SHELBY WAS IN CONSTANT SUSPENSE during the next few days. Everywhere she went, she kept anticipating that Dr. Rinehardt would step out of a doorway or from around a corner to tell her the time and place for her rendezvous with Donovan. In her hotel room she kept waiting with anxiety for the phone to ring, hoping it would not happen while Wolfgang was around.

The suspense increased as the days passed. Finally she began to wonder if Dr. Rinehardt had failed in his mission. She wasn't looking forward to talking to Donovan—she dreaded it, in fact—but she did realize it was his only slim hope of salvation. For that reason she wanted Rinehardt to succeed. But soon there were only three days before the wedding ceremony in Idor-Amstein and then two days and then finally they were back at Wolfgang's castle, their trip over and the festivities about to begin the very next morning.

The village square had been decorated for the occasion. Food and drink had been prepared. The village minister was ready and waiting. The invitations had all been sent, and in the morning the guests would begin arriving, prepared to stay for the two-day celebration, including the wedding ceremony itself on the morning of the second day. Two nights from now, Shelby reflected, she would be Baroness Wolfgang von Heller.

Thinking about the wedding, she wandered through the garden that fronted the castle. Even at this time of year, when all the flowers had long since faded, the beauty of the garden and the surrounding hillside was a pleasure to behold. She had forgotten how truly lovely it was and how bizarre it looked juxtaposed against the outside of the castle. The exterior still appeared crumbling and jagged, giving no hint of the elegance of its interior.

Wolfgang was away at the moment, completing the last details of his business trip. He was rendezvousing with a man who was far more dangerous than the others he had encountered on their trip. Shelby knew this from the night she had been with Wolfgang in that bar in Amsterdam. The seedy characters he had met there had warned him about how predatory this particular man was.

Shelby couldn't help thinking that maybe Dr. Rinehardt would appear here in the garden at the last moment, now that she was alone. But no, she knew she was kidding herself. That wouldn't happen. What would happen was that in a few minutes she would go into the castle and call Rinehardt. She had not done it so far because she feared he would say that the rendezvous could not be arranged. Donovan would continue in his self-destructive ways, and sooner or later. . . .

She turned her thoughts away from this and mused instead on how Wolfgang was displeased with her for not inviting her father to the wedding; nor had she invited any of her friends from the legation. Shelby had not asked them because this was not a joyous occasion for her, and she had no intention of pretending it was. She would find some way to make excuses to her father for not having him there—after the wedding. But for now she could only take one crisis at a time, and it was enough just worrying about getting through the wedding itself.

The sun began sinking toward the horizon. When the last rays of daylight had vanished, she returned to the castle and called Rinehardt from Wolfgang's phone in the den. The phone rang and rang without being answered. Finally she hung up. There would be no rendezvous, she was sure of this now. At the back of her mind she felt relief—and guilt about feeling it. But at least now she could let herself relax. She would not have to deal with seeing Donovan again. She poured herself a snifter of *schnapps*—strong German liquor—and curled up on the sofa. When Werner came in to ask what time she wished to have dinner, Shelby told him she wasn't very hungry, that she'd wait till Wolfgang returned and eat with him.

The tension had really been getting to her, she could tell. She poured a second snifter of *schnapps* and took a few swallows to calm her nerves. Then, before she knew it, she was asleep on the sofa and having the same nightmare she had several weeks earlier: the mean-eyed hoodlums, her children bouncing gaily on their knees, respect and warmth in her children's eyes, Wolfgang looking on fondly....

A hand squeezed her shoulder, and Shelby cried, "No!" startling herself out of her nightmare. She squinted, her eyes very bleary, and saw Wolfgang standing above her, gazing at her with concern.

"Are you all right?" he asked. "You were whimpering in your sleep."

Shelby rubbed her eyes. "I'm okay," she said, her voice husky. She felt a bit shaky. She stretched and yawned. "Did you just get back?"

"Yes. The meeting went well. It was not as dangerous as I had been told." He bent forward and kissed her on the forehead. His coat came open as he did so, and for the first time Shelby saw that he was wearing a gun in a shoulder holster. The sight startled her. She might have known in the back of her mind that he would have one of these and that there would be occasions on which he would wear it. But if she had known, she hadn't thought about it, and now, seeing it for the brief second that it was visible before he stood up again, she was stunned.

"What's that?" she asked after he was again standing, his coat closed. Her finger pointed to just beneath his arm.

"It is nothing," he said. He was upset at himself for letting her catch a glimpse of it.

"It's a holster, isn't it?"

"It's nothing." He turned away from her to fix himself a drink.

"It's a holster," she repeated. "And what's that inside it?"

"Don't be naive, Shelby."

"All right, I know what's inside it. Can I see it?"

"No." He sighed with annoyance. "Forget it."

"Come on, really, I want to see it."

He looked at her steadily, his eyes hard. "I know this disturbs you. I will tell you that I carry it very rarely, and when I do, it is for protection only. And when I carry it for protection, I do not need to use it."

Shelby couldn't let the subject drop. For some reason she felt a perverse urge to press on with it, despite the hard way he was looking at her, telling her he wanted the subject dropped immediately. "Did you use it tonight?" she asked.

"No!" His voice was cold steel.

"Did you—"

"Drop it, I said!"

She lowered her head. She knew why she was bringing this up now and why she could not let the subject drop. She knew it had been preying on her mind for a long time, and that was why she had had that nightmare again.

"Wolfgang," she said softly, feeling immense sadness. "I can't let it drop. Because it affects something very important. . .something that touches on both of us."

The way her mood had changed from petulant belligerence to subdued sadness made him realize that something was very wrong. He sat down on the sofa beside her, touching her supportively. He frowned with concern. "What is it, my love?"

It took a moment for her to gather the strength to say it. She had known it for a long time but had not been able to face it, to admit it to herself. She had been hiding it from herself, pretending that something miraculous would happen to change things so that this decision would not be necessary. But now, seeing what she had just seen, knowing all that it implied, she realized there was no way to avoid the decision any longer. She managed to keep her voice steady, but it was an effort.

"Wolfgang, we can't have any children, you and I."

"*What?* What do you say? This is crazy talk. Of course we will have children."

Now her voice cracked, despite her efforts, and the words came out in a sob. "How can we? Children should be raised to look up to their parents, to respect them and want to be like them. But I can't have my children learning to respect what you do... wanting to grow up to follow in your footsteps."

"I have told you the reasons I am what I am." He stood angrily and moved away from her. "Who are you to judge me?"

"I'm the one who will bring our children into the world if we have them, and I won't raise children who grow up wanting to be criminals or who feel loving toward criminals." Her voice was steadier, for she felt sure of her ground. She was strong now, not weak, and though she was experiencing great anguish at what she was doing, she knew she was doing the right thing.

Wolfgang lit a cigarette in frustration, scowling, and breathed the smoke in sharply. Shelby could see she had caught him off guard with her words. He didn't want to accept them. His mind was frantically searching for some way to deal with the problem.

"There are other ways to handle this," he ventured. "I can. . .hide the truth of what I do for a living from them."

"Do you think that's the way to raise children? Starting with lies and deceit right from the beginning? Intending to keep lying to them for. . .how long, Wolfgang? Forever?"

"You twist things!"

"No, I don't, and you know it." She tried to be gentle. "I don't say these things to hurt you. I didn't want to decide this any more than you want me to. I've always wanted to be a mother—more than almost anything. To love children, to raise them, to watch them as they grow. . . .'' She had to stop speaking. She was becoming too emotional.

"I know how much you want children. I refuse to let you give them up, to let you sacrifice this thing you want so badly."

"You have no choice in the matter."

"There is nothing I can do," he asked frustratedly, "to make you change your mind?"

"Yes, there is, but you won't do it."

"What is this thing? Tell me."

"You can stop being a black marketer and criminal."

"And you can go straight to hell."

Shelby said nothing. He took a drag of his cigarette and exhaled it furiously in a thin cloud of gray smoke. For a long moment he said nothing, continuing to seethe with anger. Finally he managed to regain control of his emotions. "Forgive me," he said stiffly, making an effort at apology. "This is not easy for me. This is a very hard blow you have dealt me."

He paused, then added, "My work is my life. I will continue with my business interests for which I have sweated and slaved and fought and have finally built up to this point after all these years. And I will tell you this, also. I want children, and I shall have children—if not with you inside our marriage, then with someone else outside of it."

"That's your choice," she replied icily, "but you won't have them with me."

"Tell me, is this how you expect to get out of marrying me?"

"Tell me," she said mockingly, repeating his phrase with disdain, "would you like to get slapped across the face?"

He seethed with anger, but then after a moment he said, "I should not have accused you. I know you are above that. It is just that...." He shook his head sadly, his eyes bitter. "This is a very hard blow you have dealt me," he repeated. He stubbed his cigarette butt into the crystal ashtray. "But I shall get over it," he said abruptly. "And I will not release you from your vow to marry me. I want you as my wife; I want you as my lover, and I will bear whatever crosses I must, to have these things."

He put his heels together and bowed in a formal way. "Good night. In the morning the celebration begins, and the morning after that, we will be married."

He left the den, shutting the big double doors after himself, leaving Shelby alone with her thoughts and emotions in the cold empty room.

SHE WORE a calf-length floral-print dress of raised velvet to the celebration. With it, she chose black suede boots that gave the outfit a peasant air. And because the occasion was festive and gay, she put a wreath of twisted ribbons in her hair. This was her way of trying to contribute to the mood. She knew she could not do it by smiling or pretending to be happy, so the outfit she wore was a way of showing she really did want to do her share. And she did, really. It wasn't Wolfgang's fault she was so sullen. He had done nothing to hurt her deliberately. It was what he *was* that created the problem, not what he did or how he treated her. Because of this she didn't want to ruin his wedding celebration. She felt deeply burdened, but tried hard to disguise it. She was a strong woman, she told herself; she could bear up under this pressure.

Wolfgang seemed happy as he and Shelby moved to the gaily decorated podium at the front of the village hall, urged on by Idor-Amstein's cheering townspeople. If he felt any residue of bitterness from yesterday evening's encounter, he was hiding it. This was the day he had been waiting for. There were problems, true, but still, he was soon to marry the woman he loved. He cared for her; he wanted her—and he would have her.

"*Danke,*" Wolfgang was saying over and over to the townspeople, who would not stop applauding. He was smiling down at them from the podium. His arm was around Shelby's waist possessively. In keeping with the German folk-tradition spirit of the gathering, he wore a blousy white shirt and a wide sash. His dark trousers were tucked into the tops of high boots. He looked extremely handsome as he smiled and waved to the crowd.

The townspeople were applauding Shelby, too, not just Wolfgang, and in response she tried to smile back at them. She managed only a very poor imitation of a smile, which she thought certain they must know was forced and false. But if the villagers were aware of it, they gave no sign. Their applause and raucous good humor did not diminish.

Finally the ancient seamy-faced mayor managed to quiet the crowd. As he stood at the podium, he looked down on the colorfully attired people in front of him. "My friends," he said, launching into a brief speech of praise for Wolfgang and finishing by extending Idor-Amstein's best wishes for his and Shelby's happiness. Then, just before the speaking ended and the partying began, he made one final remark.

"Tomorrow morning's wedding will be a blessing, and soon after we all expect another blessing—a new generation of von Hellers to cherish and to watch as they grow into manhood, as we have cherished and watched the baron.'' Shelby saw Wolfgang wince at this. The mayor then embraced Wolfgang and kissed him on the cheek. His next words to him were spoken in an emotional voice. ''Wolf, you are a good man. You would make your father, Manfred, very proud. We are all proud of you. Many of us thought you would never marry, that you were too hard a man—forgive me—ever to need a woman or take a wife. It makes us happy that we were wrong. God bless you both.'' He hugged Shelby, too, and kissed her on the cheek.

The crowd applauded. Shelby saw tears in many eyes. Then the band struck up the music. Wolfgang led Shelby onto the dance floor and swirled her with him for the first waltz. Because of the old injury to his leg, his waltzing was not perfect, but no one seemed to care. Soon other couples joined in, and the party was in full swing.

Shelby did her best to pretend to enjoy it all. By midafternoon the strain of her pretense was causing her a headache. She told Wolfgang she had to lie down for a few hours. He nodded and squeezed her hand. Since the celebration would last two days, lengthy rest breaks were taken for granted. He offered to let her take his car back to the castle, but Shelby had never learned to drive a racing stick shift. Instead she agreed to let one of the villagers take her back—a man who had left earlier to return to his shop. Shelby put on her coat and started down the main street to the man's shop. Before she reached it, though, she noticed that someone had begun following her, moving out from between two buildings. When she turned and saw it was Dr. Rinehardt, her heart sank.

"Not *now*," she said in despair.

"I could not arrange it earlier."

"It's too late for that! I can't talk to him now." Her words were imploring. After not hearing from Rinehardt for so long, she had allowed herself to feel relief at the knowledge that she would not have to face Donovan again. She had been girded up for it once but had let her guard down. Besides, after the past weeks of living with Wolfgang and the past hours of enduring this "wedding celebration," she knew she was in no condition to face Donovan. Her emotional defenses were in disarray.

"Please," said Rinehardt urgently, "you must see him." He maneuvered her off the sidewalk toward the side of a building so they would be less visible. "He is waiting in a clearing in the woods only two kilometers from here. I told him that the uncle of an East Berlin scientist desires to meet him to arrange the crossing of his nephew. Donovan came because he is seeking another crossing. You know how dangerous that is at the moment. You *must* speak to him. Talk him out of this insanity."

She felt dazed. She couldn't do it now; she knew that. But she also knew she couldn't refuse to do it at all. She listened with only part of her mind as Rinehardt told her where Donovan was waiting. Then she found herself driving along in Rinehardt's East

German-made Wartburg sedan that he had lent her, having refused to come along himself. "This is not the time for a threesome," he had said. Shelby was moving as if in a dream. Nothing seemed real—not the road she traveled down, nor the woods flashing by, not even the fallen tree stump she finally parked beside.

She made her way into the clearing, and it was only then that her dreamlike trance faded as reality struck her in the face. Donovan was standing there in the glade. There was a thin layer of snow on the ground, but he wore no rubbers or boots. He was studying a portfolio of notes—evidently plans for the intended crossing. He glanced up sharply as she approached. He seemed shocked to see her.

Shelby was shocked too—at the way he looked. His hair was unkempt. His eyes were almost wild. He had apparently come straight from the legation, for beneath his open black wool coat, he wore a dark pin-striped suit. But even this appeared uncared for. Most striking of all was his hardened expression. He looked like a man who had nothing to live for, who was reckless and yet still very powerful—a dangerous combination. He was strong enough to take risks and to die for what he believed in but was no longer caring about whether he lived or died.

"What are you doing here?" he demanded, glaring at her.

"I...I....." She couldn't speak. What was there to say?

He continued staring, then finally realized he had

been tricked. "Damn that Gottfried." He turned to go.

"Donovan?" she said, her voice small and soft, like that of a frightened little girl.

She thought he wouldn't turn back to her. When he did, she almost wished he hadn't. His expression was cold and bitter and accusing. Shelby still didn't know what to say. All she knew was that the torment of the past days and weeks came to a head as she saw the hateful way he looked at her—the way he, the man she loved, looked at her. She couldn't bear it. Anguish flooded her vulnerable heart, and she reacted automatically, not thinking at all.

She threw her head back and burst into tears. She began moving toward him across the clearing, her head craned backward, her eyes so blinded by tears that she couldn't see where she was going. She reached him and sank down to the ground, wrapping her arms about his knees. Her cheek was against his trouser leg. She was sobbing and could not stop.

She remained like that, on the cold ground, crying against his leg. She was out of control, no longer able to be strong or adult or responsible. She was none of those things now. She was a little child, alone and unloved, hurting to the depths of her soul. She knew nothing but her pain and her tears.

Donovan stood silently still, rigidly unmoving. Then, after an eternity, Shelby felt something. She didn't dare believe it was what it seemed, but then she knew that it was. His hand had moved to the top of her head and begun gently stroking her hair in that tender way she loved so much. She continued crying, and he continued stroking her hair.

"I don't understand you," he said finally in a low throaty voice. "You're the most complicated woman I've ever known. You're about to marry von Heller. Yet here you are, embracing me. If I didn't know better, I'd say that look in your eyes was the look of...." He let the sentence peter out uncompleted.

Shelby still could not trust herself to speak, so she didn't. Donovan put his hands under her arms and gently raised her up to her feet. His arms went around her as she continued crying against his chest, more quietly now, less violently. She felt warm and protected in the cradle of his arms. He rocked her gently. Neither of them spoke. They remained together, sharing this moment that could not last, that was doomed never to be repeated.

Finally, after a long time, Shelby pushed away from him slightly and looked up at him. He was gazing at her, confused and uncertain. Words would be useless now, she knew. This moment had to be preserved without words, preserved in her mind's eye forevermore. She kissed him on the cheek softly, then backed away from him. He watched her go. She left the clearing, climbed into the Wartburg and drove away. She did not glance back.

The celebration was still in full swing when she returned. There was dancing, laughing, loud music and a smiling crowd. She didn't know how she managed to get through the next few hours or the elaborate dinner that evening at the festively decorated long tables, a huge blaze glowing in the hall's fire-place. The false smile that was frozen on her face was so brittle, she felt that if she were to let go, it would shatter like fine china.

Wolfgang saw that she was not eating and noticed her mood. It seemed to make him somber and thoughtful. For a long time he said nothing about it. Then, toward the end of the dinner, he leaned close and gazed at her with a surprisingly intense look.

"You are unhappy, *Liebling*. I cannot have this. We will talk later, and I will tell you what I will do to make you no longer unhappy."

When night finally came, though, she did not want to talk to him. She knew that nothing he could say would make her feel any better. She went to bed early, without saying good-night. Since that first night when Wolfgang had slipped into bed beside her, she had moved to a small room of her own on the lower floor of the castle. She set her alarm for seven in the morning so she'd have time to prepare and dress for the wedding ceremony at ten. She had been fighting to keep her mind blank ever since seeing Donovan earlier, and now she continued fighting to keep it blank as she climbed in under the warm covers.

Sleep came with merciful quickness.

CHAPTER TWENTY-EIGHT

SHE WAS HAVING such an enchanting dream. Donovan was there beside her, gazing down at her lovingly. His hand was gently stroking her hair. "It's all right now, my love," he said in her dream. "Everything will be all right from now until forever."

Shelby smiled happily, like a little child comforted by the reassurance that the world *could* be a happy place for her, no matter how much she had doubted it.

Then she opened her eyes and saw Donovan's strong handsome face gazing down at her lovingly, his hand stroking her hair. It seemed so right, so perfectly natural, that she just continued smiling up at him in gratitude and love. Slowly it dawned on her that she was no longer dreaming, that her eyes were open and she was awake. She had to rub her eyes to make herself believe it. *No,* she thought, *I'm still dreaming, I must be.*

She looked at Donovan again. He was clean-shaven and clear-eyed now, as handsome as on that first day she had seen him in Washington. He wore his black coat over a blue turtleneck and dark jeans. He noticed her expression and realized she wasn't yet sure that she was fully awake, that this was really happening. He bent forward and kissed her on the lips so passionately that it wiped out any question of whether he was real or merely a dream. Dream figures didn't kiss like *that*.

Shelby's mind was reeling. She pushed away from him and sat up in bed. "You can't be here," she said disbelievingly. "How did you get in?"

He nodded toward the large casement window. It was partially open, and there was dirt on the carpet from where he had climbed in from the garden.

"What are you doing here?" This castle was in East Berlin. He was taking his life in his hands by being there.

"I've come to get you," he said. "I'm taking you away with me."

"Donovan, no! I'm about to be married."

"That's right—to me."

"Darling, no!"

He swept her up in his arms and grinned that powerful confident grin of his, which she had not seen for so very long. "I found out the truth. Diana told me. After the way you acted in the woods this afternoon, I knew you still loved me, not von Heller, so there had to be some other reason you were marrying him. I badgered Diana until she told me all about it."

"Oh, darn her!" Shelby said in frustration.

"No, bless her. She knows what's good for you, even if you don't. Besides, that story about the mix-up in prison release papers always seemed fishy to me. I should have realized the truth long ago."

"Put me down," she said.

"Never!" he grinned at her exultantly, triumphantly.

"Will you put me down!"

"All right, but only so you can get dressed."

"I'm not getting dressed," she declared as he set her on her feet.

"Then it looks as if you're going to go tromping through the woods with me in your nightgown."

"Oh, Donovan, please," she moaned, "don't you understand? I can't leave. I gave my word I—"

"Don't *you* understand?" he interrupted forcefully, his expression intense. "I love you, and now that I know you still love me, nothing is going to stop me from marrying you. Nothing! I was willing to let you go when I thought I didn't have your love, when I thought you were marrying von Heller because you wanted to—what would be the sense in pursuing you if you didn't love me—but now that I know the truth, I'll never let you go. You're coming with me, Shelby, if I have to carry you out of here kicking, and when we get back into the West, we're getting married."

Her emotions were in turmoil. She wanted nothing more than to go with him now, to live the life he promised. But she had made a deal, and Wolfgang had been honorable in living up to his part of it—at the risk of his very life.

"Donovan," she said tormentedly, "I can't go. Don't you see? I gave my word I'd marry him. I have to respect it."

"You do. I don't." He went to her closet and

pulled out several articles of clothing. "Put these on," he said, tossing them to her.

Shelby shook her head in refusal and let the clothes fall to the ground.

"Suit yourself," said Donovan happily, coming to her, swiftly pulling the coverlet from the bed over her and sweeping her up in his arms. He started toward the casement window.

"Put me down!" she protested. "You have no right to do this."

"I love you. What more right is there than that?"

She began beating on him with her small fists, feeling helpless and frustrated.

"You can't end this charade of an engagement yourself," he said, "so I'll have to do it for you."

"I gave my word!"

"And you kept it, damn it. You told him you'd be willing to marry him, and you are willing. It's not your fault if circumstances beyond your control stepped in to ruin your plans."

"I won't let you ruin them," she declared in almost a sob, struggling futilely against his overpowering strength.

"Try and stop me."

"I'll scream," she threatened.

"Then now is the time to do it," he replied, pushing open the tall vertical window with his elbow. He seemed to have regained the full use of his injured arm.

A blast of cold December air swept across Shelby as he carried her over the windowsill into the garden.

She didn't dare scream now. The stone walls of the castle were thick, but she knew that Wolfgang worked with his window open, even when it was cold. If she screamed now she most definitely would be heard. Wolfgang had his pistol, she knew. If he saw Donovan abducting her, there was no telling what he might do.

She continued struggling, but Donovan was heedless of her efforts. He carried her quickly across the garden, onto a stone staircase that led to a lower level. He began descending rapidly. Centuries ago, feudal swordsmen had clashed on these steps over possession of the castle and its keep, and perhaps, thought Shelby, centuries ago some bold warrior had fought his way up these stairs to take in his arms the woman he loved, just as Donovan was doing now.

They reached the front of the castle. They were near a window, and through it Shelby could see Wolfgang in his well-lit study. He seemed to be composing a letter or a speech, somberly intent upon what he was writing. Donovan hurried across the lawn into the bushes. Shelby shivered as she felt the night air on her face and bare lower legs. Donovan's face was illuminated by the bright full moon; it appeared determined and purposeful. He noticed her looking up at him, and he grinned. Shelby could see he was enjoying every minute of this. After the grim self-destructive way he had been the past few times she had seen him, it was almost a pleasure to see him so dynamic, confident and purposeful again.

They reached the car he had come in. It was Rinehardt's Wartburg. In the back was a knapsack on a frame, with a rolled-up sleeping bag attached. Donovan forced her in through the driver's side and came in after her. He released the clutch and let the car roll down the hill. When he was far enough away from the castle, he turned on the motor. Shelby gazed out the back window at the castle silhouetted against the moonlit sky. The bottom-floor window still glowed from the light within the room in which Wolfgang remained unaware of all that was happening.

"Where are you taking me?" she asked. He could certainly not cross at a border checkpoint.

"To the lower slopes of the Harz Mountains. It's southeast of here, away from Berlin. Part of the border between East and West Germany passes right through the Harz range. I've got a crossing all planned out." He glanced at her as he spoke. "There's a two-mile stretch of the minefield that's being worked on near the electrified fence at the border. The land mines are fifteen years old near that fence. Half of them are so corroded with rust that they're useless. The *Vopos* have dug them up to replace them with new ones, which means there's two miles that, at the moment, are protected by nothing but an electrified high fence and *Vopo* patrols."

That sounded like plenty of protection to Shelby. "Does anyone else know about these two miles of deactivated minefield?"

"Von Heller does."

"Oh, no! Donovan, you can't cross there. He'll check in on me before he goes to bed tonight. There's something he wanted to talk to me about. When he finds I'm gone, he'll know you took me. You left footprints on the carpet. He'll call the *Vopos* and tell them exactly where to look for you.''

"I don't think he'll do that." The headlights from an oncoming car illuminated his features, then passed on. "It's a risk, all right, but I've known the man longer than you, and I think he's the type who'd come after me himself before he'd call in the *Vopos* on a personal matter like this.''

"He's in love with me. I think he'd do anything to stop you.''

"Maybe," he said, dismissing the subject with a shrug. They were speeding down a main road now on the way to the mountains. For several minutes neither spoke as Shelby tried to get her emotions under control. Her efforts were shattered by a sudden flashing light that appeared from behind them, bathing the inside of the car in red. Shelby's heart leaped into her throat with fear as Donovan pulled over to the side of the road, followed by the patrol car. "Don't panic," Donovan said with cool assurance, "I'll handle it.''

Two uniformed men approached the car cautiously, one from either side. They had flashlights, which they shined inside. When they came near, Shelby saw that they were East Berlin policemen, not border soldiers. That, at least, was one small blessing.

"You were going very fast," one said to Donovan, examining his face.

"My wife had stomach pains," Donovan said. "I

thought it was something serious, perhaps appendicitis. I got her out of the house as quickly as I could to take her to the hospital.''

"That is why she is dressed in only her nightgown?" he asked suspiciously.

"You don't want to take any chances with appendicitis," Donovan said in assent.

The policeman grunted and related that his brother-in-law had had a bad appendix only a month ago and that if they had not got him to the hospital in time, he would have died. Shelby felt the danger lessen slightly; it seemed the policeman's suspicions had been put to rest. Donovan explained that the pains had gone away only a few moments earlier, meaning it had probably been nothing more than indigestion. Now he was taking Shelby home—a visit to the hospital no longer seemed necessary—but he did not want her out in the cold for too long, dressed as she was. . . .

To Shelby it was disconcerting to hear Donovan speaking in German. The only other time she had heard him doing so was at that café where he had met Kortz's granddaughter. Shelby had become so used to thinking of him as a man who needed a translator that it was jarring to hear him speaking the language so fluently.

The policeman seemed satisfied with Donovan's explanation. His partner, though, was still suspicious and asked Donovan gruffly for his papers. Shelby tensed. Donovan reached into his pocket, however, and withdrew a forged identity card and vehicle permit, which he handed over casually. Then, within minutes, the policemen were gone, and she and Donovan were once more headed toward their forest crossing.

Shelby was shaken by the incident. She knew how great the danger could have been if the policemen had been more on the ball. She made a decision. She would not try to flee from Donovan now. To do so would only increase his danger, since he would pursue her. No, instead she would wait until they were across the border, where he would be safe. Then she would leave him to return to Wolfgang to fulfill her hated obligation.

Donovan turned onto a narrow road and, after a few more minutes' driving, turned again, this time onto an unpaved dirt path. They were in the forest now, only a few hours' hike from the border. The car rumbled and jolted down the road until Donovan saw a brief on-off signal from a flashlight. He pulled to a stop and got out.

"This is as far as we go on wheels," he said to Shelby, indicating for her to get out, also. The night was cold, and she shivered. She felt dead leaves beneath her bare feet.

The man who had signaled Donovan was young and studious-looking, with rimless glasses. Donovan introduced him to Shelby only by his first name, which was Christian. Shelby recognized the name. This was the accomplice Donovan had used in taking Hans across when Dr. Rinehardt had refused.

"Do you have the explosives?" Donovan asked in a businesslike tone.

"Yes, they are ready."

"You have to blow up the electric generator at exactly seven A.M. Don't do it any earlier than that or you'll kill the night watchman, who doesn't go off duty until a few minutes before then. His replacement won't come until afterward—Gottfried has a way to delay him."

So Dr. Rinehardt and Donovan were again on good terms, Shelby thought, hearing this.

"I understand," said Christian. "Seven A.M. exactly. Then, once the generator is destroyed, you will be able to cross the fence without being electrocuted."

Donovan clapped him on the shoulder and pulled out the knapsack and sleeping bag from the back floor of the the car. He began taking something out of the knapsack. Christian was gazing at Shelby meanwhile, perplexed at her state of dress. Apparently Donovan had not told him that tonight's crossing would be a forcible kidnapping, as well. Christian's only comment regarding Shelby's nightgown was, "You must be very cold."

"I must be," Shelby agreed, hugging herself. Her teeth were actually chattering.

"Here," said Donovan, "put these on." He handed her a flannel shirt, khaki trousers and thick wool socks. Shelby put them on gratefully over her nightgown. The clothes were Donovan's and were so big on her that the sleeves and legs had to be rolled up several turns and the waist clinched with a belt. He also handed her a pair of hiking shoes that were, surprisingly, a near-perfect fit.

Christian climbed into the car and turned it around. "Good luck," he said to Donovan and Shelby. Donovan gave him the thumbs-up sign. Then the boy drove off—leaving them stranded, reflected Shelby, in the middle of nowhere, on a freezing cold night, with the entire *Vopo* force for this sector probably after Donovan in hot pursuit.

Donovan shouldered the backpack, and they began hiking. The slightly inclined hillside bristled with twigs and dead branches. Donovan had a flashlight, but it was not needed, for the full moon provided plenty of illumination. Shelby kept glancing up at the sky as they hiked. In the city the diffusion of light made it hard to see any but the brightest stars. Here, far from any city lights, the sky was ablaze with millions of twinkling stars. It was such a lovely sight that Shelby couldn't help but feel her spirits lifting.

After two hours or so, Donovan unslung his backpack and said, "We'll make camp here. We're about a mile from the border. I don't want to get any closer because they've got foot patrols every half hour alongside the fence."

"Do you think the *Vopos* will come after you from down at the base of the hill?"

"I don't think they'll know I'm here. I still disagree with you about von Heller telling them. Even if he does, though, the danger will probably come from the area near the fence. The *Vopos* might hike up the alternate route and reach it before we can cross." They both knew that Shelby was in no danger, even if the *Vopos* did block their way at the border. Donovan was, however, and at this point it was danger of death. He saw her look of concern and seemed to want to say something reassuring, but there was nothing to say.

As he had been speaking, he had been untying and rolling out the big down sleeping bag. Shelby felt uneasy watching him. When he finished, he motioned for her to climb in.

"That looks as though it'll be very comfortable for me," she said quietly, "but what are you going to sleep in."

He laughed shortly, as if she had made a joke. "It's a two-person bag."

"Good," she said, nodding in approval. "That means I'll have plenty of room to stretch out in. But I still don't know where you think you're going to sleep tonight."

He just smiled at her, feeling her words didn't deserve an answer. He set his wristwatch alarm for six o'clock, pulled off his turtleneck and climbed into the left side of the sleeping bag. He rolled his sweater into a ball and used it as a pillow.

Shelby sat down near a fallen log and hugged herself for warmth.

"You'll freeze out there," Donovan told her. "The cold didn't hit you too hard while we were hiking because you were burning up energy and creating heat, but if you plan just to sit out there on that log for the next five hours, it'll be unbearable."

Shelby tried to think of some mocking reply, but none came to her mind. She knew he was right. Already she was shivering and hugging herself to quell the quaking of her body. She looked at Donovan, who, warmly encased in the down sleeping bag, was looking at her. After a while he shut his eyes, and his breathing became more regular.

Shelby didn't believe him for a minute. He was awake, she was sure, just waiting for her to enter the sleeping bag. She couldn't make love to him now, she knew. She was still obligated to marry Wolfgang, no matter what Donovan said, no matter what her own heart yearned for. She began pacing quickly back and forth, trying to warm herself. I didn't work. She tried to concentrate on the moist scent of the winter forest, on the shadows of the moonlit trees to take her mind off the freezing cold. Nothing worked.

She gazed at Donovan again; he really did seem to be asleep. Finally she could stand it no more. She crawled into the right side of the thick sleeping bag and pulled the top over herself. It was wonderfully toasty inside, already warmed by his body heat. She was so cold, though, that it took several minutes for her to thaw out fully. Finally she felt warm and relaxed. Donovan had made no move toward her all this time. Maybe he really was asleep, she thought hopefully.

No such luck. He turned on his side to face her. His eyes were open, clear and bright. Shelby tensed. She got ready to leap out of the sleeping bag, though the thought of again enduring that freezing cold made her cringe. Donovan made no move toward her, however. He just looked at her.

"I know you don't want me to make love to you," he said, his voice surprisingly gentle.

"That's right," she replied quickly, her own voice lilting, as if in song.

"And I don't want to do anything to make you unhappy. Ever. But Shelby, you've got to realize you're mine now; you're not von Heller's fiancée any longer. I know you don't accept that. I have to make you accept it. As it stands at the moment, you probably think you're going to run back to him after we get safely across the border, once I'm out of danger." He shook his head. His voice was still gentle as he added, "It won't work, babe. Now that I know you love me, I won't let you go. Not ever. If you run back to him, I'll just come after you again. You'll just be making me risk my life all over."

Hearing him say this made her even more frustrated than previously. Now she didn't know what to do. She felt so confused and anguished that she thought she'd explode. "You're making things so hard for me," she moaned.

"You made it hard for yourself by cooking up that deal in the first place. You knew I never would have stood for it if I had known about it."

"Your life was at stake," she responded feebly.

"What is my life without you? I'd sooner be dead than have you marry another man." He had made no effort to touch her so far, but now his hand came forward and gently stroked her cheek. Shelby tried to move away from him, but she was already at the very edge of the sleeping bag. "I'm telling you all this," he said, "because I want you to know I'm not doing this to force myself on you or to torment you. But I am going to do it—to make love to you now."

She started to leave the sleeping bag. He put his arms around her and held her there. She began struggling against him. "Please, Donovan, let me go."

"No." He began nuzzling her neck and ear. His lips and breath were warm against her skin. He had her arms trapped against her sides. With his free hand he began unbuttoning the flannel shirt.

"I can't make love with you," she said desperately, "I'm not your woman anymore."

"Yes, you are."

He had the flannel shirt open now. His hand went to the collar of her nightgown and tugged at it hard, opening it. He pushed the gown back until her breasts were bare and pressing against his warm chest.

"Why are you doing this to me?" she moaned.

"To prove to you that you are...that you're my woman now and that you'll be mine always—and no one else's." His hand went to the belt holding her loose trousers in place and unbuckled it. Then he pushed the trousers down.

Shelby struggled against him, breathing in gasps, but it was useless. Within minutes he had her completely naked and was holding her against his own totally naked body. He tried to be gentle with her. Both their bodies seemed searingly hot as they pressed together in the warm sleeping bag. Only their heads protruded out of the bag, feeling the crisp cold air outside. The contrast was sensuously exciting, and Shelby felt her nerve endings come alive with raw, tingling, surging passion.

"No, Donovan, no . . . please don't."

But the more she struggled against him, the more excited both of them became. Her taut nipples rubbed against him, and her belly touched his stomach.

"I love you," he whispered, his voice raw as his hand stroked down her back and over her derriere, pulling her even tighter against him. "If this is the last time for us, if I have to die in the morning when we try to cross, it's worth it—it's worth it to have you one final time to let you see how much I love you."

Shelby couldn't stand it. The pleasure was excruciating; the powerful love and affection radiating from him were overwhelming. She could have resisted if she had had to contend with only his hands and lips, moving now all over her body. But it was his love that was weakening her so, making her defenses collapse—his dear—precious love. When his lips came down over hers, she felt herself responding, kissing him in return, despite all her efforts to hold back. His hand cupped her breast. He pushed her gently onto her back, and his body came down atop hers, preventing her from moving away.

Shelby moaned and moved beneath him, awash in wave after wave of searing pleasure, lost to his love and his passion. She stared wide-eyed over his shoulder up at the bright stars. Finally her arms went around him in the answer he sought and held him against her.

When the moment came, she gasped and bit her lip to keep herself from crying out. Donovan's body tensed, too, and a groan escaped his lips. "Oh, Shelby," he gasped in that instant, his voice rich with love, "my Shelby!"

CHAPTER TWENTY-NINE

IN THE MORNING Shelby was awakened by the sound of people thrashing around in the bushes farther down the hill. She looked at Donovan. He was already dressed and out of the sleeping bag, checking the equipment in his knapsack.

"Donovan?" she whispered, frightened.

"It's all right," he said with a calmness so deliberate she knew things were not all right at all. He handed her the clothing she had worn last night. She quickly dressed inside the sleeping bag, then got out and joined him where he stood near a tall tree, looking down the hill. In the morning sunlight a platoon of about twenty gray-uniformed *Vopos* was making its way up the hill, off to the north. "They're taking the alternate path to the fence," he said.

"Can we cross before they reach it?"

He looked thoughtful. "We can try." He slung the knapsack over his shoulder and took her hand. "Come on," he said. He left the sleeping bag behind, not bothering to hide it. The *Vopos* already knew they were in these woods so it wouldn't matter if they came across it. As they walked quickly up the hill, keeping under cover of the foliage, Donovan handed

Shelby his canteen. She drank from it gratefully. The water was wonderfully chilled from last night's coldness.

She kept glancing over her shoulder at the *Vopos* off to the side and below them. Once she saw a sight that startled her, though she knew she should have been expecting it. Ahead of the *Vopos*, not quite with the group of them, was Wolfgang. His posture was ramrod straight, and even from here Shelby could see his expression. It was not one of anger but of stern determination. He moved along quickly, not bothering to look to the left or the right. He seemed to know exactly where he was going and what he intended to do when he got there.

So Donovan had been wrong, she thought. Wolfgang had summoned the *Vopos* after all.

They traveled for only a few minutes more when finally—thank God—they reached the high fence, which was topped with coils of barbed wire. Shelby's spirits soared. There ahead of them lay freedom for Donovan. The *Vopos* had *not* reached it first, were not blocking it off. Donovan stopped her, and they peered out from the cover of the bushes near the edge of the woods, making sure no one was there.

The reason the woods came to an abrupt end just a few feet in front of them was that a strip of land running parallel to the electrified fence had been cleared of brush and made bare. Red-and-white signs were posted everywhere, reading: Warning—Minefield. As Donovan had promised, though, the dirt strip was plowed up for as far as the eye could see in both directions. Deactivated rusting old land mines were scattered here and there around their old holes, waiting to be carted away and replaced by new mines.

Donovan checked his watch, his face tense and alert. "The regular foot patrol has already passed," he said. He kept his eyes glued to his watch, marking off each second until seven, when they could cross. Shelby nervously looked around. The *Vopos* were no longer visible farther to the north. They could be anywhere. She thought she heard the sound of thrashing in the bushes near them but couldn't be sure. She was so jumpy it could easily have been her imagination.

"Five seconds," said Donovan, not looking up from his watch. He squeezed her shoulder to reassure her. She kept glancing around, frantically searching for some sign of the *Vopos* so she would know they were far away and did not pose a threat to them.

"Two seconds. . . one second. . . now!"

There was the sound of an explosive roar muffled by the hills far off in the distance. It was as quiet as the sound of distant thunder. Donovan grasped her hand, and they started toward the fence. Just as they crossed through the last line of bushes, a tall figure loomed up in front of them at the edge of the clearing, blocking their path.

"No," moaned Shelby in frustration. They had come so close. To be stopped now, at the last minute, was unbearable.

Then she realized who the tall man was as he moved out from in front of the rising sun, which had made looking at his face impossible. It was Wolfgang.

Shelby gasped. Off to the side now was the distinct sound of German voices and a crashing through the bushes as the platoon of *Vopos* drew near. Wolfgang was staring at Donovan, who held his stare. Neither spoke. Donovan did not try to go around him to the fence. To do so would be futile, for Wolfgang would only have to call out and the nearby *Vopos* would appear within seconds. Shelby expected he would call out anyway, summoning the *Vopos* to arrest Donovan.

Instead he simply stared at Donovan coldly. Shelby thought she understood why he was not calling to the *Vopos*. It wasn't necessary. The voices and the sounds of boots were coming nearer with each second. They would be upon the three of them within the minute.

Still neither man moved nor spoke. They stood there, two commanding figures, facing each other off, as if time meant nothing. They were locked in a battle of wills, neither flinching as the *Vopos'* voices grew louder.

"Over there," shouted a voice from somewhere nearby, "try over there."

Shelby couldn't take it any longer. She started to go to Wolfgang to plead with him, but Donovan pulled her back and held her firmly at his side, refusing to let her go.

"There, I think!" came a nearby voice. "I think I see something over there!"

Running boots crashed through the undergrowth. Shelby's face screwed up into a mask of horror. She wanted to scream. Then, a split second before the *Vopos* burst into the clearing from the north, Wolfgang lunged forward and shoved her and Donovan backward into the bushes.

The *Vopos* stormed through, looking about feverishly. The officer, his rank displayed on his shoulder boards, stalked up to Wolfgang. "Who are you?" he demanded. "What are you doing here?"

"I came to find the Lion of Berlin."

"You know he's here?" The officer was amazed—and eager. "We know it, also. The police on the road stopped a car last night and saw him with a brunette girl in a nightgown, but the fools did not know whom it was they were looking at. Later they recognized the face from a photo that had been circulated and alerted us." His tone became urgent. "Camping gear was in the back seat of the car. We suspect he is here in these hills, trying to make a crossing in this deactivated area."

Wolfgang nodded but said nothing.

"That is how *we* know he is here," said the officer, his expression becoming menacing and suspicious. "Now tell me how you know, before I jump to my own conclusions."

"He stole my woman. That's who the girl was. And this is the most likely place for him to try to cross."

"*Herr Oberleutnant*," said one of the *Vopos* urgently, "I saw figures standing here, at just this spot."

"Who else is with you?" the officer demanded of Wolfgang.

"The Lion," he said. He paused. "Or at least he

was a minute before you showed up. I almost had him when you frightened him off with your damn tromping through the bushes. Didn't anyone ever teach you to approach a place silently? You and your men, you are like a pack of bull elephants.''

The officer looked amazed that the Lion had been there only a moment earlier. He became furious at Wolfgang's abuse. ''Do not waste my time with this idiocy! Which way did he go? Tell me!''

Wolfgang jerked his head to the south.

''Quickly!'' the officer called to his troops. ''After him! Check every spot along the bushes in that direction. Stay away from the fence; it is electric.'' He turned to the *Vopo* who said he had heard voices from this area. ''Stay with this man. Hold him here. We will come back for him.''

The officer started off after his men. The *Vopo* who had been left behind unslung his rifle and held it in both hands at the ready, watching Wolfgang. Wolfgang sighed in disgust. With a sudden mighty blow he hit the man in the face, knocking him backward and unconscious.

Donovan and Shelby had been crouching behind the bushes Wolfgang had shoved them through. They began moving now. Donovan stood up first, offering his hand to Shelby to help her to her feet. Then he went toward the wire mesh fence at the far end of the cleared plowed strip. First, though, he stopped in front of Wolfgang. Once again their gazes locked. Donovan nodded—not so much in thanks as in acknowledgement. His expression showed he had never expected anything less of Wolfgang. His nod was a bridge of respect, a tangible sign of the bond that existed between proud strong men such as these, no matter which side of a battlefield they were on.

Wolfgang nodded back, his expression grim.

Donovan glanced at Shelby. Then he left her alone with Wolfgang while he quickly crossed the plowed dirt strip and knelt before the electric fence. He tested it for current, then bit into its metal strands with the bolt cutters from his knapsack. He kept glancing to the side as he worked to make sure the *Vopos* did not reappear.

Shelby saw that Wolfgang's eyes were on her. She went to him and stood before him. She had expected him to turn Donovan in to the *Vopos*. Her expression was filled with gratitude that he had not done so, but it was also questioning. Why, her eyes asked.

His face was as hard as granite. She could see how difficult this was for him—giving her up—and how much it cost him emotionally. "I was a fool to think I could buy your love with a 'deal,'" he said. "You are a woman, a human being, not contraband like the things I smuggle, which can be bought and sold."

"But you knew that earlier," she said, "and it didn't make a difference then." She struggled to understand.

"Shelby, many who know me say I am too hardened a man, too cold, ever to fall in love or marry. I think it is true; maybe they are right. But what I had with you—what I feel for you—is the closest I have ever come to love. For the first time in my life I care for a woman so greatly that I want her happiness even more than my own." He considered this. "Maybe it is love I feel for you, as I at first believed. I do know this: I care for you too much to see you miserable. At first I thought this would not matter. But now—" he shrugged sadly, fatalistically "—I care for you too much for that."

"Oh, Wolfgang," she murmured softly.

He glanced at Donovan to see how much time was left. Shelby looked, too. Donovan was straining hard at the fence with the metal shears, his face pouring sweat. In only a moment he would be finished.

"I saw how unhappy you were at yesterday's celebration dinner," Wolfgang said. "That was when I made my decision. I came to tell it to you last night, but when I reached your room, it was too late. Hawkes had taken you." He grinned, a tight nonjoyous grin, as if laughing at himself. "I was even writing a speech in my study to tell the villagers I was calling off the wedding."

Donovan finished with the bolt cutters and threw them down. He had cut a semicircular hole in the bottom of the fence about knee-high. Shelby and Wolfgang both were aware she had to go now.

"It was knowing you would not let yourself have children," he said firmly. "That was what made me finally decide. You are the sort of woman who should have children, who would make a wonderful mother. I want you to have them...and I want you to be happy. I release you from your vow. That is how much I care for you."

"Oh, Wolfgang," she said emotionally. She came closer and kissed him on the cheek. "I do love you."

And she did, though it was not in the way she loved Donovan, nor in the way Wolfgang most wanted. "Wherever you are, Wolfgang, know that there is someone out there who cares for you very greatly."

Through a supreme effort of will, he managed to grin at her. She could tell how false the grin was and how much it cost him. She had nothing but admiration for the way he intended to show her only his strength as her parting view of him.

Donovan came up to them. His face was hard and sweating from the major exertion. "We have to go," he said, wiping his forehead with his sleeve.

Shelby nodded.

Donovan faced Wolfgang. For a moment there was silence. Then he said, "If you're not careful, you're going to turn into a damn boy scout."

"That is right, Hawkes. Already I am thinking of quitting my activities so I can devote myself to helping little old ladies across busy streets. Or maybe I will move to Africa, buy a white suit and become another Albert Schweitzer."

Donovan grinned tightly. He clapped Wolfgang on the upper arm hard and let his hand remain there. Watching this, Shelby thought it was the most telling gesture of respect she had seen one strong man make toward another.

Then Donovan took her hand and led her with him to the fence, checking for *Vopos* as they ran. She had to get down on her hands and knees to crawl through the jagged hole, but she made it. Donovan followed quickly after, expertly gliding through in half the time she had taken. They were not safe yet, though. The electrified fence was set back several yards from the actual border to prevent West Germans from approaching it to tamper with it. They ran the remaining distance until they reached the signposts that marked West German territory.

Shelby looked back across the fence to the other side, but Wolfgang was gone. She knew he would be. There was the sound of *Vopos* rushing along the fence and someone shouting that he could see a hole. Shelby and Donovan were safe from the *Vopos* now, but still he pulled her with him into the thick woods. Then he lifted her in his arms till her feet were off the ground and twirled her in a circle, hugging her against him.

His rugged strong face beamed at her, and she saw the triumph and joy that were in his eyes. They had won. They had won against overwhelming odds, conquering their own misunderstandings, the entire *Vopo* force of East Germany and all the obstacles fate had thrown in their way to test them. Their love had weathered it all—the trials and tribulations, the cruel bitter moments of doubt—and now they were here, free at last, and she was in Donovan's arms.

"My love," he said, smiling at her tenderly.

"My life," she answered, her eyes clear and steady as she held his gaze.

His lips descended upon hers in a kiss of fire that sent her heart soaring.

Legacy of
PASSION

BY CATHERINE KAY

A love story begun long ago comes full circle...

Venice, 1819: Contessa Allegra di Rienzi, young, innocent, unhappily married. She gave her love to Lord Byron—scandalous, irresistible English poet. Their brief, tempestuous affair left her with a shattered heart, a few poignant mementos—and a daughter he never knew about.

Boston, today: Allegra Brent, modern, independent, restless. She learned the secret of her great-great-great-grandmother and journeyed to Venice to find the di Rienzi heirs There she met the handsome, cynical, blood-stirring Conte Renaldo di Rienzi, and like her ancestor before her, recklessly, hopelessly lost her heart.
